DOCTOR DENIS

The Life & Times of Dr. Denis Wright

DOCTOR DENIS
The Life & Times of Dr. Denis Wright

Roy Newsome

(based on an unpublished autobiography
and documenting the first 15 years of the NYBB)

First published in 1995 by
Egon Publishers Ltd, Royston Road, Baldock, Herts SG7 6NW

Copyright © Roy Newsome and Egon Publishers Ltd

ISBN 0 905858 92 1

Designed by Nick Maddren
Campion Publishing Services, Baldock SG7 6DB
for Egon Publishers Ltd

Printed in England by
Streetsprinters, Royston Road, Baldock, Herts SG7 6NW

Contents

List of music examples   vi
Author's Preface   ix
Acknowledgements   xi
Introduction   12

Chapter   1   Denis Wright - how it all began   16
             2   One Bulgar less - a sordid tale!   20
             3   Joan of Arc and the big day   22
             4   Confessions of an Adjudicator   28
             5   What the papers said   31
             6   What next?   38
             7   Other pre-war compositions   46
             8   Doctor Denis and education   49
             9   Doctor Denis on repertoire   58
            10   Doctor Denis on contests   65
            11   Doctor Denis on personalities   70
            12   Working for the BBC   75
            13   Life outside the BBC   90
            14   Let there be Massed Band Broadcasts!   100
            15   The BBC's overseas services   107
            16   Intermezzo - a matter of Form   111
            17   Compositions - I   115
            18   Interlude   125
            19   Compositions - II   128
            20   Compositions - III   143
            21   To the end of the '40s   152
            22   Denis the Author   161
            23   Messiah in Brass   173
            24   Denis Overseas   181
            25   The 1950s - Year by Year   200
            26   The NYBB - A Lasting Tribute   210
            27   The Final Years   239
            28   Obituary   248

Appendix 1   Compositions   253
Appendix 2   Transcriptions   255
Appendix 3   Arrangements   259
Appendix 4   Pseudonyms   265
Appendix 5   Collections   267
Appendix 6   Music not written for bands or brass solo   270
Bibliography   274
Index   275

MUSIC EXAMPLES

Ex. 1	Joan of Arc . . . . and then I got stuck	18
Ex. 2	Joan of Arc - opening	25
Ex. 3	Oliver Cromwell - opening	25
Ex. 4	Joan of Arc - from transition	26
Ex. 5	Oliver Cromwell - 2nd subject	26
Ex. 6	Joan of Arc - 2nd subject	26
Ex. 7	Oliver Cromwell - fugue subject	26
Ex. 8	Joan of Arc - fugue subject	26
Ex. 9	Tintagel - 2nd movement (opening)	47
Ex. 10	Overture in the Olden Style - Allegro	47
Ex. 11	Scottish Fantasy - 2nd movement (soprano obligato)	48
Ex. 12	Academic Festival - triplets in strings and horns	61
Ex. 13	Academic Festival - triplets removed for clarity	62
Ex. 14	Academic Festival - final section (string scales)	63
Ex. 15	Academic Festival - same passage in brass band score	64
Ex. 16	Introduction Act III Lohengrin - Denis Wright's ending	101
Ex. 17	Introduction Act III Lohengrin - as in opera	102
Ex. 18	Joan of Arc - recap. (1st subject against fugue subject)	116
Ex. 19	The White Rider - opening	117
Ex. 20	The White Rider - 2nd theme	118
Ex. 21	The White Rider - (in more aggressive mood)	118
Ex. 22	The White Rider - an air of defiance	118
Ex. 23	The White Rider - a brooding realisation of temporary defeat	118
Ex. 24	The White Rider - the struggle is renewed	118
Ex. 25	The White Rider - a joyful pæan of triumph	118
Ex. 26	Tintagel - King Arthur	119
Ex. 27	Tintagel - King Arthur - a more serene theme	119
Ex. 28	Tintagel - 1st movement (2nd subject)	120
Ex. 29	Tintagel - 2nd movement (cornet obligato)	120
Ex. 30	Tintagel - 3rd movement (rhythmical sorcery!)	121
Ex. 31	Princess Nada - Ivar's theme	122
Ex. 32	Princess Nada - transformation of Ivar's theme	122
Ex. 33	Princess Nada - Prince Ivar (further transformation)	122
Ex. 34	Princess Nada - Princess Nada's theme	123
Ex. 35	Princess Nada - 'they all lived happily ever after'	123
Ex. 36	The Sea - Introduction	124
Ex. 37	The Sea - 1st subject	124
Ex. 38	The Sea - 2nd subject i	124
Ex. 39	The Sea - 2nd subject ii	124
Ex. 40	The Sea - 2nd subject iii	124
Ex. 41	Overture for an Epic Occasion -1st subject	128
Ex. 42	Overture for an Epic Occasion - 2nd subject i	128
Ex. 43	Overture for an Epic Occasion - 2nd subject ii	129
Ex. 44	Music for Brass - Prelude (introduction)	130

Ex. 45	Music for Brass - Prelude (theme 'A')	130
Ex. 46	Music for Brass - Prelude (theme 'B')	130
Ex. 47	Music for Brass - Scherzo (opening)	130
Ex. 48	Music for Brass - Scherzo (Trio - theme 'A')	131
Ex. 49	Music for Brass - Finale	131
Ex. 50	Atlantic - Introduction	132
Ex. 51	Atlantic - 1st subject	132
Ex. 52	Atlantic - 2nd subject	132
Ex. 53	Atlantic - Recapitulation (1st subject)	132
Ex. 54	Atlantic - Recapitulation (2nd subject)	132
Ex. 55	Atlantic - a shared problem?	133
Ex. 56	Atlantic - changing colours!	133
Ex. 57	Glastonbury - Introduction	133
Ex. 58	Glastonbury - 1st subject i	134
Ex. 59	Glastonbury - 1st subject ii	134
Ex. 60	Glastonbury - 2nd subject	134
Ex. 61	Tam o' Shanter's Ride - Opening and Tam's motif	135
Ex. 62	Tam o' Shanter's Ride - 'Wife' motif	136
Ex. 63	Tam o' Shanter's Ride - Tam makes merry	136
Ex. 64	Tam o' Shanter's Ride - becoming the worse for drink	136
Ex. 65	Tam o' Shanter's Ride - his sulky sullen dame	136
Ex. 66	Tam o' Shanter's Ride - Tam sets off for home	137
Ex. 67	Tam o' Shanter's Ride - Tam blissfully rides along	137
Ex. 68	Tam o' Shanter's Ride - the alcohol takes its toll	137
Ex. 69	Tam o' Shanter's Ride - Tam's motif, wildly distorted	138
Ex. 70	Tam o' Shanter's Ride - suddenly all is dark	138
Ex. 71	Tam o' Shanter's Ride - the final argument	138
Ex. 72	Salzburg Suite - 1st movement (beginning of Allegro)	140
Ex. 73	Salzburg Suite - 2nd movement (opening)	140
Ex. 74	Salzburg Suite - 3rd movement (opening)	140
Ex. 75	Salzburg Suite - 4th movement (opening)	140
Ex. 76	St. Nicholas Eve - opening	141
Ex. 77	Scherzetto (Op 3 No 2)	144
Ex. 78	Cornet Concerto - 1st movement (1st subject)	146
Ex. 79	Cornet Concerto - 1st movement (2nd subject - 1st exposition)	146
Ex. 80	Cornet Concerto - 2nd movement (main theme)	146
Ex. 81	Cornet Concerto - 2nd movement (mellifluous accompaniments)	146
Ex. 82	Cornet Concerto - 3rd movement (theme 'A' - 1st subject)	147
Ex. 83	Cornet Concerto - 3rd movement (theme 'B' - 2nd subject)	147
Ex. 84	Cornet Concerto - 3rd movement (development section)	147
Ex. 85	Trumpet Tune - opening	148
Ex. 86	Trio Concerto - 1st movement (opening)	150
Ex. 87	Trio Concerto - 2nd movement (opening)	150
Ex. 88	Trio Concerto - 3rd movement (opening)	150

From time to time various people have suggested I should write Denis's biography. Certainly there were the first few chapters of the autobiography he himself had written, and I gave the idea some thought. In the end I decided against it - firstly because I am not a trained musician and could not give any worth while assessment in that direction and also because when events are part of your every day life you are not really aware of their significance.

We discussed new ideas and projects and my part was as the "cold water department", pointing out the practical implications and problems of whatever the proposal was. When we did decide to go ahead I was usually involved in the behind the scenes detail, and so however new or innovative to the 'public' it was an every day fact to me. This was in addition to my own fairly responsible full time job so again such events fitted into normal routine.

When Roy Newsome said he was contemplating this biography I was delighted. Since he became Music Director of the National Youth Brass Band I have come to know him and from his dedication to the NYBB, his involvement in education and his generally balanced views, I realised he would approach the task with an open mind. Until I read the Manuscript I had not realised what a skilled researcher he is. I read of events I had forgotten and saw in perspective some of those every day events and their significance.

I think this book will show, in its own way, the contribution Denis made to the musical awareness and standing of brass bands - not always appreciated at the time! It is certainly an understanding and sympathetic tribute to someone who came into the category of those who 'did what they could for music'.

I am deeply grateful to Roy Newsome for the time, effort and indeed dedication he has given to producing this book.

Maud Wright

Author's Preface

The initial motivation for this book was provided by University College Salford (at the time known as Salford College of Technology) in the form of a research project into some areas of band history. My intention was to undertake a study of the lives and music of two - possibly three - brass band composers.

An obvious starting point, wearing my hat as Music Director of the National Youth Brass Band of Great Britain, was that band's Founder, the late Doctor Denis Wright. With much support and encouragement from his widow, Mrs. Maud Wright, who gave me access to an unfinished and unpublished autobiography and to some of the original scores, as well as to other sundry documents and papers, I embarked on what proved to be a fascinating study of a musician whose name is widely known through his compositions and arrangements, but yet whose contributions to the development of bands and band music have not, to date, been documented, nor indeed fully appreciated. It soon became apparent that there was so much to say about this one composer, his life and his work - if it was to be done adequately - that other composers would have to wait for some future study.

In mid-project, as it were, I took early retirement from my position at the College as Senior Lecturer and Director of Band Studies. That was in 1989, and work on the project ceased for a time. (Perhaps I should point out that retirement was merely from that particular position, creating a situation in which I was able to become, in effect, a free-lance brass band practitioner.)

Having taken this step, calls on my time were such that I was unable to continue my 'academic' study, and it lay dormant for some two years before I received a nudge which induced me into further action. This came from Edward Gregson, via Peter Graham - now one of my successors at Salford. Both felt that the time was ripe for a new book on some aspect of band history and both were kind enough to express the opinion that perhaps I might be able to contribute something.

The temptation was such that I decided to return to my academic study, revising it somewhat to give it a less formal tone, and trying to develop it into an informative but entertaining account of the life and work of the late Dr. Denis Wright.

I have done this with something of a feeling of presumption, because there are many people who knew Dr. Wright far better than I did. My first recollection of actually seeing him was when he was guest conductor at one of the twice-yearly massed band concerts run by Brighouse and Rastrick Band in the Town Hall, Huddersfield. He was tall and slim, and came across as a person of dignity who knew the music thoroughly, understood the musicians under his control, and who had that hallmark of all good conductors, an expressive pair of hands.

A few years later I actually played in a massed band concert under his direction, which not only confirmed these conclusions, but which also demonstrated his warm, likeable personality and that beneath the dignified exterior there was a quiet sense of humour.

I also remember visiting a course of the National Youth Brass Band in the early 60s when his kindly enforcement of discipline was in evidence, as was the obvious love and respect which the members of the band felt for him.

My next recollection of Dr. Wright was an occasion when he adjudicated a contest in Huddersfield in which I conducted one of the competing bands - Slaithwaite. His results, which gave us first prize, despite being considered to be outsiders, made me into something of a local hero and contributed considerably to my own fortunes in the brass band world.

Regrettably, I had person-to-person contact with Dr. Wright on one occasion only, and that was early in 1967, the year of his death. As Bandmaster of Black Dyke Mills Band I conducted two half-hour programmes for the BBC Transcription Service which he produced, though he had long been retired from the BBC by then. It was obvious that he was quite a sick man, but little did I realise that that would be my only 'professional' association with him. Within a few months I was attending his funeral representing Black Dyke - a band which he greatly admired - so much so that in 1965, the year before I became associated with them, he had invited them to play, under his direction, in his own 70th birthday broadcast.

It was at his funeral that I first met his widow, Mrs. Wright, and again, little did I realise that some 17 years later I would receive an invitation to become Music Director of the child of her husband's maturity, the National Youth Brass Band of Great Britain.

Out of a mixture of loyalty to her late husband and, I know, a deep love of this child of his, Mrs. Wright has been very much a part of the institution of the NYBB - a faithful and long-serving Treasurer and attending some 80 of its courses, prior to her retirement in April, 1994.

The National Youth Brass Band of Great Britain, the text books and other writings, the compositions and the vast collection of transcriptions and arrangements are the monuments we still see around us which bear testimony to the life-long work of Dr. Denis Wright. But there's also much more, as I shall attempt to prove in this book which, I hope, will be seen as a small tribute to a great man.

I'm told that he was known by many orchestral players as 'The Silver Fox'; in the world of brass bands he is fondly remembered as 'Doctor Denis'.

Roy Newsome
BURY, Lancs
1994

Acknowledgements

Dr. Wright's unpublished and unfinished autobiography has been the main source of information for the first half of this book - a fact hereby acknowledged in full, along with my thanks for having it placed at my disposal by Mrs. Wright. It is undated, but covers his life and much of his thinking up to the mid-1940s.

I wish also to record my grateful thanks to Mrs. Wright for her tremendous co-operation in leading me to many of the facts, particularly from the later years, and for the loan of a huge array of scores, books, papers and cuttings of all kinds, for her patience in proof-reading my manuscripts and offering kindly suggestions for their improvement here and there.

Past copies of *The British Bandsman* have also provided much information, and I wish to record my thanks to its Managing Editor, Mr. Peter Wilson, for giving me access to the Collection stored at Beaconsfield and also to Mr. Roy Horabin of Sunderland for access to his past copies. Past copies of *Brass Band News*, published and owned by Wright & Round of Gloucester but currently in University College Salford's library have also provided further information, as have miscellaneous papers, magazines and old programmes, acquired from a variety of sources, including those in my own collection.

The help of Mr. Herbert Møller of Denmark has been quite significant, especially in the section on Norway and Sweden and in the loan of material referred to in Chapter 22.

There have been numerous letters and countless conversations with people who remember Dr. Wright. The names of many of them are recorded in the text. My thanks go to all of them, along with my thanks and apologies for any omissions. Their willingness to share with me their memories of this remarkable man has been an inspiration. Many others would, I know, have gladly made their contribution but I had to stop somewhere, or the book would never have reached completion.

I offer a special thank you to Mrs. Peet (formerly Elizabeth Lumb) and Colin Hardy (a former member) for locating and loaning me many of the old programmes from NYBB concerts and course photographs. My thanks are also due to the music publishers, R. Smith & Co., Novellos, Boosey & Hawkes and Molenaars for permission to reproduce the music examples.

My friend Mr. Manny Curtis willingly provided me with some cartoons which I hope the reader will find entertaining. Thank you, Manny.

I wish also to acknowledge the co-operation of the BBC Written Archive Centre at Caversham Park, Reading and colleagues at University College Salford (formerly Salford College of Technology) for constant encouragement and guidance.

Finally, the biggest thank you of all goes to my wife Muriel for putting up with what - especially in the last few months - has become nothing less than an obsession. Her tolerance never flinched.

R.N.

Introduction

Many people have played an important part in the development of the brass band and its music. The late Harry Mortimer introduced a more cultured style of playing - more like that of the strings of the orchestra; Elgar Howarth has championed modern music - persuading composers from the schools of the avant garde to write for brass band, and concert agents and promoters to feature bands in prestige concerts, playing modern works.

In earlier generations there have been those who have conducted famous bands with spectacular success, for example The Great Triumvirate of the late 19th and early 20th centuries, John Gladney, Alexander Owen and Edwin Swift, followed in turn by William Rimmer, J. A. Greenwood, William Halliwell and many others.

Several came from families already associated with bands. The Mortimer family is possibly THE most famous brass band family ever, the father and each of his three sons all becoming well known. Howarth, as a youngster, played solo cornet in the band conducted by his father. Rimmer came from a family with strong banding connections, his father also being a conductor.

Eric Ball, Geoffrey Brand and Edward Gregson are three more who have contributed greatly to the development of bands and band music. Having Salvation Army backgrounds, they also were in a banding environment from an early age, so there was a certain inevitability that they should become associated with bands.

There have been, however, at least three people who have each, in their own way, changed the course of the brass band, and who became involved purely by chance. Their names - Enderby Jackson, John Henry Iles and Denis Wright.

The earliest, Enderby Jackson - born in Hull in 1827 - was a flautist attached to a York opera company during the second quarter of the 19th century. He also played in the orchestra of one Lord Chichester, whose home was at Burton Constable in the East Riding of Yorkshire. On one of the home's open days - in the year 1845 - the worthy Lord had organised a band contest and Jackson, who was there to play in the orchestra during the evening's entertainment, was so moved by the enthusiasm and sincerity of the members of the competing bands that he felt he must somehow, one day, help to raise their status. Of another incident some years later he wrote,

'The autumn of 1853 found me engaged at the Doncaster Theatre for race week; after the races, chatting in the music room one of our band remarked

Enderby Jackson

Ah! they give prizes to horses at races and to cattle and pigs at shows to encourage and bring them to an extreme of excellence; but no one gives prizes to musicians to stimulate them to excel.

These words sank deep in my heart. I saw the excitement produced. Was it entirely to see the horses run the people cared for? No, thought I, it is the rivalry: and if this rivalry could be instituted amongst workmen with music instead of horses, my work would be inaugurated.'[1]

It was Jackson who organised the first series of band contests at the Crystal Palace, who thought of having a piece specially written so that all competing bands had the same starting point, and who first had the idea of having a massed band concert as the culmination of a day's contesting. The Crystal Palace contests organised by Jackson took place between 1860 and 1863, and though failing to achieve lasting success, they were an important part of band history.

It was over 40 years before the second of our three 'course-changers' came on the scene, and the occasion was that of the Belle Vue September contest of 1898, another competition which Enderby Jackson had helped to found back in 1853. John Henry Iles, a businessman from Bristol, happened to be in Manchester at the time, happened to have a free day on his hands, happened to ask the hotel porter how he should spend his day, and the porter just happened to suggest that he (Iles) should visit Belle Vue and listen to the brass band competition. Many years later Iles wrote,

'I regarded the suggestion of attending the Manchester event as anything but attractive. I was, however, persuaded to go, and then I heard these

John Henry Iles standing left

bands which had been described as wonderful. It is not too much to say that I was positively astounded. . . . . I came away from that contest a completely converted enthusiast for their cause.'[2]

On his return to London Iles, then aged 27, threw himself whole-heartedly into further raising the status of bands, taking up the banner raised by Enderby Jackson all those years earlier.

His success was equally spectacular but much more lasting. He became the owner of R. Smith and Co. which specialised in publishing brass band music and, a little later, of one of the two principal band newspapers, *The British Bandsman*. He went on to secure the interest of many influential people, including Sir Arthur Sullivan, and organised a mammoth massed band concert in London's Royal Albert Hall in aid of funds for the relatives of victims of the Boer War. Included in the programme was the first performance of a brass band arrangement of a song by Sullivan called *The Absent Minded Beggar*, and this title also became the name by which the concert was remembered.

This was but a prelude to his most outstanding achievement, the founding of the National Brass Band Championships in 1900. Initially held at the Crystal Palace, later at other venues (mainly the Royal Albert Hall), this event has been the pace-maker of the brass band movement for over 90 years. It has been the London platform for Britain's best bands and has, until recently, culminated in a spectacular massed bands finale - sometimes with an internationally famous guest conductor on the podium.

Most important of all, it has been responsible for a series of compositions, specially commissioned as test pieces, for use not only by the very best bands competing in the highest class, but also for more modest bands in lower sections and, in recent years, music for youth bands - and all this as a direct result of a chance question asked of a hotel porter in Manchester back in 1898!

For the 25th anniversary of the National Championships, John Henry Iles set up a competition to find a suitable test piece, hoping at the same time to find and encourage new talent. Quite by chance a young music teacher by the name of Denis Wright saw an advertisement for this competition, and though he knew next to nothing about brass bands he decided to submit a composition. His entry and its subsequent success brought him into the very heart of the brass band world, making him number three of this trio which came into banding by chance, and the subject of this book - well overdue as we approach the centenary of his birth.

N.B. Throughout the book all direct quotes by Denis Wright are shown between full inverted commas ("), whilst references to quotes from others are shown within single apostrophes (').

Notes

[1] From the unpublished autobiography of Enderby Jackson.

[2] From an article first published in Guildhall Music Student (date unknown) and later reproduced in *The Brass Band Movement* (Russell & Elliott, published by J. M. Dent, 1936), on p. 172.

Crystal Palace, original house of the Nationals

Chapter 1

Denis Wright - how it all began

Denis Sydney Steuart Wright was born in Kensington, London, on 22nd February 1895. He was the son of Dudley d'Auvergne Wright and Ethel (née Morse). Dudley Wright was an eminent surgeon, becoming Senior Surgeon to the London Homeopathic Hospital, Consulting Surgeon to several other hospitals, and was one time President of the British Homeopathic Congress. He was the son of a member of the Civil Service in Ceylon, where he was born in 1867. His wife, Ethel, hailed from the Isle of Wight, where her father ran a private school.

Steuart, the third of Denis's Christian names, was the family name of a friend of the Wrights and Denis referred to it later in life in some of his pseudonyms - W. Stewart, Walter Stewart and Walter Steuart.

The Wrights moved to Wembley when Denis was five years old, and it was here that his musical talents began to surface - first of all as assistant organist at St. John's Church in Wembley, a post he held before the 1914 war, whilst in his teens.

He received his general education at St. George's School, Harpenden, a co-educational public school, to which he later returned as Director of Music. On leaving this school he went to study at the Royal College of Music in London, where his teachers included C. V. Stanford[1], Walter Alcock[2], Frederick Bridge[3] and Charles Wood[4] - a distinguished group of musicians indeed. He also studied conducting for a time under Sir Adrian Boult, forming a friendship which was to be very useful in the years to come. Unfortunately, his musical studies were interrupted by the outbreak of war in 1914.

Dudley Wright was already over military age when the war started, but he was determined to do something to help. He had heard terrible stories of the plight of the French in the town of Dieppe, where medical help was urgently needed. He made his way there and offered his services to the Mayor, who helped him set up a surgical unit in a sea-front hotel (the Hotel du Rhin), prior to moving to Yvetot, a busy market town on the banks of the Seine, and some 25 miles from Rouen. Here he transformed a Jesuit College into the Hôpital de l'Alliance and was joined by his wife (whose skills as a masseuse were more than welcome) and by the 20-year-old Denis, who drove the ambulance and administered anaesthetics.

It wasn't long before Denis himself joined the army, serving in the East Kent Regiment and later in the Army Service Corps. For two years he served in Macedonia, attached to the 3rd Serbian Army. Whilst on active service he was mentioned in dispatches, and also received a Serbian decoration. (Some years later he was to refer to a Serbian legend in one of his brass band compositions.) It was here that he had his first experience of a brass band, forming one and arranging some short pieces for it. The band was made up of lorry drivers, all members of a transport unit.

After the war Denis completed his studies at the Royal College of Music and then spent a few years doing free-lance work in London. In 1920 he helped form the Wembley Philharmonic Orchestra, which grew to a strength of around 40 players, and which he conducted in a number of concerts. This orchestra closed down after a time, but Denis returned to Wembley on a number of occasions to conduct the Wembley Symphony Orchestra. He also acted as deputy conductor of various other orchestras and choral societies and, at a more earthy level, played drums for silent films! By now he had had a number of songs and piano pieces published and was attempting to set up his own publishing firm.

Next he became a school teacher. As well as having a thorough musical training he spoke fluent French and German, and so his main teaching activity was in modern languages. His first post was at St. Andrew's School, East Grinstead, where he taught from 1924 to 1928. St. Andrew's was a prep-school, later becoming known as The Abbey School, but closing down during the 1960s. During his time in East Grinstead Denis forged some links with the local Amateur Operatic Society.

It was during this time also that he first made his mark in the brass band world. The following account is taken from his unfinished and unpublished autobiography:

"The fact that there existed a Brass Band World - a self-contained musical organisation possessing very definite boundaries - had, I think, been known to me for a long while without its impressing itself very markedly on my mind, but on 3rd April 1925, I became suddenly very vividly conscious of the fact.

The previous day I had returned home for the Easter holidays; I was teaching music and other things at a small school in Sussex at the time. On 3rd April I bought the current issue of *Musical Times* and, over a cup of tea in a Lyons teashop, started to study the advertisements.

One in particular caught my attention - a prize of 100 guineas was offered for a work for brass band by a British composer, suitable as the test piece for the National Band Championship. This prize, offered by Mr. J. Henry Iles, was to mark the 25th anniversary of the founding of this Championship.

Here indeed was a good way to fill up my holidays, but what did I know about scoring for brass band? Precious little; true, I had during 1916-17 conducted a small brass band in Macedonia and Serbia, and arranged little tunes for them, but then I had only certain limited instrumentation (the band never exceeded 17 players) and I had no idea of the full scope or how many different sorts of instruments made up a proper band.

However, I went up to R. Smith & Co.'s premises in the Strand and bought the scores of the two previous test pieces, Henry Geehl's *Oliver Cromwell* and *On the Cornish Coast*, and went home to study them."

Example 1 Joan of Arc ". . . and then I got stuck"

As is now widely known, Denis won the 100 guinea prize with his overture *Joan of Arc* which, later in 1925, became the test piece for the Championship Section at the Crystal Palace contest. Still with the autobiography:

"After a few hours of studying Geehl's two scores the music grew rapidly. It wasn't called *Joan of Arc* then, but was just a concert overture in the making. Within a week I had composed and scored about half (down to the start of the fugue, fig. 16 to be exact - see Example 1) and then I got stuck.

After a miserable day of trying to get going I decided to pack it up, and I went off to Paris for an Easter binge on the spur of the moment. I wasn't very rich in those days - I'm not now, for that matter - and after three days in Paris I reckoned I'd about run out of money in another two days if I didn't move somewhere less expensive and less surrounded by money-spending opportunities. So I moved back to Dieppe[5], spending a day in Rouen on the way.

Two things happened that day in Rouen. I got the idea for continuing the overture as I was standing in the place where Joan of Arc was burnt at the stake nearly 500 years previously, and almost simultaneously came the idea to call the work after the Maid - more in thanksgiving for the idea (since the finding of good titles is not my strong point) than because the music really had any bearing on her story, so the overture was christened *Joan of Arc*."

On his return from this Easter 'binge' Denis finished the score, submitted it and promptly forgot about it as he resumed his teaching at East Grinstead. It was about a month later that he was summoned to the house of Herbert Whiteley[6], editor of *The British Bandsman*, and told that he had won the competition and the 100 guineas - the equivalent of two terms' salary at the time. Off he went back to East Grinstead and bought himself a motor cycle - though he didn't actually receive the cheque until some weeks later!

Notes

[1] *Sir Charles Villiers Stanford (1852-1924)* - composer, conductor and organist. One of the principal figures in the revival of British music in the late 19th and early 20th centuries, studied at Cambridge, Leipzig and Berlin. He was a prolific composer but is chiefly remembered for his influence as a teacher, teaching composition at the Royal College of Music from its founding in 1883, becoming Professor of Music at Cambridge four years later and holding both positions with distinction. His pupils included Vaughan Williams, Bliss, Howells, Ireland and Holst, all of whom were to write brass band pieces.

[2] *Sir Walter Alcock (1861-1947)* - organist and composer of church music. As organist at the Chapels Royal and assistant organist at Westminster Abbey, he played the organ at the Coronations of Edward VII and George V.

[3] *Sir Frederick Bridge (1844-1924)* - composer, conductor and organist. He held appointments as organist at Manchester Cathedral and Westminster Abbey and in 1903 became London University's first Professor of Music. His compositions were mainly oratorios but he was responsible for the musical arrangements for Queen Victoria's Diamond Jubilee service and for the Coronations of 1902 and 1911.

[4] *Dr. Charles Wood (1866-1926)* - composer and teacher, pupil of Stanford's at the Royal College of Music, where he later taught harmony, becoming a lecturer in harmony and counterpoint at Cambridge and succeeding Stanford there as Professor of Music in 1924.

[5] It was in Dieppe that Denis had helped his father, some 10 years earlier.

[6] *Herbert Whiteley* was the right hand man of John Henry Iles, Editor of *The British Bandsman* from 1906 to 1930, and one of the founders (in 1925) of the National Brass Band Club. During the 1890s he'd been organist and choirmaster at Saddleworth Parish Church, near Oldham.

Chapter 2

One Bulgar less - a sordid tale!

In the winter of 1917[1] when Denis was in the British Army, attached to a Serbian unit, he was asked to help a band provide music for the occasion of the visit of a British general.

His unit was camped in the Mitrovica Valley, at the foot of a high range of mountains - part of which was held by the Serbs and part by the opposing Bulgarians. The idea was for the band, made up of Serbs, to play the respective National Anthems for the visiting big-wig. Unfortunately, they didn't have the music for *God Save the King*, and Denis was asked to write out some band parts, go up the mountain, and show the band how it ought to go. This led to a situation in which he claims (no doubt with tongue firmly in cheek) that he must be the only conductor to have had a rehearsal interrupted whilst a couple of his players "went out and did a murder!"

It was a bitterly cold day as Denis set out in an old Ford van, climbing up the side of the mountain through lonely pine forests. Two thousand feet up, the road ended and he was supplied with a mule to take him the rest of the way. The mule was unco-operative to say the least, dumping Denis in a trench and galloping off back to its home! Eventually he reached a clearing, some 5,000 feet up, where the Serbs were camped. After what he described as an excellent lunch they all settled down to some serious rehearsal of *The King*.

Progress was slow, partly on account of Denis's limited knowledge of the Serbian language, and partly because the instruments being used were pitched differently from their British counterparts, and therefore some of the band parts he'd prepared were wrongly transposed.

In due course they started to make some progress, but after about an hour an orderly came in and spoke to a sergeant who was playing in the band. The sergeant jumped up and went out, taking a corporal with him. The rest of the band stayed put, but showed increasing signs of excitement, along with a corresponding decrease of interest in the rehearsal.

Some minutes later a shot was heard, not a particularly unusual thing only a few hundred yards from the trenches up in the mountains, so the erstwhile conductor didn't pay too much attention. Shortly the sergeant and the corporal re-appeared, picked up their instruments, and the rehearsal was resumed in earnest. Soon the band was playing *God Save the King* as well as could reasonably be expected and the rehearsal ended.

The sergeant apologised to Denis for the interruption, explaining that someone had found a stranger wandering near the camp. He did speak Serbian, but with a strong Bulgarian accent, and after a short discussion it had been decided that he must be a spy!

Spies in the camp were apt to be a nuisance, it was explained. When caught, they were *supposed* to be sent down to base for interrogation but, as Denis was told:

> 'A hundred and twenty miles from the base in the wilds of the mountains such niceties of conduct are sometimes disregarded and a quick bullet in the back saves a lot of time!'

It was also pointed out that war is a grim business and that anyway,

> *'One Bulgar less is always a help when the Bulgars aren't on your side.'*

Notes

[1] In a later report, Denis said that this event took place on a lovely hot day in June 1918.

Chapter 3

Joan of Arc and the big day

As he had composed the test piece for the 1925 Championship it seemed logical to the organisers to engage Denis as adjudicator - even though he'd had no experience of brass bands nor, I assume, had he very much experience of adjudicating. His colleague in the box was Lieutenant Charles Hoby[1], a Royal Marines Director of Music, and between them he and Denis seem to have made rather a mess of things. Back to the autobiography:

> "I did not realise, when I was invited to be one of the judges of the Championships, how little I really knew about brass bands - I suppose few men have had, for their first experience, to judge the highest and most momentous contest in this country. But Whiteley should have realised what I was going to be up against and should have arranged, for my assistance, that the other judge should be an experienced *brass* band musician, not a *military* band specialist, however eminent and knowledgeable in his own sphere. That the result of our combined judgement may have been bad must be blamed to a large extent on Whiteley. I have no means, other than by the general reaction of the band world, of knowing how bad it actually was, though I have been told by plenty of people who said they knew, that it was pretty awful."

Of course, this highlights the dilemma which still exists for contest organisers on a day such as that of the Nationals, for on that day many, if not all the *brass* band specialists will be actually *conducting* bands in the competition. Of the 1925 results Denis says,

> "I wish I could record the announcing of a popular favourite on this occasion. St. Hilda's, Foden's, Black Dyke - a name like those and the audience would have cheered for minutes and bandsmen thrown their caps in the air (if they were in the winning band). But no, an outsider got home - Marsden Colliery from Durham; an almost unconsidered rival of St. Hilda's and Harton Colliery, Marsden's nearest neighbours.
>
> The audience gasped, there was mild applause from one corner of the crowd, and on Iles went to the rest of the prizes. 2nd, Irwell Springs - well, at least the great Halliwell got one band in, even if it was his fourth string. South Moor Colliery 3rd - another 'turn-up'. My hat! *what* a decision! Well, there it was, and there it had to remain."

As John Henry Iles was the owner and organiser of the Nationals and also

Iles . . . he loved to conduct his favourite pieces*

the owner of R. Smith & Co., the firm which published most of the music played, it wasn't surprising that his weekly paper, *The British Bandsman*, gave the event the highest possible profile.

Iles himself was a larger-than-life figure,who loved publicly to extol *his* bandsmen. Even more, he loved to 'conduct' his favourite pieces with the assembled massed bands during the closing stages of a major band event such as the Nationals. From an artistic standpoint he left much to be desired but as a showman he was second to none.

Whilst many admired him and accepted that he was, for whatever reason, leading the brass band movement forward, he had his critics. Admirers were represented by *The British Bandsman* - the right wing of the banding press, so to speak, and others found their support in the rival monthly *Brass Band News*, published in Liverpool in those days.

Denis had already unwittingly and unintentionally created much fodder for both factions of the press and so, over the next few months, he received much publicity and almost overnight became a big name in the brass band world. Good publicity or bad, his star was in the ascendancy, and the next few years saw a complete re-shaping of his life-style. But,

"So much, then, for the events that directly led up to my being set down firmly in the middle of the brass band world. Firmly? Well, perhaps, that is hardly the right word. There were many who resented my intrusion and did all they could to get me out again. Sometimes they nearly succeeded. I wonder occasionally, had I known what a fight I was to have for many years, in order to get accepted as one of the brass band community, if I would have followed up the prize-winning incident as I did, or whether I would have decided to turn my back on an obvious opportunity and fade out of the picture once the Championship contest had been fought out."

Happily he stayed, but though his impact was so great, and though he was without doubt one of the most important figures of his generation in the band world, even towards the end of his life he still had his critics, especially amongst the older generation, many of whom resented change and sneered at progress. Later in his writings he declared,

"When, a few months later, my father asked me: *Where do you think this brass band business will lead you to?* I had to answer that I had no idea, but that it seemed to me that it might lead somewhere and I was willing to leave it at that."

We've seen why he composed *Joan of Arc*, and also some of the events surrounding its composition, but let's return to the autobiography for more background:

"*Joan of Arc* was published early in August 1925 and, judging from the reports in *The British Bandsman*, was well received by bands. I was too fresh at the game in those days to know that a chorus of praise in *The British Bandsman* almost invariably heralded a diatribe of condemnation in *Brass Band News*, and since Herbert Whiteley was still at that time keeping me, as it were, under a glass case - not to be let out till the great day of the Palace contest, I did not see a copy of *Brass Band News*, nor indeed did I know of its existence. So I still don't know the reactions of what I might call the anti-Iles clique."

These reactions weren't unduly harsh - certainly not against the composer. It is perhaps difficult to realise that in 1925 there were but a handful of original works for brass band. True, in the latter part of the 19th century a number of fantasia-style pieces had been written by people such as Harry Round, but these were no more than pot-pourris of popular-type melodies, strung together - often linked with cadenzas - much the same as in the operatic selections which were in vogue at the time.

The first piece of original brass band music to justify the title 'work' was Percy Fletcher's tone poem *Labour and Love*, composed for the 1913 Crystal Palace contest. Fletcher was a leading composer of light music and an experienced theatre conductor.

The next two brass band works - also tone poems - *Coriolanus* and *Life Divine* were by Cyril Jenkins, a Welsh composer who probably had a higher profile than Fletcher, and who had had organ lessons from Alcock and composition lessons from Stanford, both of whom also taught Denis. *Life Divine* was the most tightly structured piece up to that time, and though designated 'tone poem', was really a concert overture.

Hubert Bath wrote the next brass band piece, *Freedom*, calling it a 'symphony' when it was in reality a three-movement suite. He also wrote an opera and music for the stage. A composer with a modest but growing reputation in the musical world, he made something of a name for himself in brass bands, just as Fletcher and Jenkins had, but was to achieve more fame as the composer of *Cornish Rhapsody* for the film *Love Story*.

The composer of the next two works, though by no means a major composer, did have considerable standing in the musical establishment. Henry Geehl was born in 1881 in London. After musical studies with various teachers he decided on a career as a concert pianist, though eventually he gave up this idea in favour of conducting and composition. He conducted in a number of theatres between 1902 and 1908, and later taught at Trinity College of Music. He composed much orchestral, instrumental, piano and vocal music, his best-known composition being the song *For You Alone*.

It was with some justification, therefore, that Denis turned to Henry Geehl, the most firmly-established composer to write for brass band so far, and to the scores of *Oliver Cromwell* (1923) and *On the Cornish Coast* (1924). The former, a concert overture and, in my view, a much better piece than its rhapsodic successor, seems to have had considerable influence on *Joan of Arc*. Not that Denis used the Geehl work as a model. Quite the contrary. There's almost a reaction against the relatively easy-on-the-ear melodies of *Cromwell*; there's no slow introduction; and whereas Geehl opens with an eerie motif in C minor (Example 3) Denis begins with a rather pompous theme in B flat major (Example 2). Moreover, Geehl's compositional 'seams' are fairly obvious, whereas Denis's are quite well concealed.

Example 2 Joan of Arc – opening

Example 3 Oliver Cromwell – opening

However, each uses the term 'Concert Overture', each writes in sonata form, each writes a fugal exposition at some point, Geehl at the start of the development section, based on material from the introduction, Wright also at the start of the development section, but as new material. (For more detail about structure, refer to chapters 16 and 17.)

There are melodic similarities between *Oliver Cromwell* and *Joan of Arc* which may be pure coincidence but which, I can't help thinking, must have been part of a sub-conscious influence (see motif (a) in Examples 3 and 4 and motif (b) in Examples 5 and 6). Examples 7 and 8 show the respective fugue subjects. Here also there are some apparent motivic similarities (motifs (c) and (d)), and the subjects seem to have a common spirit.

Example 4 Joan of Arc – from transition

Example 5 Oliver Cromwell – 2ⁿᵈ Subject

Example 6 Joan of Arc – 2ⁿᵈ Subject

Herbert Whiteley had, to his credit, spotted likenesses and had phoned Geehl to ask if he had submitted an entry. On being told 'no' he had come to the conclusion that Denis Wright must in fact exist.

Example 7 Oliver Cromwell – fugue subject

Example 8 Joan of Arc – fugue subject

In the autobiography, with an obvious air of guilt, Denis writes that *Joan of Arc*

"Shows my indebtedness to Henry Geehl[2] and the thoroughness with which I had studied his two scores. (In acknowledging this indebtedness now, I hope I am atoning for never having done so in the past, an omission which I am afraid Geehl himself noticed on one or two specific occasions, such as the reading of my little book on *Brass Band Scoring*, published in 1935.)"

As a test piece *Joan of Arc* sets out to exploit and expose virtually every instrument in the band, though there are no big solos. Interpretative imagination is called for, and in 1925 it must have been quite an interesting piece to rehearse. There's no published synopsis or programme. Indeed, considering that the piece came first and the title later, that's hardly surprising. However, here again is a possible Geehl influence, because he was the first of the early brass band composers *not* to sketch out something which would give conductors an indication of the moods of the music - bearing in mind that they'd been reared on the operatic selection, where almost every phrase had a traceable extra-musical meaning.

Though *Joan of Arc* has been recorded several times, and selected on other occasions as a test piece, it has never become a part of standard band repertoire. Denis speaks quite harshly about it in the autobiography, maintaining that it was not well scored. "Hardly surprising," he says, "since it was my first attempt."

He further states that a concert overture "should possess architectural value", whilst "*Joan* was long-winded". His most stern comment, however, is,

> "Alas, my music was poor stuff enough, to represent such a magnificent story. I can only plead, in self-justification, that it was never really intended to, but a title *had* to be found!"

In 1930 Denis scored *Joan of Arc* for full orchestra, with double woodwind plus the usual brass and percussion. (Could this have been the first example of a brass band piece being transcribed for orchestra? It pre-dates Elgar's orchestration of *Severn Suite* by two years.) The orchestral version was first performed by the Harlesden Philharmonic Orchestra in March 1931, and was performed twice by the Bournemouth Symphony Orchestra the following year, one of the performances being broadcast. The orchestral version adheres strictly to the form of that for band but the figuration is, understandably, more complex, and occasionally the Italian terms are modified, and a few extras added.

Several years later Denis made a revision of *Joan of Arc* - for his own amusement. It was never played, but he felt it said as much in eight and a half minutes as the original version did in 12[3].—On the question of whether or not the overture had a programme he wrote:

> "It often amused me, later on, to read fanciful descriptions of where this or that section of the music aptly illustrated this or that aspect of the story: imagination can do a lot in that respect, though if you think it over you will admit that a piece of music - any music - which has well contrasted sections, bold, meditative, and so on, can be without any mental effort linked up with a story possessing, as Joan's does, equivalent contrasts of martial bravery and panoply of war and the mystical side represented by the voices she is reputed to have heard that spurred her on to such great valour, and eventual sacrifice."

Notes

[1] *Charles Hoby* (1869-1938), Mus. Doc. (Oxon), LRAM, ARCM - Director of Music, Band of the Royal Marines (Chatham) 1907-1928; professor of military band work at the Royal College of Music; awarded MBE in 1926; author of two books on military bands; composed several pieces both for military band and orchestra; on retiring from the Marines became Musical Director for Rhyl Corporation and was succeeded at Chatham by Lieut. P. S. G. O'Donnell (see p. 98).

[2] *Henry Ernest Geehl* died in London on 14th January 1961, aged 79. He had composed 12 brass band test pieces.

[3] This must have been the 1st movement of the Orchestral Suite he submitted for his Doctorate in 1940 (see p. 91)

Chapter 4

Confessions of an Adjudicator

It has been traditional to surround test pieces and the identity of composers and adjudicators at important contests with a certain amount of secrecy. Having composed the 1925 Crystal Palace test piece and been appointed adjudicator, Denis had to be kept out of the way. Herbert Whiteley, who looked after such protocol did, however, let him out of his "glass case" on one occasion, though taking pains to impress on him that he must not make himself known to anyone.

St. Hilda's Colliery Band were playing at the Wembley Exhibition and during the week-long engagement they would rehearse the test piece most mornings. (This was common practice for many years with bands which were able to attract these 'residential' engagements at the appropriate time of year.) Whiteley told the young composer to go and listen outside the rehearsal room so that he could 'get an idea of what a good band sounded like'.

Denis described this as "an interesting experience", though admitting that he was more interested in hearing his piece for the first time than in trying to sort out the fine tone and technical qualities of the band.

"I suppose I was doing the latter unconsciously to some extent, but my first reaction was not *how lovely the band sounds* but *how grand my music sounds.*"

He goes on to wonder how he might have reacted if the band had been a bad one. Would he have thought *What a rotten band* or *What lousy music?* "Probably, in my pride," he said, "the former."

The great day arrived - Saturday the 26th of September 1925. Our Mr. Wright arrived at the Crystal Palace at about 11.30 in the morning. Making his way past the crowded trade stands he reached the Director's office, where Herbert Whiteley introduced him to his co-adjudicator, Lieutenant Charles Hoby, Mus. Doc., Director of Music of the Band of His Majesty's Royal Marines (Chatham Division).

The two adjudicators were then escorted to the judges' box - up in the gallery. Half a bottle of whisky and a large pile of sandwiches were there - "a most thoughtful gesture," commented Denis. "But," he went on,

"The next year, when I judged the second section, the whisky had shrunk to a quarter-bottle. It subsequently changed into two bottles of lemonade, if I remember rightly, or was it a jug of water?"

Cresswell Colliery under J. A. Greenwood had drawn the dreaded number one and their performance had quite an impact on the young composer, for the first time hearing an actual performance of his composition.

"I don't think I shall ever forget how the opening by the first band thrilled me and made me feel, from where we sat almost above the band, the enormous power - not noise, but sheer dynamic energy that lies behind the playing of a good band."

But all was not well in the box. As each band finished playing, Hoby insisted that he and Denis should both read their written comments out loud.

"As can be imagined, this took the dickens of a time and it was not long before the audience was whistling and making vocal signs of disapproval during these long waits."

Denis, sensing the growing restlessness, tried to hurry Hoby up, but not until near the end, when it was becoming obvious that they were going well past the time-limit and holding up the organ recital, did Hoby relax and allow just a summary of the notes to be exchanged.

"At long last I am able thus to explain those awful waits between each band during that 1925 Championship contest, and to decline to accept any responsibility for them! Perhaps the Management thought we were occupied with the half-bottle of whisky and - awful thought - we may have been the cause of that inverted miracle whereby the bottle shrank within a year or two and finally changed into water. If that is so, I offer my apologies to all subsequent judges. It must have been a nuisance to them, to have to supply their own whisky. I don't mind, I don't care for it much anyway."

After it was all over, going back into London in a packed train, Denis heard two bandsmen discussing the results. 'What d'you make of it, Bill?' asked one. Bill's reply, heedless of ladies being present, was terse and pointed. 'The most b .... awful decision I've ever heard!'

Denis's comment: *"I was rather glad they didn't recognise me."*

Chapter 5

What the papers said

The competition offering 100 guineas for a suitable test piece for the 1925 Crystal Palace contest was first announced on the front page of *The British Bandsman* in the issue of 28th February. The following week the first of several advertisements appeared, also stating the rules of the competition. Similar adverts appeared in *The Times* and *The Daily Telegraph*, as well as in the principal musical journals of the day - *Musical Times*, *Musical Opinion*, *Musical News* and *Musical Standard*. An article on p. 2 of the 5th March issue of *British Bandsman*, headed *Composers and the Brass Band*, said that the prize offered may be regarded as a challenge to 'the present day school of composers'.

There were plenty of these around at the time, though I doubt if many of them could realistically have been expected to risk the vagaries of a composing competition, especially in a relatively unknown field. The list is nevertheless quite thought-provoking and includes Elgar, Delius, Bantock, Walford Davies, Vaughan Williams, Holst, Frank Bridge, Ireland, Bax, Bliss, Rubbra, Walton, Tippett, Rawsthorne and Constant Lambert, and in varying degrees of 'lightness' Eric Coates, Edward German, Albert Ketèlbey and Ivor Novello! Some did of course, in later years, write for brass band, but through commission rather than competition.

The article referred to went on to say that the competition offered not only the 'handsome prize', but also 'an outlet for his (the composer's) creative skill, such as no other musical medium has at its disposal.' It lamented the fact that composers were neglecting a movement which was 'young, healthy, virile and strong,' going on to say that the brass band had outgrown its resources and that there weren't, within its own ranks, the composers 'who can produce the stuff for which it is hungry.' Time has certainly proved that there's more than a grain of truth in those opinions, outlined in a column by a regular contributor to *The British Bandsman*, writing under the pen-name *The Exile*.

Advertisements continued to appear regularly up to and including the issue of 2nd May (though entries had closed three days earlier), but there were no further articles until 30th May, when the following was revealed:

"One of the rules of the competition gave the adjudicator the right to withhold the prize, but it was evident before the competition closed that there would be no necessity to enforce this rule."

Not until the issue of 15th August was the name of the winner made public. Denis himself had known for about three months, but under the rules of the competition no details of test pieces or composers were allowed to be publicised until six weeks before the event. The momentous announcement was made in an article headed:

Testpiece for the Championship
Overture: JOAN OF ARC - A NEW COMPOSER.

The article stated:

'For the 1913 and successive contests for the Championship the music had been chosen by Mr. Herbert Whiteley (musical adviser to Mr. J. Henry Iles), who adjudicated this prize competition and stated in his report of 1st June last:

Several of the compositions submitted were the work of recognised composers. Others were from unknown men. I have very carefully examined all the manuscripts and I award the prize to the composer of the overture Joan of Arc - *Mr. Denis Wright.*

As a composer Mr. Denis Wright is as yet almost entirely unknown. He has written a few orchestral pieces and songs.'

It would be interesting to know exactly who the 'recognised composers' were, but I fear that will remain a secret until the day of that other Judgement!

The story of how the title came to be chosen was not revealed to the public, though I believe Denis himself made no secret of it. In the issue of 22nd August there was a long article by one John F. Porte, explaining what a splendid topic *Joan of Arc* made for a musical composition. The following week there was a study of *Jeanne d'Arc* herself by a correspondent calling himself (or, less likely in those days, herself) *The Young Recruit*. An article in a later issue referred to the large number of composers who had based musical works on the same subject.

Over a period of months there was regular mention of *Joan of Arc* - both in articles and advertisements, but the first serious review appeared on 12th September. Written by a Leslie Aldous, the final sentence opined:

"Excellent though its predecessors have been, this veritable work of art will hold its own."

Alas, this was more optimistic than prophetic! Nevertheless, all printed comments about the overture were favourable, including opinions expressed by officials of 14 competing bands, revealed on 26th September, the day of the contest. A further review by Mr. Porte, in the same issue, hinted that he now suspected the music had little to do with the title, though he seemingly still regarded it as a good composition.

The contest-day issue of *The British Bandsman* was devoted largely to various aspects of the day's events. The following week the full results were published, along with the 'remarks' by ALL the adjudicators on ALL performances in ALL six sections. The events of the day were therefore not

4   THE BRITISH BANDSMAN.   March 7, 1925.

discussed for a further week, and there was not the slightest hint of the atmosphere at the announcement of the results, as described by Denis. If the contest *had* produced an unpopular result then the paper did a first-rate whitewashing job, though one writer did suggest that in future it might be a good idea to screen bands from the *audience*!

Such was the popularity of the piece at the time that no fewer than four commercial recordings were made - two of them complete (for the first time with a brass band test piece, it was claimed), and two abridged. The complete versions were recorded by Marsden Colliery and St. Hilda's, both for Regal. The incomplete recordings were made by Horwich on Zonophone and Black Dyke on Winner! Extracts from W. A. Chislett's reviews in *The Gramophone* appeared in *The British Bandsman* on 19th and 26th December, and were more complimentary about the music than they were about the recorded performances.

On 7th November all the recordings were fully reviewed by Harry Wild. It was apparent that he had cottoned on to the notion that there was little relationship between overture and title, but he published a rather surprising letter which he stated he had received from Denis, saying:

"I imagine Joan, in all the simplicity of her faith in the 'voices' she hears, fired with a noble resolve to save her country at any cost. I have not attempted to work any programme into the music. The story is not illustrated, as it were, by the sequence of musical events. It is more a commentary on her character; the simplicity contrasting with the grandness of her project; trials and troubles overcome, opposition put to confusion, and at the end, in spite of her martyrdom, a summing up as if to say, *You can think what you like about it, but there's no getting away from the fact that she did a marvellous thing in that she carried through her work to such an end without flinching.* It's a sad story, but very thrilling."

Evidently the composer had decided - or perhaps had been persuaded - that a word picture relating to the overture's musical content wouldn't go amiss.

So much for coverage in *The British Bandsman*. Denis's own views on the competition find some support in *Brass Band News*, though not universally so.

Brass Band News was a monthly paper, made up mainly of adverts, snippets of news about people and events, reports and results of contests, and news items and gossip about bands in different parts of the country. These latter were written anonymously under pen names such as *Northerner*, *Trotter*, *Moderato* and so on. It is very interesting to read the comments of these district correspondents in the run-up to the contest, and even moreso afterwards. Thus, Tyneside Notes in the issue of 1st September state:

'Marsden Colliery I hear are competing again at the Crystal Palace. I also hear good reports about their concert playing . . . .'

A month later and the same correspondent:

'Marsden Colliery have entered for the Championship section again at the Palace, and Secretary Cunningham informs me that they have had two practices every day since the piece came out . . . .'

Sandbach Notes, covering the area of Foden's Motor Works Band, made no mention of Crystal Palace in the September issue, but in October reported:

'The band is now hard at work on *Joan of Arc*, the Crystal Palace test piece and again I say watch Foden's.'

September's Halifax notes, taking in Black Dyke, went further:

'Dike[1] is in splendid form and will be able to get in at least a score of full rehearsals for Crystal Palace. The test piece suits the band down to the ground and bar accidents they should win.'

Confidence indeed! The issue of 1st November reflected post-contest attitudes in the regions, coloured by the success or otherwise of local favourites. Halifax's correspondent said simply:

NATIONAL BAND FESTIVAL, 1925.

CRYSTAL PALACE.

JUDGES' AWARDS.

Championship CONTEST.

FIRST PRIZE to Band which played No: 4

SECOND PRIZE to Band which played No: 7

THIRD PRIZE to Band which played No: 17

FOURTH PRIZE to Band which played No: 10

FIFTH BAND in order of Merit: 15

SIXTH BAND in order of Merit: 5

SEVENTH BAND in order of Merit: 16

Charles Hucy)
Denis Wright) Adjudicators.
)

'I can quite imagine thousands of your readers saying, What about Dike? Poor old Dike, Hard luck, etc.'

Sandbach Notes were more outspoken:

'Still another Crystal Palace contest has passed with its attendant joys and sorrows. Dissatisfaction is rife and not without good cause. I cannot remember, and I'll wager that no-one else can, a decision which caused such consternation. The decision was received in stony silence, as though the huge audience failed to understand what really was being said. One felt that the audience believed it hadn't heard aright, or that it had not heard at all and was still waiting for the announcement of the name of the band that was for 12 months to carry the high honour of the day. . . .

Ye gods, verily it passeth all understanding. Even the most narrow minded of us must admit that the greatest can have an off day, when they fall just a little short of the excellence required to place them on the pinnacle. But who can imagine that six of England's best . . . . can fail to reach their usual excellence in any given contest? When such great bands as Foden's, St. Hilda's, Dike, Wingates, Horwich, and Cresswell all fail to gain a prize then something is wrong and very much so.'

The writer of Westhoughton District Notes, covering two competing bands (Horwich and Wingates), concurs with the views of Denis himself:

'Now I am not going into details about the playing except so far as it concerns our district bands, but there are one or two things that happened, and have happened before, that I should like to mention.

The first is that the Palace contest stands condemned, not because there is anything underhand or unscrupulous about it, for I am firmly convinced that so far as the officials are concerned, they do all in their power to give every band a fair chance, but because it is too much of a lottery as things are at present.

The adjudicators were the composer of the test piece and a military man, who may have a thorough knowledge of military bands. But do they get enough practical experience of brass bands?

Certainly the composer had some claim to judge his own composition, if he was judging the same kind of musical combination that he had his experience in, but that doesn't alter the fact that if he hasn't had long experience in brass bands he is not a fit person to judge them, whatever his qualifications as a musician; and his music stamps him as a thorough musician.

How would military bands take their medicine if some brass band fellow was to judge a contest and give a decision out of harmony with other people who are in a position to know?'

Strong words, and yet things haven't changed all that much since 1925! But two interesting facts which emerge are that there was no criticism of the test piece, and no accusation that any form of skulduggery had taken place.

Understandably, the doom and gloom of the disappointed correspondents was not shared by their opposite number on Tyneside, who said,

'I saw the Marsden men arrive in Newcastle and heard them play the test piece. What a band: *Just like a huge organ* was a remark passed by the crowd where I was standing.'

In fact, there's much evidence to suggest that Marsden Colliery Band was a strong contender for the 1925 title. It was one of 19 brass bands in South Shields at the time, and these included St. Hilda's, Harton and Boldon Colliery bands. St. Hilda's had won the Nationals in 1912, 1920, 1921 and 1924 - and were to win again in 1926, and Harton had won the Belle Vue contest in 1919. Thus, there were many very experienced players in the area, which had acquired something of a reputation as 'the hot-bed of banding'.

Mines had been closed for something like 20 weeks prior to the date of the Nationals, therefore rehearsal time had been virtually unlimited, and it is said that Marsden had 76 rehearsals on *Joan of Arc*.

Not only that. Several members were former St. Hilda's or Harton players and had previous experience of Nationals wins. Incredibly, Dave Martin, Marsden's euphonium player, notched up his fifth with the 1925 victory, and when John Henry Iles travelled north to present the trophy (as he always did) he quipped that the way things were going he would soon need a season ticket!

It was the second Crystal Palace win for conductor J. A. Greenwood, and according to octogenarian Bill Blackett, until his recent death the only surviving member of the winning band, he had been very scathing in his comments about the band's playing, saying that they sounded 'like Tyneside fog!' He maintained that at one point the bandsmen were going to refuse to let him conduct.

But whatever doubt anyone may have had about the performance or the result, the following advertisement proudly appeared in the December issue of *Brass Band News*:

Marsden Colliery Band

World's Champions

Winners of 1,000 Guinea Trophy, Crystal Palace 1925
Winners of People's Challenge Shield, Crystal Palace 1922

OPEN FOR ENGAGEMENTS, SATISFACTION GUARANTEED

SOLOISTS SECOND TO NONE

Mr. Jack Boddice - Bandmaster

Note

[1] 'Dike' - old spelling of 'Dyke'.

Chapter 6

What next?

Having been so successful with his first brass band composition, it was natural that Denis should follow it up with further pieces. *The White Rider*, written for the 1927 Crystal Palace contest, was designated 'Symphonic Poem.' *Princess Nada* ("pronounced Nardah") came six years later (1933) and was described as a 'Symphonic Legend'. Both have programme notes, the former more extensive than the latter.

The inspiration for *The White Rider* came from *Kralyevitch Marko (Marco the King's Son)*, Marko being a legendary hero in Serbian history. (You will recall that Denis served in Serbia during the First World War.) The lengthy programme note ends:

> "The connection between this legend and the music is one of mood rather than an attempt to illustrate the actual story, though the music may be roughly divided into four sections: the struggle against heavy odds, leading to a brooding realisation of temporary defeat; then, after a clarion call, the struggle is renewed, but with a new hopefulness, and finally a joyful pæan of triumph signifies final victory."

Evidently from the outset Denis saw the desirability of providing a 'programme', as an aid both to interpretation and appreciation. I think that *The White Rider* would be easier on the listener's ear in 1927 than *Joan of Arc* had been a couple of years earlier. It certainly contained more singable tunes and was based on melody rather than motif. The music was continuous, but the four linked sections followed (in miniature, of course) the pattern of a symphony.

My own reaction on reading through the score was that it seemed like a backward step, compositionally speaking, from *Joan of Arc*, and I wondered if Denis was trying to achieve a more direct communication with his (in the main) musically unsophisticated audience. It was interesting to read subsequently therefore, in the autobiography, that *The White Rider* was never intended to have been a top section piece. He had actually been asked to write something a little easier for one of the lower sections, and was very surprised when he discovered it was being used in the highest section. He described its musical ideas as commonplace, saying that it was sheer programme music, lacking any musical form, and concluding, "*The White Rider* sets out to tell a little story; bereft of its story it means precious little." Harsh, maybe - but interesting!

As a matter of further interest, on the occasion of its première, at Crystal Palace on 24th September 1927, when 16 bands competed for the 1,000 guinea trophy (the Championship section), the adjudicators were Henry Geehl, whose music had helped Denis in 1925, and Edward Dunn. Their results appear to have been just about as controversial as those of 1925, with Carlisle St. Stephens winning, Callender's Cable Works coming second and Carlton Main third - leaving out Black Dyke, Foden's, Wingates and several other big names.

The selection of *The White Rider* as test piece for the 1927 contest was announced during August and both *The British Bandsman* and *Brass Band News* published articles about it during the following weeks. *"Broadacre"* in *The British Bandsman* of 24th September, however, had a slight reservation as he wrote:

'I had the pleasure of perusing the score of *The White Rider* as well as hearing it played. A very fine composition it is, but it is not so exacting in technical difficulties as some of its predecessors'.

In the issue of 22nd October the adjudicators gave their opinions, Henry Geehl saying,

'As to the music of *The White Rider,* I felt from the first glance at the score that this would be a very difficult piece - the composer has not gone out of his way to find new effects - yet there is something about the music that is fascinating. Only the most artistic band will come out on top of this, I feel certain.'

Not the most perceptive of conclusions! Edward Dunn, the other adjudicator, shared some of the doubts of 'Broadacre'.

'Mr Denis Wright gave us a work easy to comprehend and yet demanding in care and treatment, although more exacting tests of the soloists would have considerably enhanced its value, at least as the National Championship testpiece.'

As was becoming common practise, recordings of the test piece were made, including a complete version by the winners, Carlisle St. Stephens, on Regal, and an abridged version by Dyke, again on Winner. *The British Bandsman* of 17th December quoted a rave review from the *Daily Telegraph* of Dyke's recording.

My impression of the next test piece, *Princess Nada,* was that it went even further down the hill to meet its audience. The plot concerns one Prince Ivar who, having conquered a neighbouring state, decrees that one hundred maidens, led by Princess Nada, are to become his slaves. Meeting the sad procession, he falls instantly in love with Nada, forgives the conquered state, frees the maidens, marries the Princess, and of course they live happily ever after. As the music unfolds, the score displays a succession of somewhat naïve comments (see p.122).

One must ask, why this undoubted backward step? The answer seems to me to be regrettably simple. *Princess Nada* was composed for the Belle Vue contest, and though this was in the very heartland of brass band country, the

Manchester audience was less musically sophisticated than that which assembled at the Crystal Palace. The London contest, whether at Crystal Palace or, more latterly, in the Royal Albert Hall, has always been the principal pioneer for new music. For example, the first original work appeared in London in 1913, whilst Manchester had to wait until 1925. Even then, the original works meted out to the Northern audiences during these years (prior to Herbert Howells's *Pageantry* of 1934) were musically some way behind their London counterparts. Compare the following:

London	**Belle Vue**
1925 *Joan of Arc* (Wright)	*Macbeth* (Keighley)
1926 *An Epic Symphony* (Fletcher)	*A Midsummer Night's Dream* (Keighley)
1927 *The White Rider* (Wright)	*Merry Wives of Windsor* (Keighley)
1928 *A Moorside Suite* (Holst)	*Lorenzo* (Keighley)
1929 *Victory* (Jenkins)	*Sonata Pathetique* (Beethoven)
1930 *Severn Suite* (Elgar)	*Oriental Rhapsody* (Bantock)
1931 *Honour and Glory* (Bath)	*Suite: Springtime* (Morris)
1932 *A Downland Suite* (Ireland)	*The Crusaders* (Keighley)
1933 *Prometheus Unbound* (Bantock)	*Princess Nada* (Wright)

Granted, there are a few weak links even in the London chain, but it is way ahead of the Belle Vue list for musical quality and content, and I cannot help thinking that these lists, along with the aids to interpretation to be found in *Princess Nada*, are an indictment of Northern audiences - or at least a reflection of Henry Iles's opinion of them.

Denis was in the box for the 1933 Belle Vue contest at which his latest opus was to be the test. His colleagues were Herbert Bennett and George Hawkins - quite an experienced team. Brighouse and Rastrick were the winners, and as this was the second win in their ultimate hat-trick, we may assume that this was neither unpredictable nor a shock result.

Press reaction to both pieces was again favourable, though coverage less extensive than for *Joan of Arc*, which undoubtedly benefited from being a competition winner in itself. *Princess Nada* had the least press coverage of all the three test pieces, possibly because it was to be used at Belle Vue and not Crystal Palace. The September issue of *Brass Band News* tersely announced in a preview of the Belle Vue Festival:

'The test piece is a symphonic legend, *Princess Nada*, specially composed by Mr. Denis Wright. It is a good test, and will extend all the competing bands.'

The British Bandsman did rather better (as usual), its first reaction being a reprint of an article from *The Halifax Daily Courier*:

'The testpiece for the September contest has now arrived and we have already sampled it,' writes the secretary of the Brighouse and Rastrick Band. 'From a first observation it is on similar lines to last year's testpiece *The Crusaders* and appears to be a very delightful composition, being very tuneful.'

WHITEHALL THEATRE

EAST GRINSTEAD

UNDER THE DIRECT MANAGEMENT OF THE PROPRIETORS

Resident Manager -   -   -   Mr. F. C. Maplesden.

By kind permission of Messrs. Chappell & Co. Ltd.

The East Grinstead Operatic Society

PRESENT

"THE REBEL MAID"

A Romantic Light Opera in Three Acts

BOOK BY ALEXANDER M. THOMPSON

LYRICS BY GERALD DALTON

MUSIC BY MONTAGUE F. PHILLIPS

Produced under the personal direction of
PETER J. MORRIS

Musical Director -   -   Mr. DENIS WRIGHT, mus. bac.

MONDAY, TUESDAY, WEDNESDAY and THURSDAY

JANUARY 15th, 16th, 17th and 18th, 1934

AT 8 EACH EVENING   MATINEE WEDNESDAY AT 2.30

Brighouse had won first prize in the previous year, playing *The Crusaders*, and they were quite right in pointing to similarities between that and *Princess Nada*.

A couple of weeks after the contest a *News Chronicle* review of the piece was reprinted in *The British Bandsman*:

'As music, *Princess Nada* is attractive, and has character of its own. The love music contains at least one vague and fleeting reminiscence of the impassioned scenes between Siegfried and Brunnhilde in Wagner's *Ring* but the work as a whole has an atmosphere peculiar to itself'. (I imagine that is meant as a compliment!)

Finally, and in the same edition of *The British Bandsman*, Denis himself gave his impressions of the performances at the contest. His remarks were generally complimentary, but he made the point that the sub-titles had had the effect of "over-stimulation" in some of the performances. He was not to indulge in this technique again for almost 30 years, when he used it (though with far more subtlety) in *Tam o' Shanter's Ride*.

In 1926, the year following the controversial decision in the Championship section at the Crystal Palace, and the year in which he became Mr. Denis Wright, Mus. Bac., he judged the next section down - the 'Grand Shield'. The test piece was again *Joan of Arc*. The following year's contest also saw Denis adjudicating the Grand Shield, but in 1928 (the year of *A Moorside Suite*), though at the contest, he seems not to have been involved. However, his Fantasia *Hanover* was used as the test piece in the Junior Cup section.

Away from brass bands, but no doubt as a consequence of his work with them, the years following 1925 saw a considerable change in Denis's lifestyle.

He continued in his job as a school teacher in East Grinstead and must also have been continuing his studies, as he gained the degree of Bachelor of Music at Durham, an external degree which didn't require attendance at the University, except for the purpose of the examinations, which would probably have been spread over a couple of years. (Though completing his degree at Durham he apparently started it at Oxford. Neither university has a copy of his Exercise but according to the Durham Librarian it was a cantata called *Sennecherib*).

In 1929 he left East Grinstead to become Organist and Director of Music at St George's School, Harpenden, a co-educational public school, and the school at which he had been a pupil some 20 years earlier. This appointment was rather short-lived, because in 1931 he took up the post of General Music Editor for the music publishers Chappell & Co. Ltd., a post he held until 1936, when he joined the BBC.

His work at Chappell's included proof-reading and a large amount of scoring - both for bands and orchestras. He also took on arrangements for other companies, and was accepting engagements as a conductor, working with orchestras, choral societies and in opera, as well as with brass bands. Amongst his work at this time, he apparently renewed his association with East Grinstead, being appointed Musical Director of the Operatic Society.

Under his direction the Society performed *The Rebel Maid* in 1934, *The Geisha* in the following year and then in 1936, his last year with the Society, *The Yeomen of the Guard*. The 1934 show was said to have been one of East Grinstead's biggest, with 15 principals in the cast, 50 in the chorus and an orchestra of 30.

I have not been able to find much detail of the other engagements or appointments, but I'm indebted to Mr Ernest Brown, a former member of the Crystal Palace Band for much valuable and interesting information. He first

The young Denis Wright

met Denis at a Crystal Palace Band rehearsal prior to a concert being given in the Concert Hall of the Crystal Palace itself in December 1929. Denis was there to conduct a performance of his *White Rider*, commemorating the band's winning of the Grand Shield a few months earlier. But he was also continuing his work in the orchestral field, as Mr. Brown well remembers.

'Early in 1930 I was invited to play with the South London Philharmonic Society Orchestra. To my surprise at the first rehearsal for a Wagner concert I found that Mr. Wright was the sub-conductor and tympanist, and what a player he turned out to be. At that time the orchestra engaged professional players for the brass section. These players came from the London Symphony Orchestra where the conductor of the local orchestra was principal 2nd violin. The first trumpet was a player named Mr. Solomon[1].'

Apparently Mr. Wright was on the committee of this local orchestra when it was decided that the professional players hired from the LSO could no longer be afforded. Denis Wright suggested that I be approached to form a brass section of 2 trumpets and 3 trombones. I formed this brass section. . . . On our first rehearsal for *Elijah* Mr. Wright was in charge. I suppose he could see that we were a little bored with the very long tacets that brass have in this oratorio. In the last part of the rehearsal he announced that he was going to give the new brass section a chance to show their worth. He brought out *Les Preludes*. After some moments he stopped the playing to tell us we were drowning the orchestra!'

Denis's orchestral work continued spasmodically more or less throughout his life. For example, he conducted the Pinner (Middlesex) Orchestra from about 1944. He was also conducting an orchestra at Harlesden between 1947 and 1949, and as late as 1966 he was conductor of the Manor House Hospital Operatic Society[2].

These were all amateur groups, but professionally he became involved with orchestras through his BBC work, part of which was the founding of the Westminster Orchestra for broadcasts in the BBC's Transcription Service, involved in overseas transmissions.

The 1930s saw Denis doing more brass band conducting. In 1931 he conducted two bands in the 'Grand Shield' - Cambridge Railway (which came fifth) and Raunds Temperance. Again, according to Mr. Brown,

'From 1931 onwards the Crystal Palace Band played in the Massed Bands at the evening concert following the contests. Denis would instruct us for these items, then a week or so before the event John Henry Iles would come in his Rolls Royce to run through the pieces he was to conduct'.

In 1933 Denis was appointed Musical Director of the Crystal Palace Band, which by then was a regular broadcasting combination. He was able to make use of this band and it's BBC involvement to expand the brass band's repertoire, as we shall see later. Mr. Brown comments,

'Though he never won a prize at a contest he made us into a very good concert band'.

At about the same time Denis also took over Friary Silver Band in Guildford, a band which seems to have been rather more involved in contests than concerts. He was also appearing with some regularity as an adjudicator and conducting massed band concerts, no doubt achieving higher standards both in both performance and programme content than at the events which took place following the Crystal Palace contests. The April issue of *Brass Band News* contained the following:

'Mr. Denis Wright, who in renewing his advert for the following year writes: *I am managing to keep quite busy, mostly with orchestral work. I paid a visit to Leicester Contest. It was a very good contest with some fine playing.*
We would like to see Mr. Wright doing more with brass bands'.
Evidently it *does* pay to advertise!

Notes

[1] *John Solomon* was one of the four originating members of the LSO. A noted trumpet player, he later became Professor of Trumpet at the Royal Academy. He died in 1956, at the age of 96.

[2] *The Manor House* Hospital in North London deals to-day primarily with industrial accidents and sickness, but was set up originally towards the end of the first World War for the treatment of disabled soldiers and sailors. It was established to continue the work begun by Dudley Wright (Denis's father) at the hospital he had established in France during the war. He became one of the Manor House's first and leading surgeons, and Denis's involvement with the hospital's operatic society renewed his connection, after some 40 years, with a movement of which he had seen the very beginning. In more recent years there have been further developments at this hospital, its links with the Trade Union movement resulting in specialist treatment for many working musicians who have developed certain medical conditions (see *The Musician*, March 1994, p. 21).

Chapter 7

Other pre-war compositions

Despite the relatively high profile of Denis Wright's brass band pieces so far discussed, none of them achieved a permanent place in the repertoire. All were recorded, all were used as test pieces in the years before World War II and no doubt each received the occasional broadcast and many concert performances - especially by bands which won major prizes in the contests in which they were premièred. But still, unlike many of the early test pieces by Fletcher, Jenkins and Geehl, and especially those by Holst, Elgar, Ireland and company, they did not survive the war years.

However, amongst the early works there is an exception and, paradoxically, it concerns a piece which had a far less illustrious birth than the three so far discussed. *Tintagel*, composed in 1930 and therefore Denis's third major band piece, was turned down as a test piece by Whiteley and Iles on the grounds that it was too difficult. Its chequered career began on 17th November 1930 when it was broadcast by Callender's Cable Works Band. Callender's kept it in their repertoire for several years, and it was also featured regularly by Foden's[1]. Hawkes took over the copyright in 1934, but transferred it to R. Smith & Co. in 1955. It was used as test piece for the Grand Shield in 1957 (by then competed for in Belle Vue's Spring Festival), after which it became quite popular and was featured by many bands - especially by those which had a good trombone soloist!

Denis always felt that this was the best of his early pieces and that it would have made "a fine Championship test". History has proved him at least partially right, because it is the only one of those first four band pieces to have survived. Even so, it has never been used in the top section of a major contest, though it has been used at lower levels, has been recorded, broadcast and played in concert many times.

There is a beautiful but quite demanding trombone solo in the second movement (Example 9) and some unusual rhythmical activity in the third (Example 30) which, though causing few problems to-day, would have been somewhat perplexing in 1930, and may have been the cause of the piece's rejection.

Tintagel was a suite - only the fifth brass band piece with separate movements. There seemed to be a reluctance, especially on the part of minor composers, to write suites. Either they were obsessed with writing overtures, tone poems or symphonic whatevers, or they were reluctant to have a break in the middle of the piece, lest perhaps an attack of applause should break out in the wrong place! Indeed, some of the early Thomas Keighley pieces used at Belle Vue in the mid-1920s seem quite obviously to have been conceived as suites, and then had links added. Holst, Elgar, Ireland, Howells and Bliss on the other hand, all wrote suites for band, but not until after the second World War did the lesser composers adopt this form with any regularity.

Example 9 Tintagel – opening of 2nd movement

Following the example of Holst's *Moorside Suite* and Elgar's *Severn Suite*, *Tintagel* paved the way for several later suites both by Denis himself and also some excellent examples by Eric Ball. It emphasised the fact that subtlety in structure could be achieved even in the smaller forms and was the forerunner of some very fine suites, especially for lower section bands.

There is another overture, first published by Hawkes in 1933, and called *The Sea (Thalassa)*. It has the look of a test piece but seems not to have been used as such. It was broadcast once or twice but even though it was re-printed by Molenaar's in 1960 it doesn't seem to have got very far.

There are four more pieces dating from this period, all of a lighter and easier nature than those so far discussed. *Carnival Suite* was written in 1935. I don't think it was ever published in full, and the score I have seen, from Callender's library, is the original. There are four movements, *Procession, Grotesque Dance, Valse Interlude* and *Revelry*. *Valse Interlude* was later published separately by Parr.

Overture in the Olden Style is a kind of French Overture, with its slow-quick-slow formula. The allegro section is a pseudo fugue, the subject of which seems to be a parody on the opening of the hymn *He who would valiant be* (Example 10).

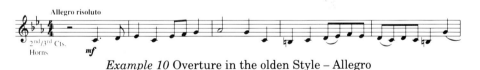

Example 10 Overture in the olden Style – Allegro

There's also a very interesting piece called *A Scottish Fantasy*. It was written in 1937 and published a year later for both brass and military band by Chappell's, the publishers of which, you will recall, Denis was Musical Editor from 1931-1936. Example 11 shows part of Denis's interesting treatment of *My Faithful Fond One* from the fantasy's middle section.

Completing this early group of what might be called 'occasional' pieces comes *A Handelian Suite* (four movements in the style of Handel). The movements are headed *Prelude, Minuet, Air* and *Gigue*. The *Prelude* is a kind of overture, whilst the rest of the suite is made up of characteristic dance movements of the period, using familiar Handelian idioms. The piece was assigned to Boosey's in 1940, but I don't know whether it was ever published or not.

Example 11 A Scottish Fantasy – from 2ⁿᵈ movement

Alas, these pieces are all long forgotten. This is a pity, because they were further examples of Denis's early attempts to put at the disposal of bands music which was unpretentious but yet which had musical integrity, and this at a crucial stage in their development.

Note

[1] There was great rivalry between Foden's and Callender's. After coming 2nd to Foden's several times, Callender's withdrew from contesting and, according to Arthur Taylor in his book *Brass Bands*, 'After plans to form a BBC Brass Band fizzled out, Callender's Senior Band became, thanks to Denis Wright, almost the unofficial broadcasting band, averaging at least one broadcast a fortnight'. They held a meeting with representatives of twenty top bands with a view to taking over the running of the Nationals. It was when this failed that they not only withdrew from contesting but also withdrew all R. Smith publications from their library, replacing them with new and difficult pieces specially composed or arranged for them by leading writers of the time including, of course, Denis Wright. According to Taylor, 'In the North, veteran brass band enthusiasts tended to turn off the radio in mid-concert - irritated by the new-fangled, modern sounds they heard.'

Here is an extract from another letter from Mr. Brown explaining the set-up at Callender's: 'The legendary band of the 20s and 30s was Callender's Cable Works Band, situated in Erith, Kent. There were three bands, Callender Senior, Callender 'A' and Callender 'B', with at least one training band. Quite a few players came from St Hilda's. . . . To secure the services of the famous trombone player Harold Laycock, Callender's gave him the position of gate keeper on a little used gate! I know this is true. . . . The conductor of the senior band was Tom Morgan, and C.A.Walters was in charge of the 'A' band.'

Chapter 8

Doctor Denis and education

Denis Wright was always interested in educational work. Even though, in 1931, he had given up his full-time job as a school master and become involved more and more in composing, conducting and adjudicating, he developed a keen interest in the musical education of members of the brass band fraternity.

Looking back it becomes apparent that he tackled the problem on two fronts - bandsmen themselves and the music they played. He encouraged players and conductors to undergo systematic musical training and to submit themselves to public examination - both as a means of stimulating their studies, and in an attempt to measure their success. At the same time, he made a great personal effort to make available to bands a higher quality of music than they had been used to, primarily by adapting and transcribing music from other sources on more authentic lines than, for example, the operatic selection and air varie type of solo, or the medley of popular tunes of the day. He did this because he believed that first-hand experience of good transcriptions would lead the bandsmen - and hopefully some of their listeners - back to the original. More of this later.

In 1936 Denis succeeded Thomas Keighley as Director of Examinations for the Bandsman's College of Music[1], and shortly after this became a visiting Examiner for Guildhall School of Music and Trinity College of Music, with special interest in their diplomas in brass band conducting, also set up at around this time.

The Bandsman's College of Music was an institution which administered grade examinations similar to those of the Associated Board of the Royal Schools of Music, but geared specifically to instruments found in a brass band, and for many years the only examinations available on some of these. Even more important, the Bandsman's College also offered a series of diploma examinations in brass band conducting, in particular the BBCM, giving would-be conductors targets and stimulating them to systematic study, formerly reserved only for their orchestral counterparts attending music colleges or universities. As Director of Examinations Denis sat on the panel of examiners for the practical examinations at diploma level - generally held twice a year in Manchester and/or London, and he also set and marked the paper work for all examinations.

Denis also became Director of Examinations for the Alexander Owen Memorial Fund Scholarship (AOMF), in which young brass instrumentalists were required to sit a theory examination, play a test at sight and then perform a solo, with piano accompaniment, in the presence of an audience. This had been set up in the early 1920s, following the death of Alexander Owen.

Both of these organisations still exist, though it must be said there was a greater need for them in those early days, when opportunities for education and examination of bandsmen were rare.

Brass Band News of October 1934 stated that more than half the holders of the BBCM Diploma were or had been pupils of Denis Wright. Denis had this to say about them, and about one in particular:

"Although a fairly large number of pupils have come and gone during the last 30 years, I cannot point proudly to a long list of outstandingly successful ones. This is probably because most of them were amateurs and intended to remain amateurs; they came to be put on the right path for studying the theory of music in a small way as a hobby. Some of these passed on to rather elementary composition, scoring for brass band and very occasionally conducting as far as one could teach it with a piano, a gramophone or the wireless as a means of producing the music.

The most successful has, I think, been George Thompson, whom I first remember coming up to me at the Crystal Palace in 1932 and asking if I would give him lessons.

At that time George would have been about 22. He was playing BB-flat Bass in Callender's Cable Works Band and it didn't take me long to find out that here was a sensitive natural musician who, had he had the chance of serious study and a cultural background in adolescence, would have turned out a first-rate musician. Lessons were rather spasmodic; I put my fees as low as possible but even so I fancy it was a real sacrifice on his part to come to London about once a fortnight for that nominal half-hour lesson that usually stretched to fifty or sixty minutes".

George Thompson went on to become a dominant figure in the band world. He conducted a number of top bands, his most successful period being with Grimethorpe Colliery in the years before Elgar Howarth became involved. He was an exceptionally fine band trainer and achieved several major contest successes, including winning the British Open Championship twice - with Grimethorpe. I co-adjudicated with George on a number of occasions. He was a fearless but totally honest adjudicator and was often very outspoken in his criticism of certain aspects of what he called brass band politics, but he looked back with pride on his association with 'Doctor Denis.'

However, Denis voluntarily gave up this side of his teaching when he was appointed Director of Examinations of the Bandsman's College of Music, as he felt it wouldn't be right to be examining his own students.

A certain young lady was making her mark at this time; her name - Gracie Cole[2]. She was never a pupil of Denis's but, as she put it to me, 'Without Denis Wright I would not have got anywhere'.

Gracie believed that she first came to Denis's attention when he auditioned Firbeck Colliery Band for the BBC. She was playing repiano cornet at the time and says that Denis was 'quite impressed' by the way she played the

Gracier Cole with her AOMF winners' certificate

underneath part in the cornet duet in Rimmer's march *Cossack*.

In fact, according to the autobiography, Denis had 'spotted' her earlier than that. At the Leicester Band Festival of 1939, Gracie had played a solo, accompanied by Firbeck, and as Denis records,

> "She had great success; her youth - her charming stage presence and absence of 'side' and sophistication, charmed the huge audience. From that day her feet were firmly placed on the upward ladder and, although an occasional unwise move may have slowed her progress musically, she has continued to charm audiences ever since by her lovely tone, her artistry and her own happy smile."

Gracie was having lessons with the legendary Harold Moss at the time. She wanted to enter for the AOMF Scholarship examination but was unable to do so at first because only boys were allowed to compete. She was by now a member of Besses o' th' Barn Band, was regularly featured by them as a soloist, and was on stage with them in the Royal Albert Hall in January 1942 when Sir Adrian Boult conducted the 1st performance of Denis's arrangement of *Themes from Symphony No. 5* (Beethoven) - to be discussed later in the chapter.

In 1941 Denis composed a cornet solo, *La Mantilla*, especially for Gracie.

This was first broadcast with her as soloist, along with a small group from Fairey Aviation (as it was in those days) in an educational broadcast called *Making Your Own Music*, in which Denis used Gracie and her contemporary and star of the trombone, Maisie Ringham, to illustrate what girls (described in the script as 'the weaker sex'!) could do, in a serious attempt to get more of them playing in brass bands.

By now the Council of the AOMF, submitting to pressures from Harold Moss had changed the rules, to allow brass band players of both sexes to compete, and in 1942 Gracie entered and won, thanks largely to the musical experience she had gained through the influence of Denis.

The prize for winning was two years' free tuition, and as Harold Moss had now left the district in which she lived, Gracie turned for lessons to that former pupil of Denis's, George Thompson. George was conducting Grimethorpe Colliery Band, but no doubt he still had contact with Denis. Denis had several times expressed the opinion that Gracie should be playing repiano with a good band and sure enough, that is exactly where George put her in Grimethorpe - despite opposition from several band members at having a female within their ranks!

Gracie still treasures letters she received from Denis, letters which gave all kinds of advice, not just on musical matters, but on the ethics of being a musician and so on. But back to Denis.

In 1935 he wrote the first of his three books, *Scoring for Brass Band,* still the definitive text book on the subject, now in its 5th edition - revised in 1967, further revised and reset in 1986. Here is what Arthur Butterworth had to say in *The British Bandsman* of 5th September 1987, following the publication of the most recent version:

> 'Before the mid-1920s band music relied almost totally on transcriptions from other sources: opera, oratorio, light music and the orchestral repertoire. His (Denis Wright's) arrangements became models of their kind, establishing a lucid practice of the art of brass band instrumentation. This expertise was systematised in 1935 with the appearance of *Scoring for Brass Band* which after more than fifty years remains the standard work.'

Denis was also, in the late 1920s and 1930s, writing articles for music journals and was assisting in the preparation of a revised edition of *The Musical Educator,* a four-volume work edited by Harvey Grace and published by the Caxton Publishing Co. in 1934, later to be revised as *The New Musical Educator.* Volume 4 contains a chapter on *The Military Band* by F. J. Laubach, revised by Denis Wright, and another on *The Dance Band* by Denis, described as 'A new article'. Both consist largely of résumés of the principal instruments used, with hints on practical arranging.

These articles constituted a major part of Denis's rôle as educator, and are discussed in detail in Chapter 22.

In 1948, Denis wrote another book, *Brass Band Conducting,* and though not achieving the lasting popularity of the one on scoring, it is an excellent book and deserves to be re-printed. A later book, *The Complete Bandmaster*

(1963) is quite comprehensive in the areas it tackles, covering conducting, teaching, ensembles as well as bands, rehearsals, programme building, concerts, brass and voices, contests, scoring, conducting diplomas and a useful repertoire section with advice pertinent to the many and varied demands made on bands. This was published by Pergamon Press and Kenneth A. Wright was General Editor of the series of which this book was one.

So much for Denis's efforts at educating the individual. In a chapter in the autobiography headed *Brass Band Repertoire*, Denis discusses in some depth the strengths and weaknesses of early repertoire and highlights reasons for them. He says, for example,

> "The brass band began as the music of the uncultured, and it has largely remained so. Its earliest music consisted of transcriptions of glees, operatic and oratorio choruses, with a few solos - mainly vocal - thrown in. But amongst all the published repertoire there has always been a scarcity of music that can be called good when judged by the highest standards. Much - indeed most - was *suitable*, but that didn't mean it was *worthy* music."

When he became Musical Director to the Crystal Palace Band, Denis seized the opportunity to introduce a steady stream of more 'worthy' pieces. He had to come to terms with the fact that most of the band's engagements were of the type that demanded popular music - football matches, firework displays, park concerts and the like, but this did not deter him from seeking to raise standards - and to EDUCATE. To quote again from the autobiography:

> "Whilst I was often appalled at the lack of interest for a musician, in much of the programme material, I was inclined to set it down to the lack of educated musicians in the wider sense of those words amongst those who worked in the band world. And who will blame me if I, as a musician whose fortune it had been to be blessed with a good education . . . , who will blame me, I say, for thinking that here, amongst these marvellous technicians, was a field for educational work. There *was* - there still *is* - such a field. But is such education wanted? I thought so, and still think so - many others thought not, and have not changed their views."

What a pity he did not live to see the wider acceptance of bands and band music in the years since his death. He really was up against 'the music of the people' attitude, which seemed to demand that music must be easy to comprehend, with melody present all the time and no underlying harmonic complexities.

He was favoured in that the Crystal Palace Band became a regular broadcasting combination and he was able to insist that every broadcast contained at least one piece which had never been broadcast previously by a brass band. He thus conducted, on the radio, during the three and a half years prior to the war, over 40 of his own transcriptions, mainly of what might be called 'popular classics'.

With these Denis brought a new credibility to the art of the transcription, with a high degree of musical integrity and a genuine desire to introduce bands and their public to a "more worthy repertoire." One piece which stands out as a shining example is his transcription of the *Academic Festival Overture* by Brahms. He broadcast this with his Crystal Palace Band in 1936, it was snapped up by R. Smith & Co. the next day, and in the following year was published and used as test piece at the Belle Vue September Championship. This transcription will be discussed in more detail in the next chapter. (Ernest Brown says that for its first broadcast Denis brought in the BBC Men's Chorus to sing the finale - *Gaudeamus Igitur*).

In 1942 another and somewhat controversial piece appeared, an abridged version of Beethoven's *Symphony No 5 in C minor*. This symphony had become something of a best-seller during the early years of the war, its opening motif being associated with the Morse Code symbol of 'V' (· · · −) for 'Victory'. There are earlier examples of the 'Selection of Themes' from a symphony, in which the themes appear in random order, and with cadenzas or other unrelated links 'composed' by the arranger. Denis, in this new Beethoven arrangement,

> "Adhered scrupulously to the composer's sequence of musical ideas, selecting such sections as are suitable for transference to brass, adding nothing . . . . and making no modulations or harmonic transitions that the composer did not write."

Sir Adrian Boult had agreed to conduct the first performance, with the massed bands of Foden's, Black Dyke and Besses o' th' Barn, in the Royal Albert Hall on the afternoon of Saturday, 10th January 1942. It was a John Henry Iles promotion and Boult had agreed to conduct the arrangement without having been told that it was an abridged version of the symphony. Denis had the job of breaking the news to the great man as to precisely "what he had let himself in for". Expecting him to withdraw his agreement to conduct, Denis was both relieved and glad to find that Boult's "keenness to show his interest in the Brass Band Movement overruled his natural dislike of playing cut versions of symphonies in public." Denis goes on,

> "The point about the success of these two works (*Academic Festival* and *Beethoven V*) is that it proves (to my satisfaction, at least) that my method of educating the brass band public towards better music is a logical one: if a work has good tunes and is worthy music, let the general listener hear it *on his own favourite music-making medium* provided that it is suitable for transference to that medium."

It is also very interesting to read Sir Adrian's comments after the performance:

> 'I am bound to say I can see no more objection to the performance of a selection of a Beethoven Symphony than that of a selection from a Mozart or Sullivan opera. Dr. Wright had done the job with great discretion, and there were moments, particularly at the beginning of the slow movement, when one felt that something fresh had been added to the normal beauty of

the passage. . . . (The) arrangement gives *all* the suitable material from the Symphony in a most attractive form, and I am convinced helps an audience to enjoy a wireless or live performance of the (whole) symphony by an orchestra.'

This seems to underline Denis's arguments about the transcription leading the performer and the listener back to the original.

In June 1940 Denis completed his Doctorate at Edinburgh University. Two famous names were involved here. Sir Donald Tovey, author of six widely read volumes of *Essays in Musical Analysis,* was the Professor at Edinburgh at the time, and the author of what must have been one of the best selling books on harmony, "that lovable old pedagogue Dr. C. H. Kitson", agreed to give Denis ten lessons "to polish up my very rusty counterpoint", although he had practically given up teaching by then. (Further details regarding the Doctorate will be found in Chapter 13.)

Still in pursuit of education for band people, Denis gave numerous talks and broadcasts. He also taught many students through correspondence courses. Peter Gartside, now living in Scotland, but when I first knew him the conductor of the very successful Blue Coat Band in Oldham, has this to say:

'I had started a correspondence course with him (Denis) on brass band arranging. Looking back it seems quite incredible. He wrote out by hand every lesson for me, about one a month, two or three foolscap sheets . . . , as well as commenting on the work I had done. And all for a few coppers!

On reflection, the fact that Doctor Denis was prepared to find time in a busy schedule to give support at a personal level was as valuable to me as the material itself.'

Later Mr. Gartside concluded that, due to his own limitations, the correspondence course wasn't working. Reading Denis's reply to his own letter explaining this - some 30 years on - and having been involved himself in running courses on tutoring and training, he feels that it does absolutely everything that a good tutorial letter should do. Part of the letter is reproduced towards the end of this chapter.

A significant side of Denis's educational work was introducing new ideas to the brass band world. Thus, the following innovations are all credited to him:

Composer of the first concerto for a brass band instrument (the Cornet Concerto). Subsequently, this was available for brass band, military band or orchestra - another first! (see Chapters 13 and 20)

The first scoring of a piano concerto to be played with brass band (the 1st movement of Schumann's Piano Concerto) in July 1946, with Eileen Joyce the solo pianist in the 1st performance with brass band (see Chapter 21)

The first scoring of an organ concerto to be played with brass band (Handel's *Hallelujah Concerto*) commissioned by Butterfield Tank Works Band in November 1952 (see Chapter 25)

Founder of the first National Youth Brass Band (see Chapter 26).

DENIS WRIGHT

17, CRAWFORD AVENUE,

WEMBLEY, MIDDLESEX.

PHONE : WEMBLEY 6322

8th November, 1957

Dear Peter,

Many thanks for your letter - rather a sad one, and
I share your disappointment that you find the sort of exercises
I have felt it necessary to give you are too mechanical and not
music!
I can quite see your point, and it is true that we started
too far away from the beginning. The working of harmony problems
is bound to be rather a mathematical business, but even so it is
possible to infuse into them some musicianship and even some
creative effort. I think the great drawback you have had to face
is not being able safely to "hear" with the eye, so that you
cannot really appreciate the sounds you are creating on paper.

That is a problem that always has to be faced, and your
inability to play the piano is a hindrance in that you cannot
check up at the piano to see if what you have written really
sounds musical, or, indeed, anything like what you expect!

So far as I can remember, you started first simply to
learn scoring; the harmony work came because I felt you needed
a knowledge of chordal structure and part writing to help you
extend a 4-part hymn tune to a full band and also to help you in
writing good individual parts for the various instruments.

Heaps of people can think out tunes; not all of them can
either write them down properly, or, when written down, can find
the appropriate harmony to fit the tune. But scoring an already
completed tune can be done without either being able to play the
piano or being able safely to hear with the eye, although this
latter is a tremendous advantage and will stop one from doing
all manner of bad things in the scoring.

I appreciate that your real interest and, so far as I know,
strong point, is the helping of others to make music and it may
be that if we were to confine lessons merely to overhauling any
scores you care to send, it will give you a certain amount of
help. That is assuming that you do not want to become a
composer! I should be quite willing to work on those lines if
you think it would be of any real use to you. If you wanted to
go back to the start of harmony exercises, I am wondering if
it would not be better for you to find someone locally to whom
you could go for personal lessons. Correspondence ones are
cumbersome and one can learn more in half an hour at a personal
lesson that in a couple of correspondence ones.

Well, there it is. Let me know what you intend doing, some
time, and you know that if at any time you think I can help you
further, I will do all I can to be of help. That so many of the
hymns you played recently were of your own scoring is fine; as
you are able thus to hear the result of your work it may be of
help in itself to you to discover if you are doing things the
best way, or not. Yes; any tune could be scored in many ways;
don't be afraid to experiment, but when you hear them, be very
self-critical.

With every good wish, and kindest regards,
Yours sincerely,
Denis Wright.

To summarise, all Denis's endeavours in the brass band world were of a pioneering and educational nature. In his various activities - composing, arranging, lecturing, teaching, adjudicating and conducting - he introduced many new ideas which were to become standard practice. His aim was to show the capabilities and possibilities of the brass band and to help bands and conductors improve their standards, their repertoire and their musical appreciation.

Notes

[1] *The Bandsman's College of Music* has no particular base - it is an examining body, takes no part in training or education, and therefore its title may be felt to be slightly mis-leading.

[2] *Gracie Cole* later became a professional trumpet player. At the age of 18, in the mid-war years she was faced with working on munitions or joining the ATS. As an alternative she could, if she wished, become a professional musician and go into the entertainment business. As she says, '18 year old girls did as their fathers told them in those days,' and father decided she had to become a professional musician. She joined Gloria Gaye's dance band - first on cornet and then on trumpet, and some time later became a member of the famous Ivy Benson All-girl Orchestra. She is now Mrs. Bill Geldard, and lives quietly in Surrey - still active in local musical circles though.

Chapter 9

Doctor Denis on repertoire

As is already becoming apparent, Denis Wright made a long and sustained effort to improve the quality of music played by bands. He was very concerned about what he called "this paucity of good music" which, he realised more than most, was one of the main reasons why musicians from other branches of music were so alienated against bands.

On page 53 I quoted some of his comments about the origins of brass band music - glees, choruses and solos. He continued:

> "From these it grew to selections from the old operas and oratorios, and for many years such works formed the 'diet' of the bands. The transcriptions were often based on the assumption that a band would have a few good soloists who could play pretty difficult stuff - cadenzas of great length and complexity were inserted, to show off the players' agility - a leaf out of the book of Italian opera. Accompaniments were often simplified to suit the less experienced players - indeed, many arrangers worked from piano scores and did not apparently worry in the least that such a score usually gave little indication of what was in the orchestral score."

The more contact he had with bands, the more Denis felt their need for a wider choice of better music, even though many band engagements were of the 'popular' sort. He reasoned:

> "Here are great numbers of men who can play their instruments amazingly well, but spend a lot of their time playing shoddy music. So let me do all I can to help them musically to a better understanding of good music, so that they can spend more time playing worth-while music and thus gradually bring their unsophisticated audiences to appreciate the better stuff."

Despite his willingness to do this for the good of bands - making transcriptions of what he called 'worthy' music - he met with much opposition. 'What can he know about a brass band? - he can't play a cornet!' was apparently a common cry. Accused of 'foisting orchestral music on brass bands,' he asked,

> "And what if I did? Were not the majority of selections by Rimmer, Gladney, Owen, Swift and Ord Hume nothing more or less than pot-pourris of bits and pieces of orchestral music?"

He found it very hurtful that though these older writers could apparently do no wrong, he regularly had to face a barrage of criticism. He had great respect and admiration for the earlier generations and what they had done, but he knew full well that the time had come when band music needed to move forward. Perhaps I could pause here to reflect on some of Denis's comments on the growing but still quite slim repertoire of original test pieces.

The first of these, *Labour and Love*, and one or two of its successors were, he felt, constructed as a sort of concession to bandsmen who understood selections but who did not appreciate form. He wrote,

"They consisted of lots of little sections with constant full stops and even cadenzas for solo instruments."

And yet, he points out, even these had their critics, for a quite different reason.

"Supporters of the old régime sneered at, jeered at, and, finding it made no difference, blackguarded the composer, the publisher, and the supporters of *this horrible new music*." Interesting!

Constructional weaknesses evident in the earliest pieces disappeared, he felt, after a few years, as Fletcher's *An Epic Symphony* and the suites by Holst, Elgar and Ireland were

"Constructionally far more closely knit and therefore interesting to the musician."

Not that even these completely escaped Denis's criticism. He said, for example,

"Holst's *Moorside Suite* was spoilt as brass band music by the unsuitable style of the 1st movement, though the final march was grand stuff."

The *Nocturne* from the same suite had provided him with one of his greatest thrills from a brass band. This was in the playing by Black Dyke (during its winning performance in the 1928 Championships) of the final chord, *pianissimo,* which he described as "A mighty chord of A flat extending over four octaves."

He obviously didn't go along with some other person's idiotic comment that *Moorside* was not a good test piece *because there wasn't a single semiquaver in the whole work.*

Denis was a great admirer of Elgar's music, but even *Severn Suite* didn't completely satisfy him. For all its "brilliant *Toccata*" and "quite organ-like *Fugue*," he didn't regard it as really good Elgar. He felt that the *Minuet* was "over-long and repetitive" and that some of the muting "was not altogether a successful innovation from a tonal point of view."

The best of all the early original works, he felt, was *A Downland Suite*, which he described as "Good music, good brass music and good Ireland."

He made many decidedly uncomplimentary remarks about his own pieces. *Joan of Arc* he described as "long-winded". Of the next piece, *The White Rider,* he felt that it possessed "no great musical value", that the musical ideas were "common-place", and the fact that it was "sheer Programme Music" meant almost inevitably a lack of real musical form. (Let's not forget, however, that he intended this to be a lower section test piece.)

He had a little more regard for his *Princess Nada,* but felt that *Tintagel* was "probably my one decent band work." (I don't know just when he wrote this comment, or whether it takes into account his later works.) He must have been very disappointed when *Tintagel* was turned down by Whiteley as being too difficult, blaming this on "a bad attack of cold feet following the Elgar piece" (*Severn Suite,* the testpiece for 1930), whatever that means, and so it would seem that *Tintagel* was intended to be the Crystal Palace test piece for 1931.

Back now to Denis's attempts to counter this 'paucity' of good music by adding more 'worthy' pieces to the repertoire.

A golden opportunity presented itself in October 1933 when he received an invitation to succeed Walter Reynolds as professional coach of the Crystal Palace Band. Founded by W. W. Grant, originally as Upper Norwood, and subsequently renamed Crystal Palace, it was a shrewd move by 'W. W.' to engage Denis, already becoming a major brass band figure. Of course, it worked both ways, because it enabled this highly talented musician - though one who was still somewhat naïve in the ways of brass bands - to familiarise himself with the existing repertoire and then to add to it in the way of transcriptions of what he now called 'healthy' music.

Crystal Palace Band gave regular broadcasts under Denis, and as I've already mentioned, he used this situation as a means by which to enlarge the repertoire, introducing into each programme pieces which had not previously been broadcast by a brass band.

Inevitably this brought regular bouts of criticism from the 'opposition' in *Brass Band News* and, it has to be said, it was not always popular with members of the band itself, though it seems they did eventually come to appreciate the value of what they were doing, and to accept the burden of the extra rehearsals needed to enable them to cope with the work.

During the remaining years before the war, when Denis was regularly broadcasting with Crystal Palace, he introduced over forty new pieces to the repertoire, many of which were later published, becoming 'standard repertoire'. There was music by Bach, Brahms, Dvôrak, Elgar, Mozart, Rimsky-Korsakov, Rossini, Schubert, Tchaikovsky, Verdi and Wagner, as well as lighter-weight pieces by Bizet, Cimarosa, Delibes, German, Grainger, Offenbach, Johann Strauss and Waldteufel.

One of the early pieces was his transcription of the *Academic Festival Overture* by Brahms. This has retained its popularity for nearly sixty years, and was the fore-runner of many successful transcriptions of overtures from opera or the orchestral repertoire. Of course, many older examples of popular overtures exist, but by and large they belong to the earlier generation of outdoor music and were utility arrangements rather than authentic transcriptions. Many of these are still played regularly and some are quite effective, but *Academic Festival* lifted the art of transcription to a new level.

Structurally it adheres faithfully to the original, and there are inescapable similarities between the sonorities of the orchestral version and those

Example 12 Academic Festival Overture—showing triplets in string and horns

obtained from Denis's transcription, through his skilful choice of instruments and textures.

There are a couple of instances where he has left out some of the orchestral figuration (Examples 12 - 15) and it is often debated as to why he did this. One view is that it was to simplify the music because of the limitations of the all-brass combination. I go along with the opposite view that, with the smaller forces, it is more effective without the embellishments. There have been performances where the conductor has chosen to amend Denis's score to make it conform with Brahms. Where there are larger groups - massed bands or the 75-strong National Youth Brass Band - the amendments can be very effective, but where a single band only is involved, I personally much prefer the Denis Wright formula.

Example 13 Triplets removed for increased clarity in brass band version

Example 14 Academic Festival Overture—final section showing orchestral figuration

So, within the space of a few years Denis had made a significant and lasting contribution to the development of brass band music with his transcriptions. The purist did not accept that these were of any value. I have already stated Denis's view - supported by Sir Adrian Boult - that by experiencing the transcription many people will be led back to the original. Another argument in support of transcriptions is the number of them made by some of the greatest of composers, both of their own works and of the works of others, introducing the music to a different group of listeners. Possibly the strongest argument of all is that because of the relatively short history of brass bands none of the great masters from earlier times could possibly have written for the medium, and therefore the only way for brass

Example 15 – the same passage in the brass band transcription, with scales removed

band players to have first-hand experience of their music is by acquaintance with it through transcription.

So, by his transcriptions alone, Denis considerably enriched the repertoire available to bands. Others have followed his example and there are few band programmes which do not include at least one piece 'borrowed' from some other source.

Appendix 2, though not claiming to be complete, gives some idea of the scope of Denis's work in this area. Appendix 3 gives a similar indication of the vast numbers of his arrangements, and though Denis would be the last to claim that many of these were of any great musical value, all bear the hallmarks of his musicianship and his ability to make this borrowed music sound well in its new medium.

Chapter 10

Doctor Denis on contests

Between 1925 and his death in 1967, Denis Wright adjudicated at several hundreds of brass band contests - probably more than any other musician who wasn't actually brought up in bands. It is therefore interesting to see what his views were on this aspect of banding.

We must remember of course that during the early years of his association with bands, a large number of contests were held in the open air - not an attractive situation for a serious musician - at the mercy of the weather, often in an unfriendly and uncomfortable tent, and perhaps surrounded by a noisy crowd. But he nails his colours to the mast straight away:

"Once you have got the contesting fever in your system, nothing, so far as I know, can get it out. You may return home, soaked to the skin after enduring an English summer afternoon and hearing nothing but inferior playing of a dull test piece, and swear that nothing will ever tempt you to go to another open-air contest. . . . But will you keep your resolutions? You will not!"

He also nails his colours to that other mast, the thorny question of open or closed adjudication.

"I have often been asked whether I prefer to be shut in or be allowed to judge in the open. Having tried both, I am firmly of the opinion that for band contests it is preferable to be screened, for the following reason: one cannot compare a band contest to an ordinary competitive music festival. In the latter the day is marked out into sessions of varying length, which allow the judge to relax a while. But suppose you have a full-length band contest, one section and twenty-four bands playing one after the other - a five or six hour session that must not be interrupted except perhaps for a hastily snatched break for tea. Human nature couldn't stand it, if one were forced to carry through without a break, sitting unscreened amongst the audience. But in the seclusion of a tent it is a far simpler matter."

He cites additional reasons for seclusion in open-air events, but goes on:

"Even were the contest indoors it is hard to concentrate over a long period if one is surrounded by people who chatter in the breaks between each band . . . and contest judging is difficult enough without any unnecessary burdens being added."

He admitted to an element of shock when he first found out that brass band adjudicators had to be shut away, "for all the world like a Beckmesser in the first Act of *The Mastersingers*."

(Beckmesser is the spindly-legged odd-ball who, in the opera, judges songs by 'marking' his slate every time he considers a rule has been broken. I think that every contest conductor's prayer should be something like, *Lord, preserve us from having a Beckmesser in the box!*) However, Denis goes on,

"If Wagner's setting, with Beckmesser shut up in a sort of tent, is indeed founded on actual fact . . . there you have the original tradition that dates back, not a single century to the start of band contesting, but at least 400 years, to the days of the Guilds that fostered music and the companion arts in Europe in the Middle Ages." The debate about open or closed adjudication continues to this day!

Changing to the subject of honesty, Denis admits that there have undoubtedly been judges who "might not have been able to stand the strain of knowing for certain which band was playing." And he confesses, "An experienced judge, hearing the same bands on several occasions, can frequently tell which band he is hearing, even when screened."

(This may have been the case a number of years ago when, I suppose, there was more individuality of style amongst leading bands. Those adjudicating regularly today will tell you that 'band-spotting' from within the box is a fruitless and positively dangerous occupation, to be avoided like the plague!)

Lord, preserve us from having a Beckmesser in the box.

Denis goes on to say that if a judge wants to be crooked, then no amount of screening will prevent him from "wangling". He also states that it was not, in his day, unknown for bands to drop hints to adjudicators with regard to what they proposed to play, or how they might give a pre-arranged signal.

"But", he adds, "do not run away with the idea that contesting is essentially a crooked business. It is not; for every one contest where the results were faked, there are, thank goodness, hundreds in which no suspicion of dishonesty could be held against the judge."

Admitting that unfortunately suspicion existed even over such contests as the Nationals and other well-organised events he said,

"Having judged at many of the contests organised by John Henry Iles, I have no hesitation in saying that I have never found any cause for suspicion."

Happily, this still applies, as all present-day adjudicators would testify. But sadly, bands and even conductors do still sometimes harbour suspicions.

In the autobiography Denis tells a couple of light-hearted stories which put it all into perspective. The first is about an occasion when a policeman was on duty outside the tent, his job being to ward off any would-be interlopers. At one point he popped his head in and declared, "Now you're going to hear a good band, sir, they won here last year".

Denis said he had often wondered whether this was "constabularian enthusiasm" or an attempt to influence the outcome of the contest.

"If it were the latter", he wrote, "I'm afraid it didn't work, as the band was, to my mind, a bad one anyway."

His other story concerned the Mortimers, and he claimed to have heard it from both Harry Mortimer and James Ord Hume, the central character in the story. Ord Hume was adjudicating a quartet contest somewhere in the Luton area. The Mortimers were based there at this time, Fred conducting Luton Red Cross Band and Harry playing solo cornet. Prizes at these events could be either money or various odds and ends - cutlery, umbrellas and so on. At this particular contest Luton's quartet was awarded 3rd prize but when, a week or two later, the same party played the same piece for the same judge and won, Fred couldn't help having a light-hearted 'go' at Ord Hume over being placed 3rd. 'Of course you really won, Fred,' said Ord Hume, 'but I thought you'd rather have the ten bob than the case of tea-spoons!'

Looking at contesting from the other side, I doubt if Denis did all that much competing as a conductor, though as we saw in Chapter 6, he conducted a couple of bands in the Grand Shield section at Crystal Palace in 1931. A few years later he was conducting Crystal Palace Band as well as Friary Silver. In connection with his work with the latter he became involved in squabbles over borrowed players and the fact that in certain situations contest organisers could be persuaded to turn the proverbial 'blind eye' in cases of transgression. More interestingly, however, and with an intriguing twist on the borrowed player issue he refers to an incident which, as far as I know, couldn't possibly happen today, though I have heard of other instances of it happening in the past, and no doubt bandsmen a few years older than I am would be able to verify that this sort of thing did actually happen.

As I have said, Denis had two bands. Both were competing at Crystal Palace, and both were in different sections, playing in different halls. Both had early draws, which made it necessary for Denis to conduct Crystal Palace Band in one hall and then dash to another where his other band, Friary, had already started its performance - conducted by the bandmaster. As was apparently the custom in such situations, Denis took the stick out of the bandmaster's hand - in mid-bar, so to speak - and conducted the rest of the performance. A side-issue to all this was that the Band Manager had, without consulting Denis, engaged a 'star' solo cornet player to assist the band on the day. It was with obvious glee that Denis reported,

> "By the time I reached the other hall, Friary, thanks to their additional cornet player, had well and truly blown themselves out of the prizes. The imported player had about the fiercest tone imaginable, and it completely wrecked any ensemble that I had tried to obtain. When I took the stick out of the Bandmaster's hand, more than half way through the piece, it was far too late to do anything about it."

Another bone of contention concerned what Denis quite rightly observed as sharp practise in the self-promotion of certain bands. He was not amused by bands which advertised themselves as '1st prize winners' without reference to which section they had actually won. This, he suggested, could be duping the people who knew nothing about the grading system of bands, amongst them often the organisers of fêtes, flower shows and so on, who were offering engagements.

As an example he cites a massed band concert which took place somewhere in the London area, with a well-known guest conductor. In the publicity for the concert the bands taking part were described as 'some of the finest in the country' - and yet Denis knew they were of about 4th section standard. He described this as "deliberate catch-penny mis-representation," but I am sure he was levelling his criticism at the bands for 'duping' the concert promoters, who probably knew no better. To the best of my knowledge this practise has now ceased, and bands which advertise themselves as champions do, without exception as far as I know, openly - even proudly - state to which section their title applies. I hope so anyway. Going back to borrowed players, he praised any band which

> "By sheer hard work, can develop its own resources to such an extent that it becomes a prize-winning combination by reason of efficiency, mutual understanding and in fact real team work."

On the question of team-work, he gives high praise to Foden's, who won the Nationals six times in the 1930s with an almost unchanged team of players. He points out that whilst at one time or another it might have been possible to have brought in a better player, the Foden team spirit would thereby have been destroyed, and they would have been in danger of losing what Denis described as "their complete homogeneity of tone and style, the lovely phrasing throughout the band, the absence of all harshness even in their most brilliant playing." He concluded,

> "Other bands in the past may have been better technically . . . but I dare wager anything that no band ever possessed finer all-round qualities nor displayed the sheer beauty of brass playing than did that Foden's team of the years leading up to the 2nd World War."

If we've learned some lessons from the past I do not think the band movement as a whole has really become aware of the value of a settled band, or of a team which has had a chance to get to know all about itself.

But for a final word on the high regard in which Denis held contesting, with all its faults:

> "In spite of everything that should not be and yet so often is, you will be drawn to the next contest, as you were to the previous one, as by an irresistible magnet. The magnet, I think, is the worth-whileness of the band contesting movement that has been its justification and the reason for its continuance for a full century in this country, although the very weaknesses inherent in the contesting field might have killed it stone dead."

Chapter 11

Doctor Denis on personalities

There must be lots of us still around who remember Denis Wright, but not too many who remember the generations before him. It is interesting, therefore, to read his personal views on some of the band world's pioneers.

John Gladney, Alex Owen and Edwin Swift were all before his time and though some of their music does now have limited availability little of it, if any at all, would have been seen or heard by Denis and so, as he wrote, "I have practically no means of making up my own mind as to its merit." He conceded though, that as teachers, "they were undoubtedly outstanding."

Moving into the next generation, he knew James Ord Hume quite well, even if only briefly, but he had little to say of him other than that he was "a better arranger than a composer." To his sorrow, Denis never met William Rimmer, who had already retired and was living "quietly at Southport" when he (Denis) first became interested in bands. However, he had heard lots of stories about him, covering many aspects of his work with bands but, he wrote,

> "Never have I heard anyone say a derogatory word." And he goes on: "A man who reached the top and who inspires such affection and respect that no one ever says an unkind word about him, even in his lifetime, must indeed be a great man."[1]

J. A. Greenwood and William Halliwell, "the next in line", he did know, though he was reluctant to say too much about their respective conducting abilities as he had never seen them take a rehearsal, and he felt that that was where one probably learned most about a conductor. He first met them on the Sunday afternoon following his "first Crystal Palace Championship experience," being introduced to Halliwell by Herbert Whiteley, outside Finsbury Park Empire. Greenwood was inside, rehearsing the winning band, Marsden Colliery, which he had conducted the previous day in the contest.

> "Poor Halliwell was very unhappy," wrote Denis. "None of his bands had scored and he wanted to know why."

Denis did not even know which bands Halliwell had conducted, so he couldn't tell him.[2] In later years he often saw Halliwell in action and felt that his great success in contests must have been due to his ability to impart "a contest-winning style" to a band, adding, "Halliwell was not an inspiring conductor to watch - or to play under."

He said that as an arranger he was practically unknown though he'd come across his arrangements of Jarnefelt's *Praeludium*, Weber's *Der Freischutz Overture* and two movements from Mendelssohn's *Italian Symphony*, all of which he said were "excellently done" - an opinion which I imagine is shared by all who know these arrangements.

Regarding the difference between Halliwell and Greenwood, apparently there was a consensus that the former won more big contests than the latter because he was engaged by better bands. Denis says,

> 'This may be true - indeed on paper it was true. For all that, I consider, having seen both men in action, that Greenwood was the better conductor. Halliwell was probably the finer teacher."

With regard to Greenwood's writing, his arrangements and the "slight pieces" he composed, Denis felt they were "always practical and playable," but that when it came to arranging from an orchestral score, "Greenwood's style was rather laboured and over-scored." Denis also said that he felt Greenwood

> "Sank his artistic instincts in order to make his work commercial; parts had to be doubled so that if a player were absent someone else was automatically playing the missing part."

(I would add, in defence of Greenwood and his contemporaries, that a large proportion of their output was meant for outdoor use, where weight would have been more important than subtlety of scoring.)

Denis described both Halliwell and Greenwood as "very gentle men." He said that they talked quietly and "seemed to love home life." He added, "After conducting at a contest they would usually fade quickly away as soon as their work was done, seldom staying for the results." On the outbreak of war in 1939 Greenwood, Denis said,

> "Found himself without bands to coach, and had to take an unskilled job in an aircraft factory. Bad luck," he went on. "Poor John's musical soul must have suffered badly."

With Halliwell it had been rather different. He was, in 1939, already on the point of cutting out most of the bands he had been coaching, intending to concentrate on two or three only. So, when the war caused the abandoning of most band contests - in particular the Nationals - Halliwell retired.

> "Thus", wrote Denis, "the latter day triumvirate, Rimmer, Halliwell and Greenwood, came to an end almost without us realising it. Their names will live, though, probably as long as those of the original trio - Owen, Gladney and Swift - for each was in his own way a great man and they all exercised a great power for good in the brass band world. The accusation that they were merely contest-winners rather than professional conductors is very far from being justified."[3]

Moving away from Denis's thoughts on band conductors, he had lots to say about the man who, through a casual visit to a band contest, became the 'Father-figure' of brass bands for almost half a century.

John Henry Iles comes in for both praise and criticism. He owned the two major brass band championships and over the years must have injected large sums of money for the benefit of the bands of which he was, without doubt, so very proud. His reward for this was two-fold - each year he conducted the massed bands concert after the Crystal Palace contest (and, on certain occasions, in other places) and he presided over the presentation of awards at both Crystal Palace and Belle Vue. His forays with the baton were the subject of scorn by the many thousands of bandsmen who had the doubtful privilege of playing under his direction, but if he was an amateur musician he was certainly very professional when it came to public speaking.

The Crystal Palace contest must have been a really great day but it did, apparently, have certain drawbacks. There was a short organ recital prior to the playing of the massed bands. Let's allow Denis to set the scene.

"I have heard bad organ playing, but never anything so bad as that provided on the occasion of the Palace contests - noise, wrong notes, complete absence of rhythm and singular inability to keep time in the most elementary way."

And that's only the start! He goes on:

"Why, oh why should such an exhibition be foisted on the band world? All this talk of 'our working men musicians' and their amazing standard of musicianship - which no one will deny - and then they are treated to a musically contemptible show that even the humblest bandsman must know is a musical disgrace."

But there were compensations.

"After the organ recital, the massed bands concert began. Those who remember the old Crystal Palace - destroyed by fire in November 1936 - do not need reminding of the wonderful sight - those five or six bands, in their varied and multi-coloured uniforms, massed on the great Handel Orchestra, the tiers of seats, not one empty, reaching up to the ceiling on each side of the great organ, behind the stage. The vast packed auditorium - a bare place, with iron girders and glaring lights - seemingly of endless length since in the haze of tobacco smoke one could scarcely see the boxes at the far end. Oh yes, I nearly forgot - the policeman, too, solemnly sitting on the right of the conductor's rostrum, guarding the box in which had been placed the sealed results of the different contests, and the curious gallows-like contraption on which later would be displayed the numbers of the prize-winning bands."

Iles was in the business of constructing fairground equipment - the Ghost Train, the Bobs, the Big Wheel and so on, and despite his ultimate bankruptcy, it is reasonable to assume that he knew more about his business than he did about conducting brass bands. Denis had little to say about the actual concert, but realised fully that 'John Henry' came into his own when it came to the results.

"For all his limitations as a conductor, J. Henry Iles is a grand showman. I

John Henry with Frances Bantin at the 'draw'

know of nobody who could so well carry off that massed band concert and the subsequent announcing of winning bands. His huge voice and impressive figure dominate the scene and even if he frequently underestimates the band public's standard of musical appreciation, no one would deny him the credit of having built, in the National Band Festival, a more worthy memorial to himself (when the time comes for a memorial to be needed) than his scenic railways and other delights (or tortures) of Belle Vue, Manchester, or Dreamland, Margate, could ever provide."[4]

The results were not announced until the concert was over, and in time-honoured manner, the prize-winners in the lower sections were announced first, the tension gradually building as the Grand Shield results were announced, reaching boiling point as it came to the Championship section itself.

"Applause and even conversation were stilled; that vast crowd became amazingly quiet as John Henry opened the last envelope, leaned over from the rostrum to compare the numbers on the sheet with the list of bands which his secretary and assistant, Miss F. E. Bantin[5] held up to him and at last, when the crowd was almost overcome by the tension of waiting, announced the winner of the Championship.

That tension just before the announcement is extraordinary; it borders on mass hysteria. Twenty thousand people will laugh as Iles, no doubt as strung up as they, pretends to drop the sheet of paper, or fingers his throat and takes a drink of water.'

What a wonderful word-picture that is. It requires little imagination to bring the scene to life, and though this was, in fact, Denis's description of the 1925 announcements - the prelude to his own personal shock result - it is no doubt typical of all similar results ceremonies presided over by Iles.

But despite the criticism and inverted praise meted out, Denis makes a final point, which none of us should forget:

"Whatever opinions one may hold of Henry Iles as a band conductor, one must acknowledge the debt of the band world to him that he was willing to sink capital in providing a repertoire of original compositions for brass, probably knowing full well that many of the works he published would never be financial successes. That many of the earlier publications were not very good musically was not Iles's fault. It was through bringing in the smaller men first of all that he was eventually able to attract the greater ones. Much credit too must be given to Herbert Whiteley, who was the visionary behind Iles and whose absorbing passion it was to see the establishing of a library of works specially written for brass. His enthusiasm for this scheme was undoubtedly responsible for Iles taking it up at all. One can only hope that the day will come when brass bands as a whole will realise what Whiteley and Iles did for the prestige of the brass bands of this country in making such a collection of works possible - even though there are tares amongst the wheat. Perhaps one day we shall be able to say of these two men *Si monumentum requiris, circumaudite*[6]. But it is up to bands to make this true."

Notes

[1] *J. Ord Hume* died on 27th November, 1927, William Rimmer on 9th February 1936.

[2] *William Halliwell* conducted no less than 8 bands in the 1925 Championships, Black Dyke, Foden's, Irwell Springs, Luton Red Cross, Nelson Old, St. Hilda's, Sowerby Bridge and Wingates Temperance.

[3] *William Halliwell* died on 24th April 1946, aged 82, *John A. Greenwood* on 21st December 1953, aged 78.

[4] *John Henry Iles OBE* was born in Bristol on 17th September 1871 and died on 29th May 1951, after an illness lasting some months.

[5] *Miss Frances E. Bantin* was Assistant Editor of *The British Bandsman*, and Secretary of the Crystal Palace National Band Festival. She later became Secretary of the London & Southern Counties Area Contest of the Daily Herald Brass Band Championships, a Director of R.Smith & Co. Ltd., and of Bandsman's Press Ltd. She was Secretary to Iles from 1921 and acquired the title The First Lady of the Brass Band Movement. She died on 5th April 1964 after 34 years' service to *The British Bandsman*. Iles said of her, shortly before his own death, 'She is my continuity girl. People come and people go, bands change, contributors change and sometimes all is chaos but there, standing in the middle of it all, is my Miss Bantin, imperturbable, knowledgeable and without an ounce of panic within her'.

[6] This Latin phrase is a slight 'mis-quote' of a famous inscription made in honour of Sir Christopher Wren in St Paul's Cathedral. Denis's version translates as *If you require a monument,* listen *around you.*

Chapter 12

Working for the BBC

During the winter of 1929-1930 Denis Wright took up an appointment as General Musical Editor for Chappell & Co. Ltd., one of the leading music publishers of the time. The work was varied and at first seemed a very attractive proposition after what must have been, for such a talented musician, the rather hum-drum life of a schoolmaster. He was involved in proof-reading and arranging or orchestrating from other people's sketches, and he regularly rubbed shoulders with well-known personalities from the lighter side of the music business of the time, including Ivor Novello, Noel Coward and Noel Gay. Several of those with quite famous names were unable to write down their musical ideas, and so Denis became a very important part of the chain which linked them with the ears of their public.

His outside work also began to blossom at this time, conducting his two bands - Crystal Palace and Friary Silver - and renewing an earlier association with East Grinstead Amateur Operatic Society.

But alas, the musical policy of Chappell's changed over the next few years and Denis found himself dealing more and more with things which just did not appeal to him. He began to feel the need for a further change in his main occupation, and it was his work with Crystal Palace Band which seems to have brought about the opportunity - though not at first.

The band had already been involved in broadcasting for a number of years - even from pre-BBC days. During 1932 they were offered a BBC engagement, and as they proposed to include *The White Rider* in their programme, Denis was invited to conduct. However, he relates,

> "There was a man in charge of the balance business who obviously understood neither brass bands nor music. The band was made to sit in two long lines of 12 players and the conductor was stuck in the right-hand corner, not even in a central position."

The outcome was that the playing lacked cohesion, the results were chaotic, and Crystal Palace Band was struck off the broadcasting list - not to be reinstated until 1935, and this is where the story becomes more interesting.

As we saw in Chapter 9, Denis was appointed Musical Director to the Crystal Palace Band in October 1933, and within a couple of years not only was the band back in favour with the 'Beeb', but Denis had been offered a full-time job there, specifically to look after all band broadcasts - both brass and military.

At this point two new names come into the picture, Kenneth A. Wright and Maurice Johnstone. Kenneth Wright (no relation to Denis) had worked for the BBC since its inception in 1922, when he became the first Station Director at Manchester, later becoming chief assistant to the Music Controller, Percy Pitt, in London. He must have had a very strong interest in bands, because he is said to have written over twenty pieces for Callender's between 1931 and 1934, and in 1935 he composed the Crystal Palace test piece *Pride of Race*.

Maurice Johnstone joined the BBC in 1935. Three years later he became Head of North Region Music, and from 1953 until his retirement in 1960, was Head of Music Programmes (Sound), in London. Johnstone also wrote a number of pieces for band, including three well-known marches, *County Palatine, Pennine Way* and *Beaufighters*, as well as the 1944 Belle Vue test piece, *The Tempest*.

Maurice and Denis first met on the day of the 1925 Crystal Palace contest. In conversation they discovered that they had attended the same school (St. George's, Harpenden), though as Maurice was Denis's junior by some five years they didn't know each other at that time. They also discovered they had several other things in common, including a passion for the music of Elgar and a growing love of brass bands. In 1925 Maurice was running a small shop in Manchester so he and Denis saw little of each other for a few years. In 1933 he moved south to London to become Sir Thomas Beecham's secretary, and also an ssistant to Beecham in the British National Opera Company. He joined the BBC two years later and this, as it were, is where we came in!

So, the year was 1935, Kenneth Wright had composed the Crystal Palace test piece and Maurice, a new boy at the BBC and Kenneth Wright's junior, wanted to hear it before the day of the contest. Denis must have heard about this, and invited him to one of his rehearsals with Crystal Palace Band.

To recap, the band had fallen out of favour with the BBC as a result of their unfortunate broadcast some three years earlier, but Maurice was so impressed with what he saw and heard at Denis's rehearsal that it wasn't long before he was using his influence to get the band another broadcast - without having to re-audition.

He eventually succeeded and was rewarded with a good broadcast of a quite substantial programme which included *Egmont Overture, Severn Suite* (minus the Fugue) and four movements from *L'Arlesienne*. The band and its music obviously found favour with the 'powers' and was immediately re-instated as a broadcasting combination, to be heard on the air quite regularly until shortly after war broke out when, for fairly obvious reasons, the band was unable to maintain the standard required. By then Denis was working for the BBC, and it was he who had to say, "No more broadcasting for you until you can do better than that!"

Here's another amusing anecdote from Mr. Brown, who I mentioned earlier:

"Besides playing on the BBC programmes broadcast during the day in this country, we often played to other countries in the middle of the night. We would travel by coach to the studio. On one occasion we had three announcers in different languages, and as one would be announcing, the other two would try to 'de-bag' him. Denis would stand at his rostrum with his baton in his right hand and the finger of his left hand across his mouth. We knew we dare not laugh."

Several of the Crystal Palace Band broadcasts were special. On one occasion, for example Sir Arthur Bliss conducted *Kenilworth* and on another Maurice Johnstone conducted one of his compositions.

Going back to 1935, the BBC was still in its infancy and band broadcasts - no doubt in common with other specialist areas - had really not found a satisfactory pattern. There was a National wavelength and several Regional ones so that, wherever you lived you would be able to pick up the National and your own Regional programmes and, depending on your wireless set, your location and your aerial, possibly some of the other Regional programmes, which were all transmitted on different frequencies.

Ironically, what few decent bands there were in and around London took care of most of the band broadcasts on the National wavelength as well as their own Regional broadcasts, while the best bands, mainly from other parts of the country, did most of their broadcasting only on their own Regional programme. Most of the Regional Directors and their assistants "knew nothing about and cared little for brass bands", so it was by no means an ideal state of affairs. Denis explains:

"In actual effect, Callender's Cable Works Band had become a sort of unofficial BBC brass band and fulfilled the majority of the sparse number of engagements going for brass bands. Other first class bands such as Foden's, Black Dyke and Luton got an occasional look-in, mainly on their own regional wavelength, and for what was called regional policy reasons an occasional performance by a third or fourth-rate band was slipped in. But there was no settled policy as regards brass bands and the band world really has a great deal to thank Kenneth Wright for, in that he had vision enough to realise the need for brass bands to take their rightful place in broadcast programmes alongside (though possibly in smaller quantities) orchestral concerts, solo recitals, chamber music and other sections of Music Departmental activities."

Maurice Johnstone, it seems, was over-seeing broadcasts by London-based bands "as a sort of sideline to his orchestral programme planning work" but, along with Kenneth Wright, was looking towards creating a Band Section within the Music Department.

This was the situation at the BBC when, in May 1936, Denis was invited to lunch with Kenneth Wright, Maurice Johnstone and B. Walton O'Donnell, conductor of the BBC Wireless Military Band.[1] The up-shot of this was that Denis was invited to join the BBC, and to work under O'Donnell to form the new Band Section.

He was taken aback somewhat a few weeks later when he saw the job he thought he'd actually got, advertised in the *Daily Telegraph*. This could have been awkward to say the least, as on the strength of the lunch-time meeting he had given his notice at Chappell's. Anyway, all was well and eventually the appointment was confirmed - despite competition from several other applicants!

Most of Denis's broadcasting experience to date had been with his Crystal Palace Band, though there was one other broadcast he had been involved in, details of which I think are worth recording for posterity. From the autobiography:

> "My first experience of broadcasting, apart from visits to Marconi House in the very earliest days before the BBC was formed, consisted of conducting a massed band concert at Carmarthen, which was relayed by the old Swansea transmitter. This was in 1929; the occasion was a West Wales Association band contest and the weather was quite the worst British summer specimen imaginable. Throughout the broadcast a man stood holding an umbrella over the microphone for a solid hour - though I fancy the drumming on the umbrella made more noise than if the rain had been allowed to fall on the 'mike'.
>
> Seven bands took part - they filled the covered grandstand on the Carmarthen football ground and I stood on a dais in the open. The audience numbered fewer than the band, thanks to the weather, and the programme (not of my planning) was colossal. It included amongst other things such major works as *Egmont Overture*, Rimmer's selection of *Liszt's Works*, Keighley's *Lorenzo* and a selection from *Der Freischutz*. I had about an hour's rehearsal (I had asked for two), I got soaked to the skin and caught a chill; my sole recompense was - ten shillings!"

But let us return to Denis and his new job, which started in July 1936. Little is recorded about the early years, though it was during the three and a half years before the outbreak of war that he introduced many of his new transcriptions into the repertoire through his broadcasts with Crystal Palace Band.

However, things were certainly improving for bands through his efforts, because by the time the war arrived and changed everything, there were six or seven brass band broadcasts per week, one or two of them on the National wavelength and the others in various Regional programmes. Denis had also changed the situation in which all broadcasts on the National programme were provided by London bands. He did this by asking for national slots to be allotted, in turn, to the regions where they had the better bands. One problem he was never able to resolve satisfactorily was that of a number of bands appearing at the same time but on different regional wavelengths. This meant that out of those six or seven band broadcasts no-one could pick up more than three or four - even if they had been able to tune into ALL the regions. Decisions on the timing of these programmes was in the hands of the Regional Directors and, try as he may, Denis could not persuade them to avoid these regional clashes.

Things were to change dramatically on the outbreak of war, on 3rd September 1939. The last band to broadcast before hostilities began was Edge Hill LMS Band, which appeared in a North Regional programme on the Thursday before war was declared.

The immediate impact of the war on the BBC was staggering. Many existing programmes were cancelled and replaced, for a time, by the playing of gramophone records. The effect on bands was no less dramatic. With military call-up, voluntary war-work, and with over-time being demanded of those working in munitions factories and the like, regular rehearsals became difficult, if not impossible, for many.

Denis had a note published in the band press asking secretaries of all broadcasting bands to let the BBC know whether or not they would be able to carry on. Some works bands were able to continue, almost unaffected, and some others were able to undertake broadcasts with the help of borrowed players.

But there was another problem, that of finding studio accommodation. The London studios were out of use, as were several regional venues, due to the possibility of air raids. Bristol, Manchester and Glasgow became the main broadcasting centres, with a further small studio being opened in Evesham,[2] where much of the Corporation's 'normal' broadcasting was resumed. There was only one programme, broadcast nationally on two different wavelengths, with a virtual end to regional broadcasts.

This, coupled with the availability of fewer bands, meant a reduction to two periods of band broadcasts per week for the time being. It also meant that, in order to maintain the standard, only bands which were good enough for national broadcasting were offered engagements, and many of the bands classified as grades B and C, which had been used only at Regional level, were not offered any more broadcasts. As a result of this, whereas some 180 different bands had had broadcasts in the two years before the war, only fifty were now being used - and the number was reduced even further as wartime conditions created more and more problems. This policy caused some dissatisfaction in the band world, reflected in the band press but, Denis maintained,

"The average technical standard shown by the broadcasting bands was higher than before the war, simply because the lower grade ones had been weeded out."

Band broadcasts were actually re-commenced during October 1939. The studio situation was eased somewhat by allowing Callender's to broadcast from their own bandroom. Their first war-time broadcast was on the 16th November, and shortly after this - on the 25th - the first war-time broadcast from a London studio was given. According to the autobiography, with but a few exceptions, band broadcasts were provided by the North Region - using mainly the Manchester studio - and by Scotland (though my Black Dyke records show that most of their war-time broadcasts were from the Woodhouse Lane studios in Leeds, and if my memory serves me right, so were those of Brighouse & Rastrick).

Broadcasts by military bands now started to build up. Before the war there were only about two per month, but it was soon realised that both because they were popular and, up to a point available, they could to some extent be used instead of brass bands. Also, according to Listener Research figures, they commanded a slightly greater listening public.

Of course, availability of Service bands was subject to War Office approval and quite early in the war it was decreed that all line regimental bands should be scrapped. This rule was rescinded within a few months, but I assume that few, if any, of the bands in this category would have been used for broadcasting anyway.

The bands of the Guards regiments, the Corps staff bands and the various Marines and RAF bands were not affected, so about a dozen Service bands were available, though at first little use could be made of them because of their geographical locations and the problems of studio accommodation.

The BBC did, of course, have its own Military Band, though this was disbanded on the outbreak of war. Happily, it was soon re-formed and started to broadcast again. As this meant a partial re-opening of studios in London it also provided the opportunity to make more use of Service bands.

By early 1940 things were looking better on the band broadcast front, with more bands available, and some studios re-opening. The advent of a second programme, "The Forces", also increased the scope, and by September there was a weekly average of four brass bands, two Service bands and three broadcasts by the BBC Military Band. The actual figures for the first year of war-time broadcasts were:

Brass bands	199
Service bands	97
BBC Military Band	149
Total	445

So, despite all, the Band Section of the BBC's Music Department was being kept pretty busy. From 21st September the situation was to change again.

"The BBC Military Band was sent to Glasgow in order that enemy action, which had become intense in London, should not hold up their transmissions, and the band itself came on a new contract, under which they were to be called on up to six times a week instead of only three times. Moreover, the old method of allotting certain definite periods to the BBC Military Band whilst those for other bands, brass or military, were given to me to allot amongst the various regions, was superseded by an arrangement whereby I received a blank list of so many periods per week to share out between the BBC Military Band and all other bands. That was not a difficult thing to do, but what was bad was that, since the BBC Military Band had now had its hours doubled (or nearly so; one or two periods per week were used for overseas programmes) we still had about the same total number of periods allotted to the bands in general as we had before the BBC Military Band's hours were increased.

The immediate result was to decrease the number of available periods for brass and Service bands, and since the Controller of Programmes issued instructions that Service bands were to be given preferential treatment over brass bands, a thin time began for brass bands, and for weeks at a time we seldom got more than two brass band periods against a total of 5, 6 and even 7 military bands. The final totals for the second complete year were:

Brass bands	127
Service bands	128
BBC Military Band	195 (excluding purely overseas transmissions)

"This gave a grand total of 323 military bands to 127 brass, a proportion of roughly 2.5 to 1 in favour of the military band. If the Listener Research figures of comparative popularity were any real criterion, this proportion represented a grossly unfair state of things."

The other side of the coin was, of course, the difficulties under which many bands were functioning. Several had to suspend their activities or at least decline broadcast engagements. Some completely closed down. For many, evening rehearsals were impossible because of the blackout and therefore they were restricted to one rehearsal per week. Overtime made full attendance at rehearsals, and in many cases engagements, virtually impossible, and it wasn't surprising therefore that "even our best bands had temporary lapses from their normal high standards."

And of course most, if not all broadcasts in those days were live. There was no question of spending nearly a whole evening getting a programme right by means of re-takes!

By present day standards, the potential audiences for band broadcasts were enormous. There was, of course, no TV, a choice of only two programmes, and little social life or going out in the evenings. Listener Research figures suggested that rarely would there be fewer than a million listeners. Often there would be three or four million, and on one Christmas Day broadcast by Foden's there was an estimated six million.

It was also calculated that not more than 10% of listeners would be "what one might call brass band practitioners," and therefore a fairly tight reign had to be kept on programmes played on the air, bands constantly being encouraged to "get away from music they had played over and over again for many years." Not surprisingly, this policy was unpopular amongst the 'die-hard' school of band supporters, who wanted to hear nothing but their old favourites, but it was nevertheless enforced with much success.

From the listeners' point of view there were the regular - and often justified - carps about unsuitable timing of broadcasts, complaints about programme content and so on, but still the listening figures continued to be encouraging, which caused Denis to conclude that

"You simply can't start trying to please everybody, even once, let alone all of the time. But that conclusion should not be used as an excuse for failing to adopt a progressive outlook. In the brass band world in particular, though in the military band world to a not inconsiderable extent, hindrances and objections to any form of healthy progress are so much in evidence that you have either to grow a tough hide, go the way you decide to be right, and damn the consequences, or sink your aspirations (and artistic integrity, if any) and be virtually useless."

In these days of only one regular band programme per week the reader might wonder what kind of programmes bands were involved in when there were so many. There was, of course, a *Music While You Work* broadcast every morning and afternoon on week-days, and invariably a band was featured at least once during the week. Then there were programmes like *Saturday Bandstand*, *Sounding Brass and Voices* and *Command Performance*. There were also occasional features of particular bands or band personalities, and later in the war several massed bands concerts were broadcast.

Denis became quite heavily involved in finding a suitable format for *Music While You Work*. There were two programmes on each working day, one in the morning and the other in the afternoon. The programme was first broadcast in June 1940 and its object was to provide half an hour's continuous music, suitable for playing in factories and workshops, and aimed at encouraging even greater effort from the workforce, as part of the 'war-effort'. A wide variety of musical combinations was used and choice of groups and items played had to be carefully monitored. Even though the scope of the programme extended far beyond brass and military bands, Denis was one of those who had to see to it that the programme did actually work.

Ensuring that this and all the other programmes were of interest to the general listener must have created many problems, and the success of a programme often depended not on how well the band played nor indeed what the band played, but how it was presented. Denis often wrote the scripts, but generally they were read by one of the BBC's regular announcers.

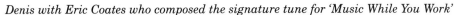

Denis with Eric Coates who composed the signature tune for 'Music While You Work'

Gracie Cole (referred to earlier) took part in one or two special broadcasts in which Denis was, again, trying to inform and to educate his listeners about certain aspects of playing a brass instrument. She showed me scripts of two of these.

The first went out on Sunday afternoon, 16th June 1940 in the Home Service. It was called *Blowing Your Own Trumpet* and in it, with the help of Foden's Motor Works Band, Denis demonstrated each of the band's instruments in turn. He then set about trying to persuade his listeners that they should take up the playing of a brass instrument. Fred Mortimer chipped in with comments about the need for regular practice and then Gracie played part of *My Old Kentucky Home* to show what could be done by a 15-year-old after a mere three years on the cornet.

The second programme was transmitted in the Home Service again but 18 months later, and this time at 7 o'clock on Friday evening, 16th January. (What splendid times for these broadcasts!) This was called *Making Your Own Music* and this time Denis enlisted the aid of six members of Fairey Aviation Works Band plus three ladies - Gracie herself, Maisie Ringham the trombonist and at the piano, Violet Carson - famous as the pianist in Wilfred Pickles' quiz programme *Have a Go!* and even better-known in later years as the infamous Ena Sharples of *Coronation Street*.

In this programme Denis demonstrated the delights of getting together to make music in small groups. Some of his demonstrations were of one or two instruments playing with piano accompaniment; there were a couple of quartets - each using a different set of instruments, some octets and three pieces using the whole group of eight brass instruments and piano. This must have been a delightful programme, and one from which we could learn even today.

Gracie also took part in a programme called *Music Makers' Half Hour* and another called *Two Girls and a Band,* in which Denis was trying to convince his listeners that the brass band need not be thought of as an all-male domain - and look at the results of THAT theory!

Good programme ideas were always in danger of being 'pirated' by some other department, for example,

"The BBC Military Band's request programme *Command Performance* was killed by an American variety relay that was given the title even whilst the BBC Military Band was still using it. *Brass Bandstand* was snatched away from us to become *Saturday Bandstand* in which, if you please, music was provided by - The Variety *Orchestra!*"

A programme which receives special attention in the autobiography is one which was set up as a tribute to Sir Granville Bantock on the occasion of his 73rd birthday, in 1941.

"Two things remain particularly in my mind: the first item was Bantock's *Festival March* which I put on the programme without having heard it previously. It turned out, at the first rehearsal, to be very long-winded - and rather dull, and took seven and a quarter minutes whereas I had only allowed four and a half minutes for it. So, without telling Bantock, I made a large cut in it which, although it wrecked the form of the march, improved it in all other respects. After the broadcast (given by the Fairey Aviation Works Band, which the Manager, Bill Hume, and Harry Mortimer their Musical Director, allowed me to conduct) I wrote and apologised to Sir Granville, who replied that I need not have apologised because he hadn't even noticed the cut!

The other thing was Bantock's reply to the story I told about him. Some years previously, at a dinner given by Munn and Felton's Works Band at Kettering before one of the special concerts they put on annually for three years prior to the war, Bantock had made a little speech in which he said he would rather listen to a good brass band than to an orchestra. I knew he was a great brass enthusiast, but to cover him in case the remark had been merely a courtesy one, I said, after telling of his words on that occasion: 'it may be that this statement was born of the enthusiasm of the moment, but I like to think that Bantock meant in fact exactly what he said'.

Bantock's reply was that he *did* indeed mean it; his enthusiasm for brass bands was the measure of their own enthusiasm - it seemed to him that 'banding' is so tremendously worthwhile - the best form of real amateur music making. Indeed, if any justification were needed for the brass band it is to be found in its very environment: amateur musicians making music - often surprisingly good music - for the enjoyment (not education, mark you) of those whose lives are set in drab and depressing surroundings and whose chances of finding beauty in their everyday occupation - often the occupation of maintaining a bare existence - are remote."

And please, dear reader, let us not lose sight of the fact that many of today's bandsmen and band enthusiasts still lead very hum-drum lives, and that they do look to bands for entertainment, as well as perhaps for moral and spiritual up-lift.

So there was still a great deal going on in the Band Section and, understandably, there was also plenty going on behind the scenes. One very time-consuming activity was that of auditioning bands which hoped to get on the air. This had been completely suspended on the outbreak of war, Denis being 'evacuated' to Evesham in fact on the day before war was declared. He returned to London a couple of months later, but it wasn't until March 1940 that the first war-time audition took place. Even after that, auditions took place only spasmodically, though applications were being received regularly both from Service bands and brass bands - particularly from within the North Region. Travelling wasn't easy of course, so nothing in the way of an auditions tour was carried out and in fact, bands were not visited unless they were fully expected to be of the required standard.

In September 1940 the Band Section, along with the BBC Military Band, was evacuated to Glasgow, enabling Denis to make periodic visits to bands in the North and the Midlands. The first war-time auditions 'tour' took place in April 1941, but the standard of the bands was apparently not high, and so not many passed.

Several of those auditioned were Home Guard bands. Most of them were not successful, but it is perhaps worth recording that the first such band to be given a broadcast was the Halifax Home Guard Band. Under the direction of Tom Casson, this band included amongst its members players from both Black Dyke and Brighouse and Rastrick - each located within a few miles of Halifax.

The year 1942 proved to be quite an eventful one. The BBC Music Department, which had spent some time in Bristol, had been moved to Bedford during 1941, and at the end of January 1942 Denis was also moved there, though in fact he spent most of his time in London. He had been a member of the Home Guard in Glasgow, and in London, some months later, he discovered that the BBC Home Guard ('E' Company, 5th London Battalion) was looking to form a brass band. He offered his services, was given a commission, and the job of recruiting players and forming the band. Despite a host of problems the band was formed in 1942. It was started originally as the BBC's own Company Band, but as there were insufficient recruits it became the Battalion Band and made its first public appearance on Sunday, 10th January 1943, marching into Regents Park to practice its parade routine. Denis takes up the story.

A broadcast with the Home Guard Band, October 1944 (Ernest Brown is on soprano and Ivor Walsworth, BBC sound engineer, on bass drum!)

"Snow overnight and fog in the morning rather spoilt the attendance, but we put out a band of 16 and had 15 buglers from the Cadets attached to the Battalion, so it didn't look too bad, though it could have sounded better. As the Colonel said afterwards: *It sounded quite nice - from a distance!*"

Denis apparently arranged a number of marches for band, bugles and drums. On another occasion:

"March 7th 1943; the Band turned out for a General Inspection - the General had to see each platoon - Signallers, Pioneers, Medical and so on, doing their stuff. So, after waiting in a side street till a runner gave us the tip, the Band, Drummers, Buglers, some three dozen in all, marched past Company Headquarters, on the steps of which stood the General, our Colonel and a few others. We played 'Georgia' so that the Buglers could have a show. After counter-marching I got a signal from our Company Commander to halt the Band.

Those who were in the Band that day may, for all I know, still be wondering why I gave that particular order. I still wonder myself. But they obeyed it to a man, though they could not have been more surprised at the result than I was. For the whole Band right-turned with almost Guards-like precision, and finished up amid awful silence - *with their backs to the General.*"

Mrs. Wright tells of an interesting sequel to this incident. Not surprisingly, Denis was hauled before the Commanding Officer and asked for an explanation. She says,

'He solemnly explained he had noticed that if he had given the correct order the bass drum would have collided into the player next to it, so to avoid this clash he'd had to make the Band turn right round. The explanation was accepted.'

This couldn't possibly have happened under Captain Mannering (or should it be Mainwaring) - or could it?

In 1944 Denis took his Home Guard Band to Belle Vue to compete in Class A of the May Championship Festival. The test piece was *Coriolanus* by Cyril Jenkins but alas, the only Home Guard band to figure in the prize list came from Halifax!

During its brief life the London Home Guard Band gave three broadcasts, played regularly in the London Parks and fulfilled nearly 50 Battalion and Company functions. When it was disbanded - around the end of 1944 - it boasted 45 players, including 10 buglers.

Stepping back into that all-important year of 1942 and to 7th April; Kenneth Wright, by now the BBC Overseas Music Director, travelled to Bedford to see Denis, and to offer him the job of Assistant Overseas Director - a position just vacated by Arthur Bliss.

Denis accepted, and on his recommendation Harry Mortimer was appointed to take over his old job as the BBC's Brass and Military Band

Harry Mortimer was appointed to take over his job . . .

Supervisor. Denis thus moved into a completely different area of work, but one which still allowed him to maintain some contact with band broadcasting. More of this later.

Some of Denis's 'firsts' were listed on page 55. Here are a few of his broadcasting innovations:

The first broadcast of combined voices and band, with the BBC Men's Chorus and Crystal Palace Band. He scored the music and conducted the programme (1937)

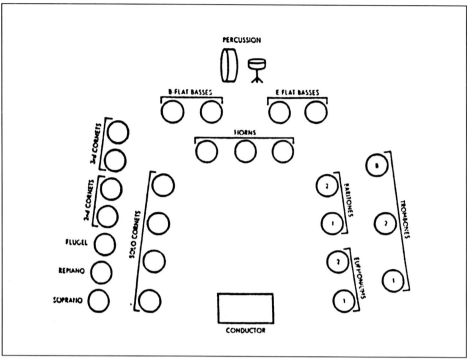

Above: Standard formation used during 30s nd still used quite regularly

Below: Broadcast formation, devised by Denis Wright in late 1930s

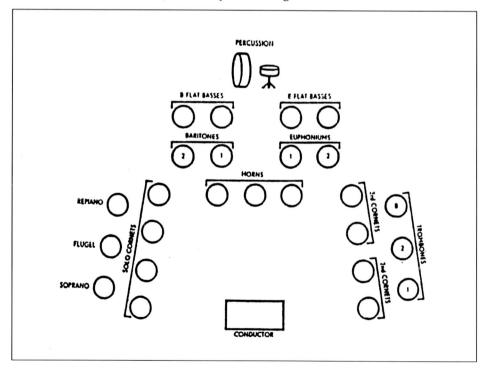

The first broadcast of a solo singer with brass band. This was with Walter Widdop and Crystal Palace Band. The pieces sung with band accompaniment were the *Prize Song* from Wagner's *Mastersingers* and Handel's *Sound an Alarm*. Again he scored the music and conducted (1938)

(These two broadcasts paved the way for the popular and long-running series 'Sounding Brass and Voices')

The establishment of 'Broadcast Formation' - devised in 1939 in conjunction with a BBC sound engineer, Ivor Walsworth (*see diagram*)

The first broadcast of a massed bands concert in which the players were seated as a composite band and not as individual bands. This was from Butlin's Holiday Camp in Skegness (1939)

Denis's promotion to the post of Assistant Overseas Director signalled the end of an era. He had spent just over six years

"Trying to get the BBC to appreciate the difficulties of amateur brass bands and in trying to get brass and Service bands to appreciate what a large number of friends they have in the world who would be so glad *not* to be treated as musical nitwits."

Those six years - half of them war-time years - had obviously not been easy. Amidst the turmoil of forming a new section in the BBC and the turbulence of war, Denis had undertaken over 500 auditions and had directed broadcasts with over 80 bands. He was now disposed to say,

"So now I could sit back and watch someone else hold the baby - a baby I had at times enjoyed holding, but which didn't always show signs of enjoying being held by me. It bit my hands a good deal and I have had to wait a long time before I could smack it in return."

Notes

[1] *The BBC Wireless Military Band* was a group of professional musicians assembled by the Corporation to give regular broadcasts of military band music. Formed in 1927, it was temporarily suspended on the outbreak of War in 1939, then reformed and sent to Glasgow. Many famous players were associated with the band over the years, including Gilbert Vinter on bassoon and Philip Catelinet on euphonium. The band was finally dissolved on 16th March 1943. (See page 98 for information about its two conductors, the O' Donnell brothers.)

[2] The **Evesham** location is still used by the BBC, primarily as a training centre for its sound engineers. It still has the 'underground' features of a war-time emergency unit, but is, I am told, serving its purpose well.

Chapter 13

Life outside the BBC

The arrival of World War II affected the lives of virtually every man, woman and child in Britain - and not only in Britain! We've seen some of its effects on bands, and in particular, band broadcasts. But it also brought about considerable changes in the way of life of Denis Wright. From the autobiography:

> "It was only natural that at the start of the war there should be a partial closing down of normal music-making activities during the weeks of uncertainty and before the country became stabilised and adapted to new conditions. My evacuation to Evesham with the BBC Music Department meant that, even if things had gone on normally in London I was not in a position to do much myself, but I was back in London ten weeks later - thanks to a persuasive pen which justified in official eyes my return there when the rest of the Department was moved to Bristol.
>
> The Crystal Palace Band was still meeting on Sundays, though several players had left for the Forces or other war work that made it impossible for them to attend regularly, and it was not until April 7th 1940 that we gave our first war- time broadcast."

Apart from the occasional guest conducting or adjudicating engagement, life outside the BBC was quiet, to say the least, but a couple of months into the war Denis met someone who had recently obtained a Doctorate at Edinburgh, and from his account of what he had to do it occurred to Denis that he could do the same. I've already mentioned the preparatory work that he did with Dr. Kitson (page 55), which obviously paid off, because by June, 1940, Denis had reached the height of his academic career, becoming a Doctor of Music. His main thesis, as he says,

> "Took the form of a short history of *The Evolution of the Wind Band*. Not a very detailed history, since in about 20,000 words I covered well over 2,000 years! I added to this, as an appendix, my published book, *Scoring for Brass Band* and threw in as makeweight, so as to give me a second string to my bow, an orchestral suite and a short work for 8-part chorus and orchestra."

The *Evolution* will be discussed in Chapter 22 and *Scoring* is now pretty standard reading for the brass band student. Edinburgh University was unable to provide any details of the musical part of the submission and for a time I feared it had been lost. To my great relief and joy, however, I located a bound score in Mrs. Wright's collection which is, without any doubt, the "makeweight" to which Denis refers.

For this compositional side of his submission, Denis returned to earlier material. The suite has four movements, three of them revisions of brass band pieces, and the choral work is an expanded version of a song dating, co-incidentally, from 1925.

The movements of *Suite for Orchestra* do not have separate titles, but the first is a re-working of the overture *Joan of Arc*, while movements II and III are based on the 2nd and 3rd movements of *Tintagel*.

In the autobiography Denis describes his original version of *Joan* as "long-winded", going on to say that, for his own amusement, he later wrote an 8½ minute version, making more economical use of the same material. I believe the opening movement of the *Suite for Orchestra* to be that particular 'amusement'. I said earlier that Denis had scored the overture for orchestra. He probably did that in 1931 and it followed faithfully the structure of the band version. However, there are penciled comments on the original score which obviously refer to the 1940 version which, though it contains large sections of the original orchestration, also encompasses some re-worked passages and some abridging.

In the two *Tintagel* movements (*Elaine* and *Merlin*), however, he has gone the opposite way, expanding each in order to exploit more fully the additional resources of the symphony orchestra. He contrives to end *Merlin* quietly so as to make it less conclusive and also to make an appropriate lead-in to the final movement, which begins softly. This appears to be new, and takes the form of a passacaglia - a set of variations on a short theme which recurs over and over again, mainly in the bass.

The other work in the doctoral submission, *Pibroch of Donuil Dhu*, could be described as a secular cantata. Its words come from a poem by Sir Walter Scott, and the music is based on an unaccompanied part-song by Denis, published in 1925 for 4-part choir (SATB). The 1940 version calls for full orchestra and double chorus (SSAATTBB) and demonstrates that Denis was very much at home writing this kind of work for these sort of forces.

Interestingly, Harold Hind went for the Edinburgh Doctorate a year later than Denis, also writing a thesis dealing with the history of the wind band, "but with a difference," as Denis says.

"He covered about 500 years, but with truly amazing thoroughness and at great length - it must have been about five times the length of mine and involved far more research than I had given to the subject."

He goes on, with characteristic charity,

"I feel pretty sure that, had Harold gone up to Edinburgh before me or even at the same time, I should not have passed, as the examiners could not fail to have compared the scholarship and exhaustiveness of his thesis with the brevity and incompleteness of mine - to the detriment of the latter!"

Be that as it may, Denis did get his Doctorate, and his next project was to write a *Concerto for Cornet and Orchestra*, a virtuoso work which he hoped would prove that the cornet was

> "Entitled to rank with other wind instruments as a worthy soloist in its own right, fit to associate with horn, trumpet, clarinet and any others that have had concertos written for them and are accepted and not merely tolerated."

He had been toying with the idea for some years but had not had the chance to get to work on it. Alas, as so often happens, now that he had the time, he could not come up with suitable musical ideas. And anyway, in London at this time there was the small matter of the Battle of Britain, with its enforced visits to the studio air raid shelters, sleepless nights, and "too much tea-drinking in the small hours," all adding up to "not much scope for quiet concentration."

He had also joined the Local Defence Volunteers (the LDV - forerunner of the Home Guard, or as it's since been dubbed, 'Dad's Army').

> "A handful of us, armed with broomsticks, solemnly paraded in the big studio at Maida Vale and learned or relearned our drill and, when the authorities weren't around, flopped on our tummies in one of the corridors and 'potted' at a miniature target - with an airgun. We also did our turn of all-night guards at Maida Vale, getting on occasions well and truly mixed up with the blitz."

Despite all this, ideas for the *Cornet Concerto* were slowly forming in his mind. In September 1940, he was whisked off to Glasgow, along with the BBC Military Band, in an attempt to make broadcasting easier for the band than it had been in London, and it was here, billeted in "a singularly depressing unlicensed private hotel" that he started to get the *Concerto* down in writing. It came out in the remarkably short space of three weeks - and that was by working on it only in the evenings and at week-ends - largely because he had been thinking about it for so long.

First came the short score, after which he made the decision to write it initially not for orchestra, but for military band. This was good thinking as there was, on hand, a fully professional group. He had Harry Mortimer in mind for giving the Concerto's first performance, and within a month of finishing the actual composition he had scored it for military band, and also sent a piano and cornet version to Harry,

> "With a request that I might be allowed to dedicate the work to him. There was no doubt whatsoever in my mind that not only was he the most artistic cornet player in this country at the time - although perhaps on a test of virtuosity and sheer technique Jack Mackintosh might have beaten him - but also that the particular lay-out of the solo part, mainly melodic but not overwhelmingly difficult technically, would appeal to him and suit him."

With typical thoroughness, Denis scored a brass band version so that Harry could rehearse it with Foden's, where of course he was still playing.

'HM' obviously liked the *Concerto,* and I'm sure he would feel very honoured about the dedication and at being asked to première it.

The first performance was in a broadcast from Glasgow on 4th March 1941. Harry Mortimer was the soloist, with the BBC Military Band conducted by P. S. G. O'Donnell.[1] Harry had not only learned the Concerto for that first performance, he had actually memorised it.

"The sheer loveliness of his playing on that occasion - as at many subsequent performances - fully justified my desire at the outset that Harry should be associated with the work."

The orchestral version was completed during the summer of 1941 and first performed by the BBC Northern Orchestra, conducted by Denis's old friend and colleague, Maurice Johnstone, again with Harry as soloist. Such was Johnstone's enthusiasm for the work that another performance was arranged, to take place a mere four weeks later. This was with the Scottish Orchestra, forerunner of the present RSNO, under the baton of Warwick Braithwaite.

"Braithwaite was then in his second season with the 'Scottish'; he put the work down for a Sunday afternoon popular concert at the Paramount Cinema, Glasgow. At the last moment Braithwaite asked me to conduct. It was not an easy decision to make; I wanted to because apart from preliminary rehearsals with the BBC Military Band I had never conducted the work but on the other hand one hears it better from a seat in the auditorium. However, the lure of conducting finally triumphed."

The broadcasts brought mildly favourable comment from the press, but a commercial recording released by Decca at around the same time as the second broadcast created more interest than either of the broadcasts, even though Denis didn't think very highly of it. The recording was by the Royal Artillery (Woolwich) Band under Captain Owen Geary, with a Sergeant-Major Lewis as soloist. *Musical Times* gave good coverage in a well-informed crit:

'It may be that since the days when its repertory ranged from *The Lost Chord* to *Variations on a Popular Tune* the cornet has been surreptitiously compiling a store of original music. I doubt, however, whether it has ever had a concerto, at least in England, or has advanced to the stage where a concerto is a long-felt want. Perhaps it has lingered on the upward path for want of a virtuoso to do for it what Tertis[2] has done for the viola and Rascher[3] for the saxophone; perhaps if the great Levy[4] were alive now he would have surrounded himself with a school of cornet compositions, including not only concertos but Cobbett Fantasias[5] and arrangements of, say, horn music beginning with the Brahms E flat Trio.

Mr. Denis Wright may be acquitted of any desire to start such a movement with his new and romantic *Cornet Concerto* (Decca M 508-9); he is more likely to have written it out of sheer affection for the cornet. Mr. Wright does not modernize or militarize the cornet. He dwells rather on its capacity for lyrical sentiment; by which I do not mean sentimentality -

there is nothing here of tearful street-corner minstrelsy. The music belongs to the region of, say, early Elgar, where well-cut melodies lie upon irreproachable harmonies and music hath charms.

The soloist is given his opportunities to prove himself a virtuoso, but he is not allowed to hold up the music while he performs stunts, for which relief much thanks. This is a composition first and a show piece second. Among the technical specialities to be noted are some wide, rapid arpeggios up and down common chords, and a good deal of triple tonguing. Most of the time, however, the cornet is proving its readiness to play more or less anything that comes along. One bit of treatment that the average composer would not think of is a melodic passage in the lowest register, round about middle C and a fifth downwards; from these depths the instrument brings out a tone of striking quality and expressive value.'

There were several more reviews, in various papers and magazines, not all totally complimentary, but supportive on the whole.

The *Concerto's* first brass band performance was given by Foden's Motor Works Band on 2nd February 1942. Again, the soloist was Harry Mortimer and though brass band enthusiasts declared it (not surprisingly) to be the best version, Denis himself thought it to be "the least successful of the three; as the band part being all brass tone there was not sufficient contrast between the solo part and the tutti work." But he goes on:

"I think I'm right in saying that this was the first instrumental concerto to be performed by three different types of ensemble - orchestra, military band and brass band. So whatever its musical value, it has at least created a record."

There is a BBC recording - still in existence - made by Harry Mortimer with the Band of the Irish Guards conducted by Captain G. H. Willcocks - later Major Willcocks and Professional Conductor of Fairey's and Black Dyke. In recent years the Concerto has become one of the most played of all Denis's compositions - mainly in its brass band version, but also as a very popular choice, with piano accompaniment, in examinations.

Obtaining the Degree of Doctor of Music and composing the *Cornet Concerto* were Denis's main projects outside of his BBC work during the early years of the war. But other things were going on also.

An important new development in the brass band world at this time was, aided and abetted by the BBC, an escalation in the number and quality of massed band concerts. They proved to be a means of getting substantial-sized audiences into big halls, were capable of boosting flagging spirits - being spectacular events both visually and aurally and, given the right type of programme, were capable of engendering a feeling of patriotism during those dark and troubled times.

The massed band concert which receives fullest treatment in the autobiography is the one mentioned previously, in which Sir Adrian Boult conducted the first performance of Denis's arrangement of *Themes from Symphony No 5* by Beethoven. The concert, organised by John Henry Iles, took place in the Royal Albert Hall, London, on Sunday, 10th January 1942 -

within a few days of the anniversary of the famous 'Absent Minded Beggar' concert of 1900 in the same hall (see page 14).

Iles had approached Denis towards the end of 1941 with a view to getting the BBC involved, and in turn, Denis had notified the Assistant Director of Music, with a strong recommendation that part of the concert should be broadcast. Initially it was agreed that there would be an hour's broadcast, from 4 p.m. to 5 p.m. on the Forces Programme, but it was reduced to 40 minutes.

Denis had meanwhile suggested to Iles ("with my tongue in my cheek") that the programme should include a shortened version of Beethoven's 5th Symphony, with its 'V for Victory' connotations and all that (see page 54). This work

"Had suddenly become a popular classic in the worst sense of the word, and had taken to itself sundry titles, such as the *V Symphony,* the *Victory Symphony* and so on; titles that made all sensitive musicians writhe and gnash their teeth. Little did I guess how my suggestion was to add to the writhings and gnashings, chiefly by the BBC Music Staff, or what a hornet's nest I was stirring up."

Iles liked the idea and asked Denis to go ahead and make an arrangement.

"The Selection, containing music from all four movements, worked out at about nine and a half to ten minutes' playing time and was thus of a suitable length for any band programme without wearying the unclassically-minded listener."

Also included in the massed band programme was Sullivan's hymn *Onward Christian Soldiers* - with Eva Turner singing. The reason for the inclusion of this was that it had also been included in the 1900 concert, conducted in fact by Sullivan himself.

Iles offered Sir Adrian either *Onward Christian Soldiers* or Beethoven's 5th Symphony. Not surprisingly he chose the latter, though as I have explained previously, he had not been told that it was an abridged version, little more than a third of the length of the Symphony itself.

Boult did, as we have seen, conduct the 'potted' version though he asked that it should be in the non-broadcast part of the concert. He was, of course, one of Britain's foremost orchestral conductors, and also the BBC's Director of Music. However, both his Deputy and his Assistant had already decreed that on no account was the arrangement to be broadcast. Further, they had expressed the view that Sir Adrian 'should not conduct a mutilated symphony in public at all.'

Poor Denis. He returned to Glasgow feeling that he had started something which was going to do nothing but cause friction.

The broadcast part of the programme had now been further reduced,

"To a miniature Crystal Palace Massed Band concert, consisting of massed items - marches and two hymn tunes - the inevitable *Sandon* and *Eternal*

Father, Strong to save - conducted by Iles, with solo items by the three bands taking part interspersed between the massed numbers."

Another of Denis's criticisms of the concert was that it had been advertised as *"including* Foden's, Dyke and Besses" whereas, in the event, it included *only* those three bands, a publicity trick which Denis felt was less than honest. There's even stronger criticism on another matter.

"Both Sir Adrian and I suffered from another instance of the disregard of professional etiquette in connection with a deal made with a gramophone recording company."

It seems that dear John Henry had negotiated for the recording of the event, and had actually 'given' the services of both Sir Adrian and Denis, without consulting either, though as Denis said, "If in my case it were more the principle of the thing that mattered, in Boult's case it obviously involved him in a considerable financial loss."

And so to the day of the concert. Iles had arranged for a two-hour pre-concert rehearsal and then proceeded to use up the first hour on his own pieces. But then,

"Sir Adrian's rehearsal was an object-lesson to the band conductors and bandsmen. He asked me first of all to take the bands through the whole selection, so that he could, as it were, get his bearings, since brass bands were almost an unknown medium to him. Then for about 40 minutes he gave them a rehearsal, which, for musical interest and painstaking insistence on correctness, style and the understanding of the music they were playing was an eye-opener and an education to those who had never before heard a conductor of Boult's standing at work. He accomplished far more in that short period than the average band conductor would have accomplished in six such rehearsals - if ever. It was a pity that there was no time left for a final run-through of the piece; it was here that we saw the need for that extra hour I had asked for. I was left with the final quarter of an hour in which to rehearse my two numbers. Luckily they were both pieces familiar to the bands, so the fact that I had time for not much more than getting a mutual agreement on tempi did not matter very much."

As was to be expected, the Beethoven was the highlight of what was in other respects a fairly undistinguished concert, and Denis got what he described as "the biggest thrill I have ever had from brass bands out of the 'travesty' of the *Fifth Symphony*." Sir Adrian and the bands were accorded a great ovation and even many of those who had been sceptical had to admit to the arrangement's unqualified success.

In these days of so little media attention to what brass bands are trying to achieve, it is interesting to read the good coverage given by newspapers to the more important band events of 50 years ago. As we have seen, the *Cornet Concerto* was discussed quite thoroughly by the press, in its debut year of 1941, and the Royal Albert Hall concert of 12th January 1942 attracted interesting and varied comments in a range of newspapers.

Sir Adrian Boult

The *Daily Telegraph,* much to Denis's delight, attacked the programme in that it had given a false idea of modern brass band music. Both *The Times* and *The Daily Mail* were enthusiastic about certain aspects of the concert, but both gave it the metaphorical patronising smile at the mixture of selections, trivial solos and hymn tunes.

The Beethoven came in for both criticism and praise. *The Telegraph* attacked it fiercely as 'an arrangement of Beethoven's C Minor Symphony which purists would have called a disarrangement and pedants a travesty!'

On the other hand, the critic writing for *The Times,* had this rather spectacular comment:

> 'The effect was a magnified projection of the music which had moments of real magnificence'. And *The Daily Mail's* comment -

> 'If not exactly Beethoven, the result was a brilliant piece of music.'

Sir Adrian derived "considerable pleasure", with no apparent feelings of "having assisted at a massacre or desecration." His letter to the BBC Controller of Programmes (part of which was quoted on page 54) is evidence of this.

So much for the Royal Albert Hall concert in January 1942. Iles was undoubtedly pleased with it and decided to have a re-run at Belle Vue a couple of months later, with Fairey Aviation Works Band being added to the original three and with a specially assembled mixed-voice choir of about 600. However,

> "The question of another broadcast came up. Having had such poor reports as to the Albert Hall one - bad balance in the case of solo bands (owing to the formation in which each band had to sit) and complete absence of clarity when the massed bands were playing, I came to the conclusion that our gesture to Mr. Iles having once been made, was not worth repeating on the score of actual value received for our money."

However, the final decision on whether to broadcast the Belle Vue event or not was left to Maurice Johnstone, as North Region Music Director, who decided that 'it was not an important enough event musically to justify his asking the Programme Planning Department in London to make room for it.'

So, in the end, the concert went ahead without BBC involvement - and a good thing too, according to Denis.

> "The choir did not come to a rehearsal, so it would have been impossible to achieve a balance test; in actual effect it was a case of a choral mountain giving birth to the smallest of small vocal mice - not through any fault of their own."

According to Denis, John Henry allowed the massed band to play "as if it had nothing to do with any singers." Nevertheless the crowd enjoyed it all and *The British Bandsman* gave the usual glittering account, but Denis was quite vitriolic about the whole affair, even dubbing Iles as *"The Barnum of Brass Bands".*

Notes

[1] *The O'Donnell's* were a famous family of military bandmasters - three of them in all - and brothers. B. Walton O'Donnell, with whom Denis worked in forming the Band Section of the BBC's Music Department, had been a bandmaster in the Royal Marines from 1914 to 1927. He conducted the BBC Wireless Military Band from 1927 to 1937, when he took up an appointment as Music Director for the BBC in Northern Ireland. His brother, P. S. G. O'Donnell succeeded him as conductor of the BBC Military Band until it folded in 1943. The third of the brothers, R. P.

O'Donnell, was a Director of Music in the Royal Air Force. According to Harry Mortimer 'RP' was the first to address him as 'HM'.

[2] *Lionel Tertis* (1876-1975) was a celebrated British viola player who devoted his life to the cause of his chosen instrument, regarded at the time as the 'Cinderella' of string instruments.

[3] *Sigmund Rascher* (b. Germany, 15th May 1907) holds a unique place amongst saxophonists, having inspired many works for the saxophone, several of which are dedicated to him.

[4] *Jules Levy* (1838-1903) was the self-elected 'King of cornet players', a pioneer creating the instrument's popularity in the 19th century, and described by one authority as *the most celebrated cornetist in the history of the musical world!* He was born in London but spent much of his life in America.

[5] *Walter Cobbett* (1847-1937) was an English businessman and amateur violinist who promoted concerts and presented prizes both for performance and composition. He commissioned several composers to write works for chamber groups in the Elizabethan fantasia form and also endowed the Cobbett Medal for services to chamber music.

Chapter 14

Let there be Massed Band Broadcasts!

At around the same time as Denis handed the band broadcasting reins over to Harry Mortimer in 1942, Arthur Bliss became more involved in programme planning at the BBC, and following a very successful massed band concert Denis had conducted in Sheffield and which was broadcast, the BBC Programme Planners said (in Denis's words), "Let there be massed band broadcasts!" For starters four were arranged on Sunday afternoons - one per month - during the first part of 1943.

As the BBC's new Brass and Military Bands Supervisor, Harry Mortimer took the brunt of the organisational side of these, and as he was still playing, as well as having become one of the most successful brass band conductors, he took on a variety of rôles. Denis also was quite heavily involved and his views on such things as programming and the seating arrangement of the bands were very much in evidence. As far as programme content and presentation was concerned, old ideas of the limitation of massed items - mainly marches and hymns - had to go - and not only that:

> "A professional standard of programme - good music adequately prepared - was aimed at. No more describing - for such is the bandsman's love of description that every piece must have some designation other than its title - so, no more describing the 1st movement of the *Unfinished Symphony* as an *Intermezzo* (which indeed I have actually seen!) or mixing up composers' names with those of the publishers, whereby *Lohengrin* appeared as a composition by *R. Smith* and a selection from *Faust* by *Wright and Round*."

Denis and Harry would have liked to engage top orchestral conductors to work with the bands, but owing to the limited time available for planning and organising this early series, that idea didn't come to fruition until later.

Denis was also able to put into practice his ideas of seating the players in groups - all solo cornets together, all trombones together, and so on. This we now take for granted, and it seems incredible that massed bands used to be seated as a collection of individual bands. No wonder they played only marches and hymn tunes.

Denis had first evolved a logical way of seating in 1939, in a massed band concert held at Butlin's Holiday Camp in Skegness. He had used the plan again in the Belle Vue concert described towards the end of the previous chapter, though Iles claimed the credit for it.

The basis of his massed formation, as in his 'broadcast formation' (also devised in 1939) was that all the upward-facing instruments (horns, baritones, euphoniums and basses) should be seated in front of the conductor whilst all horizontally-played instruments were to the conductor's left and right (see diagrams on page 88) Denis's thinking behind the 'broadcast formation' was the positioning of the various instruments in such a way that the geography of the band matched the geography of the score, with treble solo instruments grouped together, euphoniums close to E flat basses, baritones close to lower horns, and 2nd and 3rd cornets seated immediately in front of trombones, with which they are frequently 'paired' in Denis's scores. There were also advantages for the 'miking' of the band with this kind of grouping - more-so in the days of mono than today.

His recommendation for the massed formation is an extension of this, but with repianos and flugels now on the right instead of being out on the left flank, possibly behind several rows of solo cornets.

In recent years other seating arrangements have been devised, especially with regard to the positioning of the flugel horn which, these days, takes on a much more dominant rôle as a major treble solo instrument than was formerly the case.

The logic of seating lower cornets close to trombones - though rarely done these days, is demonstrated in Example 16 (bars 9-12), and this leads nicely into another anecdote of Denis's about a massed band concert in the Royal Albert Hall in April 1944, when Sir Henry Wood was Chief Guest Conductor. Denis's transcription of the *Introduction to Act III* of Wagner's *Lohengrin* was one of the pieces Sir Henry was to conduct, and a full score of Denis's transcription of this had been sent to the great man in good time.

Example 16 Denis Wright's ending to the Introduction, Act III of Lohengrin

Now, there is something of a history to the ending of this piece. Contrary to the wishes of Wagner himself, who patently disapproved of the playing of excerpts from his operas, the Introduction to the 3rd Act quickly became a popular addition to the concert repertoire, though it needed a more conclusive ending than Wagner's which, not un-naturally, leads straight into the final act (Example 17), and *Here comes the bride*.

(The Curtain rises.)

Example 17 The ending to the Introduction to Act III in the opera

Sir Henry used an ending given to him by the German conductor Felix Mottl, who had actually worked with Wagner at the first Bayreuth Festival. When Denis made the transcription he incorporated, from memory, the Henry Wood/Felix Mottl coda. Alas, his memory had played a trick on him and it was a bar short. Wood was having none of this and it was not long before Denis received a letter from him, with a re-scoring of the concluding bars - including the one omitted by Denis. But there is a rather curious twist to all this.

"On the day following the Albert Hall concert much of the programme was repeated at Wolverhampton with Sir Adrian Boult as Chief Guest Conductor. Before the morning rehearsal Sir Adrian decided he liked my version of the ending, even if not authentic, more than Sir Henry's, so we reverted to the printed copy. We never told Sir Henry, of course, but even though my ending may be a bar short (seven bars from the end) Sir Henry's scoring was not as effective as it could have been, as he robbed it of brilliance by putting the 1st trombone down an octave where it merely blended with 2nd and bass trombones, instead of giving a tremendous 'lift' to the 2nd and 3rd cornets."

This highlights one of the many examples of the advantage of seating the lower cornets close to the trombones, though for normal concert work with a single band this lay-out is hardly ever used these days, and even in the broadcasting or recording studio, with more sophisticated microphone techniques and the demands of stereo, bands are usually free to choose whichever lay-out they prefer, and almost without exception, you will now find all cornets seated in their traditional two lines on the conductor's left.

Throughout the remaining years of the War and beyond, massed band concerts were both frequent and popular. Much of the conducting was shared by Harry Mortimer and Denis, and usually some part of the concert was broadcast - either live, or via a BBC recording - already becoming common towards the end of the War. Whenever possible, conductors of the stature of Sir Henry Wood, Sir Adrian Boult and Doctor Malcolm Sargent (not knighted until 1947) were engaged, bringing prestige and musical credibility to the concerts and also helping, along with the transcriptions, to build bridges from the hitherto isolated position of the brass band across into the wider musical world of the mid-20th century. It was also from around this time that the BBC announcer Frank Phillips began a lasting relationship with the brass band world with his delightful and witty, yet intelligent and informed compering of major band events.

I mentioned Harry Mortimer's multi-rôles in these concerts. Denis also was capable of his own brand of versatility.

H.M. discusses a point with Frank Phillips, while Denis looks on

"Harry played solos sometimes and once or twice I accompanied him on the organ. I was seldom happy with the modern cinema type organ we often met in these concerts. *By a slip of the finger one can produce such extraordinary effects!*"

Massed band concerts flourished throughout the 1940s and into the 1950s, some of them broadcast and others not. Conductors introduced to bands on these occasions, as a result of the joint efforts of Denis and Harry Mortimer included, as well as Boult, Wood and Sargent - already referred to - Sir John Barbirolli and Sir Granville Bantock.

Two of these concerts are of particular interest, both of them taking place in the Philharmonic Hall, Liverpool. In the first, with the aid of Black Dyke, Foden's and Fairey's, Boult conducted the 1st performance of Denis's transcription of the opening movement of Schubert's *Unfinished Symphony*. As this was a complete movement it did not cause the stir created when *Themes from Symphony No. 5* by Beethoven was premièred by the same conductor some four years earlier. In September the following year the noted Hungarian-born pianist Louis Kentner performed the 1st movement of the Schumann *Piano Concerto*, which had been premièred in Denis's version a few months earlier by Eileen Joyce (see page 158). This time the bands were Black Dyke, Foden's and Brighouse and Rastrick, and the conductor - Stanford Robinson.

Nor were these concerts restricted to the North of England. *Brass Band News* of May 1943 contains a report of one which took place in Glasgow in

By the slip of a finger . . .

Preparing for the massed bands at a Yorkshire Miners' Gala

April. Denis himself conducted, the bands being Scottish CWS, Clydebank Burgh and Parkhead Forge. The same paper, in March 1945, tells of a concert in Hanley, at which Sir Granville Bantock was guest conductor. The associate conductors were Fred and Harry Mortimer, Colin Clayton and Bram Gay were soloists, and the bands were Foden's, Fairey's and Brighouse and Rastrick.

In Yorkshire, an annual event was established during the late 1940s which was the forerunner of the CISWO Band Festival still held in the City Hall, Sheffield. It consisted of a contest followed by a massed band concert, held in the open air, as part of the Yorkshire Miners' Gala. David Read recalls playing in several of these, and he says that Denis was usually the adjudicator and conductor. David was with Carlton Main Frickley Colliery Band at the time and says that Denis seemed to have quite a liking for that band - an opinion confirmed by James Scott.

During the second half of the 1940s the annual Grand Festival Concerts which rounded off the National Brass Band Championships at the Royal Albert Hall became spectacular affairs and began building bridges with the rest of the musical world. The 1946 concert was opened by the Trumpeters of the Royal Military School of Music, Sargent conducted, HM was the soloist in two movements from Haydn's *Trumpet Concerto*, the distinguished soprano Gwen Catley was featured - accompanied by Fairey Aviation, and concert pianist Eileen Joyce gave the first performance with brass band of Denis's transcription of Baraza by Arthur Bliss (see also page 159). Eight bands took part, and several Denis Wright transcriptions were included in the programme.

Boult and HM shared the podium the following year, when again eight bands (the previous year's National Champions plus all the current Area winners) took part. This time they were joined by the Trumpeters of the Life Guards, the Luton Choral Society, Arnold Grier at the organ and with special guests Anne Ziegler and Webster Booth. Again several Denis Wright scores were featured in the programme, including the *Academic Festival Overture* and a special arrangement of *The Blue Danube* as a choral waltz, with the Luton Choral Society and three of the bands.

And so it went on. The seeds, many of which had been sown by Denis, were beginning to flower. Sadly, in our quest to 'do our own thing' in more recent years, we seem to have lost our way, and with it, many of the friends which we were obviously winning as we emerged from the dark days of the 1940s.

Chapter 15

The BBC's
overseas services

Here's an extract from a 1945 BBC publication called *Special Music Recordings*:

'During the war it became urgently necessary to represent music of Britain and music of the Allies in the BBC's Overseas programmes. Commercial catalogues offered some of the necessary material, but this became less and less available as titles were withdrawn. In any case, some of the most significant aspects of our music-making were hardly covered, others not at all. Therefore, the BBC itself made many permanent recordings which remain available, under certain conditions, for use in its various Services; and also to broadcasting organisations overseas. This music, which ranges from folk songs and dances of the simplest kind to symphonies and choral music, and brass and military bands, is representative not only of Britain's musical life but also that of the Dominions and the Allies.

This catalogue offers the complete list of the special music titles, all of which are 78 r.p.m. records similar to commercial discs.

The catalogue contains the first recordings ever made of a substantial part of the fine repertory of original British music written for that most British of institutions, the Brass Band.

The BBC hopes, as war conditions pass, to bring back its orchestras and give an ever greater proportion of its programmes *live*. In the meantime, recorded music is unavoidable, and indeed valuable, in that it recreates for the listener unique performances, and assembles a range of talent which is otherwise impossible to achieve at this time. This is especially true of the recordings presenting the picture of Britain's astonishing musical vitality in wartime.'

Another publication dating from around the same time adds,

'These Special Music Recordings have been passing into use, especially in the Overseas Services, and the London Transcription Service has given generous recognition by sending them all over the world.'

This vast collection of records was always meant to be confined to broadcasting, and has never been available for any other purpose. First as *Assistant Overseas Director / Music Programmes Organiser* (1942-1946) and for the next ten years as Transcription Music Organiser, Denis was heavily involved in the production and distribution of much of this material.

The books go on to list all the recordings made for the Transcription Service between September 1941 and early 1946, showing the breadth of music recorded for the Service, not only by brass and military bands, but by the BBC Symphony Orchestra and the BBC Salon Orchestra, State Trumpeters, chamber groups, a host of soloists - both vocal and instrumental, the BBC Men's Chorus and other choirs, a group called The BBC Overseas Players and another called The Irish Rhythms Orchestra, Fred Hartley and his music, the London Studio Players, the BBC Theatre, BBC Scottish and the BBC Northern Orchestras, a set of recordings by a shantyman with male chorus and accordion, the BBC Empire String Orchestra, one R. J. O'Meally playing his Uillean pipes (whatever they are),[1] a 'Fiddler', a Ceilidhe band, the BBC Midland Light Orchestra, BBC Variety Orchestra and BBC Revue Orchestra, William Hannah's Scottish Dance Band and the Pipes and Drums of the Army School of Piping.

The Band of the Scots Guards heads the list of military band recordings, with a total of 81 sides. The BBC Military Band, naturally, features quite strongly, along with the United States Army Air Forces Band, the Irish, Welsh and Grenadier Guards, the Horse Guards, the Royal Marines and the Central Band of the Royal Air Force.

Brass bands listed are Fairey Aviation Works Band with 26 sides, Foden's Motor Works with 24, Bickershaw Colliery and Black Dyke with seven sides each, Grimethorpe Colliery and Parc & Dare with two sides each and Carlton Main Frickley Colliery with just one.

The following are just some of the more interesting entries in the catalogue of band recordings made for the Overseas Service between 1942 and 1944:

Fairey Aviation (Harry Mortimer)

31.10.42	*Pageantry* (Howells) 1st & 3rd movements
20.02 43	*Labour and Love* (Fletcher)
20.02.43	*Academic Festival Overture* (Brahms, arr. Denis Wright)
03.08.42	*Severn Suite* (Elgar)
06 02.44	*La Belle Americaine* (Hartmann)
	(Solo euphonium: Harry Cheshire)
06.02.42	*Overture - Sea Dogs* (Maurice Johnstone)
06.02.42	*Pageantry* (Howells) 2nd movement
06.02.42	*Honour and Glory* (Bath)
29.10.44	*Peddar's Way* (Kenneth A. Wright)
29.10.44	*Lullaby* (Brahms, arr. Denis Wright)
	(Cornet soloist: 13 year old Colin Clayton)[2]
29.10.44	*Fantasia: The Tempest* (Maurice Johnstone)[3]

Fairey Aviation (Denis Wright)

05.08.43	*The Killigrew's Soirée*[4] (Kenneth A. Wright)
05.08.43	*March: Belvedere* (Kenneth A. Wright)
05.08.43	*March: Australasian* (Rimmer)
05.08.43	*March: Brilliant* (Ord Hume)

Foden's Motor Works (Fred Mortimer)

31.10.42	*Dashing Away With the Smoothing Iron* (arr. W. Stewart)
16.05.43	*Kenilworth* (Bliss)
16.05.43	*Tintagel* (Denis Wright)
12.08.43	*A Handelian Suite* (Denis Wright)
12.08.43	*Yorkshire Moors Suite* (Arthur Wood)
29.01.44	*Princess Nada* (Denis Wright)
29.01.44	*Serenade* (Schubert)
	(Trumpet soloist: 12-year-old Bram(well) Gay)[5]
29.01.44	*Robin Hood* (Geehl)
29.01.44	*Trumpet Tune in 17th Century Style* (W. Stewart)
	(Cornet soloist: Harry Mortimer)
30.01.44	*A Scottish Fantasy* (Denis Wright)
28.10.44	*The White Rider* (Denis Wright)
28.10.44	*Overture: Comedy* (Ireland)
28.10.44	*Bravura* (J. A. Greenwood)
	(Cornet soloist: 14-year-old Bramwell Gay)

Black Dyke (Arthur O. Pearce)

15.11.42	*A Moorside Suite* (Holst)
15.11.42	*Calling All Workers* (Coates, arr. Denis Wright)
24.07.43	*Three Dale Dances* (Arthur Wood)

Bickershaw Colliery (William Haydock)

01.11.42	*Pride of Race* (Kenneth A. Wright)
01.11.42	*March: Pennine Way* (Maurice Johnstone)
16.05.43	*A Downland Suite* (Ireland)

Grimethorpe Colliery (George Thompson)

15.11.42	*My Old Kentucky Home* (arr. Rimmer)
15.11.42	*La Mantilla* (Denis Wright)
	(both featuring Gracie Cole, the young lady cornet soloist)
15.11.42	*Heroic March from 'An Epic Symphony'* (Fletcher)

Parc and Dare (W. Haydn Bebb)

15.02.45	*March: A Joyful Heart* (Maldwyn Price)
15.02.45	*A Welsh Fantasy* (Maldwyn Price)
15.02.45	*March: Hob-y-derri-dando* (Maldwyn Price)
15.02.45	*From the Welsh Hills* (Idris Lewis, arr. Denis Wright)
15.02.45	*March: Heroic* (Maldwyn Price)

Carlton Main Frickley Colliery (Albert E. Badrick)

14.11.42	*Britain on Parade* (W. Stewart)

Irish Guards (Capt. G. H. Willcocks)

18.05.43	*Concerto for Cornet and Military Band* (Denis Wright)
	(Soloist: Harry Mortimer)
25.09.44	*2nd Suite in F* (Holst)

Central Band of the Royal Air Force (R. P. O'Donnell)
17.01.44	*Suite No. 1 in E flat* (Holst)
17.01.44	*Fantasy: Australia* (Gilbert Vinter)
17.01.44	*March: The Cobbers* (Gilbert Vinter)
19.09.44	*The Chantyman* (Gilbert Vinter)
19.09.44	*The N. F. S. March* (Margaret Longstaffe, arr. Denis Wright)

United States Army Air Force Band
(Capt. G.S.Howard* & W/O. J.R.Barrow)
20.03.45	**American Symphonette No. 2*
	(Morton Gould, arr. Paul Yoder)
20.03.45	*Newsreel Suite* (W.Schuman)
20.03.45	*Carribean Fantasy* (John J. Morrisey)

It is reasonable to assume that Denis would have been the producer of most, if not all of these band programmes made for the Transcription Service, and he would also, more than likely, have been involved with many of the others.

The book, *Special Music Recordings*, contains details not only of all the works recorded and the bands and orchestras recording them, but it lists the conductors (a veritable *Who's Who* of the time) and soloists. There are also programme notes on most of the pieces recorded, for the benefit of future producers who may have need of the recordings, and I detect the mind and hand of Denis behind many of these highly informative thumb-nail sketches.

Notes

[1] I am reliably informed that *Uillean Pipes* are of Irish origin, that they are smaller than normal pipes and that they are played sitting down, with the instrument on the knees.

[2] Colin was the son of Elgar Clayton, principal cornet of Fairey's. Some years later the family moved to New Zealand.

[3] Fairey's had won the British Open Championships playing *The Tempest* a month earlier.

[4] Spelled *Kelligrew* on the band parts.

[5] Bram Gay was a pupil of Harry Mortimer's, succeeded him as principal cornet at Foden's and followed him into the orchestra, playing principal trumpet with the CBSO and the Hallé. Later he became manager of the orchestra of the Royal Opera House, Covent Garden, brass music editor of Novello's and a noted adjudicator.

Chapter 16

Intermezzo - a matter of Form

Before entering into a discussion of Denis's compositions I would like to reflect - for the benefit of the non-expert who may find it of interest - on some of the elements of composition. The techniques involved may be considered under five headings, melody, rhythm, harmony, colour and form. Whilst I may from time to time touch on any of them, the last one, *form,* is the element I will be considering most fully. It concerns the way in which compositions are built up - their structure.

In the same way that a succession of words may not make a sentence, a succession of notes does not necessarily make a melody, nor a succession of musical ideas a composition. So, though a musician may have mastered the techniques of melody, rhythm, harmony and even scoring, unless he or she has the ability to link musical thoughts together in a coherent way, then he or she cannot be classed as a composer. Indeed, the word itself implies an ability to set out a collection of ideas in a meaningful manner.

Throughout musical history composers have striven to find interesting and varied ways of constructing their works. Conventions have become established, often to be modified or improved - possibly being discarded by later composers. The creative composers are, to a large extent, those who have been able to develop new forms or to devise new ways of using old ones.

Three basic forms used with great regularity are *binary, ternary* and *rondo.* Though any one of these may be used as the basis of an extended and complex composition, there is an easy way to understand each of them. Brought down to its simplest terms, *binary* is 2-part form - basically a question and an answer - symbolised as A-B. Predictably, *ternary* form has three parts but not, as you might expect, with three separate ideas. Musical composition demands unity as well as variety, and repetition is quite important. Therefore, *ternary* form is symbolised as A-B-A, a form which schoolboys like to call the 'musical sandwich'.

A *rondo* is an extension of the *ternary* idea, making further use of the unity and variety formula. It may be an A-B-A-C-A, may be taken further as A-B-A-C-A-D-A (etc.), or it may go for more unity, as A-B-A-C-A-B-A.

During the Classical era *sonata form* developed and was used in larger compositions - especially as the 1st movement of a sonata, symphony or a chamber work. Each of these types of composition settled down as four-movement works. An extended movement came first, usually in sonata form. Next there would be a slow movement which might also be in sonata form, or it may be a set of variations or an extended ternary form movement. This was followed by a minuet and trio (or, later, a scherzo and trio) in which the two sections, considered separately, may be either binary or ternary but in which, by repeating the minuet (or scherzo) after the trio, the complete movement made a compound ternary shape. The finale, generally lively, was often in rondo form, sonata form, or possibly a combination of the two, sonata-rondo. Thus, sonata form is not restricted to 1st movements; it is frequently found in 2nd and 4th movements, and is also often used as the basis of the concert overture.

A later idea still was the *symphonic poem* which did not have any set shape, but rather followed a course dictated by something non-musical, a poem or a historical incident or character. It is a single-movement work and often contains thematic links between sections. These links are also to be found between movements in some later symphonies.

Sonata form is by far the most important musical structure, and even a basic understanding of it enhances an appreciation of the vast number of pieces or movements on which it is based. Though there are three main sections in a movement in full sonata form, historically it developed from binary form, and should never be thought of as being a ternary structure.

The first main section of a movement or work in sonata form is called the *exposition,* and is where the composer 'exposes' his principal themes. It consists of two musical ideas or groups of ideas, often in a contrasting style, and with the second theme or group in a key different from that of the first. These two ideas are called, respectively, *1st subject* and *2nd subject.* Following the exposition comes the *development section,* and here the composer builds on his ideas, using them in a variety of ways and sometimes also introducing new material. The third and final section is the *recapitulation,* in which the composer restates the themes used in the exposition, often with modifications and not necessarily even in the same order, but generally without the change of key for the 2nd subject - an important feature of the exposition. Thus, the movement ends in the same key in which it began.

Sonata form has been likened to a lecture, in which the speaker outlines his topics in the *exposition*, discusses and argues them in his *development*, and restates them in the *recapitulation*, their meanings hopefully becoming clearer as a result of them having been discussed and argued.

A work or movement in sonata form - or indeed in any of the other forms mentioned - may also have an *introduction*, a *coda,* and various links or '*bridge passages*' (also known as *transitions*).

Another and totally different musical shape which uses the word subject is *fugue*. Fugue is often described as a style rather than a form. It is a composition based mainly on a single theme, called the 'subject'. There are a number of 'voices' (even though it may be purely instrumental) - usually three, four or five, which enter one after the other and then proceed to combine with each other, introducing further ideas, some of which will have grown out of the subject. Being made up of a number of horizontal strands of music, fugue belongs to that branch of musical composition known as *counterpoint*.

One last form which has already been mentioned, and which is one of the oldest types of form, is that of *theme and variations (variation form)*. In this, the composer takes a theme, preferably one with easily recognisable characteristics, and reiterates it a number of times, varying its melody, its rhythms, and/or its harmony. In the hands of modern composers connections between a theme and its variations are not always obvious, but they are always there.

The foregoing is only a thumb-nail sketch of some of the basics of musical form. It is a fascinating branch of musical study, and the greater the understanding of it the greater will be the appreciation of many of the subtleties of musical composition.

Before ending this chapter perhaps I should say something about key-relationships and how they are linked with the notes of a scale.

Most readers will have heard of *tonic sol-fa*, used mainly by singers as an aid to music-reading. To keep matters simple I will refer only to the major scale in which, in *tonic sol-fa*, successive notes are called *doh, ray, me, fah, soh, lah, te* and *doh*.

Doh may take any letter-name and in the key of C major will be C. In A major it will be A, in E♭ major it will be E♭, and so on. It is the most important note and is often referred to as the *key-note,* though its technical name is *Tonic.* The note second in importance within any key is the 5th note of the scale - *soh,* and this is called the *Dominant.* Each note of the scale has its own name, as follows:

	1st	2nd	3rd	4th	5th	6th	7th	1st
	tonic	supertonic	mediant	subdominant	dominant	submediant	leading-note	tonic
	doh	ray	me	fah	soh	lah	te	doh
Key C	C	D	E	F	G	A	B	C
Key A	A	B	C#	D	E	F#	G#	A
Key E♭	E♭	F	G	A♭	B♭	C	D	E♭

From this it should be quite simple to work out the technical name of any note in any key.

These same names also apply to chords and keys. Thus, in the key of C major, a chord whose root is C is the *tonic* chord, a chord whose root is G is the *Dominant* chord and a chord whose root is A is the *submediant* chord. Similarly, if a piece is in the key of A but modulates to E, the music is said to have gone to the *dominant* key, and if it modulates to D it has gone to the *subdominant.*

Keys which have several notes in common with each other are said to be closely related, or nearly-related, and this principal takes into account minor as well as major keys. The closely-related keys are as follows:

home key (major)		its dominant		its subdominant
and its	AND	and its	AND	and its
relative minor		relative minor		relative minor

Thus, the keys closely-related to C major are G and F majors and A, E and D minors. If the home key is minor then the process is reversed, so the keys which are closely-related to A minor would be E and D minors and C, G and F majors.

Much music from the Classical era and earlier stays almost entirely within the cycle of closely-related keys. Conventionally, we should expect the 2nd subject in a movement in sonata form in a major key to appear in the key of the dominant. If the movement were in a minor key, however, then the 2nd subject would more than likely be in the relative major - though in some instances it goes to the dominant minor.

The Romantics and later composers modulated more freely, often going to more remote keys in order to heighten tension or to create a wider range of tonal variety. As we shall see, Denis was often quite unconventional in his choice of key relationships.

I would like now to proceed to a brief analysis of some of Denis's brass band compositions, but please be assured that there is far more to the business of analysing pieces than can possibly be attempted in a book such as this.

For the student or serious musician, reference to relevant scores will help towards a clearer understanding of a substantial part of the next and subsequent chapters.

Chapter 17

Compositions - I

No doubt in his student days Denis Wright saw composition as one of his principal aims in life. But as we've seen, though he entered the brass band world as a composer, his musical activities were spread over such a wide area that composition is now seen as only a small part of his contribution.

Appendix 1 (a) lists Denis's original test pieces - a mere twelve of them, only two or three of which are played with any regularity these days. Nevertheless they were important contributions in their day and I believe that they played an important rôle, paving the way for later developments already taking place in the years prior to his death in 1967. Time has been rather cruel to the series as a whole, and perhaps one day we may witness a revival of some of the pieces, part of our heritage of band music. I propose now to take a brief look at them from a mildly analytical point of view.

Overture - JOAN OF ARC

This was Denis's first brass band composition. Its background and the debt it owes to Henry Geehl were discussed in Chapter 1. Though the musical ideas used in the Overture are obviously the work of a minor composer, its structure demonstrates considerable facility in linking together and developing these ideas, and it is clearly the work of an already skilful writer.

The principal key of the work is B♭ major[1] and, typical of the concert overture, its structure is that of sonata form, but with certain irregularities. For example, when the 2nd subject appears in the exposition, it is centred around G, the sub-mediant of B♭, an unusual departure from the norm (but see comments on the 3rd movement of *Tintagel* for a possible explanation of this).

The 40-bar 1st subject is a long, continuous melody, making several references to the opening idea (Example 2), but also introducing other short motifs, to be utilised and developed later. In keeping with convention it is very rhythmical, in contrast to the more lyrical 2nd subject, based mainly on the idea shown in Example 6. A short *codetta* (the name given to the closing section of the exposition) leads into the development section. Here, a 6-bar introduction (fig. 15 in Example 1) leads into the fugue mentioned in Chapter 1. The subject[2] of this, stemming from a bar in the codetta, may also be seen in Example 1.

For the technically-minded, this is a 5-voice fugue with a real answer and a regular countersubject. As the fugue unfolds there are increasingly strong references to the 1st subject, and at the start of the recapitulation part of the fugue subject is heard against the first subject itself (Example 18).

Example 18 Joan of Arc - fugue subject heard against 1st subject at start of recapitulation

The recapitulation, though using the same material as the exposition, is extended and quite differently scored. A short coda, based on both 1st subject and fugue subject, brings the Overture to a close.

Symphonic Poem - THE WHITE RIDER

As already explained (Chapter 6) *The White Rider* was intended as an easier piece for lower section bands and Denis was taken aback when he found it had been selected as the Championship test. Being a symphonic poem it had no need to adhere to any standard shape. In the event, Denis wrote a tuneful piece with four principal sections, each portraying a mood symbolic of the particular part of the legend which inspired it. This legend comes from Serbian history (you will recall that Denis had served in Serbia during World War I), and is about Marko, a King's son and a hero from Serbia's history. In it Marko lies sleeping in a cavern in the mountains, his sword driven into the rock and his horse nibbling moss. The legend states:

> 'Some day the sword will fall to the floor of the cave, Marko will awake, mount his horse and ride forth to lead his people to a victorious onslaught against their enemies.'

The music, though continuous, depicts the following moods:

a) The struggle against heavy odds,
b) A brooding realisation of temporary defeat,
c) A clarion call, after which the struggle is renewed with a new hopefulness, and finally
d) A joyful pæn of triumph which signifies final victory.

Compared to *Joan of Arc*, *The White Rider* contains more singable tunes, is based on melody rather than motif and in a simplistic way follows, in miniature, the pattern of a symphony, with a slow introduction leading to a 1st movement-type Allegro, a 'brooding realisation' slow movement, what may be seen as a duple-time Scherzo (following the Clarion Call) and a bold, rousing Alla Marcia finale.

Highly chromatic and rarely settling in a key for long, the mode is mainly minor, in keeping with the dour story-line, and the tonal centre for much of the work is D. The 'struggle' begins with a sombre bass motif (Example 19), giving way to an even more sombre theme, growing out of the first (Example 20). A more aggressive mood is portrayed in the Allegro (Example 21) and an air of defiance may be detected in its sequel (Example 22).

Example 19 White Rider - opening

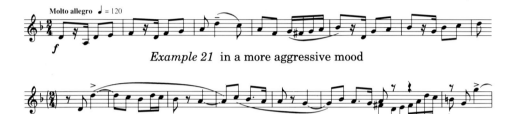

Example 20 2nd theme

Example 21 in a more aggressive mood

Example 22 an air of defiance

Surprisingly, the 'brooding realisation of temporary defeat' of the 2nd section centres around B♭ major, though still in a melancholy mood (Example 23). B♭ major is, of course, the subdominant of F major, the relative of D minor, and therefore one of the 'related' keys. (Note the odd use of phrase marks - a give-away that Denis was not yet completely at home writing for brass).

Example 23 a brooding realisation of temporary defeat

The 'Clarion Call' is quite modulatory, but leads clearly into D major (the tonic major of the first part of the piece) for Section 3, where 'The struggle is renewed, but with a new hopefulness.' This opens with a *fugato,* that is, a section in the style of a fugue - its subject shown in Example 24. This is developed at length, making a reference to Ex.22 from Section 1, before gliding into the triumphant key of C major for the final section - 'A joyful pæn of triumph' - signalling final victory (Example 25).

Example 24 the struggle renewed - but with a new hopefulness

Example 25 a joyful paean of triuph

Despite its lack of form and irrespective of the absence of long-term acceptability, I see *The White Rider* as a significant contribution to the band literature of its time, especially as it was intended for the lower sections which, in reality, were not seriously catered for until the post World War II years.

Symphonic Suite - TINTAGEL

Tintagel is reputedly the birth place of the legendary King Arthur (of Round Table fame) and Denis headed each of the three movements of this symphonic suite with the name of one of the characters from the legend. On the original score these headings were initially *Arthur (The Great King)*, *Elaine (The Romantic)* and *Merlin (the Magician)* but they have been changed to *King Arthur, Elaine* and *Merlin The Magician* - which is also how they appear in the R. Smith published edition.

The piece was discussed briefly in Chapter 7. As was said there, it is by far the best of the early group so far as content is concerned, though its construction is simpler than that of *Joan of Arc*. Its principal key is F major and the 1st movement, opening with a lively, heraldic type of theme portraying *King Arthur* (Example 26), is clearly in sonata form. Rhythmic interest is created in the 1st subject by the juxtaposition of triplet quavers with the dotted-quaver/semiquaver pattern, and the odd 4/4 bar slipped into the prevailing 3/4 grouping adds a touch of the unexpected. This theme modulates freely and becomes quite chromatic for a few bars before leading into a more serene theme - still part of the 1st subject group (Example 27).

Example 26 King Arthur

Example 27 King Arthur - a more serene theme

A passing reference to the 1st theme leads to a short transition (or bridge passage), taking the music, as expected, into the dominant key (C major) for the 2nd subject, which provides a further mix of simple and compound rhythmic groupings (Example 28). (Incidentally, there is no logical reason for the use of both simple and compound time signatures here. A straight 9/8 would have sufficed for the whole band.)

Example 28 2nd subject (1st movement)

The brief development refers to both 1st and 2nd subjects and the abridged recapitulation is quite conventional. A short, terse coda, referring to the opening, draws the movement to a somewhat abrupt close, avoiding any feeling of finality and paving the way for the 2nd movement.

Elaine is portrayed in the reposeful subdominant key (B♭), starting with a lovely romantic trombone solo, played 'con tenerezza' (Example 9) and repeated immediately with an added cornet obbligato (Example 29). The movement is in ternary form but is unusual in that after a short, modulatory and episodic 'B' section, 'A' returns in the key of E♭ major, the movement's subdominant. The scoring here is most interesting, all cornets (except soprano) playing in unison, in combination with tenor trombones at the sub-octave, giving a rich, full line. After eight bars of this the solo trombone returns - in the home key - to round off a most beautiful slow movement.

Example 29 2nd movement

The 3rd movement - *Merlin The Magician* - a brisk rondo taken 1-in-a-bar has three points of special interest - its key structure, a piece of rhythmical sorcery whereby a 3/2 band section is accompanied by a 2/4 cornet obbligato (Example 30) and a reference, in the coda, to the opening of the 1st movement. The key scheme is particularly interesting because it gives a clue as to Denis's usage of the sub-mediant as a complementary key (as, for example, in the 2nd subject in *Joan of Arc*). Beginning in F he goes, for his first episode, to the related key of D minor. He returns to F for a restatement of the main theme but then goes into D major for the second episode. This is heard now, not so much as the key of the sub-mediant of F, the home key, but rather as the tonic major of D minor, the key of the first episode.

Clearly, *Tintagel* is the most interesting of Denis's early brass band essays. Less intellectual than *Joan of Arc*, its lasting success is due to the quality of the ideas, coupled with the musically satisfying nature of its form and key scheme.

Example 30 3rd movement — a piece of rhythmical sorcery

Viewed as a test piece it would certainly not stretch any of today's top bands, but it is a great pity it was rejected at the time it was written. It would surely have been an outstanding success, and may well have influenced the style of Denis's later compositions.

Symphonic Legend - PRINCESS NADA

In *Princess Nada* Denis makes use of the device known as 'thematic transformation' or 'thematic metamorphosis', whereby a theme can be transformed to change its character, whilst yet retaining its basic, recognisable shape. Franz Liszt was one of the first composers to use this device successfully, and Denis acknowledges the symphonic poems of the Hungarian composer as the source of inspiration for his own.

Denis maintained that in *Princess Nada* "there was far more constructional interest than in *The White Rider,* which hadn't anything much in the way of real instrumental counterpoint." The legend on which it is based and which is retold on the title page of the score runs as follows:

'Prince Ivar, having conquered the neighbouring state, orders the captives to send a hundred maidens, led by their Princess Nada,* to be slaves at the Court.

Meeting the sad procession on the way, he falls instantly in love with the beautiful Nada, who pleads with him to spare her people. He readily forgives the conquered state and frees the maidens, and in return the Princess gives him her hand in marriage'. What a nice chap he must have been!

This is a more substantial piece than *The White Rider* and is more sophisticated in its construction than *Tintagel* but, along with *Joan of Arc* and *The White Rider,* it has been condemned to obscurity.

Again the hallmarks of Denis's craftsmanship are demonstrated, but though so well constructed, its musical content is less appealing than that of *Tintagel.* It seems to me also that it is devalued somewhat by the comments printed on the score, no doubt with the 'musically unsophisticated' band people of the North of England of the time in mind!

Unlike *Joan of Arc* - which was supposed not to have a 'programme' - and *The White Rider* - which loosely portrayed four main ideas or situations, *Princess Nada* set out to illustrate the legend quite graphically with the aid

*"Pronounced Nardah"

of sub-titles placed in relevant positions above the score, indicating precisely the meaning of the music at those particular points. Here are the sub-titles:

Prince Ivar's theme

Lamenting of the conquered people

Unrest and agitation under Ivar's domination

Princess Nada's theme

Anger of the conquered as the Princess and maidens set out, to be slaves at Ivar's court

The Prince approaches

Prince and Princess meet

The love duet

She sinks into his arms

The captives are pardoned and all go in triumphal procession to the court

They all lived happily ever after

Denis's use of thematic transformation, though not extensive, does create some interest. Prince Ivar's theme (Example 31) dominates, turns up in various fairly obvious transformations (Examples 32 and 33), and pervades the whole piece.

Example 31 Ivar's theme

Example 32 Transformation of Ivar's theme

Example 33 Prince Ivar - further transformation

Princess Nada's theme (Example 34) is much less in evidence than that of the Prince, though both appear in the final section, when 'They all live happily ever after' (Example 35).

Example 34 Princess Nada's theme

Example 35 "They all lived happily ever after" – final transformation of both themes

There is an undated work for chorus and strings by Denis called *The Ballad of Princess Nada*. Though the text comes from the same legend, there's no apparent musical connection.

Overture: THE SEA (THALASSA)

The origins of this work are somewhat obscure. It was first published by Hawkes in 1933 and then re-issued by Molenaar's of Holland as late as 1960. There seems to be no record of it having been used as a test piece during either period, but I can't say whether this was due to rejection or to non-submission. Perhaps it was intended to be a concert piece. Who knows?

The Programme Note reveals that the basis of the overture is a poem by Charles G. Mortimer, in which the varying moods of the sea are described:

'The broad expanses of the ocean, the fierceness of the breakers on a rocky shore, and contrasted with this, the peaceful moonlit summer sea, bearing with it a hint of the eternal mystery'.

It goes on to explain,

'The music is written in free overture form, the two main contrasted ideas remaining predominant throughout and rising to a climax typifying the close of the poem: Break, O light! Rise, O Sun! . . . . Awake, to shed God's splendour o'er the deep.'

In 'free overture form' it certainly is, with many of the characteristics of sonata form, but in some respects more of a tone poem.

The introduction (Example 36) displays two motifs, the second of which grows out of the first, and together they form the basis for much of the work. The 1st subject, in B♭ (Example 37), seems to illustrate the 'broad expanses of the ocean' referred to in the programme note. The 2nd subject is more complex, and though the central part of it (Example 39) is in the expected key of the dominant (F) it is flanked by a section in G minor (Example 38) and one in G major (Example 40), again showing Denis's fondness for pairing a minor with its tonic major. The development section uses ideas from the introduction.

Example 36 Introduction

Example 37 1st subject

Example 38 2nd subject – i

Example 39 2nd subject – ii

Example 40 2nd subject – iii

In the recapitulation there is considerable change in the region of the 2nd subject, 2nd subject (i) appearing in C minor before making its way to G minor, the key in which it appeared in the exposition, then proceeding straight to 2nd subject (iii) - in G major as before, but directed to be taken a little faster. A reference to the 1st subject, in G minor, leads back to 2nd subject (ii), in the same key as in the exposition, but with its rhythm changed from 4/4 to 12/8. The short coda refers mainly to the introduction.

It was more than a decade before Denis wrote his next test piece, and a great deal happened during the intervening years, as we shall see in the next chapter.

Notes

[1] *Keys* referred to in these analyses are at B♭ pitch.

[2] *Subject* is the name used for the theme on which a fugue is based. It should not be confused with *1st Subject*, which is the first theme or group of themes in the exposition of a movement in Sonata Form.

Chapter 18

Interlude

Denis's fortunes as a brass band composer slumped after the selection, in 1933, of *Princess Nada* as the test for the Belle Vue September contest. Following *The White Rider* in 1927, the organisers of the Nationals commissioned a series of works by major composers - *A Moorside Suite* (Holst - 1928), *Severn Suite* (Elgar - 1930), *Oriental Rhapsody* and *Prometheus Unbound* (Bantock - 1930 and 33), *A Downland Suite* and *Comedy Overture* (Ireland - 1932 and 34) and *Kenilworth* (Bliss - 1936). The gaps were filled with works by minor composers - *Victory* (Jenkins - 1929), *Honour and Glory* (Bath - 1931) and *Pride of Race* (Kenneth Wright - 1935).

Belle Vue stayed with minor composers, with the exception of the 1934 test, *Pageantry* (Howells), though in 1937 Denis's transcription of the *Academic Festival Overture* (Brahms) was selected.

Crystal Palace was, of course, destroyed by fire in 1936. Following this, the Nationals were held at the Alexandra Palace for a couple of years, and the test pieces were revivals of earlier works - *Pageantry* and *An Epic Symphony*.

Denis, by now up to his ears - so to speak - with BBC work, was beavering away at his transcriptions, striving to increase the availability of more 'worthy music', and was also arranging a colossal amount of what might be described as commercial music. A glance at the Appendices will show the scale of this side of his work.

During the war years the Nationals were suspended, whilst Belle Vue had a rather ad hoc, make-shift series of test pieces. A new piece had been written for the 1939 contest (*Clive of India* - Joseph Holbrooke), but due to the outbreak of war - coinciding almost to the day with the original date of the contest - the event was put back a few weeks and, for the convenience of competing bands, the new piece was replaced with the more familiar *Downland Suite* by John Ireland. Holbrooke's piece was, however, adopted as the test for the following year. 1941 saw an odd combination - a choice of three pieces offered in an attempt to make life easier for the competing bands. These were all 'revivals' - Denis's by now celebrated arrangement of the Brahms *Academic Festival Overture*, Geehl's *Robin Hood* (1936) and Keighley's *The Crusaders* (1932).

1942 saw a choice of either *Lorenzo* (Keighley - 1928) or *Pageantry* (Howells - 1934), and the 1943 contest provided a further outlet for Denis's controversial arrangement of the supposedly patriotic *Themes from*

John Henry announcing the 1946 Nationals results. Also in the picture the 'three wise men' - J. A. Greenwood, Frank Wright and Henry Geehl

Symphony No. 5 (Beethoven). The only new original test piece to emerge during the war years appeared in 1944 - Maurice Johnstones's fantasy *The Tempest*. In 1945 *Pride of Race,* Kenneth Wright's 1935 Crystal Palace test piece was set at Belle Vue but, of much greater importance, this year saw the end of the war and the re-commencement of the Nationals in London.

This in itself is an important part of brass band history. The war years had seen a big change in the fortunes of John Henry Iles. Not only was he now in his 70s, but he had forever lost his beloved Crystal Palace, and though in 1944 he was awarded the O.B.E., his personal finances were not such that he could continue pouring money into his favourite ventures.

He had obviously been concerned about all this for some time and, with the end of hostilities in sight, had decided to seek the support of a national newspaper. Though at first things didn't look too hopeful, early in 1945 the now defunct *Daily Herald* announced that it would organise and sponsor a series of area contests. These would be used as a means of selecting a nationwide representation of bands to perform in the National Finals later in the year.

The idea met with plenty of opposition but Iles was adamant that this was positively the only way to guarantee a revival of the Nationals, and he put all his still considerable powers of persuasion behind the idea.

Despite one or two hiccups the area contests went ahead and the finals took place in the Royal Albert Hall later in the year. This proved to be a spectacular event in a splendid venue and was an unqualified success, the only complaint being that *the Albert Hall wasn't big enough*!

There can be little doubt that Denis Wright had become a dominant figure on the brass band scene during the war years - despite the absence of new compositions from his pen. It would therefore come as no surprise when a piece composed by him was chosen as the test for the first post-war National Championships. The piece had been composed during the latter part of 1944, and the title chosen was appropriate both to the times and the event:

OVERTURE FOR AN EPIC OCCASION

Chapter 19

Compositions - II

OVERTURE FOR AN EPIC OCCASION

This Overture had the distinction of being chosen as test piece for the first post-war National Brass Band Championships, held in the Royal Albert Hall, London, under the banner of the *Daily Herald* - in October 1945. Its programme note reads:

"An epic occasion (such as the overthrow of Nazidom, in anticipation of which this overture was written) is not so much an occasion for rejoicing as one for proud thanksgiving. One's thoughts go out in particular to those who made the occasion possible, but came not home again to share in the triumph of their comrades. Thus will be explained the music's moments of quiet reflection and the chorale-like section of the overture."

Example 41 1st subject

Example 42 2ⁿᵈ subject i

Example 43 2ⁿᵈ subject ii

It is a single-movement work, in sonata form, but veering considerably from the conventional - particularly in its key-scheme. The 1st subject begins in C major, but after a short, chromatic passage, appears briefly in the subdominant - F (Example 41). A transition leads to the 2nd subject which, though under a key signature of three flats, begins in A♭ major and modulates to B♭ major (Example 42) before settling in E♭ major - as per key signature - for another theme, a broad, Elgarian melody, still part of the 2nd subject group (Example 43).

All three themes are used in the development section. In the recapitulation the 1st subject follows the same course as it did in the exposition. The transition is modified, however, and the 2nd subject appears in the key of B♭ major (dispensing with the A♭ section), in a somewhat modified form, to be played 'maestoso' and with its accompaniment beating out a compound-time rhythm. This, in turn, leads to the Elgar-like theme, but now in F major. In the coda the music returns to the key of the opening (C major) and refers to all three main themes before leading an unconventional overture to a conventional ending.

The overture's key scheme is therefore as follows:

Exposition	1st subject	C - F
	2nd subject i	A♭ - B♭
	2nd subject ii	E♭
Development		Mainly in C
Recapitulation	1st subject	C - F
	2nd subject i	B♭
	2nd subject ii	F
Coda		Mainly in C

Suite: MUSIC FOR BRASS

This was the test piece for the Belle Vue September contest of 1948. It comprises three movements - *Prelude*, *Scherzo* and *Finale* (*Rondo*).

Formerly, 'Prelude' was a term used as the heading for a piece of music which preceded something, perhaps a 'Prelude and Fugue', or an orchestral introduction to an opera or an act of an opera. Later it was often used as the title of a short, self-contained piece. Chopin, Debussy and Rachmaninov composed many such pieces. From early times composers had used 'Prelude' as the title of the 1st movement of a suite, in which case it might fulfil both rôles, being a complete piece in its own right, yet preceding the other movements of the suite. Denis had many precedents for calling the 1st movement of *Music for Brass* 'Prelude', though in fact the movement is not quite self-contained, as it leads into the Scherzo, without break.

This *Prelude,* in ternary form, has several points of constructional interest - a slow, sombre introduction (Example 44), some fascinating links between the main sections, and a coda which uses material from the introduction, transformed into a brighter mood.

Example 44 Prelude - introduction

The key of the movement is D minor, with the middle section taking its dominant key - A minor. Towards the close D major appears momentarily, but this leads back to the minor mode for the Scherzo. Themes A and B are shown in Examples 45 and 46, but though there's little out of the ordinary about the melodies, Denis's harmonic language goes up a gear, with hints of Wagner and even Debussy.

Example 45 Prelude - theme 'A'

Example 46 Prelude - theme 'B'

Example 47 Scherzo - opening

A 'Scherzo' is a jest or a joke. The term is often applied to the 3rd movement of a symphony, where it became successor to the Minuet. Beethoven did most to establish it in symphonic music, the humour behind his musical jokes often being rough or sardonic - even satanic! This Denis Wright *Scherzo* is somewhat in that vein, though skittish rather than fiendish. It is a fairly conventional structure, in ternary form, the main theme being shown in Example 47. The mood is more relaxed in the Trio, the tonal centre of which is B♭, the subdominant of the relative major of the Scherzo (Example 48).

Example 48 Scherzo (Trio - theme 'A')

The *Finale,* clearly in rondo form, is more exuberant than the other movements, and is predominantly in D major, but with the 2nd episode settling for a time in G minor - tonic minor of the subdominant. By ending a piece which has a minor-key beginning in its tonic major, Denis conforms to a practise common in the Romantic era, implying the triumph of good over evil, or of right over wrong. The main theme is shown in Example 49, and I must say, I find Denis's non-use of E♯ in this passage for championship grade bands as late as 1948 quite revealing!

Example 49 Finale

There are no apparent thematic links between the movements of *Music for Brass,* but within each movement there is plenty of scope for studying how Denis develops his basic ideas in the links, some of which are almost mini-development sections - not uncommon in 19th century music.

Symphonic Sketch: ATLANTIC

This work was selected as test piece for the Area Championships (top section) of 1951, and has the following statement on the title page of the score:

"Daybreak: slowly the mist rises off the cliffs of Cornwall. The sea is smooth, yet pulsating with life. As the sun rises, the clouds throw dark shadows on the water. The wind freshens, the clouds pass away inland and as the tide sweeps in from the south-west the ocean becomes fully alive.
   High noon and flood tide; strong wind and blue sky. The spray of the breakers in your face as you stand on the rocky shore; the mainland behind you and in front - the vast Atlantic."

I suspect that this was put in for the benefit of those who like to use non-musical images in their preparation for performance rather than as a genuine 'programme'[1], though I suppose there is an implication in the word 'sketch' which suggests that other ideas may aid the interpretation of the work. Symphonic it certainly is, being in sonata form, and indulging in a certain amount of thematic transformation and development.
   The key centre is F major, and the short introduction (Example 50)

provides the material on which much of the work is built - though other ideas are also introduced during the course of the piece which is, to all intents and purposes, a concert overture.

Example 50 Introduction

Unusually, the 2nd subject (Example 52) appears in the key of the supertonic in the exposition (perhaps regarded as the dominant of the dominant) and both it and the 1st subject (Example 51) are changed considerably in length, content and basic rhythm in the recapitulation (Examples 53 and 54). The development section uses motifs from 1st subject in the main, but also introduces several new ideas.

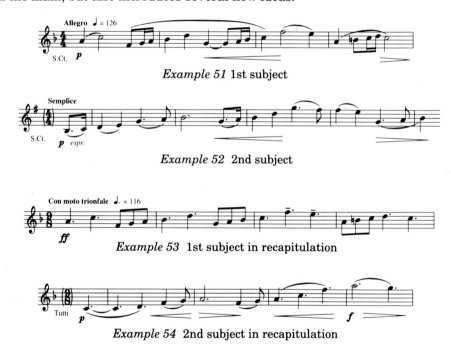

Example 51 1st subject

Example 52 2nd subject

Example 53 1st subject in recapitulation

Example 54 2nd subject in recapitulation

Though not a difficult work technically, there are some interesting points in the scoring, including some double-tonguing, the breaking up of a semi-quaver passage - either for effect, for technical simplification, or for elements of both (Example 55), and the shifting of a continuous melody line to different instruments in turn, as in the continuation of the 2nd subject (Example 56). There is also, in the coda, the most unusual (for the period) time signature of 15/8. It is really a 6/8 + 9/8 and, paradoxically, gives the effect of a shortened bar.

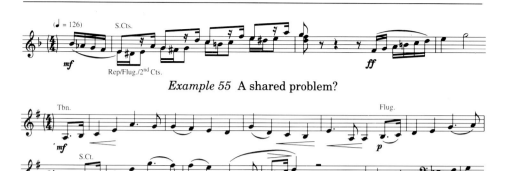

Example 55 A shared problem?

Example 56 Changing colours

Atlantic was the first of three of Denis's works to be selected as test pieces for Area Contests, the series of regional events instigated in 1945 by the *Daily Herald,* in which bands compete for the honour of appearing in the National Finals later in the year.

Overture: GLASTONBURY

Glastonbury is an ancient market town in Somerset, and tradition has it that Joseph of Arimathea founded England's first Christian church there. The ruins of a 10th-11th century Benedictine abbey dominate the skyline, and during some excavations in 1963 the site of the graves of King Arthur and Queen Guinevere were thought to have been identified - though as this happened ten years after the overture was written, we must be very careful NOT to recognise this discovery in the score!

However, there can be little doubt that the abbey and the chanting of monks of a by-gone age are reflected in this attractive overture, which was selected as the Area test piece for the 3rd section, in 1954.

Structurally it is another of those pieces with characteristics of sonata form, but which seem to avoid convention in their key scheme. A brief introduction (Example 57) leads straight into the 1st subject (Example 58). The tonal centre is A minor though the music rarely settles there. After what appears to be a transition a new theme appears which is, in effect, 1st subject ii (Example 59). This is clearly in G minor, but it leads to a re-statement of 1st subject i in G major. A further transition grows out of this, leading to the 2nd subject - also in G major - which may be thought of as the dominant of the relative major of the opening.

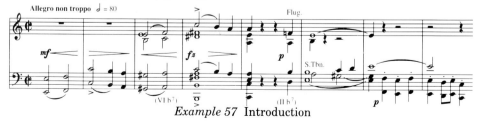

Example 57 Introduction

Example 58 1st subject i

Example 59 1st subject ii

This 2nd subject (Example 60) is a beautiful song-like theme, further enhanced by some imaginative and colourful scoring. It is first heard as a quartet comprising cornet, flugel and two horns, with additional 'comments' from baritone. On its first repeat the theme becomes a euphonium solo accompanied by three trombones, and with the baritone joined by solo cornet for the 'comments'. It is repeated yet again, with the full band playing fortissimo, and leading into a short development section based mainly on 1st subject i and the introduction.

Example 60 2nd subject

The recapitulation follows roughly the same course as the exposition, with no change in the key scheme, but with both transitions extended, the second one becoming virtually another development section, using material from the introduction, 1st subject ii, and 2nd subject, and also introducing new ideas - even at this late stage. Having used the 2nd subject in three different versions in the exposition, and also having referred to it in this latest transition, Denis uses it only once in the recapitulation - in the same key as before but in a full-throated tutti, and leading to a short coda based on 1st subject i, bringing the overture to a close in C, the relative major of the opening, and a key which seems to have been systematically avoided up to this point.

For the student there are a few things worth noting, including some of the earliest examples of the use of secondary 7ths in brass band music (see Example 57), and also some early examples of time signatures changing in mid-phrase (Example 59) There is also an example of mirror harmony in the 2nd subject quartet, seen towards the end of Example 60.

Glastonbury may not be great music, but it is a particular favourite of mine and was undoubtedly an important contribution to the literature of lower section bands.

Symphonic Sketch: TAM O'SHANTER'S RIDE

Denis's last major work for brass band is the one by which most people know him as a composer. It was selected as test piece for the Belle Vue September contest of 1956 and was possibly influenced by the time he spent in Scotland during the war. *Tam o' Shanter's Ride* is a symphonic poem - one of the most effective and successful in all brass band literature. It is based on the famous poem by Robert Burns[2] which begins:

> 'When e'er to drink you are inclined,
> Or cutty-sarks run in your mind,
> Think! you may buy the joys o'er dear -
> Remember Tam O' Shanter's Mare.'

As in *Princess Nada,* Denis adds a series of sub-titles to the score, revealing precisely what the music is illustrating. However, the comments are much less child-like than in the earlier piece, and the musical imagery much more sophisticated. There are six principal sections, with an introduction and a coda. Here is a brief résumé of some of the more important points:

Introduction: A cautionary tale of the dangers of taking too much strong drink and interfering with the Devil's business.

The opening seems to be devoid of any key (a brief visit to the world of atonality?) with a series of consecutive augmented triads and a motif for Tam which is only vaguely tonal (Example 61). The 'Wife' motif, though highly chromatic, leads clearly back to normality with the aid of a pedal point and a dominant 7th chord, but via some mirror harmony and a pair of super-imposed augmented triads - flutter-tongued (Example 62).

Example 61 Opening and Tam's motif

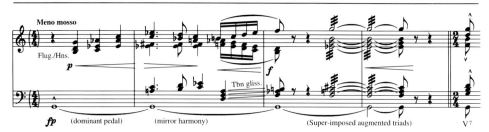

Example 62 'Wife' motif

Section 1: Tam makes merry with his friends in the inn.

Here an important theme appears, growing out of Tam's motif, completely tonal and with a distinct Scottish flavour (Example 63). This is immediately repeated with fuller scoring and then, third time round, trombone glissandi, changing time signatures and solo cornet adding a sort of 'Devil's pipe' tune - all seeming to indicate that Tam and his friends are by now becoming the worse for drink (Example 64).

Example 63 Tam makes merry with his friends

Example 64 Becoming the worse for drink

Section 2: Tam remembers his sulky sullen dame sitting at home, nursing her wrath to keep it warm.

Here a second important theme appears (Ex.65), built on the 'Wife' motif. Introduced as a cornet solo, it is repeated on euphonium along with a showy cornet obbligato.

Example 65 His sulky sullen dame

Section 3: Tam mounts his horse and, rather unsteadily, sets off for home.

Tam is by now quite definitely 'under the influence'. There are passing references to both motifs, and the music is in 8/8 time, with the conductor instructed to 'Beat 3' - the earliest example of the irregular beat (as far as I know) in brass band music (Example 66). As the horse gains in confidence the rhythm of the music becomes more regular (4/4 time) and both motifs combine in a giocoso theme portraying Tam's 'blissful' state (Example 67). Alas, the feeling is short-lived and the section is rounded off in dour mood, with bass trombone epitomising Tam's feelings after having been well and truly shaken about by the horse (Example 68).

Example 66 Unsteadily, Tam sets off for home

Example 67 Tam rides blissfully along

Example 68 The alcohol takes its toll!

Section 4: He comes to the church.

This is a distinctly sobering experience with trombones, transformed into a male voice choir, singing a beautiful chorale. Amongst the rich counterpoint provided by the rest of the band may be heard the occasional reference to one or other of the two motifs.

Section 5: Looking through the arch into the brilliantly lit grave-yard he sees witches and warlocks dancing to the piping of their Master, the Devil.

Tam is by now at the hallucination stage, seeing witches dancing a reel which becomes ever faster and more furious. Soon *Tam recognises some of the witches as his friends from the village, including Maggie, who wears the shortest of short night-shirts*. The music darts quickly through a succession of themes but with little reference to either motif. At the height of the fury

Maggie leaps higher than all the rest, revealing much that should not be revealed. Tam cheers her on: Weel luppen Maggie, wi' the *cutty sark! This is shrieked out by the full trombone section playing as loudly as it can in a wildly distorted version of Tam's motif (Example 69), and quickly followed by a most startling effect - an augmented chord with added 7th and 11th, and a sudden change of instrumentation and dynamic, indicating that *all is dark* (Example 70).

Example 69 Tam's motif, wildly distorted

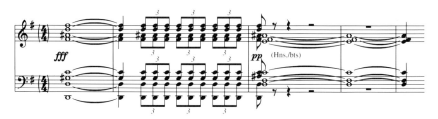

Example 70 Suddenly, all is dark

Section 6: Tam, scared, jumps on his horse. He rides off, pursued by all the witches led by Maggie.

A new theme appears, forming a tenuous link with Tam's motif. The link becomes more positive as trombones hammer out the motif in chords, while basses make reference to the scale of the opening bar. The music becomes more agitated as *He remembers his wife's warnings and makes for the river bridge - (no evil spirits can cross running water).* The 'Wife' motif now becomes more prominent but, *As they approach the bridge Maggie grasps the mare's tail. Maggie pulls, the mare pulls. The tail comes off and Maggie falls head over heels backwards off the bridge.*

All this is graphically portrayed in the music and the section closes with soft chords on muted cornets, flutter-tonged as, *Breathing sighs of relief, Tam rides on home.*

Coda

The 'rounding off' begins with a reprise of the 8/8 section, leads to the final argument, shown in Example 71, and presumably leaves poor Tam back where he was before we found him 'making merry with his friends in the inn'.

Tam o' Shanter's Ride must rank as Denis's best test piece. Less technically demanding than many later pieces by younger composers it is, nevertheless, full of musical interest, and it really does intensify the meaning of the words with which it is associated.

* cutty-sark = short shirt

Example 71 The final argument

SALZBURG SUITE (four movements in the style of Mozart)

This was written for the 3rd Section Area contests of 1960, and dedicated to Herbert Møller and Concord Band, Copenhagen (see page 190).

The Suite has four movements, following the plan of the classical symphony - in miniature of course - and is the type of piece which a later composer might have described as a *Sinfonietta*, though in the time of Mozart it would probably have been called a *Serenade*, or perhaps a *Divertimento*.

The *1st movement* begins with a short, elegant slow introduction but leads quickly into the main Allegro. This is in ternary form and in C major, with the 'B' section in the relative minor. The *2nd movement*, in the key of the subdominant, is slow, also ternary, and reminiscent of the equivalent movement in Mozart's famous *Eine Kleine Nachtmusik*.

The *Minuet*, also reminiscent of its opposite number in *Eine Kleine Nachtmusik*, follows the conventional plan for such movements. The tonal centre of the Minuet (in ternary form) is A minor, with its Trio (also ternary) in C major. As is customary, the Minuet is played again after the trio, without repeats, giving the movement as a whole a compound ternary shape.

For the *Rondo-Finale* the music returns to the home key (C major) and seems to parody a Mozart Horn Concerto finale. It follows the plan A-B-A-C-A and a short, crisp coda rounds off the movement and the work.

The beginning of the Allegro of the 1st movement, and the opening of each of the other movements is shown in Example 72-75.

Example 72 1st movement - beginning of 'Allegro'

Example 73 2nd movement - opening

Example 74 3rd movement - opening

Example 75 4th movement - opening

Prelude: ST. NICHOLAS EVE

Denis's last competition piece, this short work was commissioned by the BBC in 1962 for the semi-finals of *Northern Brass,* a radio knock-out competition for 'up-and-coming' bands. The following appears as a programme note on the title page of the score:

> "In many countries, notably in Europe, St. Nicholas Eve (December 6th) is as important as Christmas Eve. St. Nicholas (Santa Klaus) is the patron saint of young people and on the eve of his Day gifts and sweets are distributed.
>
> The music of this Prelude sets out to portray the gaiety and excitement of the occasion, with, perhaps, a tinge of sadness that another happy year is nearly ended. But this mood does not last and the excitement of the moment soon returns."

The work has remained unpublished, though presumably copies may exist in the libraries of some of the bands competing. In addition to its use in *Northern Brass,* it was performed by the National Youth Brass Band in April 1962 under the baton of Sir Adrian Boult, and Denis himself conducted it in his own 70th birthday broadcast in 1965 - with Black Dyke as his guests.

Though musically quite attractive, the Prelude's duration - less than five minutes - and the fact that it has never been published have combined to prevent it from becoming widely known. Its structure is quite loose, in ternary form, with a group of ideas forming 'A', and another group, including references to 'A' forming the 'B' section. As with several of Denis's other pieces, there seems not to be any logical key scheme, except that it begins and ends in B♭ major. The opening theme, which is used almost constantly throughout the piece, is shown in Example 76.

Example 76 Opening

CONCLUSION

So ends Denis's modest series of original test pieces. The composition of these twelve works spans a period of over 40 years, covering the period from just before Holst's *Moorside Suite* to the advent of Gilbert Vinter's contribution. There can be little doubt that, despite regular performances of only two or three of them today, they fulfilled important rôles in their time, and contributed significantly to the development of brass band music.

Notes

[1] *Programme Music* is defined as music which tells a story, illustrates literary ideas or evokes pictorial scenes (Oxford Dictionary of Music). Several of Denis's works are good examples of programme music.

[2] Correspondent James Forrest, in *British Bandsman* of 11th August 1956, pointed out that Denis's version of *Tam o' Shanter's Ride* didn't adhere strictly to that in the Burns poem. The composer admitted that he had made some references to the same story as told in a 17th century book - earlier than the Burns version. The explanation went on: 'Just as Richard Strauss, in his *Til Eulenspiegel,* did not stick closely to the original Dutch story of Til, but chose episodes that he could best illustrate in music, so Dr. Wright built up a composite story from the two sources which, while keeping broadly to the outlines, varies in detail if one compares his synopsis with the well-known poem.'

Chapter 20

Compositions - III

Having discussed in some detail Denis's test pieces, in this chapter I'd like to make a brief survey of some of his other music - band and otherwise. Lists are to be found in the Appendices. These don't claim to be complete, and they do include a number of pieces which I have so far been unable to verify.

I have seen, however, manuscripts of some piano pieces he wrote in 1910 and 1911, when he was aged 15/16. Of course, there is no comparison between opportunities then and now, so whilst there are no doubt many budding composers around today with more advanced music techniques than Denis had at the same age, there is much promise evident in these early attempts (but see his own comments on page 165). He also, apparently, had ambition even then, as he gave the pieces not only titles, but also Opus numbers, as follows:

Op.1 No.1	Petite Suite for Piano	Op. 2	Christmas Bells
2	Funeral March	Op. 3 No.1	Liebstraum
3	Albumblatt	2	Scherzetto
(Dated December 1910)		(Dated February-April 1911)	

Op. 5   Overture: King Lear
(Dated November 1911)

I don't know what happened to Op. 4, but even as early as the Op. 2 pieces there is a commendable fluency in harmony, modulation and the use of chromatic chords, and despite his imagination being ahead of his technique (not at all unusual) they make interesting reading. Op. 3, No. 2 is shown in Example 77.

Appendix 6 lists some of his non brass band pieces, a few of which come from the pre-brass band period, though there was a return to vocal music in the 1960s through his work as Musical Editor of the firm Ascherberg, Hopwood and Crewe. (L. J. Cary was also a branch of this company). There are probably several other works in this category, but the ones I have listed are all that I have actually seen. The orchestral/choral works shown represent his relatively few contributions here, including his doctoral pieces, and as will be seen, there are a number of collections of educational pieces.

The earliest of the concert pieces for band seems to have been the *Fantasia - Hanover*. This is a set of variations on the well-known hymn tune, *O Worship the King*. There is an introduction, theme and five variations and the score is marked 'Copyright R. Smith & Co. Ltd., 1926' (the year after *Joan of Arc*). Interestingly, this was chosen as test piece for the Junior Cup, sections A and B, at Crystal Palace in 1928.

A few years later Denis chose another well-known hymn tune on which to build a composition. The *Chorale Prelude - Deep Harmony* is based on the

Example 77 Scherzetto (Op.3 No.2)

famous tune by the Yorkshire hymnologist Handel Parker. The Chorale Prelude (or Choral Prelude) was brought to perfection by Bach. Rather more complex than a set of variations, it often takes the melody, line by line, embellishing and surrounding it with free counterpoint. *Jesu, Joy of Man's Desiring* and *Sleepers Awake!* are two well-known examples. The *Deep Harmony* prelude, first published in 1936 was a transcription of an organ piece written earlier in the year. Not a classic example of the chorale prelude, it is more a set of variations, but with links based on motifs from the tune itself. The original edition was published by Joshua Duckworth, the copyright owner of the tune.

Four more pre-war pieces, mentioned on page 47, are *Carnival Suite* (1935), *Overture in the Olden Style* and *A Scottish Fantasy* (both dating from 1937) and *A Handelian Suite* (assigned to Boosey's in 1940 but more than likely written earlier). *A Scottish Fantasy*, also published for military band, is dedicated "To my many friends in Scotland's bands" and though the music is continuous it uses three contrasting Scottish tunes in a quick-slow-quick structure, based on the following plan:

Wi' a Hundred Pipers an' A - an extended section - almost a fantasy in itself.

My Faithful Fond One - a simple setting of a beautiful slow melody, and with an interesting soprano obbligato (Example 11).

Green Grow the Rushes O - a more complex section with a part for xylophone (something of an innovation in a band score of the time!)

Green Grow the Rushes O also forms the basis of the fantasy's introduction and *My Faithful Fond One* is referred to in the coda, creating a feeling of unity. Not just a medley of tunes, this piece anticipates the Gordon Langford fantasies of some twenty-five years later.

The 1930s saw the composition of two run-of-the-mill cornet duets - popular in park bandstands at that time. The earlier of the two, *Two Little Finches*, is rather more successful than the latter, *Merry Mountaineers* which, despite its pleasing Alpine flavour, is un-idiomatic and somewhat dis-jointed.

Early in 1941 Denis wrote a short but attractive cornet solo, *La Mantilla* (*The Hat*), described as a 'Spanish Caprice'. It was written for Gracie Cole, who went on to win the AOMF Scholarship (see page 51) in 1942, and who became a sort of protégé of Denis's, appearing in several concerts and broadcasts at his instigation. Gracie and *La Mantilla* were referred to in Chapter 8. Following the success of this solo Denis sent Gracie a short, reflective piece, without title. This later appeared as the slow movement of the *Cornet Concerto*, by far Denis's most important piece during this period. Much was said in Chapter 13 about the background of the Concerto, the first of its kind and indeed, still one of only a handful of true brass band concertos.

Like most works in this genre it has three movements. The first is in sonata form with a double exposition - a structure developed in the time of Mozart, who is regarded by many as the supreme master of the concerto. The

1st exposition is played by band alone and, in accordance with convention, remains in the home key throughout (B♭ major for B♭ instruments). The soloist enters with something of a flourish - nothing unusual there either - and then comes the 2nd exposition, following convention with the 2nd subject this time in the dominant key. 1st and 2nd subjects, as they appear in the 1st exposition, are quoted in Examples 78 and 79.

Example 78 1st movement - 1st subject

Example 79 1st movement - 2nd subject (1st exposition)

The short development section is built around motifs from 1st subject, and the recapitulation is quite conventional, given that the soloist's part is modified considerably. A showy cadenza leads to the coda, taking a final look at 1st subject, leading to those now famous lip glissando effects, and ending with a short burst of triple-tonguing.

Example 80 2nd movement - main theme

Example 81 2nd movement - 'finely - women mellifluous accompaniments'

The 2nd movement, headed *Canzonetta* (literally 'little song'), is a particularly beautiful slow movement, giving scope for some lovely, sensitive cornet playing. It is in ternary form but in true concerto style, the principal melodies shared between soloist and band. From time to time the soloist adds some finely woven mellifluous 'accompaniments' to the melody as it is taken over by the band (see Examples 80 and 81).

The form of the finale, *Rondo*, is really that combination of sonata and rondo known as 'sonata-rondo' form. In this, though cast in the A-B-A-C-A-B-A shape of a rondo, the 'B' theme is in the dominant key on its first appearance and in the tonic on its second, taking on the rôle of a 2nd subject. Thus, the first A-B-A is regarded as the exposition, C as the development section, and the second A-B-A as the recapitulation. The features of this particular development section (C) are a new theme played in the cornet's very lowest register and a reference to the 2nd subject from the 1st movement. (The three principal themes from the finale are shown in Examples 82, 83 and 84).

Example 82 3rd movement - 1st subject (theme 'A')

Example 83 3rd movement - 2nd subject (theme 'B')

Example 84 3nd movement - development section

Along with *Tam o' Shanter's Ride,* the *Cornet Concerto* represents the high point of Denis's compositions.

It was completed in 1941, and in the following year Denis wrote two short but useful pieces under the nom-de-plume W. Stewart (Stewart being a deliberate mis-spelling of his third Christian name, Steuart). They were published in 1944 by Paxton's as a pair - i.e. back to back on the same sheets of paper. (Remember, this was war-time and economies such as this had become standard practise!) The more popular of the two was another piece for cornet, *Trumpet Tune (in 17th century style),* the score headed 'For Harry Mortimer'. It is a simple but effective solo, in rondo form, often played featuring the full cornet sections in those one-time popular massed band concerts. The main theme is shown in Example 85.

Example 85 Opening

The piece on the 'flip side' was the *Scherzo - Dashing Away With the Smoothing Iron*. This is one of those (like many by Langford and others a quarter of a century later) which falls somewhere between composition and arrangement because, though based on a known tune, there is a considerable degree of creativity in its construction.

Returning to 1935, *The Empire Jubilee March* was the winner of the 'Daily Record' National March Contest and a prize of £50. First published as a piano solo by Chappell's, its Trio section is a setting of some words by one Harold *Stewart* (a possible though unlikely further pseudonym). Versions for both brass and military band appeared later, the brass band version turning up in a broadcast by the Glasgow Corporation Gas Board Band. There are also some more marches, long forgotten, and a Fanfare which was played weekly in a series of overseas broadcasts during 1942.

Moving now into the 1950s, the *Two Lyric Pieces* were performed by the National Youth Brass Band in 1952. Headed *Morning Song* and *Evening Song*, they seem to represent the only serious compositional work in this category from the first half of the decade.

The march *Commonwealth Star*, published in 1956, heralded a small flurry of pieces. It is a fairly straightforward march in 6/8 time, but rather than the unrelated string of tunes associated with the average brass band march, Denis adopted the minuet and trio idea, writing both halves of the march in ternary form, with the usual D.C. to complete the compound ternary structure. 1957 brought the *Echo Minuet*, described by Denis himself as 'an easy novelty piece'.

Also in 1957 he was commissioned by the BBC to write a piece for its Light Music Festival, combining both brass band and orchestra. *Cornish Holiday* was the result, an attractive overture utilising the well known *Floral Dance*. (See pages 206-7 for more information about this.) The following year he wrote an overture called *Casino Carnival*, a similar piece for similar forces.

The early 1960s saw the composition of four ensemble pieces - *Age of Chivalry* for four trombones, *Romantica* for the standard brass band-type quartet of two cornets, tenor horn and euphonium, *Sonatina* for a septet comprising two cornets, tenor horn, baritone, trombone, euphonium and E♭ bass, and *Miniature Suite* for the same combination plus soprano cornet.

In 1966 Denis wrote what was to be his penultimate band piece, another of those 'creative arrangements' (if you wish to be pedantic) - *Carol Sinfonietta*. This is a 3-movement work, the 1st concentrating on the carols *I saw three ships* and *Here we come a-wassailing* which appear both separately and in

. . . winner of the 'Daily Record' National March Contest

combination with each other. The 2nd movement is a chorale prelude on the *Coventry Carol,* and the 3rd movement introduces *God rest ye merry, gentlemen* and *Angels from the realms of glory.* A stirring setting of *O come, all ye faithful* (also hinted at in the introduction to the 1st movement) rounds off the work. This *Carol Sinfonietta* has been overshadowed by the more spectacular *Christmas Festival Overture* of Leroy Anderson and Gordon Langford's *Christmas Fantasy,* but it was the first of its kind to find its way into the repertoire of the brass band, and may well have been inspired by the *Carol Symphony* of Victor Hely-Hutchinson, a member of the BBC's music staff from 1926 to 1947, and its Director of Music from 1944.

Denis's final work was his *Trio Concerto*, first performed by the National Youth Brass Band of Great Britain on its 1967 Easter course, Denis conducting and with soloists Phillip McCann, Eoin McCallum and Russell Booker. It was Denis's last course as Music Adviser, Geoffrey Brand having already been invited to take over the reins for the following course in August. The course was held, incidentally, at St. George's School in Harpenden, where Denis had been both pupil and master.

The three movements of the *Trio Concerto* are headed *Prelude, Elegy* and *Finale*, and they are bound together by a common motif (Examples 86-88). In 1968 the CWS (Manchester) Band under the baton of Alex Mortimer recorded it for Fontana and this is what Dr. Harold Hind had to say:

Example 86 1ˢᵗ movement – opening

Example 87 2ⁿᵈ movement – opening

Example 88 3ʳᵈ movement – opening

'The *Trio Concerto* was the late Denis Wright's last composition, a magnificent and scholarly work in the form of the 17th century concerto grosso, in which the soloists, in this case Derek Garside (cornet), Ian Richards (trombone) and Robert Richards (euphonium) play as a group in contrast to the rest of the ensemble.'

The following year CWS performed it in the Festival Concert following the Nationals at the Royal Albert Hall (the same concert, incidentally, that my *Concerto for Piano and Band* received its 1st performance), and the following note appeared in the programme:

'Trio Concertos are rare enough even in the orchestral repertoire, and Denis Wright's work is probably the only one of its kind yet conceived for brass band. In classical form, it provides an extended conversation between the three soloists and band. The melodic contours are wide-ranging and technical demands are considerable: but this is not merely a show-piece - all is subservient to the form and mood of the music. There are three movements: *Prelude* (introducing a trio-cadenza); a dignified, deeply-felt *Elegy*; and, following without break, a gay fast-moving *Finale*.'

Again, this work has been overshadowed by later similar works, for example by Edward Gregson, Derek Bourgeois and Philip Sparke, each using the title Concerto Grosso. It is a further example of Denis's pioneering work and may yet, with the mature approach to repertoire which seems to be developing, gain more recognition than it commands at present.

There are a number of lighter-weight pieces which seem not to warrant attention, beyond recording them in the Appendix. No doubt there are also others, but I doubt if their discovery will radically change the course of musical history!

Despite the problems and criticism of the brass band and its repertoire which we regularly hear, it is a fact that but for the likes of Dr. Denis Wright and Eric Ball in the 1940s and 1950s, there probably would be no band movement as we now know it, and it is a great pity that so much of the music which was written in a period when bands were fighting for their very survival has seemingly gone out of fashion.

Chapter 21

To the end of the '40s

'The name Denis Wright will never be forgotten whilst our brass band movement continues, if only because it appears so frequently at the head of the music played, either as composer or arranger. In this particular field, his work will ever stand as a pattern of meticulous technical accuracy to our writers of the future. He will also be remembered for his great work as conductor, teacher adjudicator and author. . . . The movement generally owes his memory a deep debt of gratitude, for all his efforts to bridge the gap that did exist between it and other forms of music making, and in a most dignified manner.'

This is part of a tribute paid by the late Tom Atkinson in *The British Bandsman* of 13th May 1967, shortly after Denis's death.

I would like now to take a cool, dispassionate look at Denis's personality, and at his work - in brass bands - from around the time he entered the scene in 1925 until the end of the 1940s. We may, perhaps, regard this as his 'middle period', or perhaps his 'bridge-building period'. First of all, what sort of a man was he?

Ernest Brown first met Denis in 1929. He says,

'We were very impressed with this softly spoken slim man with pinz nez glasses. Two outstanding features of Dr. Denis Wright at the rostrum I shall never forget - he never raised his voice in any way, and he would always stand with his feet apart and his hands across his chest with his baton in his right hand when discussing a point with whatever band he was training.'

Arthur Irons also had very clear memories. He was appointed by Denis to succeed Leonard Davies as bandmaster of Crystal Palace Band in 1938, held the position for several years and had this to say:

'The relationship between a professional conductor and a bandmaster can be rather sticky, but I never felt this with Denis. He treated me as an equal. We worked amicably, and trotted home in one or other's car after rehearsal.'

He goes on to say that Denis had 'a terrific sense of humour, despite giving the impression of being somewhat humourless on the contest platform.'

Geoffrey Brand first met Denis at a contest in Godalming in the mid-

1950s. Denis was the adjudicator and Geoffrey, with the John Dickinson Band, picked up 1st prize. Geoffrey was working for the BBC at the time, though in a different department from Denis but, possibly through this meeting at Godalming, the two came to know each other very well and, as I have already said, Geoffrey was chosen by Denis to be his successor as Music Advisor to the NYBB. Geoffrey's recollections of Denis are particularly vivid.

'He was a man with a broad knowledge of the wider world of music and we must not forget, he didn't come into music through the brass band, but rather the reverse, and he consistently and conscientiously tried to use his knowledge to broaden the musical thinking of all connected with bands.'

About Denis as a person he says,

'He was always very polite and thoughtful - with all the courtesies of a bygone age. He would never miss an opportunity to either open a door or hold a chair for a lady, nor neglect to help her on with her coat. Nevertheless, he did not always get on well with his contemporaries, and if he disagreed with them he didn't hesitate to let it be known.'

Despite keeping outside what we might call brass band politics, he often became embroiled in arguments with the brass band public. In the January edition of *Brass Band News* in 1945, for example, a correspondent signing himself *Young Trotter* says,

'I noticed that Denis Wright had been throwing his weight about at Edinburgh on the subject of modern test pieces. I wonder what business it is of his what the bands play in an own choice contest.'

In the following month's edition there was a lengthy reply from Denis justifying his comments which, in any case he maintained, had been mis-quoted. But all to no avail. A third party, signing himself *Proletarian* entered the arena in March with a quite vitriolic letter, advising Denis against *Trying to teach his grandparents how to suck eggs*!

This sequence of correspondence is typical of much of the barrage of criticism which Denis faced - especially during this 'middle period'. And it is interesting to note that *original* and *modern* were considered even dirtier words in the 1940s than they are today. Here's part of another letter from *Brass Band News* of February 1946:

'The first modern original test piece was foisted on us more than 30 years ago. I still see no keenness for its use, or any popular craving for it.'

This was from a correspondent signing himself *Open Mind* (please believe me - it's absolutely true!) and must have been referring to Percy Fletcher's *Labour and Love*. So, I think we've made SOME progress!

Kenneth Dennison, associated with Fairey's for over 25 years - first as principal trombone and later as conductor - remembers Denis for his meticulousness. He says,

'You could never find a mistake in anything Denis Wright had done; it was proof-checked to the last dot!'

Ken also makes the point that 'He would never flaunt himself.' He recalls that Harry Mortimer used to refer to Denis as 'Digger' - because 'he could dig out anything.'

Here are a few views by a later and younger generation - members of the National Youth Brass Band of Great Britain.

Richard Evans, a founder member and now one of brass bands' leading and most colourful figures, held 'Dr. Denis' in awe - even at times bordering on fear. John Berryman, later to become one of our most celebrated cornet players and now a much respected conductor and adjudicator, joined the NYBB a few years later. He doesn't go as far as Richard, but he does say that 'with his long face and pointed nose he was quite severe-looking - rather like a headmaster.'

On the other hand Allan Mead, now teaching in Hampshire and part of the Hampshire Youth Band set-up says, 'Oh, he was a very kindly gentlemen. He once gave me a lift to the station in his Jowett Javelin!'

Tony Cresswell, Managing Director of Mostyn Music, and a member of the NYBB in the early 1960s, remembers Dr. Denis as 'a very gentle and kind person, respected and even loved by everyone in the Band.'

What about Denis's work with bands?

By the end of the War in 1945 he was 50 years old and had already contributed more than most manage in a life-time. His work at the BBC between 1936 and 1942, when he established the Band Section of the Music Department, was obviously very important. His pioneer work here was built on by his successor, Harry Mortimer who, sadly, was not only the second, but the last to carry the title Brass and Military Band Supervisor, and as the years have passed since Harry's retirement in 1964 the BBC's interest in bands has waned to the point that there is now only one regular weekly band programme on network radio the whole year round.[1] Denis would not be amused!

In 1942 he transferred to the Overseas Service and his links with bands were greatly reduced. Nevertheless, in 1943, along with other leading band figures, including Harry Mortimer and Frank Wright, he was involved in attempts to form what is now the National Association of Brass Band Conductors. It took a couple of years for it to become firmly established, but Denis was always at the forefront of its activities.

As the 'National Association of Band Conductors' the first Convention was held in London on 25th March 1945. Following the formal part of the meeting Denis gave a lecture about *Conducting - as contrasted with training.* Giving the usual advice on the use of the baton, wrists, fingers, forearm and so on, he went on to stress the need for independence of the hands and caused something of a stir by beating three with his right hand at the same time as two with his left - not an unusual technique these days but virtually unheard of in bands 50 years ago. Pleading with conductors to develop a *graceful* style, he gently dropped in one of his famous quips:

"There are quite a few *ungraceful* conductors, apart from the *DISGRACEFUL* ones!"

When, in 1946, the Association published its own magazine, *The*

Denis . . . with his long face and pointed nose

Conductor, Denis became a regular contributor. In the very first issue his topic was *The Left Hand* and in the second, he posed the question *What Sort of Baton?* In March 1949 he directed the first of what was to be a whole series of classes for conductors. This was under the auspices of the NABBC, was part of its Annual Convention and followed a talk given by Sir Adrian Boult. With the aid of a composite band and a group of volunteer conductors, Denis was able to illustrate some of the points made by the maestro.

In the studio with the Westminster Orchestra

The decade spanning the 1940s was, of course, a grim period in British history. During its first half, for the second time this century, the country was embroiled in a war which was supposed to end all wars. During the second half the nation was busy trying to pick up the pieces and get things back to normal, to say nothing of counting the cost.

Bands were attempting to re-group or re-form, but the odds were very much against them. Many former bandsmen had not returned from the War. Of those who had, a good proportion did not become involved in banding again, and there were insufficient replacements to cover the losses, as not all that many youngsters had taken up brass playing during the war years.

Furthermore, fashions and tastes had changed considerably, but the brass band and its music had not. Small wonder then that during the later war years - and for the remainder of the 1940s - Denis seems not to have been too heavily involved in the practical side of band work.

Let us now look at his various fields of activity with bands. As a conductor, even though so widely experienced, he failed to reach any degree of eminence, to a large extent being overshadowed by Harry Mortimer, Eric Ball and others. During the late 1940s Denis's brass band conducting was rather spasmodic. He did the occasional massed band concert, one or two broadcasts in the *Sounding Brass and Voices* series, and was still associated with Crystal Palace Band. His lack of success in the contest arena obviously worked against him, though his knowledge of orchestral music and opera made him a key figure in widening the repertoire of bands, and also contributed to his success as a conductor of the many massed band concerts he directed over the years. His transcriptions also helped form a bridge between bands and the orchestra, paving the way for well-known orchestral conductors to work with bands, several at Denis's instigation. And we also have to realise that though not doing a lot of brass band conducting, there was, particularly towards the end of the 1940s, quite a bit of conducting involved with orchestras within the BBC. As Transcription Music Director he conducted many orchestral and choral concerts for overseas broadcasting, particularly with the Westminster Orchestra which he formed, and also with what was called the New London String Ensemble.

Ken Dennison, to whose comments about Denis's meticulousness in his writing I have already referred, insists that this quality was also there in his conducting. Perhaps lacking the charisma of some, he says that Denis was nevertheless very clear and precise, and that he was extremely good with young bands.

Contests were few and far between during the war, but even when they began to appear in the second half of the 1940s Denis seems not to have been very heavily involved as an adjudicator. He took on a few contests each year, however, including the Irish Championships in Belfast in 1948.

Denis told Richard Evans an amusing story about the Belfast contest. Apparently there was no adjudicator's box and so, in the interests of secrecy, Denis was housed in a small room under the stage. Let me explain that at the Irish Championships there are four categories of band - brass, military, accordion and flute, the category for flute being billed as the World Championship. In these flute bands, some of which reach incredibly high standards of performance, there is a variety of sizes of flute, and also a bass drum and a side drum.

As you would expect, considering the nature of the instruments, the music produced by the flute bands is always relatively soft, and on this particular occasion in Belfast, it seems the members of one band all had that dreadful habit of tapping their feet in time with the music. The effect of this was that poor Denis, in his 'hole' beneath the stage, heard nothing but the tapping of 20 or 30 feet - and barely a squeak from the flutes. I'd like to have read the adjudicator's 'remarks' on that performance!

Denis's adjudicating skills at this time were more widely accepted in the lower echelons of bands than at the top, no doubt because he could analyse a performance and offer helpful suggestions for the improvement of the band, though he admits to having "to be escorted in Cornwall by two policemen, along a mile-and-half road to the railway station, after giving a decision that was not in accordance with popular wishes."[2]

At the top level, his inability to play a brass instrument was held against him, along with the fact that he had actually conducted bands in contests, with little or no success. I suspect also that Denis may have belonged to that group of adjudicators which attaches greater importance to interpretation than to the actual playing. This never goes down well with bandsmen, who anyway take the view that it is *they* who *win* contests and *conductors* who *lose* them. As we saw earlier, Denis adjudicated at Crystal Palace in the 1920s and early 1930s - once in the Championship and also in lower sections. During the 1940s he adjudicated only once at the Royal Albert Hall, and that was at the very first event, in 1945, for which he had composed the test piece (*Overture for an Epic Occasion*). His only appearance at the Belle Vue September Championship prior to 1950 was back in 1933, when the test piece had been his *Princess Nada*.

Regarding Denis's output of music, in the Appendices I've classified this under three main headings:

COMPOSITIONS - which also include some pieces which might be regarded as arrangements but which have a strong element of creativity about them;

TRANSCRIPTIONS - pieces transcribed from other sources, without major alteration except, perhaps, for some abridging;

ARRANGEMENTS - being anything from a selection or medley of tunes to a straight transcription of a march, a solo, a pop song or something similar, but of a lighter nature than is implied by the term 'transcription'.

Chappell & Co. published more of his arrangements and transcriptions than did any of the other publishers - getting on for 250 scores, the vast majority of which were published in or before 1950, and including over 100 under the pseudonym *Frank Denham*.

Surprisingly, the peak years for Denis's published works seem to have been the late 1930s, after he had left Chappell's and joined the BBC. Not that he produced scores only for Chappell's at this time. He had quite a lot of pieces published by Boosey and Hawkes, was adding to the titles already in the catalogue of R. Smith & Co., and doing work for Novello's and Paxton's, as well as scoring pieces for a whole range of other publishers, probably because they owned the copyright for those pieces. There were also many pieces which, as again in later years, were never published, remaining in manuscript to this day, although in some cases photo-copied sets are to be found in various band libraries. Surprisingly, the large number of manuscript pieces are undated and therefore, where a date is shown in the Appendices, it often refers to the first known performance or broadcast.

One manuscript transcription which, though undated, is very well documented, is Denis's masterly version of Handel's *Messiah*, made in 1946. This was a major part of his 'bridge-building' and will be discussed fully in Chapter 23.

In between the scoring (begun in February 1946) and the 1st performance (in November) of *Messiah* Denis became involved in trying out another important link-up - between piano and brass band. The problem of pitch was more critical here because of the fixed pitch of the piano and the fact that brass bands were still playing in high pitch. I say fixed pitch, although in reality, given time, the piano's pitch can be changed.

Denis made use of this possibility when he scored his first two works for piano and band - presumably not having considered at that time the possibility of lowering the band's pitch. Because of key considerations he went for the semi-tone transposition when he scored the first movement of Schumann's *Piano Concerto* and had the piano tuned down. Eileen Joyce was the soloist, in one of the still popular massed bands concerts. The performance was organised in such a way that a single band played the actual accompanying parts, whilst full band took on the tuttis. This was scored in the Summer of 1946 at about the same time as another piece involving the piano - *Baraza* - by Arthur Bliss, from the film *Men of Two Worlds*. He went the opposite way with this, transposing conventionally and having the piano tuned up - a more difficult job because of the danger of breaking strings through the extra tension needed. *Baraza* was first performed in the Grand Festival Concert following the National Championships at the Royal Albert Hall on 19th October 1946. Eileen Joyce was again the soloist and Sargent conducted, with the Fairey Aviation Works Band and 12 trombones.

Of these transcriptions Denis wrote (*Musical Progress & Mail*, July 1946):

> "It is all an experiment which may or may not come off, but at least it is well worth trying. If it succeeds - and with good bands, a good conductor and good soloists, there is no reason why it should not - it will be one step further forward in increasing the versatility, musicianship and general usefulness of bands."

So, 1946 had been quite a momentous year, though it must be admitted that the bridges Denis built have not yet taken us very far.

In his later ventures into this very effective and still neglected field of piano and brass band, Denis called for the use of a band in low pitch where possible, and transposed accordingly. Probably the first such piece was his transcription of the very attractive *Scherzo* from *Concerto Symphonique No. 4* by Henry Litolff. Since its first brass band performance in June 1947 with solo pianist Iris Loveridge and the London Brass Players (a 'posh' name for Fairey Aviation or Foden's, whichever happened to be available), this has become easily the most popular piece of its kind, and has had many performances, broadcasts and recordings. It was followed by a transcription of the first movement of Grieg's *Piano Concerto*, broadcast by Fairey's later in 1947, with Alan Soulsby.

Chapter 8 was devoted to Denis's rôle as an educator, and among other things, it touched upon his three published books, *Scoring for Brass Band* (1935), *The Brass Band Conductor* (1948) and *The Complete Bandmaster* (1963), and also his involvement with the examinations for the BBCM and other diplomas in Brass Band Conducting, and the AOMF Scholarship. During the post-war years there were BBCM diploma examinations twice a year, generally in both Manchester and London, for which Denis set and marked the papers in harmony and scoring.

He took a particular interest in his work with the AOMF, and perhaps I should point out that the two things, despite apparent similarities, fulfilled very different functions. The BBCM - and those conducting diplomas offered by Guildhall and Trinity - was (and still is) awarded to *conductors* who could prove, through public examination, that they had reached an acceptable standard in practical and theoretical aspects of brass band conducting. Over the years a comparatively large number of candidates have prepared for and passed these diploma examinations. (There have also been some quite notable failures!)

The AOMF, on the other hand, is purely for young *instrumentalists,* and though covering theory of music as well as playing an instrument, it is highly competitive, and seeks to reward real excellence. Thus the winner, having a proven outstanding ability, is entitled to free lessons from a professional teacher for up to two years, the costs of which are paid through the scholarship.

As Director of Examinations Denis again had the job of setting and marking the theory papers, but as the results were announced on the day Denis had to be present - in Manchester - to mark the papers there and then. I have already mentioned that Gracie Cole won this scholarship and went on to become a professional trumpet player. Other famous names amongst the list of winners includes Elgar Clayton (1926), Arthur Butterworth (1939), Bram Gay (1945), Ken Dennison (1946) and Elgar Howarth[3] (1951).

Returning to his educational writings, even though two out of the three books I have mentioned are currently out of print, they are obtainable through public libraries, and every now and then one turns up in a second-hand book shop. The reader will be well rewarded by a close study of any or all of these books. The Scoring book is of course readily available, now in its 5th (revised) edition.

None of the books need be discussed because anyone who really wishes to, will certainly be able to obtain them somehow and study them in detail. There were, however, over a hundred short articles written between 1923 and 1941, and which have been preserved in a scrapbook. There is also the unpublished *Evolution of the Wind Band,* submitted as part of Denis's Exercise for the Doctorate he obtained at Edinburgh in 1940. There seems to be sufficient in these writings to warrant a special section, and so the next chapter will be devoted to a glimpse at the range of musical topics covered by this extraordinarily active mind.

Also on the educational front, Denis contributed to Kenneth Cook's *Oh Listen to the Band,* published just before the end of the decade, and wrote the 'Foreword' to the same author's *The Bandsman's Everything Within',* published early in 1950.

Finally, during these years Denis became an Executive Member of the *National Brass Band Club,* a society which had been founded in 1925 - the year of Denis's introduction to brass bands - 'to foster and facilitate the musical aspirations of those interested in brass bands, and to further their social welfare and musical advancement.' The club played an important part in this advancement both before and after the 2nd World War but has gone into decline since. Denis was one of the driving forces behind its activities during the 1950s, as we shall see later.

Notes

[1] Due to pressures from producers Bob McDowall and Paul Hindmarsh there are a number of shorter series being broadcast from time to time, but *Listen to the Band,* at the time of writing, is the only brass band programme being relayed 52 weeks per year.

[2] This anecdote is taken from *The Evolution of the Wind Band* (p. 42).

[3] In 1993 Elgar Howarth succeeded the late Harry Mortimer as President of the NYBB.

Chapter 22

Denis the Author

In the previous chapter I tried to give some indication of the scope of Denis's work - as conductor and adjudicator, as examiner, and as composer and arranger. In other chapters I have discussed in more detail his work at the BBC and also his compositions.

Earlier in the book I suggested that one of his great aims in life was to educate the 'brass band movement' (though he didn't like this phrase, and rarely used it). Much of this was done through his writings, and though at this distance in time it is difficult to assess what effect they had, I suspect that over the years their cumulative effect and influence has been considerable. It is quite conceivable, in fact, that his literary work was second in importance only to his work at the BBC. His writings comprise the following:

Articles written for various musical journals	1923-1946
Articles for *The Musical Educator*	1933
Scoring for Brass Band	first published 1935
The Evolution of the Wind Band (part of submission for doctorate)	1940
The Brass Band Conductor	1948
The Complete Bandmaster	1963
The Autobiography	date unknown

The three published books have already been referred to. All serious students of the brass band should read them and I guarantee that any trouble taken in obtaining copies will be amply rewarded. The articles in *The Music Educator* were reprinted in the later *New Musical Educator*, also mentioned in Chapter 8, and as much of the information from the autobiography has been used in earlier chapters of this book no further comment is necessary.

That leaves the contributions to musical journals and the doctoral thesis, and these form the basis of the present chapter. I am indebted to Mr. Herbert Møller for the loan of the scrapbook containing articles from a variety of journals, and to Mrs. Wright for giving me access to *The Evolution of the Wind Band*. I propose to look at these in roughly chronological order and in the context of Denis's other work in the various periods of his life.

Pre-1925

These were his post-student years when he worked as a free-lance musician in London. He wrote a number of songs and piano pieces at this time but seems to have first appeared in the 'columns' on 3rd November 1923 in *Music News and Herald,* with some observations about the audience at an organ recital in Westminster Cathedral the previous month. The recital received no mention, and the article was credited to 'D.S.W.'

In the following month we find him in *The Writer* with a lengthy article headed *Markets for Song Lyrics,* giving advice to lyric writers. Though admitting to having "but a few published songs", as 'Denis S. Wright' he claims to be musical editor to a music publisher. (The publisher is un-named but I wonder if it might be his own company, which Mrs. Wright believes he formed in the 1920s).

The third and last article from this early period showed up in *Opera* of April 1924 as *My First Opera - by an office-boy.* (I am assuming that its presence in the scrapbook indicates that it was in fact written by Denis). It is a charming story about the office-boy himself (Tony) and a typist (Peggy) hearing musical strains coming through the office window, emanating from a wireless set in a neighbouring office. They listen, enthralled, for most of the evening and discover from the concluding announcement that they have heard part of Wagner's opera *The Mastersingers.*

Tony, knocked out by it all discovered, a day or two later, that this opera was to be performed at Covent Garden. He bought a ticket and went to his 'First Opera'.

This seems a harmless little story but it was, I believe, possibly the first of Denis's 'parables'. There was a school of thought in those days which forewarned that music on the wireless, or indeed on gramophone records, would lead to dwindling concert audiences and ultimately to the demise of all live entertainment. Denis took the opposite view, maintaining that those who 'listened-in' to music would be tempted to go to *more* concerts! Was this story written in support of that view? I think so.

1925-1928

During these years Denis taught at St. Andrew's, a prep-school in East Grinstead. He also became involved with brass bands (through *Joan of Arc*) and, in 1926, completed his Bachelor of Music degree.

After those first three articles there was a lull. Doubtless much of his spare time would be taken up with his academic studies, and in any case he composed *Joan of Arc* in 1925, a fantasia on *Hanover* the following year and *The White Rider* for the 1927 Championships. No other band pieces seem to have been written until 1930, so suddenly there was more time for his literary pen to get to work. It started - not surprisingly - with *The British Bandsman,* and between 1926 and 1928 seven articles appeared, though only two of them used the name 'Denis Wright'.

Reading these it soon becomes obvious that Denis enjoyed being controversial, that he would not shy away from taking an unpopular stance if he believed in it, and that a major part of his scheme to educate included criticism of the status quo.

Three of the articles used the pseudonym 'Historicus' - one of them continuing the theme mooted in *My First Opera*. In it, he extols the virtues of amateur performers, with all their imperfections, saying that they are, "en masse", pupils of the professionals, and expressing his opinion that "By listening to the wireless they receive encouragement and stimulation for their own efforts."

In another article, 'Historicus' tells of *The Origin of Contesting*. This is highly satirical and was obviously a dig at the band contest as he saw it at the time. It refers to Greek mythology and to a challenge between Appollo playing the lyre and Marsyas performing on a reed flute. (As an aside we are informed that this particular reed flute was formerly owned by Minerva, who had thrown it away when she discovered that blowing it was causing her to lose her good looks. This, it is reasoned by 'Historicus', is probably the cause of the dearth of ladies in brass bands!) To return to the first contest: King Midas had been appointed adjudicator and had declared Appollo to be the winner. Whereupon Marsyas cast a spell on Midas, causing him to grow a pair of ass's ears. The moral of all this was that if you must contest, it did not pay to be either a loser or a judge!

The final contribution from 'Historicus' was in a letter headed *Whence Comes Progress?* It was in answer to earlier writings by Dr. Thomas Keighley and a Mr. E. C. Moore. In it Denis (alias 'Historicus') seems already to be taking on the rôle of 'Educator of Brass Bands', explaining the difference between teaching and conducting, advocating improvements in both, and begging for a more careful choice of music.

Under another pseudonym, 'Musicus', there's an article headed *The Great Squeeze - Performing Rights*. Performance fees had just been imposed by publishers and Denis was putting forward the case that when a band had *bought* music it should be free to *play* it. (He added that he believed in this principle even though, as a composer, he stood to gain by the new regulations.)

The remaining articles in *The British Bandsman* during this time, penned under Denis's own name, appeared in 1926 - only the second year of his involvement with bands. Yet he ploughed straight in with his views, pulling no punches. In January he discussed what he called *The Conductor Problem*, attempting to persuade bandmasters to try to emulate orchestral conductors, to increase their efficiency, and even to indulge in a little showmanship. *The Summer Programme* provided his hobby-horse in March, when he said that conductors should think more seriously about their programme-planning. Finally, in a December issue under *Face the Facts* he advocated the formation of an all-star band, to be assembled for a tour, properly promoted and advertised, on which would be played only good, original brass band music.

Leaving the subject of brass bands he published, in 1927, an article in *The Preparatory Schools Review* in answer to an earlier article complaining of the poor standard of piano playing amongst boys who came to public schools from prep-schools. Denis defended work done in the latter, giving the distinct impression that at least part of his work at East Grinstead was teaching piano-playing to boys destined for public schools.

One thing which becomes apparent from the scrap-book is that there were more journals taking at least some interest in brass bands than is the case today. A light-hearted article by Denis headed *A Busman's Holiday - even in Switzerland*, doesn't call for comment beyond the fact that it appeared in the October 1928 issue of *The Melody Maker (Military & Brass Band News)*!

By far the most substantial series of articles was published in *The Musical Mail* (fore-runner of *Musical Progress & Mail*) in which, between July 1927 and August 1928, there were eleven articles on the basics of harmony, which would have made quite a handy booklet on the subject. The series began:

THOSE HATED WORDS
HARMONY, COUNTERPOINT and THEORY
by DENIS WRIGHT, Mus. Bac.

It began:

"Considering human curiosity and the general fondness of people for finding out 'how it is made', it is surprising that a very great number of those interested in music - singers, bandsmen, orchestral players, and so on - have a horror of the words harmony, counterpoint and musical theory, and all that such words imply. They seem to think that these things should be left to the dry-as-dust professors and to those unfortunates who have to sit for academic examinations, and that to themselves a knowledge of music's whys and wherefores is quite unnecessary and liable to be a very dull subject at the best of times. Yet an acquaintance, if only slight, with the theory underlying the construction of music, not only increases one's musicianship, but enables one to derive far more enjoyment from one's musical activities, be those activities banding, orchestral playing or merely listening!"

There he was again - educating. By September he was already having some reaction from readers, and along with the article for the month, *How Chords are Made and Used*, he drops in this 'Interlude':

"I have been told by a reader, quite politely, of course, that he was bored by last month's chat on triads, though he admitted that he knew nothing about them. He said he wanted to get on to *Practical* work. For the benefit of others like him may I lecture seriously for twenty seconds? These articles, being intended primarily for those who have not studied harmony, must necessarily start at the beginning of things, and I must explain rather more wordily than would be necessary if I and a piano could be put down for half an hour in each one of your homes. So bear with it if you wish to enjoy the more advanced work I hope to reach. You can't run until you know how to walk, and in any case I believe my old nurse was quite right in principle when she used to say 'Bread and butter first, young man, *Then* you can have some cake!' So let's get over the bread and butter stage, and the cake will be all the more enjoyable."

The articles were lively and refreshing, and must have been very enlightening to the more serious-minded amongst the readership.

There were also other miscellaneous articles in the same journal during 1928. One, headed *Taming the Lion of Stage Fright* was an informed article about combating the problem of nerves. *Musical Nonsense - the Press*, criticised what Denis called "the musical drivel we are given in the daily press," suggesting that, perhaps 'The Tout' of the racing column is often also 'Orpheus' of the music notes.

It is already becoming obvious that Denis was not one to suffer fools gladly, and one of his most vitriolic articles came as a follow-up, in *Musical Nonsense II - Ultra-modern Tendencies,* 'inspired' by an evening spent at a studio party in Chelsea. Amongst the so-called advanced thinkers he met was "an anæmic flat-footed lady who declaimed some of her own verses by way of a prelude." And then:

"There followed a composer who played music that might have been produced by a child banging its hands at random on the keys. It represented, he said, moonstones in a wild, wan waste."

Denis was not impressed, but he tried to put things in perspective with another of his parables.

"If you want to paint an ugly man you will, if you are a good artist, make him just as ugly as he is in real life - but you won't paint him badly. The whole difference lies in the fact that ugliness can be produced by good technique where wanted, but must not be confused with the ugliness resulting from poor technique."

1929-1930

During this brief period Denis was Organist and Director of Music at St. George's School, Harpenden. His only brass band composition from this time (as far as I know) was *Tintagel* and there were no transcriptions or arrangements. Therefore, the writings continued, but almost exclusively in *The Musical Mail*.

Between February 1929 and April 1930 there was a series following on from the earlier one on Harmony, about different aspects of composition. Topics covered included *The Power of the Title*, *Planning Your Work*, *Writing Longer Works*, *The Value of Inspiration* and *Dont's for the Amateur Composer*, for example:

"*Don't set out* to write music for its money-making possibilities;
Don't believe the people who tell you that studying harmony and the more technical side of composing will tend to make you write dull academic music;
Don't be afraid to experiment and make mistakes - above all, don't be afraid to acknowledge to yourself that you have made mistakes;
Don't think that the first pieces you write are wonderful. I did, and it caused me much sorrow and bitterness when I found out that those who

knew what they were talking about did not hesitate to show me how poor they were;

Don't be afraid of studying form. You are more likely, in the first stages at any rate, to gain more success with fairly short pieces in some definite form than with long rambling pieces, made up of lots of sections in different styles, times and keys;

Don't forget that variety is essential."

Characteristically, as his Coda to the series he wrote:

"*Finally* (did you say 'thank goodness'?) don't be afraid of hard work. Nothing in music, worth doing, is ever accomplished without real hard work. 'One-tenth inspiration and nine-tenths perspiration' sums the matter up. You won't all be Beethovens or Schuberts, but if you have the necessary talent and are willing to serve your apprenticeship by means of constant study, practice and self-criticism, you will at least give yourself a chance to make good. A kindly publisher and the public opinion of your work may do the rest."

This is all very sound advice and I wish it was given out today to more students.

During these two years there were also several more miscellaneous articles, a couple of which deserve a mention. Both concerned Denis's attitude to live music versus radio and the gramophone. We have already seen how he disagreed with those who said that the wireless was going to kill amateur music-making and live performance. In July 1930 he wrote a strongly-worded article, supported by Leslie Boosey (of Boosey & Hawkes), giving his personal guarantee that he was right on this issue, but at the same time stressing how important it was for conductors to make rehearsals interesting, so that young players would be eager to continue. (And how true that is again today, when we see great problems in maintaining numbers in bands.)

The article in the following month's *Musical Mail* appeared as a result, Denis said, of having "put my foot right in it by suggesting that conductors might have studied gramophone records of a particular test piece." He had apparently caused a barrage of criticism (he was becoming expert at doing this) by the comment and he went to great lengths in the article, headed *Learning from the Gramophone*, to try to persuade his readers of the sense in the comment. He could not resist the sting in the tail though, and ended with these words:

"The man who feels that it is beneath him to learn from a greater man's experience - or indeed from *any* man's experience, whether greater or less, so long as there is something worth learning, is virtually signing his own death warrant as far as his musical career is concerned. *And the brass band world has its fair share of such men.*"

By the end of 1930 this journal had acquired its new title of *Musical Progress and Mail.*

Another magazine pops up with the name *Bandsman's World* and in April

1930, Denis wrote a substantial article headed *This Antagonism*. It was a real 'soap-box' sermon on Old versus New, commenting on different adjudicating methods, but mostly on the reluctance of brass band people to progress musically. He concluded:

"The man who does not believe progress either possible or desirable, in the brass band world or in any other community, has no right to be a member of that community."

1931-1935

During these years Denis worked as General Music Editor for Chappell & Co. Away from the stringency of the school time-table and the extra duties imposed by life in a boarding school, he was free to devote more attention to bands, scores and his writings.

He conducted a number of bands during these years, as well as being called upon to direct massed band concerts. He also did some adjudicating, private teaching, teaching through correspondence courses and became involved as an examiner for diplomas in Brass Band Conducting. He was now also becoming fairly heavily committed with composing and arranging.

On the literary front Denis wrote articles for *Musical Progress and Mail* every month from January 1931 to March 1933 - quite a commitment. The first 17 were devoted to a series under the general heading *The Descriptive and Illustrative in Music*. This was a fairly specialised course - I'd say in Music Appreciation rather than directly about Musical History, though it covered developments chronologically from the 14th century through to Elgar, Strauss and Debussy. He didn't go later because, as he explained, he was too close in time to make informed comments.

The course illustrated Denis's intimate knowledge of an incredibly wide range of musical works, at a time when many of them were far less accessible than they've become in recent years through the LP, the CD, videos and the much wider range of books and scores now available.

He followed this course with a 3-article series about music *A Hundred Years Ago* - gleaned from a set of a musical journals he had acquired, called *The Harmonicon*, and dated 1823-24.

Then came a further string of miscellaneous articles, generally of an informative or educational nature. Two of these caught my attention, *Pride and Prejudice* and *The Quartet Party - a Suggestion*. Both were written in 1932 and in the first, Denis was slamming, in no uncertain terms, a decision of the officials of the South Wales National Eisteddfod to remove brass bands from their competition. He goes to town on what he calls "the snobbish attitude" and "the prejudice displayed by the 'superior' type of musician." He goes on,

"The brass band movement has a greater number of devotees than either the amateur orchestras or choral societies of the country. It brings music to far, far more people - who would get little music but for the bands - and one of these days musicians from outside the band world will wake up to the existence of this great music-making movement."

And all this in *The Musical Mail*, 'A Monthly Journal devoted to the interests of Brass, Military and Orchestral Musicians'. Characteristically though, he ended by throwing the ball back into the court of bands saying,

> "But the bands themselves must work to wear down all prejudice and to show that they are indeed pride-worthy."

In the other article to which I have referred, Denis was advocating the inclusion of an occasional quartet piece in a band concert. He also took the opportunity to spell out the difference between contest playing (generally the home-ground of the brass quartet) and concert work. He seemed to be stating the obvious but I wonder how many of us have seen the problem as clearly as Denis saw it - even in 1932. He wrote:

> "At a contest the players are using the music as the medium for showing their technique, but at a concert they should be using their technique as a means of showing the beauties of the music."

In a later issue (September 1933) he returned to this theme in *As Others See Us,* but this time from the point of view of choice of music. He begged conductors to show off *music* rather than *the skills of players*. He also begged for appropriate choice of music according to the type of engagement, but insisting that whether the choice be light or serious, it should always be of good quality. He concluded,

> "There has yet to be much 'pulling-up of socks' in the band world if it is ever to become the great musical force that it could - and should - become."

There were but three articles in *The British Bandsman* during this period - his impressions of the 1933 Belle Vue September Contest, when *Princess Nada* was the test piece and Denis one of the adjudicators, comments on the 1935 Belle Vue July Contest - which he had adjudicated, and an article in December of the same year, about Brass Bands and the BBC.

Denis was back in teaching mode in a contribution to *The Bandsman's Little Book* in an article dated May 1933 and headed *The Compleat Bandsman*. In this he was exhorting bandsmen to take all of their music-making seriously. His opening gambit provided evidence of his wit and of his highly individual way of 'putting things across'. He wrote:

> "If one may adopt the doggerel three R's, *reading, 'riting and 'rithmetic,* as the first essentials of one's ordinary education, one might take the three P's, *playing, perception and 'preciation* as representing the necessary equipment of the good bandsman."

1933 was also the year in which Denis wrote his articles - to some extent revisions of earlier work by a different author, for *The Musical Educator* (later revised and published as *The New Musical Educator*). These are mentioned on page 52, and call for no further discussion here, as there are still plenty copies of these books around.

From May 1932 Denis seems to have become the unofficial brass band consultant of the lordly *Musical Times*. Several of his contributions were answers to readers' queries about various wind instruments, but during

October and November he contributed two substantial articles on *Scoring for Brass Band*. Quite obviously, these were intended for practising musicians who may be tempted to produce a brass band piece - either original or transcribed - rather than for beginners who needed to learn basics. The first discussed suitable styles and idioms, along with instrumentation, transpositions and practical ranges. The second went deeper, dealing with the characteristics of the instruments, some conventional combinations and more general comments. They would be very useful articles at the time, and in fact form the basis of his book *Scoring for Brass Band*.

Other contributions to *Musical Times* included an article headed *The Prisoner-Judge*, in which Denis gave his views on closed adjudication - apparently being mooted for choral competitions at the time, a critique on a march score which had been submitted, and reviews of the newly-published book, *The Brass Band* by Harold Hind, and of the 1935 National Band Festival at Crystal Palace.

To conclude Denis's journalistic writings for this period, there was a review of a concert given by the International Staff Band of the Salvation Army in Harlesden late in 1934, and some programme notes for *The Amateur Orchestra of London* for a concert in Kingsway Hall in December. The highlight of the ISB concert for Denis was *Exodus* by one Captain Eric Ball.

The big thing of 1935 was, of course, the publication of Denis's first and most successful book, *Scoring for Brass Band*.

1936-1942

1936 was the year in which Denis took on the momentous task of setting up a Band Section within the Music Department of the BBC, and the ensuing years saw him becoming an increasingly dominant figure within the world of brass bands. He introduced several of his innovations in broadcasting (see pages 87 and 88) and towards the end of the period he became Doctor Denis Wright.

The years 1936-37 seem to have been the peak years for publication, though it is possible that some of the pieces were in the pipe-line before he joined the BBC.

As life became more hectic at the BBC, the number of band pieces dwindled, and apart from a surge in 1950, when Gilbert and Sullivan came out of copyright and he arranged selections from several of their operettas, the mid-1930s remained as the peak years.

Literary works also became fewer and further between. In *The British Bandsman* he reviewed a School Orchestra and Junior Band Festival which took place at the Queen's Hall in 1936. He also gave some background information about the *Academic Festival Overture* and his impressions of classes A, B and C which he had judged at the Belle Vue Spring Festival, also in 1936.

In *Musical Times* he reviewed a book on Military Band Instrumentation by Charles Hoby (his co-adjudicator at Crystal Palace in 1925), the 1936 Crystal

Palace Band Festival, a published work for military band and he answered reader's query about the oboe.

In the issue of *BBC Empire Broadcasting* dated 19th-25th September 1937 Denis penned an article on *The Evolution of the Military Band*. It is quite brief, discussing the early development of military bands and the current state of British Army bands. At the head of the article the following appears:

> 'Denis Wright, who is well-known as an arranger of music for military bands, throws some light on the evolution of military bands. The part played in that development by the Band of H.M. Coldstream Guards will be illustrated in a programme which the band will give this week.'

And that is exactly what the article is - a prelude to a radio programme. It is certainly not a prelude to his thesis which, at this point in time, I don't believe he had even begun to think about.

There is a tribute to B. Walton O'Donnell in *Ariel* (the BBC Magazine). O'Donnell had been a colleague in Denis's early days at the BBC, and had worked with the BBC Military Band before taking up another BBC appointment in Belfast. He had died on 20th August 1939 - hence the tribute.

Whilst demand for contributions would have waned during the war years, it is also likely that his BBC work was becoming all-consuming, and there was also the small matter of the Edinburgh Doctorate.

In the *Radio Times* issue of 28th February 1941 Denis wrote a review of bands on air during the forthcoming week. It included the broadcast of the 1st performance of the *Cornet Concerto,* with Harry Mortimer and the BBC Military Band. I would imagine that Denis wrote fairly regularly in *Radio Times,* but that is the only write-up from there in the scrapbook.

I stated in Chapter 12 that Denis wrote many of the scripts for brass band broadcasts. He also, occasionally, gave radio talks about bands, band personalities or band history. Transcripts of a couple of these talks have been preserved in the scrapbook, one for a programme called *The Brass Band Movement*, broadcast in the Midland Region on Monday, 27th September 1937 from 9.25 p.m. to 9.40 p.m. and the other, *Brass Bands of Britain in War-time*, which appears to have been broadcast in the BBC's Overseas Service. This was some time in January 1942, but no further details are given. The former script gives a brief review of the history, development and current state of brass bands, whilst the latter concentrates mainly on those bands which had taken part in a weekly series of quarter-hour programmes transmitted in the Overseas Service.

That brings us to the submission for the degree of Doctor of Music at Edinburgh. The part we are now concerned with is his *Evolution of the Wind Band*, a dissertation which was completed in April 1940. For Denis's own comments on it, see page 91.

Despite that view it is worth reviewing as, to date, it has remained unpublished and is therefore not available to the student. It follows the usual pattern of such works, with a résumé of the history and development of the various families of instruments - woodwinds, brass and a particularly interesting chapter on percussion before giving an outline of the growth of bands - both military and civilian.

There is the usual information about the early domination of the French, followed by German superiority, and the reliance in early English military bands on German musicians and is all very readable - no question of 'dry-as-dust' academic jargon. There are several references to other authorities - Adkins, Farmer, Kappey, etc., though some of their statements or conclusions are questioned. Denis still can't resist the occasional amusing anecdote. Take, for example, his reference to the 19th century horn bands which flourished in some countries, in which "each player was responsible for the sounding of one note only, as in the playing of hand-bells."

The monotony of this is illustrated, Denis asserts, in a letter which appeared in one of the 1823 issues of *The Harmonicon* (referred to above), signed by *F-sharp to His Imperial Majesty The Emperor of all the Russias.*

The Evolution of the Wind Band differs from most other similar treatise in that it includes a substantial chapter on *The Brass Band*. This, surprisingly, makes no mention of the Russell and Elliott book *The Brass Band Movement*, published in 1933. It does, however, reveal several interesting points, including Denis's attitude to the use (or non-use) of trumpets, flugel horns and French horns in the British-style Brass Band.

He begins by posing the rhetorical question as to why trumpets and French horns are not included in the instrumentation - a question regularly asked even to-day. Denis's answer to his own question is as follows:

"Admittedly the addition of, say two trumpets and two French horns would be a very useful addition to the very limited tone colour, provided that special parts, characteristic of the instruments, were written for them. In certain passages the trumpets would make a better treble to the trombones than cornets can ever make, whilst the French horns could be very effective, especially for solo work.

French horns, however, do not blend so well with the rest of the brass when used for the usual type of 'filling-in' that saxhorns are mostly called on to do.

As in the case of French horns, there would seem to be no reason, other than the absence of any special part for them, why trumpets should not be included for concert work. The chief drawback to their use, just doubling existing cornet parts, is that the tone of the trumpet does not blend with that of the cornet. An experienced ear can always detect the slight 'edge' on the cornet tone when, as happens occasionally, a trumpet is included at one of the solo cornet desks."

Denis takes the opposite view regarding the flugel horn, a view shared by many.

"It is a pity, too, that the standard instrumentation admits only one flugel; at one time it was usual to have three in a band, a very useful tonal extension of saxhorn tone into the upper register of the band."

On the wider issue of what he calls "the comparative failure of the brass band to acquire real musical standing" he concludes,

"It is sufficient to say that the band world (a very large community, having its own weekly and monthly journals) has consistently stood in its own way, on account of its ultra-conservatism of outlook. On the other hand, it must be recognised what valuable work the movement does, not only of a social nature, but in bringing music to a great number of people for whom life is apt to be drab and beauty hard to find."

Denis used material from this chapter as the basis of some of his later writings, for example in an expanded version, also taking on board scoring techniques, I believe, for a further edition of *The New Musical Educator*. He doubtless also made use of it in many of his lectures in later years.

There are just a few more articles, but it seems obvious that as Denis became more involved with the BBC's overseas work and less involved with bands, the published writings steadily dried up, and his compositions, transcriptions and arrangements were now also well past their peak.

I hope the foregoing has given an insight into the scope of Denis's literary writings, spanning some 20 years. A close study of them reveals that in general he praised the brass band when speaking or writing to the musical world at large, but that when addressing band people themselves he was constantly trying to convince them that, given the right attitudes, things could be so much better.

I believe that, despite a host of problems still unsolved, things are much better, and that if Denis could return and see conditions today he would feel that in spite of ourselves we *have* made progress, albeit not as much as we *could* have done had more people taken more notice of all the things he had to say.

His work has, without doubt, been continued by a number of people, some of whom were named in the Foreword, but the movement needs someone else with the vision, dedication and experience of a Denis Wright, to continue the bridge-building and to secure firmer links with that very large musical world outside our own relatively small one.

Chapter 23

Messiah in Brass

By the mid-1940s Denis had produced an impressive array of transcriptions (to say nothing of his compositions and arrangements). As we saw in the early part of the book many of these were designed to educate members of the brass band movement - be they conductors, players or listeners. He had also started building bridges to try to link brass bands with other forms of music-making. His *Sounding Brass and Voices* series on the radio had been very helpful, introducing choir audiences to the sound of the brass band and making bands more aware of choirs and indeed of solo singers.

The natural progression from this was to score a large-scale work involving voices and bands - an opera or an oratorio. He chose the latter and went for the obvious, Handel's *Messiah*. But there was a snag.

Almost the whole of the rest of the musical world had adopted, by an international agreement of 1939, a standard pitch. This had become necessary because of the problem faced by travelling orchestras in having to tune to the varying pitches of organs and pianos in different venues. It was not a problem shared by brass bands and so they maintained their own pitch, almost a semi-tone higher than the standard A=440 of what is now commonly (but wrongly) called concert pitch.

During the late 1940s and early 1950s, when the 'elite' bands were being asked to combine with pianos and organs in some of Denis's transcriptions of concerto movements they resorted, as we have seen, to the use of specially lengthened slides to bring the instruments to the right pitch. When, in the 1960s, instrument makers virtually refused to go on making high-pitched instruments, bands were forced to conform to the rest of the musical world's agreed pitch - initially by the use of low-pitch slides, and later by buying standard instruments.

But in 1946, when Denis transcribed *Messiah,* none of this had happened and so he scored parts of it in the 'wrong' key. He did this for the convenience of both singers and instrumentalists. Much of *Messiah* appears in the 'sharp' keys G, D, A and E majors, and therefore had Denis transcribed conventionally, B♭ instruments in the band would have been playing in A, E, B and F# majors and the E♭ instruments in E, B, F# (or possibly its enharmonic, G♭) and C# (or D♭) majors. Not only this, he would have taken the singers almost a semitone higher than normal, causing problems for sopranos in their highest register.

By taking these sections down a semitone he made life easier all round, the A, E, B and F# of the B♭ instruments becoming A♭, E♭, B♭ and F, with corresponding adjustments to keys for the E♭ instruments, and the voices singing a little *lower* than in conventional performances.

So, the transcription of the orchestral accompaniments of *Messiah* for brass band was done with this adjustment to its keys and, despite the anomaly, Denis produced the score in the hope that it would prove a blessing to the many choral societies which performed *Messiah* regularly each Christmas, often struggling through with very poor orchestral support. He felt that even a decent band would be able to create a more satisfying result than did some of the pretty awful 'philharmonics' of the time.

The first performance in the new version took place on 13th November 1946, with Denis conducting Blaencym Choral Society and Parc and Dare Band in Treherbert, in the Rhondda Valley. It was the first of three performances given on successive evenings (Wednesday, Thursday and Friday) in a local chapel and there was a half hour broadcast, on the BBC's Welsh Home Service, of part of the Friday performance. In the programme's Foreword Denis wrote,

"This series of performances of Handel's *Messiah* breaks new ground and

---

LIBANUS CHAPEL, TREHERBERT.

❖❖❖❖❖❖❖❖❖❖❖

WEDNESDAY, THURSDAY & FRIDAY,
NOVEMBER 13TH, 14TH & 15TH, 1946.

❖❖❖❖❖❖❖❖❖❖❖

'THE MESSIAH'
(Handel)

BY THE

BLAENYCWM CHORAL SOCIETY

ACCOMPANIED BY

THE PARC & DARE WORKMEN'S BAND.

❖❖❖❖❖❖❖❖❖❖❖

The Performance will be Broadcast on Friday Evening
from 8 to 8.30 p.m.

Programme for the first performance in the new version

Preliminary Announcement

AN EVENT THAT NO BAND ENTHUSIAST SHOULD MISS

The National Association of Brass Band Conductors

presents

M E S S I A H

(Handel)

with brass band accompaniment

KINGSWAY   HALL,   LONDON

Saturday, April 3rd, 1948 at 2.30 p.m.

THE ALEXANDRA CHOIR *(200 voices)*

THE LUTON BAND

Millicent Ward
(Soprano)

Sara Buckley
(Contralto)

Alfred Hepworth
(Tenor)

Arthur Copley
(Bass)

Harry Mortimer *(Trumpet)*

Conductor : DR.   DENIS   WRIGHT

MAKE A NOTE OF THE DATE AND KEEP IT FREE

Tickets ~~will be~~ ready ~~early in January~~, but as we are already having requests for reservations it would be advisable to make your request NOW

to:—   Miss M. Thomson, 45 Sutherland Avenue, London, W.9.

Prices : 7/6d., 5/-, 3/6d. and 2/6d.

There are seats at each price both on the ground floor and in the balcony ; please say which you would prefer. If you have never heard this grandest of all oratorios here is your chance. If you **have**, it is worth hearing again, especially with brass band accompaniment (Dr. Denis Wright's arrangement), which adds grandeur to the massive choruses.

Any profits from the performance will be handed to the Alexander Owen Memorial Fund. So in giving yourself a musical treat you will be helping the Fund that is doing so much for the Bandsmen of tomorrow.

opens up a new chapter in musical history. For the first time, a complete oratorio is being given with brass band instead of orchestral accompaniment, thus uniting more completely than ever before the two greatest amateur music-making forces, choir and brass band.

That it will be done again I have little - if any - doubt; indeed I hope we may in all humility echo the words of a very great man and feel that . . . . *we shall this day light such a candle by God's grace . . . . as I trust shall never be put out.*"[1]

Though it received many more performances it was a source of great disappointment to Denis that it did not really light that metaphoric candle, nor did it ever achieve the popularity he felt it deserved.

Not that he expected anything like universal acceptance of the idea. Elsewhere, he wrote:

"When I set out last February to score the usual concert version of *Messiah* (some 40 numbers) for brass, I was not blind to the possibility of my getting a few more brickbats on the score of vandalism, but in twenty years or so amongst brass bands I have got hardened to that, coming as they have done from both sides, so a few more won't matter. . . . The scoring occupied about ten weeks of my spare time."

These first performances were well received - even *Musical Times* giving a favourable review, and there followed a succession of quite prestigious performances. The first London performance was given by Luton Band and the Alexandra Choir in the Central Hall, Westminster, with Denis again conducting. It took place on 2nd April 1947 and was so successful that it was performed again the following April - this time Harry Mortimer playing the solo in *The Trumpet Shall Sound.*

I myself recall attending a performance in Halifax around 1951, with Halifax Choral Society and Black Dyke - conducted by Alex Mortimer. The choruses and some of the arias were quite magnificent but I have to say that few of the recitatives came off, because they were not understood by the band.

In 1954, Stockport Citadel Band and Songsters gave a performance in their own town, following it up a year later in Manchester, and again in 1956 in Oldham. One of the principals on those occasions was Alan Jenkins, later principal tuba with the LSO and now a journalist and features editor for *Brass Band World.* Going further afield, the first Australian performance took place late in 1956. This came about as a result of a meeting the previous Easter between Denis and a Handel scholar - Dr. Robert Dalley-Scarlett. The expert had not shared Denis's enthusiasm for the brass band version, expressing doubts about both its effectiveness and its suitability.

However, he had thought about it and decided to put it to the test by directing a performance himself. This took place on Saturday, 24th November in Brisbane Town Hall, with his own Brisbane Choral Society and a composite band made up of the better players from four of Brisbane's bands.

Reports indicate that the singers enjoyed the experience, that the bandsmen were quite thrilled, and that the audience gave Dalley-Scarlett a big ovation. The press was apparently less enthusiastic but Dalley-Scarlett conceded that it was 'quite a good idea', adding that he hoped to do it again the following year and saying he thought that 'it might spread into the country districts.' That, of course, is precisely what Denis had hoped would happen here in Britain - but it never did.

What must have been one of the most exciting performances of all took place in Belfast in December 1957. This was in St. Patrick's Church, filled to capacity with an audience of over 1,400, with Templemore Avenue Band and a chorus of 140, drawn from five local church choirs, together with the Ulster Singers. The average age of the band was only 15, and many of the singers were in their teens; Denis conducted, and the performance attracted rave reviews. The Bishop of Down was present and complimented both Denis and Alfie Bell - founder and conductor of the Templemore Band.

Quite obviously there were other performances of *Messiah* in its brass band version and there were also fairly frequent performances of excerpts, including the following - all of which were broadcast:

1946 Blackburn Choral Society and Bickershaw, conductor Denis Wright
1947 Sheffield Philharmonic Choir and St. Hilda's,[2] conductor Denis Wright
1948 Dewsbury Music Society and St. Hilda's, conductor Denis Wright
1950 Huddersfield Choral Society and Black Dyke, conductor Herbert Bardgett
1956 Composite choir and Timaru Band (New Zealand), conductor Denis Wright

Peter Gartside tells me that during the early 1950s he attended a rehearsal and recording of extracts with the Hallé Choir and CWS (Manchester) Band in the Free Trade Hall, Manchester, for a *Sounding Brass and Voices*, again with Denis conducting. He recalls,

'I shall never forget the impression which the combined sound of the Band and the Hallé Choir made.'

Encouraging as these performances must have been, Denis's wish that his transcription would become a regular feature in performances by some of the many local choral societies which perform *Messiah* annually has never been fulfilled.

When brass bands finally adopted low pitch to come into line with the rest of the musical world, it could have been reasonably assumed that Denis's transcription would never again see the light of day except, perhaps, for the occasional performance of extracts. But that has not been the case. Though still never becoming all that popular, it has continued to be performed at intervals - with at least a couple of performances in the United States. In the summer of 1971 Black Dyke and Bradford Festival Choral Society recorded excerpts for PYE and there has also been one very high profile broadcast. *The British Bandsman* of 18th March 1989 made this announcement:

AMBITION ACHIEVED - by Ron Massey

'It was a long, hard day for everyone concerned. But Harry Mortimer stood up well to the ordeal. He was in Huddersfield Town Hall to conduct Black Dyke Mills and Britannia Building Society, together with the town's famous Choral Society, in Dr. Denis Wright's setting of Handel's *Messiah*. Maurice Murphy was there, and so was Roy Newsome, this time at the console of the mighty organ rather than wielding a baton.

It was HM's ambition to conduct the work, and it came from a comment made in an interview two years before. Now it's all on tape, and you can hear the end product on Radio 2 next Saturday.'

The background to this was that in a radio interview, Harry had been asked if there was anything he had not done that he would like to do. His reply was to the effect that if he could conduct *Messiah* with Huddersfield Choral Society and a good brass band, he would die a happy man.

Well, the BBC took this to heart and arranged to record the work in Huddersfield Town Hall. As Ron Massey says, it *was* a long, hard day, and none of those of us present knew how the 87-year-old H.M. stood up to it. For him, it began with radio and press interviews during his 7.30 a.m. breakfast, and continued with him standing (or just occasionally sitting) on the podium from 9.30 in the morning until well after nine o'clock in the evening, with only minimal breaks for refreshments. Mrs. Wright, who was also there,

Black Dyke, Britannia and Huddersfield's famous Choral Society

Maurice Murphy was there . . . [+]

Mrs. Wright with the original score [+]

commented that when the choir arrived for the evening session and struck up with *Hallelujah Chorus*, 'you could literally see the years roll off Harry.'

The resulting programme, *Messiah in Brass*, was nothing short of sensational and a tribute not only to Harry himself and Denis's score, but also to the BBC, and in particular to Antony Askew, the producer who thought up the idea. It was broadcast on Radio 2 on Easter Saturday, and again shortly before Christmas. There was also a Radio 4 documentary, *The Making of Messiah,* which went out a few days before the Easter broadcast. Music critic John Wainwright in *The Northern Echo* of 1st April 1989 said of *Messiah in Brass*:

> 'I have heard it in churches, chapels and concert halls. I have memories of its performance by professional musicians and by amateurs. I have seen Barbirolli on the podium. I have seen Malcolm Sargent there and I have seen George Solti there. I have heard the LPO, the BBC Symphony Orchestra, the Hallé, the Liverpool Phil and heavens knows how many other orchestras send those notes belting at me.
>
> I kid you not. Had anybody asked me, before last Saturday, I would have assured the questioner that I knew every note of Handel's *Messiah*, back to front, top to bottom and whether it was played on anything, from a four-manual organ to a penny whistle.
>
> At 7.30 pm on Saturday, March 25th on Radio 2, an 86-year-old whizz kid showed me what Handel really meant.
>
> I ask that you believe that I've both heard and seen Huddersfield Choral Society more times than I care to count. Equally, you may take my word for it that, when they take the bit between their teeth with the chorus *Unto Us a Child is Born* they take some catching.
>
> But, on that evening, the combination of Black Dyke Mills Band and the Britannia Building Society Band not only caught them, it rode alongside them, note for note and created sound more magnificent than I'd thought possible.'

This was certainly one of those occasions of which I can say, 'I'm glad I was there.'

Notes

[1] This is part of a quote by Hugh Latimer (1485-1555), Bishop of Worcester, to Bishop Ridley.
[2] Not the legendary St. Hilda's Colliery Band, famous in the 1920s and 1930s, but one which was formed near Leeds during the early 1950s.

Chapter 24

Denis Overseas

These days it is commonplace for bands and band personalities to spend time overseas. European countries - particularly Holland, Switzerland, Norway and Belgium, all within an hour or two's flying time of the major British airports - frequently call on British band people to conduct, adjudicate, lecture or perform in their band functions. There are also many band tours to these countries.

Further afield, the former dominions - Canada, Australia and New Zealand have brass band communities, and for many years they have called upon the services of British adjudicators. There have also been occasional visits to these countries by British brass bands, the most spectacular being by Besses o' th' Barn when they undertook their two famous World Tours before the 1914-18 war.

In recent years, as inter-continental travel has become more commonplace, visitors from America and Japan have visited our country, have formed British-style brass bands on their return home and then, from time to time, have invited well-known conductors - and occasionally a band - to visit them, to teach and to stimulate interest.

But not until the late 1940s did the international brass band scene start to develop on anything like the scale we know today. Australia and New Zealand, with their large numbers of British immigrants, were the principal overseas developments pre-1940, but at a distance of 12,000 miles it was very much a luxury to have visitors from the 'old country'.

Denis's influence in Europe was confined mainly to Holland, Sweden and Denmark - and in particular the latter. He was able to visit these countries for a few days at a time, and frequently did. But he undertook a series of far more extensive visits to places much further afield. The first of these longer-range trips was in 1951 when he visited New Zealand, staying there for about a month - adjudicating and conducting.

After retiring from the BBC at the end of 1955 he had more freedom for travel and was able to pursue, with even more vigour than before, the musical education of band people, wherever they were. But as time went by the scope of his work widened, as we find him conducting more orchestral and choral concerts and working for four overseas universities as lecturer, tutor and conductor. He also fulfilled over 100 broadcast engagements in the Commonwealth during the course of these tours.

Freed from the shackles of full-time employment for the first time in 35 years he launched himself, within a matter of weeks, into a tour lasting over four months, during which time he visited Ceylon, Malaya, New Zealand, Australia, Johannesburg and Rhodesia.

Three years later (1959) and he was off again, this time visiting Australia, New Zealand and Canada. This tour spanned 18 weeks - from late February to early July, and provided Denis with over 100 engagements and 30,000 miles of travel. His 1961 trip, though taking in only Australia and New Zealand, was even longer, stretching from May to December. A year later he went to Canada to adjudicate a chain of music festivals covering the length and breadth of the country, but lasting a mere four months! His final long-range trip was in 1966 when, at the age of 71, he visited the Far East. I will try to outline his overseas work country by country.

Holland

British-style brass bands were virtually unknown in Europe before the late 1940s and Holland - very pro-British, within receiving distance of BBC broadcasts, and reaping the benefits of post-war brass band tours - was the first European country to make a serious attempt at forming our kind of brass band.

Fairey Aviation and Foden's were amongst the first British brass bands to visit Holland, and the Dutch were quick to see possibilities in this kind of amateur band - especially in the north of the country. By chance, Denis was in Holland in 1949 when Fairey's arrived for a tour which incorporated an appearance in an international competition. The reader will recall that part of Denis's early musical training was as a percussionist, and when it was discovered that Fairey's were a bit deficient in this department, Denis found himself dragooned into augmenting their 'battery' - in particular, displaying his skills on the glockenspiel.

The British Bandsman of 4th June announced that Fairey's had had an outstanding success at the International Music Festival, their five 1st prizes ensuring that they picked up the title of International Champions. It makes no mention of Denis's involvement, but this is recorded on a plaque presented to Fairey's a few years ago by Mrs. Wright. Displayed on the bandroom wall it says, tongue in cheek,

Aalsmeer, Holland, April 23rd 1949

The members of the Fairey Aviation Works Band, having informed themselves that, within the precincts of their rehearsal room in Aalsmeer, Holland, on April 23rd 1949, there strayed an eminent Doctor of Music with unsuspected talents as a Glockenspieler, such members discreetly cajoled the eminent Doctor to augment the percussion.

Their success in the subsequent Contest was, in no small measure, due to the dexterity of the Glockenspieler, cum Adjudicator, and it is with gratification coupled with amazement that we subscribe our appreciation to the Doctor for his invaluable contribution.

On the plaque is a caricature of Denis playing the glock, with four beaters in each hand and the instrument balanced on two stools. Signed by each member of the band it was, at the time, presented to Denis by Fairey's, but it is fitting that it has now found its way back to the bandroom in Stockport, a valued addition to the band's memorabilia.

Denis returned to Holland late in 1951 and spent a week rehearsing three British-style brass bands. In *The British Bandsman* of 17th November he told of his experiences with these bands - based at Groningen, Leeuwarden and Drogenham - all in the North of Holland. They existed largely because of the enthusiasm of Drogenham's conductor, a cornet player called Hilke de Vries. The band from Leeuwarden was conducted by his father, and the conductor of the other band was Mr. A. van Kammen, who was also a choral conductor. Denis spent his week rehearsing each band individually, in preparation for a massed band concert in the city of Leeuwarden.

In the article Denis outlined the strengths and weaknesses of the three bands and also told of the difficult conditions under which they existed. He said, for example,

> "The chief tonal weakness lies with the horns and the basses. Groningen's two saxophones are out of place; I hope they will eventually be able to discard *those two musical interlopers,* whose reed tone does not blend with the brass."

He was nevertheless very impressed by the keenness of the players, who all listened regularly to band broadcasts from the BBC. English sheet music was very expensive in Holland, so Mr. de Vries had appealed for help through *The British Bandsman.* He had been rewarded with gifts amounting to about 100 sets of band parts.

I am indebted to my friend Jurien de Koning of Utrecht for further information about this visit, and also for a copy of the actual programme. From this it emerges that the Kroningen Band was called 'Crescendo', Drogenham 'Hallelujah' and the third, 'Leeuwarden Fanfare Orchestra'. The massed band was under the direction of 'the English composer/conductor, Dr. of Music Denis Wright of the BBC.'

'Crescendo' and the 'Leeuwarden Fanfare Orchestra' played individual items, and pieces played by the combined bands included Denis's *Handelian Suite,* his arrangement of the *Impressario Overture* and the march *B.B.&C.F.* Before the finale Denis made a short speech - in Dutch!

The event was reviewed in the Dutch brass band magazine *Binding,* edited by de Vries (junior), and there was also a substantial article in a local newspaper, *Zealander* headed *A Milestone in Dutch Brass Band History.* This reveals that some five years earlier, Mr. van Kammen, a former bandmaster of Groningen Salvation Army Band had formed 'Crescendo', and that Mr. de Vries (junior), a former member of Leeuwarden Salvation Army Band had spent some time in England, playing with Rushden Temperance. The article also tells of the antagonism of other Dutch bands to these developments, referring to them as '*the English disease*'.

The three bands gave each other moral support during these difficult early years and hence the idea of a combined concert under the direction of Denis, which really was a milestone. The concert was recorded by Vara Radio - a broadcasting company well known to most bands which have visited Holland in recent years.

A detailed résumé of Denis's impressions of the three bands was published in *Binding* - covering tone, technique, phrasing and *concentration,* along with a plea for a deepening of emotional feeling in the playing and less superficiality, concluding,

> "It is the music only which is important for the band, and the music we play must come out of our heart, to reach the heart of the audience."[1]

Denis would be very happy to know of the high standards achieved by Dutch brass bands since those early days. He returned in 1952 to work with the Leeuwarden Band, following which Hilke de Vries wrote an article in *The British Bandsman* of 26th July referring to the impact of Denis's visits and saying,

> *We strongly believe that in the not-too-distant future brass band playing - as you know it - will cease to be a purely British affair.*

Truer words were never spoken!

And so ended Denis's 'gospel-spreading' activities in Holland. We will look now at his work in a country where brass bands were already well established, but where there was a strong desire to improve standards.

New Zealand

Denis made four trips to New Zealand - in 1951, 1956, 1959 and 1961. The first was primarily to adjudicate at the National Championships in Wellington (always a 5-day event in New Zealand). This was the first time since World War II that a British adjudicator had officiated at these Championships. Denis also conducted a massed band concert and delivered two lectures - one in Wellington itself (capital city of North Island and a sea-port situated on the Island's south-western tip) and the other in a small town called Hawera, home of the new New Zealand champions and some miles further up the west coast. Denis described the massed band concert as something of a novelty for the New Zealanders but a successful one, even though some of the bands taking part turned up without music, expecting it to be provided on the night by the organisers! There were eight bands in all - the whole of the A Grade entry in the competition, in fact, and this was the first time an adjudicator had taken part in such a concert.

There is lots of information in the British band press about the 1956 tour, but I'm also indebted to John Harrison, Chief Executive of the New Zealand Brass Band Association and to John Jennings and Miss Rachael Hawkey of the University of Canterbury for help in filling in some of the gaps.

Denis's work began with a series of lectures, delivered in Canterbury University College. (Canterbury is the most heavily-populated region of the South Island, is equivalent to an English county, and its principal city is Christchurch.)

From 5th-10th March Denis was Chief Adjudicator at the National Band

Championships way down south at Invercargill. In this contest, by winning the D Grade set test and quickstep competitions, the Dunedin Ladies' Band became the first women's band in the world to win a national title. Following the Championships Denis gave a series of broadcast talks on brass band subjects, some lectures in Christchurch under the auspices of Canterbury University College, and interspersed with all this was a series of concerts in several major towns and cities, as well as a trip to Australia to adjudicate at the Queensland Championships in Brisbane.

He gave five lectures in Christchurch and for two of these he enlisted the help of Woolston Band (now Skellerup Woolston). The first was *The Plain Man's Guide to the Brass Band,* an illustrated talk, devised the year before and recorded for the BBC Transcription Service with Fairey's; the other was a talk entitled *The Brass Band and its Music.* His other Christchurch lectures were *Youth and Music,* in which he stressed the need for playing as an aid to appreciation, *What is this Modern Music?* - discussing the critical approach and the need to sift the good from the bad and finally, *How do YOU Listen to Music?* Two other lectures given later on this tour were on the subjects of *The Transcription of Classical Works* and *The Enjoyment of Music.*

Early May saw Denis visiting the South Island's west coast bands in preparation for a Choral and Brass Band Festival in Hokitika - with three bands and 170 singers. This venture was organised by the Adult Education Department of Canterbury University College, in association with the west coast brass bands. The only anecdote I have of this venture comes from Mrs. Wright, who says there was a bit of a scare when it was discovered that half the players of one band had to make a round trip of about 80 miles in between the afternoon rehearsal and the evening concert, *in order to milk their cows!*

Two more concerts followed, at each of which Denis met former bandmasters of Fairey's. The first was at Timaru where Frank Smith was in charge, and the other was with the Napier Band, then under the direction of Robert Mulholland (senior). He found the Timaru concert very rewarding, with a good Grade A band and a fine choir. Together they performed 40-minutes of extracts from *Messiah.*

At this point in the tour Denis had fulfilled 94 engagements in 85 days - and that in spite of all the travelling around.

Much of the success of the 1956 tour of New Zealand was due to the work of the late Dr. Vernon Griffiths, Dean of the Faculty of Music at Canterbury University College. Dr. Griffiths had met Denis in London in 1952 and had assisted as an examiner for the BBCM conductor's diploma. This eventually led to Bandsman's College of Music examinations being set up in New Zealand and Australia, with Dr. Griffiths the Chief Examiner.

But the travelling wasn't over yet. Denis had a few more days of broadcasting to do, including a rehearsal 'on air' in Wellington - and then he was back in Australia to attend a UNESCO[2] Conference in Melbourne.

In 1959 Denis was again 'Down Under', once more hopping across the 2,000-mile stretch of ocean which separates New Zealand from Australia. The Australian leg found him again adjudicating at the Queensland Championships, and also at the Nationals in Brisbane.

Rehearsing Dunedin Choral Society and St. Kilda Band, 1959

His first two weeks in New Zealand were spent working for the University of Auckland, with visits to several bands and the running of two courses for conductors. This was followed by a week of radio recordings, including two illustrated talks about the National Youth Brass Band. He was also able to offer advice to the organisers of New Zealand's first National Youth Brass Band School - being planned for the following August.

After all this he travelled down to the west coast of South Island where he rehearsed a number of bands and choirs for a series of rural music festivals. This involved further travelling, often in bad weather - July being the middle of winter in New Zealand. About these festivals Denis commented:

"Although the musical standard was low, it was considerably higher than when I did similar work there three years ago. The enthusiasm these festivals create and the incentive to work at the music cannot fail to have beneficial results."

Following this he went to Christchurch, then down to Dunedin and all the way back up to Wellington. In Dunedin he worked for the New Zealand Broadcasting Service, recording talks and concerts, including a *Sounding Brass & Voices* featuring Dunedin Choral Society and St. Kilda Band - both conducted by Elgar Clayton (a former principal cornet player at Fairey's). The programme included excerpts from both *Messiah* and *Elijah* and also a new cantata for choir and band by Dr. Vernon Griffiths, mentioned earlier.

He organised a National Brass Band School in Christchurch, where he also gave a lecture - *Music and Youth in Great Britain*. In this he used tape recordings of the National Youth Orchestras of Great Britain and Wales, of the National Youth Brass Band of Great Britain, and of miscellaneous groups of children singing and playing anything from recorders to bagpipes.

This lecture was under the auspices of the Department of Music of the University, in association with the Regional Council of Adult Education and the Workers' Education Association - a body with which Denis had had some contact in Britain (see page 200).

It was now becoming obvious that he had raised his sights far beyond the education of the British brass band public, and also that he was putting a lot of effort into helping and encouraging the young people of New Zealand.

This must have been a very strenuous time. In a period of 38 days he did 24 rehearsals for 10 concerts, including one with the New Zealand National Orchestra.

In June of 1959 Denis left New Zealand to do some work in Canada (to be discussed later in the chapter).

During his fourth and last visit to New Zealand, in 1961, the emphasis on brass bands was rather less than during previous tours. He arrived in New Zealand in August (still in the depths of winter) after an exhausting seven weeks in Australia. Here he had a comparatively relaxing ten days, with just three rehearsals for the first broadcast performance of his transcription of excerpts from Handel's oratorio *Judas Maccabæus*. This was with the current New Zealand champions Waitemata Silver Band and Auckland Choral Society, and received no less than eight broadcasts, spread over a period of five weeks, from regional transmitters in various parts of the country.

This exercise was followed by a week of visits to a number of bands in the South Auckland Association, culminating in a concert in Hamilton, another of North Island's university towns. Though described as an 'All-Star Band' the players on stage came mainly from lower section bands, limiting somewhat Denis's sense of professionalism.

Next came four days in Hawera, spent with Mr. and Mrs. Harry Farrington,[3] rehearsing for the first public performance of Denis's version of *Judas*. Also featured in the concert was a performance of Denis's transcription of the 1st movement of Grieg's *Piano Concerto*, with a 14-year-old solo pianist.

Next he went to Wellington to record four talks and a studio massed band recording, during which he met a former member of the NYBB - Rex Hurst.

This was followed by a 14-week engagement on the staff of Canterbury University Adult Education Department, lecturing at the University, taking part in the New Zealand National Youth Band School, judging the Junior Solo Championships, directing a one-week course for conductors and with no less than 16 concerts - choral, orchestral and band - throughout the province of Canterbury. The conductors' course was described as the first National Band Conductors' Training School, and was made up of conductors from both North and South Islands, as well as one from Fiji.

Early September saw another lecture series. *Youth and Music* was again high on the agenda, along with a talk with the thought-provoking title *Sanity in Musical Composition*. There was also a session in a school concentrating on the theme *Music Played and Sung by High School Pupils Overseas* and a session in a girls' high school dealing with music of special interest to girls. All this demonstrates Denis's acute sense of the needs of the occasion, and the breadth of the work he was prepared to undertake.

The musical climax of this tour - possibly of all his work in New Zealand, was his work in the Canterbury area with choirs and an orchestra, rehearsing and performing music by Coleridge-Taylor - *Hiawatha's Wedding Feast* and *The Death of Minnehaha*.

There were also talks in schools and some theory classes with an army band. The final engagement was a two-day massed bands festival at Nelson, for Wellington University. After what must have been another exhausting tour of the Antipodes - and his last one - Denis arrived safely back on English soil on 9th December. I imagine that Christmas would have been even sweeter than usual that year.

This brought to an end Denis's association with New Zealand, encompassing four tours spanning ten years. Though there seem to be few people around now who remember much about these visits, I'm sure they had considerable influence on the musical life of New Zealand at the time.

Australia

In addition to articles in *The British Bandsman* I am also indebted to Ted Edsall of the Australian band magazine *Ozoompah* and the Historical Research Officer of the Band Association of New South Wales for much valuable information.

Denis's first visits to Australia were part of his big 1956 tour when, as already mentioned, having adjudicated at the New Zealand Championships he took on a similar rôle in the Queensland Championships in Brisbane. Here he listened to 259 entrants in the solos, duets, trios and quartets classes and 108 full band performances, in an 8-day event.

He also directed two week-end courses for bandsmen and bandmasters, one in Sydney, organised by the New South Wales Brass Band Association. As was usual on these occasions the delegates - some of them making a 400-mile round-trip - formed a composite band and took turns to conduct, under Denis's watchful eye. The other involved a trip of about 150 miles inland, well into the Bush where, under the auspices of the Orange City Band, Denis rehearsed the Western Group Concert Band and then gave local conductors the opportunity of conducting and receiving a written critique.

The Australasian Bandsman of January 1956 made the following announcement:

'Examinations for the coveted award BBCM are to be held in Australia during 1956 under the personal supervision of Dr. Denis Wright. The BBCM is one of three bandmasters diplomas granted by the Bandsman's College of Music, England. Dr. Denis Wright has been the Hon. Director of

Examinations for many years. Any examinations that may be held in Australia will be directly under the ægis of the Bandsman's College of Music.'

While in Brisbane Denis set up these examinations, testing one candidate for the diploma of BBCM. When he returned to Australia in May to attend a UNESCO Conference in Melbourne, he examined four more.

In 1959 Denis returned to Australia - again combining it with his work in New Zealand. This visit was mainly under the auspices of the University of Western Australia Adult Education Board, and I'm indebted to Emeritus Professor Sir Frank Callaway C.M.G., O.B.E., a member of that board at the time, for information about Denis's programme on this visit.

Denis began with ten days in Perth, giving talks and rehearsing bands. He also held a 3-day school for conductors in which Perth City Band was rehearsed by conductors both from the city and from country districts. Whilst in Perth he gave a talk to a group of 80 music teachers about the value of having a brass band or brass ensemble in school, and he also directed a concert with the Western Command Band - an Australian Army brass band.

The day on which he left Perth lasted 30 hours and included three sessions in Perth followed by a 2,100 mile flight, involving a 6-hour time change, five hours' rehearsal on arrival in Sydney and a live broadcast with a string orchestra. Whilst in Sydney there was also another orchestral concert and a series of talks for the Australian Broadcasting Corporation, including two about the NYBB. Travelling inland to Bathurst, not far from Orange, visited in 1961, he directed another of his schools for conductors.

Easter was spent adjudicating at the Queensland Centenary Brass Band Solo and Quartet Championships, again an 8-day affair, this time at Mackay in the region of the Great Barrier Reef, 1,000 miles north of Sydney, and complete with torrential rain on most days!

After this Denis flew south to Brisbane and then across to New Zealand for the 2nd leg of the tour.

In May 1961 he was in Australia again. As in 1959 he went first to Perth where, attached to the Adult Education Department of the University of Western Australia, he spent three weeks in various parts of the State. He also adjudicated the Western Australian Championships followed by three days of adjudicating at the Latrobe Valley Eisteddfod, en route to Sydney for some assignments on behalf of the New South Wales Band Association.

During seven weeks in Australia he travelled 6,000 miles, whilst undertaking 74 engagements.

In mid-July he flew to New Zealand, but during the last week in October he returned to Australia to adjudicate at the famous South Street brass band contest in Ballarat, Victoria. By coincidence, this was on the very same day as the *Daily Herald* Finals at the Royal Albert Hall in London.

The Australasian Bandsman of November/December 1961 featured an article headed

Adjudicator's High Praise at South Street Competitions.

It went on, 'The musical adjudicator Denis Wright of London said the

Ballarat competitions had such a wide reputation as being the home of good music, that he was delighted to be asked to adjudicate in the section most known to him - the bands.' In his adjudication speech following the playing, Denis said,

> "I have heard some superb playing during my visit, and were any of the A grade bands to visit England or New Zealand they would give the best bands a run for their money. In my adjudication, I have tried to seek for artistry, and it is the combination of artistry and science that makes a good rendition. Science is the art of playing the instrument, and artistry the human feeling that is put into the playing. The music at these competitions has been alive!"

And there ended the Australian connection.

Denmark and Sweden

During the German occupation of Denmark between 1940 and 1945 there developed a strong feeling of 'heavy' German cultural influence and in the years following the end of the war came the feeling of a need for 'cultural liberation'. In the sphere of amateur music-making no-one felt this need more strongly than a young bandmaster of an FDF[4] Youth Band called Herbert Møller. As a teenager he had heard an English Salvation Army band playing in Copenhagen. The band was from Rugby and its sound - so different from that with which he was familiar - was destined to change the whole Danish band tradition.

During the late 1940s and early 1950s Herbert Møller did much pioneering work, changing the instrumentation of his band and striving to bring its sound closer to what he thought of as 'the British sound'.

By the mid-1950s he felt he needed help. He was, at the time, playing tuba in a Danish army band and in the band's library he found a copy of *Who's Who in Music*. Working his way through it he found the name and address of a certain Dr. Denis Wright. (He must have dearly wished that he had been called Appleby or something rather than Wright!) He sent a letter to him asking for help and advice on the future development of bands in Denmark. This was in 1956.

A friendly and positive reply came back, as can be seen from the copy of a page from Herbert's scrapbook (reproduced on page 191). (The photograph in the bottom left hand corner is of Black Dyke - National Champions 1947-8-9).

This letter led to an immediate and lasting friendship between Herbert and Denis, who subsequently visited Denmark many times, conducting, lecturing, and adjudicating at Denmark's very first all-brass band competition, though in Herbert's own words,

> "His most important contribution was in the use of an ability to make music and to improve performances - firmly and friendly, with determination, but also with great charm."

From the time of these early communications between the two individuals,

DENIS WRIGHT

17, CRAWFORD AVENUE,

WEMBLEY, MIDDLESEX.

PHONE : WEMBLEY 6322

Dear Mr. Moeller,
                    I have read your letter with great interest;
that I have not answered sooner is because I have been away in
France for a short while, so you must forgive me.

        May I congratulate you on your English writing - it is very
good, and I am ashamed that I know not one word of Danish, though
I speak French and German and a little Dutch.

        It pleases me very much that you are so interested in the
English style of brass band playing. It would not be possible in
a letter to tell you just how to set about training your boys to
play in that style, but from my work with several bands in Holland
I know how the European amateur bands are heavy and sometimes
spoil their tone by forcing the notes too much.

        Do you think I could help you if I came to Copenhagen some time
on holiday? I may tell you that a few years ago I went to Holland
for this same purpose, to help some of their bands (who had changed
to the English instruments, with no clarinets or saxophones) and
during the week I was there I gave lessons each night to three
different bands and on the last night we had a massed band concert.

        I did not make any charge for this, as it is work that I am so
interested in and I would be prepared to come, perhaps next year,
to your band for, perhaps, a week, if you could arrange hospitality
for me - to stay with a family without cost to me. I would not ask
any fee for the work with your band.

        I am sending you as a gift a copy of the two books you ask
for; I hope you will find them of interest. I am also enclosing
a short list of some pieces you would find suitable for your
players, with the names of the publishers. I do not know the
cost of each, but usually this runs from about 7 to 12 shillings
for a set of parts. Not many pieces have full scores, which is a
great pity.

        I hope you will be able to come to England some time and hear
our bands; the Belle Vue contest at Manchester in September or
the national championship in London in October would be of the
greatest interest to you.

        Please do not hesitate to let me know if I can help you.

cerely Denis Wright.

Denis being greeted by a Danish band

a strong bond developed between Denis and the whole Danish band movement. According to Herbert, Denis more than anyone else was responsible for the improvement of playing standards and for the introduction of a new repertoire and a more cultured style of playing.

In 1957 Herbert's FDF Band changed its name to *Concord Brass Band* and became the spearhead of the Danish brass band movement. In a letter published in *The British Bandsman* of 5th October that year Herbert painted a picture of banding in Denmark. There was no such thing as a 'band movement' he said, as he complained of a 'catastrophic lack of good bandmasters.' He went on to say that most Danish bands played in what he called a 'heavy, old-fashioned German way' and that in their one band contest per year, brass and military bands were mixed together, a fact which often led, he said, to 'contentious results'. In an attempt to popularise the 'British sound' Herbert hosted a programme on Danish State Radio, playing recordings by well-known English brass bands.

In the letter Herbert also announced that Dr. Denis Wright was to visit Denmark for a week of rehearsals with his own band.

Some weeks later a letter appeared in *The British Bandsman* from Bertil Hansson of Limhamn Church Youth Band in Sweden. The band scene in Sweden was, he said, quite similar to that in Denmark, as described by Herbert. He went on to ask if it would be possible for Dr. Wright to pay a visit to Sweden when he came to Denmark. A quick response said that this was being looked into.

Dr. Denis Wright

(London)

Concord Brass

COPENHAGEN,   31st May, 1958

BAND no. 3

Tuning (20)   Technique (20)   Musicianship (20)

17   16   16   ℨ

TOTAL   49

Minuet   Some wrong notes going on in 6th & 7th bars.
Tone is well blended except when cornets go high and
force the tone.   I think you are inclined to pull
the music about too much and spoil its flow.
6th bar of 2nd section someone plays F♮ instead of #.
Individual technique shows some weak spots, such
as the 4 semiquavers not smooth or even.

Nabucco   Well controlled quiet playing in the opening, but
when ff the Top cornets get fierce and rough. The
phrasing is well managed, basses etc, 2 bars before
the Allegro.   Some very nice playing after C; effective.
But it got loose in the Andante after D.
      Cort's tone rather hard in the 3/4 and he flattens on some
upper notes.   Perhaps more attention could have been made
to the quiet moments — you do not often get down to a real p!
      Allegro — not quite enough "snap" in it at first, a bit
more stacc. wanted. But from J it is good.
      This performance was full of interest & showed a well
trained band, in spite of a few individual weak spots.

Grotesque   Spirited playing, nicely neat & well together. Soprano
does his little bit well.

Exultation   This is played with musical understanding, & the
dynamic contrasts are well made. Internal balance good.
This band has been making _music_ ! Well done.

The first of Denis's many visits to the two countries took place between 31st May and 9th June 1958. It was an eventful and productive few days, the bulk of the time being spent rehearsing Concord, but Denis also 'nipping across the water' to spend a couple of days in Malmö rehearsing the Limhamn band which, like Concord, had originated from a church voluntary youth organisation.

The week was almost a repeat of that which Denis had spent in Holland some seven years earlier, and on the Sunday the two bands combined for a concert in the Tivoli Concert Hall, with Denis conducting, and with an enthusiastic audience of around 800.

Denis also adjudicated a mini-contest and gave a lecture to some 40 bandmasters of FDF bands from all over Denmark. The bands taking part in the contest were Concord and Limhamn, along with another Danish band taking an interest in developments, FDF Lynby. On page 193 can be seen a copy of the *Remarks* for Concord's performance, showing a most caring mix of criticism, praise and encouragement.

In 1959 Denis returned to Copenhagen to repeat the exercise, though this time there were four bands.

Denis's work with Concord in these early years introduced a new standard of musicianship to Danish bands and during the course of the early 1960s more and more of them decided to change over to British instrumentation.

The British Bandsman of 2nd July 1960 reported that Denis was to return to Denmark again to run a training course for conductors, and to rehearse Concord prior to a concert in the Tivoli Concert Hall. Herbert paints a picture on a broader canvass though:

'Massed band concerts also took place in Sweden, and the ferryboat travel to Malmö and back provided many happy hours - especially the return journeys after the concerts, with modest drinking and lots of fun. The young ladies of the bands loved him; he was a perfect English gentleman, very charming and extremely polite, and here also he gave us new standards.'

In 1961 Denis again worked with Concord, this time in preparation for a concert at the Hamlet Castle Kronborg in Helsingør - a prelude to the famous Hamlet Festival, starring Sir Lawrence Olivier.

Herbert's high regard for Denis never waned. He wrote,

'Denis was always ahead of his time; he had tremendous ability in doing things before anyone else thought of the idea. In Denmark, he recognised the need for the better education of bandmasters, and he programmed courses for them in a most efficient way. He also suggested a number of people who would be able to help - Eric Ball, Harry Mortimer and the then young Geoffrey Brand.'

Leaving Denmark for the moment, let's look at some more of Denis's influence in Sweden. I mentioned Bertil Hansson's input to Denis's first Scandinavian visit. Another Swedish band musician, Kurt Hedberg, wrote to me about his memories of Denis in Sweden during the early 1960s.

(Above) Denis lecturing in Copenhagen.

(Below) With members of Concord before a concert in Frederiksborg Castle.

'When I met Denis Wright the first time, I played trombone in the LKU Band in Malmö, which he was guest-conducting. A few years later he conducted the LKU Band, together with the Concord Band of Copenhagen. We played one concert in Malmö and one in Copenhagen, and I can still remember how nervous I was when we played *Nabucco*.'

Kurt went on to form a new brass band in the village of Vaxtorp in the county of Halland. This was in 1963, and later that year he visited Denis whilst he was in Copenhagen, and told him of his new band and of the young players he was teaching. Denis suggested that he bring four of them to Britain to take part in a course with the NYBB. This suggestion was taken up in 1964 when three boys and a girl from Vaxtorp joined the Band's August course in Cardiff. (See page 235 for further details).

Following the Cardiff trip, Kurt was in regular contact with Denis. The Vaxtorp Band is still going strong, though Kurt retired as conductor after its 25th anniversary in1988. It was Peter Gartside who put me in touch with Kurt Hedberg, and Peter himself recalls attending one of Denis's courses in Sweden, as part of a Summer Camp.

'During the week sessions were held for bandmasters, under Dr. Denis Wright, and opportunity was given for the men to receive advice on conducting and band training. On the first Sunday night a contest was held between individual bands who had sufficient members in camp to play, and four bands competed before three judges - Dr. Denis, Paul Ivan Møller, solo trombone with the Danish Radio Orchestra and Peter Iversen, solo trumpet in Aalborg Symphony Orchestra.'

In June 1964 Denis was again in Denmark, working with Concord in Copenhagen, a band of selected players from FDF in Aarhus and directing yet another week's course in Silkeborg, training young conductors.

In 1965, Denis took part in a big FDF Summer School at Aalborg.[5] The King of Denmark - Frederick IX - was present and conducted the massed bands. Denis and he had quite a chat about music and music-making, and later Denis declared, "If this man was not a king he would be a professional conductor!" Earlier in 1965 Denis had visited a number of Danish bands, including Concord, ending with a massed band concert in Copenhagen.

Denis's last visit to Denmark took place in the Autumn of 1966. First he worked with Concord for a concert in Tivoli Gardens, and then he ran a wind band course in Jutland. Herbert Møller was there, and he recalls how much Denis enjoyed himself, both musically and socially. On one evening he became 'guest conductor' of a Tyrolean band and, as Herbert says,

'There he was; standing on a table, hair down, and doing all the things you should not do! To see him enjoying himself, and giving us all a good laugh, showed him to be a man with a great personality, and with the ability to combine hard work with having a good time.'

Sadly, Denis had passed away six months later, but there is no doubt in Herbert's mind that in the decade or so of his involvement, it was Denis who helped to make the Danish Amateur Band Movement into 'An onward-looking organisation, with strong musical ideas and the will and ability to work in the future to an even higher level of musical abilities.'

The Rest of the World

The foregoing represents Denis's contribution overseas mainly - though not exclusively - to the world of brass bands. His other overseas work was largely of a non-brass banding nature. For example, en route to New Zealand in 1951 he did some sort of broadcast - probably a talk - during a stopover in Singapore.

The British Bandsman of 26th November 1955 announced that Denis was to leave the BBC at the end of the year. It also gave details of an epic tour he was planning for the New Year:

'On February 12th (1956) Dr. Wright leaves England for a 4-month tour during which he will visit Ceylon, Malaya, Australia, New Zealand and Rhodesia. He has a long list of engagements: band and orchestral concerts, University lectures and teachers' training courses, and a large number of broadcast talks. He is to judge the New Zealand Band Championships at Invercargill in March, and has also been invited to judge the Queensland Championships at Brisbane at Easter.'

After a week in Colombo (in what was then Ceylon, but since 1972 renamed Sri Lanka) giving 12 broadcast talks, he moved on to Singapore for two broadcasts on Radio Malaysia. This was followed by a week in Sydney, Australia, where he directed a short course for bandsmen before finally moving on to New Zealand.

After three months of intensive work there (discussed earlier in this chapter), he now started to head for home, but not without a couple of stopovers - one in Johannesburg where he conducted a couple of orchestral concerts for the South African Broadcasting Corporation, and the other for a few days in Rhodesia (now Zimbabwe) for a concert with the Bulawayo Symphony Orchestra, arriving back in England on 23rd June, after a tour lasting over four months.

During the early part of 1959 his work for UNESCO took him to Strasburg, as Britain's representative on a committee convened to draw up rules for international band contests, and around the same time, he went to Paris to represent Britain on an international panel of judges in a competition for new music for bands.

Then, following the work he had done in Australia and New Zealand in 1959, he returned home via Canada. To his surprise, he found quite a number of flourishing brass bands here, even outside the Salvation Army. He spent his first week in the Toronto area, giving talks, broadcasting and doing some conducting, including a massed band concert in Oshawa, on the shores of Lake Ontario, and part of a concert given by two Salvation Army bands in Toronto itself. Interestingly, the bandmaster of one of these was from Britain, and had been a student on the first of Denis's WEA Summer Schools (see page 200).

At the Hong Kong Music Festival

Following a few days' holiday in the Canadian capital, Ottawa, Denis moved on to the French-speaking city of Montreal for the last two concerts of this strenuous tour. These were with the Montreal Brass Ensemble, a group which at that time had a rather peculiar collection of instruments, including trumpets and French horns as well as a tenor horn and some euphoniums, and an unusual instrument which Denis had apparently not come across previously, an E♭ soprano flugel horn.

He felt that the players in this group were of a higher standard than those in some of the the brass bands he'd come across in Canada, though he complained of a hardness in their tone, and that he had experienced difficulty "in inducing them to play softly."

He returned to Canada in 1963 for a coast-to-coast tour on which he adjudicated at 11 major music festivals during the space of three months. He was one of a team of five adjudicators who all started off in Toronto, split up to work individually in smaller towns and then linked up in one of the major cities in the West - possibly Vancouver, according to Mrs. Wright.

On 27th February 1966 Denis left England for what was to be his last long-distance tour. Much of his travelling abroad had been alone. Providentially, on this one he was accompanied by Mrs. Wright and, mixing business with pleasure (the business side being adjudicating at the 10th

Hong Kong Schools Music Festival), the two followed this up with some holiday in Ceylon, Thailand and India, before returning home on 19th April.

The Hong Kong Festival is one of the largest of its kind in the world. In 1966 there were 3,000 entries in 900 classes, spread over a period of 17 days - and Denis was one of a team of five adjudicators. For the preliminaries, the adjudicators visited little schools in country districts, and the Finals were in Hong Kong's City Hall, which Mrs. Wright recalls was 'most impressive'. Denis remarked that standards varied considerably, but were pretty low in brass and woodwind classes. He also said that due to a shortage of good band trainers, the standard of bands in Hong Kong was not good. There were great language problems for Westerners, as most people spoke only Chinese.

A few months later, Denis was off to Denmark again, as already explained, and that brought to an end his 'missionary' work. It had been of mammoth proportions and there can have been few people who have exceeded - or even equalled - this amout of overseas work, combined with a heavy schedule of work in his own country at the same time.

Notes

[1] This must be one of Denis's deliberate 'mis-quotes'

[2] *UNESCO* - the United Nations Educational, Scientific and Cultural Organisation - a specialised agency of the UN established in 1945 to promote international cooperation in education, science and culture. The United Kingdon withdrew from membership in 1985.

[3] *Harry Farrington* played solo horn for Munn & Felton's and Fairey's before emigrating to New Zealand in the mid-1950s.

[4] *FDF* (Frivilligt Drenge-Forbund), or Boys' Voluntary Organisation was formed in Denmark in 1902, taking its inspiration and objects from Britain's Boys' Brigade.

[5] This was apparently one of the festivals held every 5 years by FDF for its bands. On this particular occasion 1100 boys assembled in Aalborg in North Jutland for the 9th 'Landsorkestertaevne' - with 500 brass instrumentalists and 600 drummers. There was also a military band from the Finnish Boys' Brigade and the Drum and Pipe Band of the 92nd Belfast Company of the Boys' Brigade.

Chapter 25

The 1950s - Year by Year

As we saw in the previous chapter, throughout the 1950s Denis was doing much of his work abroad, extending his policy of educating far beyond the realms of Britain and its brass bands, and in 1952 he founded the National Youth Brass Band of Great Britain - which would inevitably take up much of his time, and to which the next chapter is devoted.

He also continued with the usual round of on-going activities such as examining for the Bandsman's College of Music (both in the practicals and the setting and marking of paperwork), the Alexander Owen Memorial Fund Scholarship, adjudicating and conducting, and of course he remained on the staff of the BBC until the end of 1955. He apparently founded what was known as *The Westminster Orchestra,* a group of close on 50 musicians which broadcast quite regularly, sometimes under Denis's baton, and generally in a series known as the *London Studio Concerts.* Even after his 'retirement' he continued to work for the Corporation, producing specific programmes or projects, on a one-off contractual basis. There was also a great deal that he did in the way of special events, and it is mainly on these that I wish to concentrate in this chapter.

1950

Early in the year, Denis delivered a lecture to the English-Speaking Union on the subject of *Amateur Music-Making.* April saw him in the chair for the Annual Convention of the National Association of Brass Band Conductors, and later in the year he officiated at a 'hymn tune and judging' competition for the Association. He also wrote the Foreword for a new book published towards the end of the year - Kenneth Cook's *The Bandsman's Everything Within.*

But one of his most significant engagements during 1950 was directing a brass band conductor's course for the Workers' Educational Association (WEA). Thirty students attended - including some Salvation Army bandmasters. They formed a band and took turns at conducting under Denis's guidance. The course was hailed as a great success. One visitor to the course, just for a couple of days, was a Norwegian so, even though Denis didn't ever go to Norway, he may just have planted a few tiny seeds there. This was one of the first of many conductors' courses which Denis ran, though he did the WEA one only for one more year, after which Leonard Davies took over.

Backstage at Huddersfield, 1950 (Jack Atherton, Jack Mackintosh, Denis, Fred Mortimer and Milnes Wood - B & R's Bandmaster)

Amongst the contests which Denis adjudicated this year was the Edinburgh Festival, where he awarded 1st prize to CWS (Manchester) for what he described as "an almost flawless performance." His conducting appointments included the first of his 11 appearances as guest conductor of the massed band concerts organised by Brighouse and Rastrick Band in Huddersfield Town Hall. This was in March, the bands were Fairey's, Foden's and the hosts, Brighouse and Rastrick and, unusually for this series, there was a guest soloist - Jack Mackintosh.

Denis also conducted the massed bands at the Dome, Brighton this year, and a special one-off concert in Doncaster in aid of the terrible Creswell Colliery mining disaster. Three colliery bands played under his baton on that occasion - Carlton Main, Markham Main and Cresswell. This engagement reflected his close involvement with the mining bands of Yorkshire. In addition to these and other brass band concerts, he also conducted the British Imperial Military Band, the Pinner Orchestra, and a number of concerts with the Westminster Orchestra for the Trancription Service.

1951

The most important event for Denis this year was his visit to New Zealand (31st March-17th April - see page 184). There were a couple more NABBC competitions and his second WEA Summer School for conductors held in Shrewsbury.

Amongst his conducting work this year there were a couple of occasions when he was invited to guest conduct *Sounding Brass and Voices* for the BBC - one with Brighouse and Rastrick and the other with Fairey's, and he took part in a massed band concert in the Royal Albert Hall in May, sharing the podium with Sir Adrian Boult and Harry Mortimer.

W.M.A. Brass Band Conductor's Summer School 1951. Denis with Leonard Davis (right) and Will Sahnow, organising secretary

Amongst his transcriptions this year one calls for special comment - even though I'm not sure it had more than one performance, and that is his score of the Cherubini *Requiem*, made in June and performed by the famous Treorchy Male Voice Choir from the Rhondda Valley.

1952

This seems to have been a quieter than average year - except that it was the year in which Denis founded the National Youth Brass Band of Great Britain. He did, however, write a series of three quite illuminating articles in *The British Bandsman* called *This Drumming Business*, and in November he ran a conductors' course in Workington. One small point of interest, and a link with Denis's overseas activities, is that Dr. Vernon Griffiths of New Zealand sat in as examiner for the November examinations of the Bandsman's College of Music, leading directly to similar examinations being set up in New Zealand and Australia.

1953

Amongst Denis's adjudicating appointments this year was a return visit to the Belle Vue September Contest - his first time there since 1933, but also the first of nine appearances before his death 14 years later.

As well as the usual round of conducting engagements he was invited to Dublin, in February, to conduct a performance of *Messiah* - not his brass band version, but with the Adelaide Choir and Orchestra. He returned later in the year for a repeat performance, and also to conduct Mendelssohn's *Elijah*. In addition to all this, he conducted more orchestral concerts for the BBC Transcription Service.

By now, Denis was on the Executive Council of the National Brass Band Club and in 1953 he was elected to represent the Club on the National Music Council, and to act as its British representative in Paris at UNESCO.

Another interesting appointment in 1953 was as an adjudicator, along with Eric Ball and Gordon Jacob in the preliminary stages of a Fred Mortimer Memorial Competition for new music for brass band.

1954

The NABBC continued to feature in Denis's schedule, and when his *Glastonbury* was selected as 3rd section Area test piece, they set up a lecture-demonstration, given by Philip Catelinet with Cable and Wireless Band. Denis was present and at the end gave a half-hour talk on points which had been raised. But the Association's most enterprising activity in 1953 was a debate on the question *Is Brass Band Music Too Old?* Dr. Greenhouse Alt, Principal of Trinity College of Music acted as President, the distinguished conductor and broadcaster Antony Hopkins put the case that it WAS too old, whilst Denis, with support from Messrs. Mortimer and Mackintosh defended the opposite view. The event is recalled vividly by my colleague Bill England, secretary of the NYBB and for many years closely linked with the National

With leader and principals of 'Messiah', Dublin 1953

Brass Band Club. Again, Cable and Wireless were on hand to give musical demonstrations, but though the debate was quite a lively affair alas, it seems that Denis and his team failed to convince and came second!

An interesting question raised by Hopkins during the debate was, *Why can't ALL brass band instruments be muted?* Well, these days they can, and we also have a wider choice of mute than did brass band players in 1954.

In a June issue of *The British Bandsman* this year, Denis revealed his 'method' of adjudicating. He said he did not fill in details of points for this or that aspect on the remarks sheet, "partly because one needs to be a very quick mathematician (which I am not) and partly because I believe the method used in ordinary music festivals is fairer." This involved awarding 50% of the marks for technique and the other 50% for musicianship. Contesting appointments this year included Belle Vue in both May and September.

Another Denis Wright special arrangement received its first performance this year. It had been commissioned by Butterfield Tank Works Band from near Bradford and was included in a concert which they gave and in which Denis appeared as guest conductor. It was yet another of those bridge-building exercises, in the shape of Handel's *Organ Concerto in Bb Major* ('*Hallelujah*'). Also included in the concert were excerpts from *Messiah*.

Later in the year Denis undertook his third trip to Dublin to visit the Adelaide Choir and Orchestra to direct a performance of the Brahms *Requiem*.

1955

It was the National Brass Band Club (NBBC) which figured high in this year's work, and quite early in the year Denis was one of several leading band personalities invited, as a representative of the Club, to the Service of Dedication of the Musicians' Memorial Chapel in the Church of St. Sepulchre in the City of London. In this Chapel now stands the Book of Remembrance for bandsmen who gave their lives in the War. This was an idea initiated by the NBBC as part of its Empire Memorial Trust.

Denis's work for UNESCO on behalf of the NBBC continued, and *The British Bandsman* this year contained several lengthy reports about his efforts towards the standardisation of pitch, and the rationalisation of the different names and keys of instruments used in bands throughout Europe.

The annual round of Dublin concerts this year saw Denis conducting *Messiah* and Haydn's *The Creation*. He wrote a couple of lengthy articles in *The British Bandsman* on the subject of 'This Test Piece Business' - pleading for a balance between technical demands and musical quality, and also pointing out the economical problems faced by music publishers. Towards the end of the year he held one of his week-end courses for conductors - this time on behalf of the London and Home Counties Amateur Band Association.

In November Denis and Miss Maud Thomson were married, then finally came the dramatic announcement that after 19 years with the BBC he was to leave. He did so on 31st December 1955 and was then, technically, out of work!

1956

Denis Wright out of work? Never!

Freed from the shackles of his work at the BBC, he now planned his momentous four-month tour - discussed in Chapter 24. Another event worth recording this year was the directing of a Ministry of Education course, in collaboration with Elizabeth Lumb (also a key figure in the founding of the NYBB), for school teachers wishing to start up a school brass band - more pioneering and educating.

After an absence of several years his name appeared in the list of composers of test pieces for the Belle Vue contests, with the selection of his *Tam o' Shanter's Ride*.

There was the usual round of adjudicating and conducting, including his regular trip across the Irish sea to conduct oratorio, and at the conclusion of the Belle Vue September Contest (of which he was also a member of the adjudicator's panel) he was awarded the Iles Silver Medal of the Worshipful Company of Musicians 'For services to brass bands'. This was the first of several awards to come his way.

One sour note which creeps into the annals this year is that, along with one or two other noted personalities, he had a difference of opinion with the NABBC and resigned his Vice-Presidency.

The BBC were apparently reluctant to let Denis cut completely loose, and during this year he was contracted to assemble 13 programmes for the Transcription Service from the Edinburgh Festival.

A couple of years earlier Denis had started displaying a 'Professional Card', and in December 1956 he began a series of advertisements which read;

BRASS BAND SCORING

Dr. Denis Wright is now available to help composers with the scoring of their works for brass and military band, also harmonisation, revision and editing of MSS. Tuition in Theory, Composition, etc. (Personal in London or by correspondence).

1957

Without doubt, the outstanding event this year was the BBC Light Music Festival which took place at the Royal Festival Hall in June. Taking part were the BBC Concert Orchestra and Harry Mortimer's All-Star Band. Two things were of special interest to brass band people - a competition, 'New Music for Brass', and a new composition for orchestra and brass band.

Denis's involvement in the first of these was as one of a panel of six adjudicators whose task it was to select five pieces to be played on the night by the All-Star Band, when a different panel nominated the actual winner. As a matter of interest there were two winning pieces, *Automation* by Frank Stokes and *Honeymoon Express* by Hanley and Field. Both achieved a degree of short-term popularity, but one piece which made it into the finals and had more lasting success was *Mosaic* by the young Elgar Howarth. The adjudicators commended it as a piece 'of outstanding musical value', but adding that it was some way outside the terms of the competition, which required it to be 'playable by the average brass band and with popular entertainment value'. I think time has proved their comments to be well founded.

But to the other point of interest and to the concert itself, broadcast live in the BBC Light Programme. Shared by the Concert Orchestra and the All-Stars, its climax came when both combined for the première of a work for orchestra AND brass band - the first of its kind, as far as I know. Denis had been commissioned to write and conduct that historic first performance. He chose as the basis of the work the *Helston Furry Dance* more commonly known these days as *The Floral Dance*, and he gave it the title *Cornish Holiday*. It was hailed as a brilliant success, and as light music in its truest sense. Part of the report from page 1 of *The British Bandsman* of 29th June is worth quoting:

'. . . the musical content, and particularly the orchestration, carried the judgement of the many eminent musicians present, and it was felt that this unique work was a considerable achievement.

Dr. Denis Wright himself conducted, and brought out the many and felicitous effects with clarity and elan. Not only were the two contrasted groups used in ensemble and antiphonally, but sections of both were used together with excellent effects, many of which underlined the possibility of the extension of the brass band instrumentation. For example, a theme for cornets, repeated immediately by orchestral trumpets clearly demonstrated how variety could be added to the treble instruments of the band; and an orchestral french-horns solo, accompanied by a pulsating rhythm from brass band horn and baritones, was similarly revealing.

Strings riding high over the accompanying brass band of something like 50 players must have proved to any anti-brass listeners that our bands are not alone in being able to produce a great and joyful noise - in this case a thrilling effect; and it was noted, as we already knew, that in a tremendous fortissimo by the whole ensemble, a piccolo could ride above everything else.'

Obviously a piece such as this was not going to have many performances in its original version, so Denis re-scored it both for brass band and for military band, as well as in a version for orchestra alone, recorded by the Concert Orchestra the day before the Festival Hall Concert for the Transcription Service. The Irish Guards (under Capt. C. H. Jaeger) featured the military band version on its Australian tour and this led directly to another orchestra and band performance, in Adelaide the following January.

Other activities this year included being involved as one of a panel of three international adjudicators in a competition for a military band composition, adjudicating the Grand Shield contest at Belle Vue (where *Tintagel* was the test piece) and contributing a chapter headed *Brass Colour Contrasts* to a book edited by Frank Wright called *Brass Today*. He continued his work for the Bandsman's College of Music, but it seems that around this time he stopped examining for the Alexander Owen Memorial Fund Scholarship, though he continued to set the theory papers.

1958

By now the National Youth Brass Band was in its sixth year and was beginning to have a small but significant effect on the brass band movement as a whole. Other bodies were soon to be looking to do the same kind of thing - though perhaps on a smaller scale - and it was in 1958 that the first of these took effect.

From early on in the year there were discussions about a 'Music School for Youths', to take place in St. Andrew's, Scotland. It was to be under the auspices of the Scottish Amateur Music Association - then only two years old, having taken over some of the activities of the Music Committee of the Carnegie Trust.[1] An approach was made to the NYBB for advice, and David Merchant, the Music Adviser for Fife, spent a day on a Youth Band course to find out exactly how it worked.

Drake Rimmer was put in charge of the venture and he invited Denis to be Guest Conductor of this, the first course of what was to become the National Youth Brass Band of Scotland. Rather like our own NYBB courses, it lasted a week. There were 53 young people on it, including six girls, and the music was borrowed from the library of the NYBB. At the end of the week a concert was given in the Young Graduates Hall of the Madras College in St. Andrew's Fife, where the course had been held and, to everyone's delight, Harry Mortimer turned up to record part of the concert for the BBC.

Following the success of *Cornish Holiday* in 1957, the exercise was repeated this year, the outcome being *Casino Carnival*.

Two years earlier, Denis had been presented with the Iles Silver Medal, following the Belle Vue September contest. At the conclusion of the Nationals in October 1958 he was honoured in the Royal Albert Hall in 'Spotlight on Service', when he was presented with a Baton of Honour 'for long and valued service to the brass band movement.' The presentation was made by Edric Cundell, Principal of the Guildhall School of Music and Drama, and following the presentation Denis 'Directed the assembled massed bands in a colourful performance of some marches.'

1959

This was another big overseas tour year, Denis spending a total of 18 weeks in New Zealand, Australia and Canada. This obviously restricted the work he did closer to home. Or did it?

The year began on a high note when he received his highest honour, the O.B.E. The recommendation had been submitted by the National Brass Band Club, with support from a number of eminent conductors, and the citation made special reference to Denis's work as Founder and Music Director of the National Youth Brass Band of Great Britain.

Mr. Molinari, Secretary of the NBBC had, to a large degree, instigated the submission and, characteristically, Denis sent him the following note:

> "It pleases me that this award would seem to imply official recognition of approval of our own NYBB and I am very, very grateful to all of you good people who have done so much to make that Band a success."

Edric Cundell presents the Baton of Honour

On his return from the 18-week venture he was almost immediately off to Llangollen in North Wales to join the panel of adjudicators for the choral classes of the famous International Eisteddfod. This was the first of a number of times he was so involved.

Having successfully helped in the launch of the National Youth Brass Band of Scotland in 1958, Denis now became involved in the inauguration of the Cornwall Youth Band, taking the form of a 4-day course in St. Austell, culminating in a Drumhead Service and Concert on the Sunday afternoon. Denis was also Guest Conductor for the second course of the Scottish National Youth Band. 61 players attended the Cornish course, whilst 73 - representing an increase of 50% - attended in Scotland.

The 3-year estrangement between Denis and the NABBC had apparently been resolved, because in February it was reported that he had again become a Vice-President. This resulted in a number of events with which the NABBC was associated. The first was a School for Conductors which they organised in conjunction with Brighton Silver Band.

During the week-end, Denis did a rehearsal demonstration with the band and also gave a talk, with tape recordings of the NYBB and called *My Work*

With Minors. Leonard Davies and Alfred Ashpole were also involved in the week-end, and together with Denis they formed a 'Brains Trust' for a Saturday evening session of *Any Questions?* He also adjudicated another NABBC competition for composers and arrangers, announcing his awards during the Convention later in the year.

On 3rd October Denis appeared for the seventh time as Guest Conductor of the Brighouse & Rastrick massed band concerts in Huddersfield Town Hall. Brighouse's guests on that occasion were Black Dyke and Besses, and part of the concert was recorded for the BBC Transcription Service.

So far, Denis's involvement with the National Brass Band Championships had been fairly minimal since that first post-war event when he had composed the test piece, *Overture for an Epic Occasion.* Granted, he had been featured in *Spotlight on Service* in 1958, and perhaps it was this which spurred the 'powers' into involving him more. Be that as it may, in 1959 he adjudicated the Championship Section in the Royal Albert Hall, along with Frank Wright and Harold Moss and was also one of the two Assistant Conductors to Sir Arthur Bliss in the Gala Concert.

Later in the year he adjudicated at the contest of the Wessex Brass Band Association in Bournemouth and appeared jointly with Charles Groves, then Conductor of the Bournemouth Symphony Orchestra, as Guest Conductor in the evening concert.

Thus we come to the end of the 1950s, a decade during which Denis cut loose from his work with the BBC whilst yet maintaining important links, a decade in which he had founded his beloved National Youth Brass Band of Great Britain, when he had done a vast amount of work abroad, and during which time he did so many other things - diverse as well as constructive, and seemingly always with a sense of purpose.

Note

[1] *The Carnegie Trust* is one of a number of Trusts and Foundations which benefited from the 70 million pounds legacy of Andrew Carnegie (1835-1919). *The Scottish Amateur Music Association* was founded in 1955 and, helped by a grant from the Carnegie UK Trust, took over the work of an informal Music Committee, created in 1940 by the Trust, to help with war-time music policies in Scotland. Since its founding, SAMA has funded a number of brass band commissions and has also helped greatly with the financing of the National Youth Brass Band of Scotland.

Chapter 26

The NYBB - A Lasting Tribute

On Saturday, 25th April 1992, in London's Barbican Concert Hall, there was a Gala Concert in celebration of the 40th anniversary of the National Youth Brass Band of Great Britain. This organisation has been dubbed 'The lasting tribute of Dr. Denis Wright', and it has often been said that had he done nothing else but found this institution, his life would have been worth while.

> 'The National Youth Brass Band of Great Britain was founded in 1952 and exists to provide an opportunity for young people to play brass band music to the highest standards. Residential courses lasting for one week are held twice each year at various centres, with intensive rehearsals culminating in prestige concerts. More than 2,000 players have taken part in the courses since the Band's formation. Many are now leading players and conductors in the band world. Others have become professional orchestral players and soloists, some with international reputations.'

So begins the Band's publicity hand-out, putting in a nut-shell what it is all about.

Returning to the 40th anniversary concert, guest soloists included Phillip McCann, the NYBB's Leader (principal cornet player) from 1963 until Denis's last course at Easter, 1967. In the finale former Leaders joined forces with the NYBB. These included Maurice Murphy (now principal trumpet of the LSO), Richard Evans (Musical Director of BNFL Band), John Berryman (Musical Director of Rigid Containers Group Band), John Clay and Jennifer Gillingham along with Phillip, now Musical Director of Sellers Engineering Band. All of these had been Leaders of the Youth Band during the 15 years in which Denis was its Music Adviser. Eleven other Leaders from later years were also on stage, creating both a great sight and a great sound.

But let's look back and examine some of the background to the founding of the NYBB.

Instrumental teaching in schools in some areas had begun during the 1940s, and *The British Bandsman* of 23rd August 1947 reports on 'the newly formed Boys' Band Association of Yorkshire', and preparations for a massed band concert, to be held in the Eastbrook Hall in Bradford.

It was during the evening of this concert, on 25th October, that the idea for a national youth brass band was first mooted. The concert had been organised by Elizabeth Lumb (later Mrs. Peet), Arthur Atkinson (Bradford Boys' Band) and Ralph Nellist (Hall Royd). Denis conducted, and present in the audience was Ruth Railton, who formed the National Youth Orchestra of Great Britain, and was on the look-out for good young brass players. During a post-concert conversation with Miss Railton (later Dame Ruth Railton), Denis posed the question,

"If we can have a National Youth Orchestra, then why can't we also have a National Youth Brass Band?"

To which Miss Railton replied 'Why not, indeed?' And thus the seed was sown.

It was some time before the buds began to appear, and the next step is not recorded until 19th August 1950, when *The British Bandsman* had a feature headed

YOUTH MASSED BAND AT LEEDS

It referred to a concert to be organised by the National Association of Brass Band Conductors (of which Denis was an Executive Member) to take place in Leeds Town Hall on 26th November, with about 100 boys and girls from school and youth bands. The article stated:

'For some months plans have been on foot to establish a Youth Brass Band of national status on much the same lines as the National Youth Orchestra and already several Educational Authorities have shown interest in the idea. The Leeds concert, it is hoped, will demonstrate to the various music advisers what can be accomplished by the youth of this country in ensemble brass playing.'

The feature goes on to say that plans for the 'Youth Brass Band' include a holiday school in which, 'Collective instrumental training by the best teachers available will play as large a part as the actual massed rehearsals.'

Then, *The British Bandsman* of 24th February, 1951 announced:

THE NATIONAL YOUTH BRASS BAND - Inaugural Meeting

This is a report of a meeting held in Manchester on 27th January, 'attended by a representative cross-section of the brass band movement and Educational Authorities at which it was decided to proceed with the organisation of a National Youth Brass Band.'

The idea was to give children of school age who played brass instruments opportunities to meet together for music-making for a week at a time, to receive group tuition on their instruments from the finest teachers available, and to form a composite band to rehearse under a recognised conductor, with a concert at the end of the week's activities. Everyone would live together during these weeks under properly supervised boarding school conditions. Students would pay fees, but these would be kept as low as possible - which probably meant running at a loss - and which is exactly what has happened throughout the history of the NYBB.

Sir Malcolm Sargent had shown interest in the scheme and expressed a willingness to become the first President as long as he wasn't expected to DO anything, while Messrs. J. Henry Iles, who had promised his support in *The British Bandsman* and Harry Mortimer, Herbert Bennett and Dr. R.

Maldwyn Price, representing England, Scotland and Wales respectively, had agreed to become Vice-Presidents. Denis was appointed Acting Chairman, and Leonard Davies - as Acting Secretary - wrote to prominent brass band personalities in all parts of the country, asking if they would serve on the controlling Council. He also offered the free use of his office at the Parr School of Music as the postal headquarters of the band.

As a result of the response to his enquiries, a further meeting took place in Manchester, on 26th May, when the original Council was formed, comprised of the following:

Miss Elizabeth Lumb, Bradford teacher and leading figure in Yorkshire school bands
Mr. R. E. Austin of East Anglia
Mr. John R. Carr, conductor and composer from the North East
Mr. A. V. Creasey, Chairman of No. 1 Centre NABBC
Mr. W. F. Hannaford, JP, President of the Scottish Amateur Brass Band Association

---

THE NATIONAL
YOUTH BRASS BAND

President :
SIR MALCOLM SARGENT

Vice Presidents :
HARRY MORTIMER, O.B.E.
DR. R. MALDWYN PRICE   HERBERT BENNETT

Founder and Chairman :
DR. DENIS WRIGHT

APPLICATIONS for membership of The National Youth Brass Band are invited from young Brass Band players. Applicants should be 18 years of age and under.

The band will meet in Bradford, Yorks, for a week's training during the Easter Holidays in 1952 (April 12th—19th inclusive).

The week will be under the direction of a well-known Conductor and individual tuition will be given by the best teachers available.

Closing date for applications—29th February, 1952.

Application forms and full particulars can be obtained from :—

LEONARD DAVIES, Secretary, The National Youth Brass Band, Wellington Chambers, 2 Victoria Street, Manchester, 3.

Mr. William Haydock, Musical Director of Bickershaw Colliery Band
Mr. W. J. (Bill) Hume, Band Manager of Fairey Aviation Works Band
Mr. W. G. Jerwood, MBE, a well-known band personality in the West Country
Mr. Reg Little, Musical Director, Rhyl Urban District Council (also a noted conductor)
Mr. Tommy Morcombe, Band Manager of Morris Motors Band
Mr. R. H. Penrose, Secretary of the South West Brass Band Association
Mr. I. Perrin of Birmingham
Mr. Maurice Teasdale, Secretary of Cresswell Colliery Band
Mr. F. G. Tyrell of Cardiff
Mr. A. J.Williams of Swansea

Denis, as Founder, was elected Chairman, and Leonard Davies became Secretary. A Constitution was agreed and plans put in hand for the first course. At a further meeting in Manchester in September the raising of finance was discussed, and plans made for the assembling of the band. From the outset, the work of the NYBB was intended to supplement, not to replace, the training which the young players received in their own bands. The idea was to add musicianship to the technical training they were already getting, and to provide a training in artistry which would make them of more value in their own bands.

Early in 1952 the organisation of the course started in earnest with advertisements in *The British Bandsman* and *Brass Band News*. *The British Bandsman* of 12th January 1952 revealed,

'The syllabus for the week has been drafted; on most days this includes half an hour's ear-training, two full band rehearsals of 1½ hours each, and periods for group instrumental tuition.'

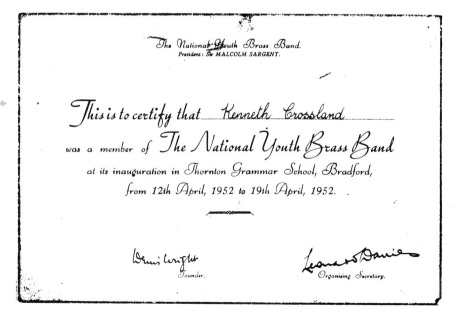

The National Youth Brass Band.
President : Sir MALCOLM SARGENT.

This is to certify that Kenneth Crossland was a member of The National Youth Brass Band at its inauguration in Thornton Grammar School, Bradford, from 12th April, 1952 to 19th April, 1952.

Founder.   Organising Secretary.

Applications were invited from young brass players between the ages of 13 and 18 wishing to take part in 'this unique week of music-making.' In *The British Bandsman* of 8th March more information was given:

'We can now announce the names of the tutors who have kindly undertaken to give group instrumental instruction under the general supervision of Harry Mortimer, OBE. These are: Willie Lang and Joe Wood (Black Dyke), C. J. (Cliff) Edmunds (Morris Motors), Tom Atkinson (Bradford Victoria) and George Kaye, BBCM, (Hepworth Silver).'

And so, the National Youth Brass band of Great Britain was founded in 1952, and the first residential course held in Bradford. It was a huge success and the final concert received good coverage in the band press. The Yorkshire correspondent 'Broadacre', in *The British Bandsman* of 3rd May wrote:

'One of the best brass band concerts I have ever heard was held at Bradford on the 19th ult., given by the National Youth Brass Band, composed of 90 boys and girls drawn from all parts of England. This was the finale of a week's Convention held at Thornton Grammar School during Easter week, under the direction of Dr. Denis Wright. The hall was packed with bandsmen, conductors and friends. The programme was by no means an easy one, but the way in which every item was played made them appear to be child's play to these youngsters. First, a new march *On Your Way*, was excellently played; then *Tancredi* and two new *Lyric Pieces* by Dr. Wright, the caprice *Zelda* was played by Maurice Murphy, a quintet in which the top cornet player was little Michael Blackburn from Leicester, aged 9, *The War March of the Priests*, *Nimrod*, Beethoven's *Mignonne* suite, euphonium solo, *The Allegro Spiritoso*, played by Martin N. (Norman) Burnham, *The Londonderry Air* and *Shepherds Hey*, a trombone canon - *Lover and His Lass*, the waltz *Espana* and finally, *The Grand March from Aida*.

All these items held the audience spellbound. This is the first appearance of the NYBB, and can only mean one thing; it will not be the last. The next session is to be held at Reading in August.'

Denis himself gave a full factual account of this first course in three articles in *The British Bandsman* during May and June. Everything had gone according to plan and he was obviously well-pleased with the results. On the Thursday the NYBB made the first of its many recordings for the BBC, playing a short programme for the North Region Children's Newsreel. Though the course was in Thornton Grammar School - some three miles from the centre of Bradford - the final concert was in the hall of another school - larger and in the city itself - at Carlton Grammar School.

Returning to the Barbican programme for the 40th anniversary, Mrs. Wright says:

'My greatest impression, looking back, is the contrast on the practical side. In 1952 young people did not normally go away from home to attend Summer Schools. These didn't exist, nor were there the residential colleges which exist today. Those early courses were held in ordinary day schools;

beds were borrowed, hired or otherwise acquired. Classrooms became dormitories; the school dinner ladies did the catering, and all staff, including the tutors, were on a rota for 24-hour duty, including dormitory patrol. These days, of course, excellent facilities are available, usually with accommodation in individual study bedrooms.

Much work and planning behind the scenes is involved throughout the year, and we have been well served by our administration. During these 40 years there have been only three organising secretaries: the late Leonard Davies, Stan Reakes, and the present secretary, Bill England. To them, much of the success belongs, and the fact that in such a long period there have been only three is proof enough of their dedication. Dedication is, in fact, the description that could be applied to all tutors, house staff and officers, most of whom have given many years' service.

This anniversary also celebrates those other essential founders of the NYBB - the parents of the students on that first-ever course. They were prepared to let their children take part in something new and unknown. Without their goodwill and foresight, we would not be celebrating *Forty Years Young*.[1]

CARLTON GRAMMAR SCHOOL

MANNINGHAM LANE, BRADFORD

SATURDAY, APRIL 19th, 1952, at 7 p.m.

THE
NATIONAL YOUTH
BRASS BAND

INAUGURAL

CONCERT
Conducted by
Dr. DENIS WRIGHT

PROGRAMME - SIXPENCE

Finally, those special people, the thousands of players who have attended courses over the years, and whose company and the results they have achieved have been the reward of those of us who have been closely involved with them. The man who started it all would, I know, be so very proud and grateful.'

Leaving the 40th anniversary and turning to the programme for the historic first concert in Carlton Grammar School on 15th April 1952. There's much to be gleaned from the somewhat austere-looking programme, which sold for sixpence (2½p).

As we have already seen, Denis himself directed the course and conducted the concert. The music played - obviously chosen with great care, considering the unknown quality of the 96 players who had applied to attend the course - adhered closely to Denis's principles of playing 'worthy' music. The concert opened with the first performance of a march specially written for the occasion by Mr. H. B. Hawley, a noted Yorkshire brass band personality. The title of the march was, appropriately, *On Your Way'*.

There were also some ensemble items - a feature of many future NYBB concerts - always played *without* conductor. Norman Burnham of Bradford, a past winner of the AOMF Scholarship played the euphonium solo *Allegro Spiritoso* (the 2nd part of the famous Senaillé piece) and Maurice Murphy,[2] as the Band's first Leader, was the soloist in *Zelda*.

Amongst the 96 players listed as the first members of the National Youth Brass Band in addition to the two just named, were John Clough and Brian Broadbent - both to become long-serving euphonium players with Black Dyke, Peter Teal - who gave many years valuable service as a cornet player, first with the now defunct Crossley's Carpet Works Band and later with Brighouse and Rastrick, Richard Evans - already mentioned as Musical Director of BNFL, Geoffrey Boult, who went into the profession, playing trumpet with the Scottish National Orchestra and Ken Butterworth, a future member of the top cornet section of CWS (Manchester) Band during its vintage years under Alex Mortimer. Colin Monkman, also on that first course, became principal trombone with Black Dyke.

Four out of the 96 were girls, in contrast to the present ratio of about one third girls to two thirds boys. The young ladies on that first course were Renee Amyes of Bacup, Judith Brown of Doncaster, Grace Dinsdale of York and Ann Robinson of Upton.

Robert Mulholland, Managing Director of *Brass Band World,* one of brass bands' two leading journals, was also on that first course. On a later course he was to become the first of several young men to meet their wives-to-be in the NYBB when he met Jennifer Longson, the future Mrs. Mulholland.

Maurice Murphy remembers Denis as being pleasant, always very helpful and, in fact, 'a perfect gentleman'. John Clough, who played in the top cornet section on that first course has a clear recollection of Denis, saying, 'When he spoke he seemed to sing. There was a sort of rhythm in his speaking - and he *never* raised his voice.'

John remained with the NYBB for several courses, as did Richard Evans who, like John, was a founder member, but just a bit older, so he had to be 'pensioned off' after the fifth course. This is always a sad time - the parting from friends after that final concert. In Richard's case it was not as final as he thought, because Denis invited him back to course No. 6 to join the team of tutors, and also to have the honour of conducting the band - in just one piece.

During its early years the Band really had to fight for survival - both socially and financially. Many in the band world viewed it with suspicion, believing that those running it were 'on to a good thing' - lining their pockets from the huge profits they imagined the Band was making. This has never been the case. Another fear was that the Band would become a vehicle for steering young players from lower sections into better bands. I suppose the NYBB must plead guilty to this charge to some extent, because it must be admitted that, through their experiences in the Youth Band, many players have, sooner or later, been looking to 'better themselves'. Many of those who did became key players in famous bands. However, many other former members have preferred to devote their talents to teaching players and training youth and lower section bands. Thus, a cycle has become established in which talented young players come into the NYBB, have their musical development enhanced as a result, and in due course repay the band movement in one way or another.

Suspicions at this social level have no doubt contributed to the Band's constant fight for survival financially. Even with minimum fees and basic expenses, a staff of around 16 does cost money to assemble for two weeks every year, and there are inevitably certain year-round administrative costs. The cost of food and accommodation for band members and staff is considerable. Yet fees charged to students have to be realistic and affordable, and there has always been a substantial shortfall between the cost of running the Band and its income from student fees and profits (if any!) from concerts.

From the outset, to meet this shortfall the Band has relied on donations and gifts, and from time to time appeals have been made to the band movement to support its National Youth Brass Band. In those early years many thousands of letters were sent, begging for money from bands and individuals, from instrument makers, music publishers and the like.

Of course, bands also have their own financial problems and whilst several have been quite generous, contributions have never been on a scale which would give the NYBB the security it surely deserves.

The band press has always been supportive and even in those early years there was plenty of coverage - glowing accounts of courses and concerts - laced with constant appeals for funds. Visitors were always welcome to come and see the Band at work, and to find out for themselves how worthy of their support it was. I can't help thinking that it must have been Denis himself who coined this parody of a well-used phrase:

"Critics and cynics are also welcome. They may come to scoff and remain to praise!"

This comment was a reflection of much of the band world's attitude towards the efforts of the staff of the NYBB. For several years the band fought hard for both recognition and financial support. Although waxing and waning during the 40-plus years of the Band's history, recognition in musical terms has often been there, but the financial support which many believe the movement as a whole ought to be giving has never really materialised.

However, an article in *The British Bandsman* of 12th July 1952 said that provided the support of the movement was forthcoming, two courses a year would be held in the future. Well, so far this *has* happened so the support must have been there even though, at times, it may have seemed like getting blood out of the proverbial stone.

A far-sighted and even prophetic comment appeared in Eric Ball's Editorial Comment in *The British Bandsman* of 23rd August, shortly after the second course.

'Those who organise and teach the National Youth Brass Band can comfort themselves (if comfort they need!) with dreams of more distant future years, when the youngsters of today have become the conductors, players and counsellors of a brass band movement even finer, more musical and more widely recognised than it is today.'

Richard Evans was Leader for the Band's second course, held in Reading, when Harry Mortimer was Guest Conductor. This was the first of seven occasions on which Harry conducted the NYBB. The Band's third course was in Didsbury, Manchester, the first of nine courses taken by that other doyen of brass band conductors, Eric Ball. With such talent fronting the Band how could it fail?

John Berryman joined the NYBB for its fourth course, held at Southall. He tells me that in those days you did not have to pass an audition as is the case today - but that it simply needed a recommendation from some noted band personality. They did, however, have seating auditions, exactly as still happens. The tutors spend the first day testing their own sections and drawing up an order of merit. Prior to the first full rehearsal, all Band members assemble but don't take their seats. The tutors then read out the names, starting at the bottom and working up - from BB♭ Bass number whatever to the top solo cornet - the Leader. It is a tense moment and there are invariably some disappointments, but once the rehearsal starts all settle down to the serious business of learning their parts - most of which they will be sight-reading at that first rehearsal.

John also says that to save lips they sometimes held a quartet contest on the day of the final concert, forming double quartets to minimise the strain even further. Senior members of the Band conducted these groups, and John recalls that Richard Evans conducted the first group in which he played. This, John's first course, was the last one of Richard's and of Maurice Murphy's, and he became Leader on only his second course, holding the position a record nine times.

John also recalls sailing on the night boat to Belfast for the Easter, 1956 course. This has been the Band's only trip across the Irish Sea to date, and band members on that course included Brian Evans (one of the greatest soprano players of our time), Bryce Ford (another AOMF Scholarship winner), Anthony Parsons (now Principal Trombone with the BBC Symphony

National Youth Brass Band of Great Britain - inaugural course, Bradford, Easter 1952

Orchestra), and David James (John's successor as Leader). This was the first course that Denis had missed and the reason - he was adjudicating the Australian Championships.

David James[3], a future Leader of the NYBB apparently became the 'biter bit' on this Belfast course. The march, *Penine Way* had become a sort of signature tune for the Band and the warm-up period before full rehearsals often ended up with the Band busking its way through the opening strains - and with young James jumping up to 'conduct'. On the Belfast course *Penine Way* was on the programme and Leonard Davies, the Guest Conductor, had spotted David, the self-appointed conductor. In the concert he brought him out to conduct the march properly, a totally unexpected experience for the red-faced David which, he says, he'll never forget.

John Berryman's penultimate course was rather special. It was held at Cranleigh in the summer of 1958 and was the first of two occasions when Denis's old mentor, Sir Adrian Boult appeared as Guest Conductor. This was the course referred to by Mr. Ernest Brown in one of his letters (mentioned earlier in the book). He wrote,

> 'In 1958 Denis rang me asking for help in meeting trains from all over the country with players for his National Youth Brass Band. I worked out a team from the Chobham Band to meet these trains and to act as stewards for the final concert.'

This is typical of help received over the years from bands and band people, contributing enormously to the success of the NYBB, and though Denis's original idea, which was to have a nationwide network of helpers hasn't quite come to fruition, there is still a great deal of goodwill and, of course, over 40 years on, many former members are now actively involved in the promotion of the Band.

The team of tutors by now included Norman Ashcroft, Kenneth Dennison, Harry Farrington and Harry Heyes. Ken recalls advising Anthony Parsons to 'drop the trombone'. Not that he took any notice, which was just as well, because he went on to become Principal Trombone with the BBC Symphony Orchestra!

Returning to John Berryman's first course in 1954, a fellow 'new boy' was Douglas Taylor, at that time living in Meltham, near Huddersfield, later working as a peripatetic teacher in Bedford, now living in Halifax, conducting Gawthorpe Juniors and playing with the band where I started both my playing and conducting days, Elland Silver.

He has vivid memories of his four years in the NYBB, and of Denis. Following the seating auditions Doug was put, to his amazement, on his very first course, on top soprano cornet, and he can still feel the thrill he experienced when, at the beginning of the first rehearsal, the Band struck up with the National Anthem (a tradition which still survives). I asked him for his view of Denis, and he said,

> 'He had a great sense of humour and was terrific with young people. He was a stickler for detail, but in a gentle sort of way - and there was often a twinkle in his eye.'

During the courses there were theory classes, and at that time not many youngsters had previously done anything of the sort. Doug was one of the exceptions - he was taking 'O' level music at school, so was placed in Denis's advanced group. After working at some simple scoring exercises, he was told to get hold of a brass band score when he got home, and to find a suitable section to reduce to a 4-part harmonisation. He returned to the next course and proudly presented Denis with such a reduction of the whole of *Tam o' Shanter's Ride,* but he felt the sharp end of Denis's tongue for being too ambitious, and for attempting the impossible!

I asked Douglas if his experience in the NYBB had changed his musical horizons in any way and he had no hesitation in saying yes. He says he already had ambition, and feels that he would still have made his mark even without the experience of the Youth Band but, whereas formerly his ambitions were centred on himself, he now began to feel that the band was far more important than the individual. He went on to play with several leading bands and has devoted most of his professional life to teaching young brass players.

Returning to Denis, Douglas recalled his penetrating eyes, his character of steel, but above all else that he was a *Gentle Man.*

In the summer of 1953, remembering that it was the National Youth Brass Band of *Great Britain*, the Band had its first course outside England, visiting Ogmore-on-Sea near Porthcawl in South Wales. On this course Denis and Leonard Davies changed rôles, Leonard conducting and Denis organising - and also T. J. Powell ('The Welsh March King') joined the instrumental staff.

Another first was the 'coming of age' of Richard Evans and Norman Burnham. They had both reached the retiring age of 19 and became the first two members to be 'pensioned-off'.

John Henry Iles, one of the first Vice-Presidents, died shortly after the founding of the Band. Two more followed him in 1953 - H. B. Hawley and Dr. R. Maldwyn Price. They were replaced by Eric Iles (son of J. H.), Sir Reginald Thatcher (Principal of the Royal Academy of Music) and Eric Ball. There were also a number of staff changes at this time.

Appeals for cash continued, and with each of the quite frequent reports in the press there was a list of all those who had given donations, or who had agreed to give annual subscriptions. In February 1954 it was revealed that an appeal had been made to 2,000 bands. Only 116 responded - "mainly the little ones!"

A TV appearance had been promised for Easter 1954 but unfortunately it did not happen. However, it was announced that a BBC recording made in Manchester the previous Easter had recently been broadcast by West Berlin Radio in a schools programme. Denis, speaking in German, had introduced the programme and talked about the Band. This had been so successful that the Transcription Service had invited the NYBB to record another programme.

As Easter approached the course and concert were pushed as hard as possible. The course was being held at Southall in Middlesex and the Band was to give its first London concert - in the Central Hall, Westminster. It was being stressed that here was not just an enlarged school band playing juvenile music. Indeed, the programme would include music by John Ireland and Denis's latest composition, his overture *Glastonbury*.

Alas, the concert was greeted with apathy, the Band playing to rows and rows of empty seats. There had again been many visitors to the course. All had been impressed with what they saw and heard, and over the next few weeks there were glowing reports of the Band in the press, along with scathing condemnation of the lack of support from the band fraternity of the South.

For its summer course in 1954 the NYBB headed north to Scotland. Here the course was held in Musselburgh, near Edinburgh, and heralded the Band's first live broadcast. Two concerts were planned for Saturday, one in the afternoon in Pittencrieff Glen, Dunfermline and an evening concert in the famous Princes Street Gardens in Edinburgh. These were to be the Band's first open-air concerts, and the conducting was being shared by the tutors - Tom Powell, Elizabeth Lumb, by now Mrs. Peet, but the same Elizabeth Lumb who had been involved with the Leeds schoolchildren's massed bands concert in 1948 and therefore one who, along with another member of the same team of tutors, Tom Atkinson, really had been involved from the start. (Elizabeth was a member of the original Council, and Tom became a member during the Band's first year.) George Kaye, Cliff Edmunds and Richard Evans completed the list of tutors on this course. Richard had been the Band's Leader on its second course and had been one of the first to have to leave on the grounds of age, so it was a nice thought to have him join the tutors for the following course. He was asked to conduct Maurice Johnstone's march *County Palatine* but though pretty good with the cornet, to say that he was a novice at conducting was an understatement.

The first time he stood in front of the Band he started somewhat tentatively, and hadn't progressed more than a few bars before Denis, sitting behind him, clapped his hands and stopped them.

'Richard', he said, 'all your beats are down-beats. You mustn't do that'.

After a hurried discussion and a bit of instruction Richard was carving again - but not for long.

'Richard', came the voice again, 'there was a wrong note in the trombones. Didn't you hear it?'
   'No', said Richard, 'I don't think there was'.
   'It wer me', piped up one of the 2nd trombone players.
   'I could have killed him', said Richard as he retold the story.

However, Richard was no worse for the experience and still treasures the letter of thanks he received from Denis (see page 223). In more recent years Richard has taken on the rôle of Guest Conductor on three occasions - the only former member of the Band to date to do so. Almost as these words are being written he has been elected Chairman of the Council of the NYBB, so he has indeed been one of the most influential of all playing members.

There are one or two other matters worth recording pertaining to the Band's first (and to date, only) appearance North of the Border. Alas, just as the Dunfermline concert was about to start the Scottish weather decided to intervene and the concert was hurriedly re-arranged indoors. Unfortunately the stage was too small and the players had to stand up for the whole concert, many of them having to manage without music stands. Nevertheless, they played to an enthusiastic audience af about 600. The evening concert met with better luck and though it wasn't a particularly pleasant evening the Band played to an audience of about 5,000, one of its biggest ever.

Up to now the Band had had only one percussionist. When it was discovered that he couldn't make this course, a special appeal was made and suddenly the Band had four - more in keeping with its size and status.

Amongst the many visitors to this course was Mr. Hannaford, President of the Scottish Amateur Brass Band Association and a member of the NYBB Council. He was accompanied by Mrs. Hannaford who had very generously provided two scholarships, enabling young Scottish players to attend courses without cost to themselves. During the week at Musselburgh she also gave a medal, to be presented to the student considered to have made the most progress. This must have been the first of many special awards presented over the years, and on this occasion it went to a bass player from Gomersal Mills Band in Yorkshire, Frank Rothery. The Hannaford Medal was presented annually for a number of years.

An encouraging sign on the financial front was a couple of collections made at brass band contests. As a result of one made at the Belle Vue Spring Festival the Band fund benefited to the tune of £36.15s.8d, whilst at the Fairford Carnival in Gloucestershire a further £37 was raised.

DR. DENIS WRIGHT

no reply needed!

Please reply to : MISS M. THOMSON
5a, CAVENDISH MEWS SOUTH,
HALLAM STREET,
LONDON, W.1.

TEMple Bar 4383 (day)
LANgham 2298 (evening)

31st August 1954

Dear Dick, I ought to have written to you sooner, but since Musselburgh I have been up and down the country and not a moment for letter writing.

I want you to know how much I appreciated all you did for us on the course. I was very happy over the way you "fitted in" with us all — it is not everyone who can!

I hope you yourself felt your efforts were worth while and that you enjoyed the experience — I'm sure you did, once you got over the "new boy" feeling.

I wish I could say that we want you as a permanent tutor, but of course you know the position. What I will say, though, is that when we need another cornet tutor, permanent or deputy, you will be given first refusal.

So once more my grateful thanks and my very best wishes for your continued success in music. If ever you think I can be of help to you, please don't be afraid to ask.

Yours very sincerely

Denis Wright.

Early in 1955 the Band's publicity machine told of the NYBB's widespread influence. Still only in its fourth year, it had already had 238 members. They had come from all parts of England - except East Anglia - and also from Scotland, Ireland and Wales. However, the Band was advertising vacancies for baritones and BB♭ basses - an on-going problem! Leavers were now inevitably on the increase, but newcomers were regarded as being well up to standard, and therefore the Band was maintaining, even increasing its quality.

The Easter course was held in Nottingham where, as in London a year earlier, the audience was very disappointing. An innovation on this course was a solo contest organised by Mr. Ernest Tetley. It took place on the final day and Mr. Tetley very generously donated five prizes.

And so to the August course, held in Torquay, with Eric Ball the Guest Conductor. There were three concerts here. Publicity continued to be good, and in addition to the regular features about the NYBB it was frequently mentioned - in passing - in reports on unrelated topics.

Incidentally, there is a note in an August *British Bandsman* that Shirley Silver Band of Birmingham sent four of its members to the August course, including one David Seville, who in later years was to follow Denis as a member of the editorial staff at Chappell's, was instrumental in introducing the Chappell Shield in 1967 and is now a Divisional Director for Yamaha-Kemble and a great supporter of the NYBB.

Like other members from those early years he has vivid memories of Denis. He recalls that he had a wide musical background and exceptionally good ears, that his conducting was 'very precise', that though he knew so many famous people he was never a 'name-dropper', and that he generally wore light-coloured clothes!

The Easter course in 1956 was in Belfast and has already been mentioned. The August course was notable from a number of points of view. For the first time a guest conductor from outside the brass band world was engaged - Captain C. H. Jaeger, Director of Music of the Band of the Irish Guards, and later a mentor of mine, as Professional Conductor at Black Dyke. He was a big hit with band and staff and became a great admirer and supporter of the NYBB.

Beds were apparently a problem on this course, held at Cromer in Norfolk, and these were eventually supplied by a nearby American Air Force Base - to which the Band said its thank-you by giving a concert at the base on the Friday evening.

A couple of other points worth mentioning about Cromer are that it was the first course of one of the Band's longest serving tutors, Alf Jarvis, and that on this course we see the first mention of Mrs. Maud Wright. On previous occasions she had been Miss Maud Thomson, but there had obviously been a wedding!

In *The British Bandsman* of 1st December there was an irate letter from Denis in reply to one he had received from the secretary of an un-named Brass Band Association complaining that 'The NYBB intends bringing Army conductors into the Youth Band Organisation and they will pinch our budding bandsmen for the army!' - an obvious reference to the Jaeger connection.

Great efforts were still being made to prise money out of the band movement. Leonard Davies made an appeal for every member of every band to donate one shilling (5p) to the NYBB. How successful this was we are not told, but one positive move came from a lady in Huddersfield, Mrs. Connie Huntley, who was collecting signatures and embroidering them on a large table-cloth. A donation had to be given for the privilege of having your signature embroidered, and the cloth was to be offered to the band which raised most money for the Youth Band. During this year the Band was pleased to receive a donation of £50 from the Bandsman's Empire Memorial Trust, and for many more years, received welcome donations from this body, instigated by the National Brass Band Club.

1957 marked the centenary of the birth of Elgar and on the Band's Easter course, held at Wallasey, Denis paid homage by including some of the great composer's music in the programme. The first obvious choice was his only original brass band work, *Severn Suite* (though played on that occasion without the rather difficult Toccata). There were also two of the Pomp and Circumstance marches - No. 4 and the rather less well-known No. 2, plus Denis's own transcriptions of the pair of salon pieces, *Chanson de Matin* and *Chanson de Nuit.*

There was a live broadcast for the North Region Home Service on the Friday evening, and part of Saturday's concert was recorded for the Transcription Service. Again the size of the audience was disappointing, but the blame for this was laid at the door of the local organisers who had apparently not advertised it properly.

There were several changes amongst the Council members during 1957, one addition being Stanley Wainwright of Burnley. Stanley remained on the Council and one of the Band's most ardent supporters right up to his death a few years ago.

The August course was held in Weston-super-Mare and it was on this course that Mrs. Huntley presented her famous table-cloth, containing 1,987 signatures, and having raised £166 - which was also presented to the NYBB at Weston.

Leonard Davies, in an attempt to drum up as much support as possible, had invited members of No. 4 Area of the NABBC (of which he was Chairman) to visit the course, and there were all the usual pleas for support. On this occasion it worked and press reports commented not only on the usual high standard of playing in the concert, but also on the good attendance.

1958 saw yet another initiative from Leonard towards securing financial help. He sent out collecting books to a large number of bands and individuals. The band which made the biggest contribution was to be presented with the Connie Huntley table-cloth, while the NYBB member (past or present) who did likewise was to receive a copy of the Oxford Companion to Music. It is not recorded who received the book, but the table-cloth went to Daw Mill Colliery Band, which quite recently presented it back to the Youth Band.

1958 also saw the founding of another award - the Newman Cup. This was presented by Mr. Clarence Newman, a member of the Executive of the National Brass Band Club and now a member of the NYBB Council. It was to be awarded 'for outstanding ability and improvement on the theoretical side of the week's music-making - aural training and harmony'. The first recipient of this award was Allan Mead - then of Manchester but now of Winchester and the Hampshire Youth Band organisation. The Hannaford Medal this year went to Brian Harris, of Arley Welfare Band.

The year also heralded the policy of auditioning all applicants for membership of the NYBB - a policy still maintained.

Boult rehearsing the NYBB

Amongst the 'sales talk' for the Easter course was an article in *The British Bandsman* by Denis headed 'Do we care what they play?' The thrust of this was that by and large, brass band audiences were interested only in which *Band* they were going to hear, not what *Music* would be played and therefore, instead of waiting to give a report on 'The music they played', he took a leaf out of the book of orchestral concerts, reporting on *The music they are going to play*! On this occasion the programme was to include Beethoven's *Egmont Overture*, the *Elegy* from John Ireland's *Downland Suite* and the *Largo* from the *New World Symphony*, and Sir Adrian Boult was to make the first of his two appearances as Guest Conductor of the NYBB.

This and other ploys of promoting the Easter concert, given in the Friends' Meeting House in Euston Road, London, paid off to some extent, subsequent reports being of a 'big success'. Denis shared the conducting with Boult and amongst the glowing reports of both course and concert, one correspondent wrote 'We have heard youth make *music*, and it fills us with hope.' However, another report castigated the London bandsmen again for their poor attendance. *Musical Times* gave a good account of the concert under the heading 'Resounding Brass' and the Band made its first appearance on television.

The British Bandsman revealed that a number of Local Education Authorities were now assisting students with financial grants. This happened for many years but alas, in these days of cut-backs few, if any present-day students receive this form of help.

The August course of 1958 was held in Sunderland and was the last of John Berryman's nine courses as Leader. He was rewarded by being invited to play the 2nd and 3rd movements of Haydn's *Trumpet Concerto*. It was also revealed that there were now over a hundred works in the library - each with parts for over 100 players - and that Denis himself 'acts as librarian'.

It was decided at this time that all future applicants for membership would be auditioned, and an ambitious network of 23 centres was set up, from Scotland to Cornwall, from Wales to East Anglia and even one in the Channel Islands. 173 auditions took place and the results, plus the publicity, were thought to justify the exercise, even though it had been very costly.

Denis missed the Easter course in 1959 as he was again adjudicating the Australian National Championships. Harry Mortimer took the course, and the final concert, in Birmingham, attracted an audience of over 1,300. *The White Rider* was included in the programme as a tribute to Denis in his absence, and amongst the band personnel was its first member from the Channel Islands, and the first to come to a course by air.

David James became the new Leader, having played No. 2 to John Berryman on a couple of previous courses, and Trevor Cardwell of Bradford (a founder member) left after an all-time record 15 courses. The Birmingham & District Brass Band Association acted as hosts for this course. Its Secretary, Stan Reakes, had done much to ensure the success of both course and concert and he was, in a couple of years' time, to succeed Leonard Davies as secretary of the NYBB.

On the final Saturday morning of this course a rather novel contest took place. The Band was divided into small groups, each to rehearse a short piece, with various senior members appointed as conductors. After ceremoniously drawing for the order of play, they performed before

Eric Ball with the NYBB, August 1959

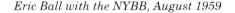

adjudicator Alf Jarvis, for a rather splendid set of prizes. The 1st was three bottles of pop, the 2nd two bottles and the 3rd, one. The group which came 4th in order of merit received an empty pop bottle from which the members could recoup threepence deposit from the tuck-shop!

The tuck-shop has, incidentally, always been an important part of the NYBB's paraphernalia. Opening at strategic times in order to sell appropriate refreshments so desperately needed in the middle of strenuous rehearsal it has, at the same time, earned a small profit for the Band-fund.

Alf awarded the top prize to a group calling itself *Turves Green Toolmakers' Temperance Band.* It was conducted by one David Seville, already mentioned, and by then playing baritone for John Thompson's Works Band. (This course was held in Turves Green School).

The August course, held in Portsmouth and with Eric Ball as Guest Conductor was also very successful. David James, now on his second course as Leader had, it was announced, won a scholarship for three years' study at the Royal Academy of Music in London. He was also apparently taking an interest in conducting, because he formed a band of volunteers from the NYBB and put on an informal concert for Southsea Silver Band.

At a Council meeting later in the year two very happy courses were reported and it was stated that auditions were in hand for the following year, with a declared age range of 12-18. In fact, the tradition of holding auditions during courses started at Easter, 1960. There were again some staff changes, and amongst the 'new boys' was Jack Emmott, Bandmaster of Black Dyke. The theoretical side of the Band's work was now being emphasised more, Edith Alston and Elizabeth Peet being responsible for developments in this field. An outward sign of its effectiveness was seen in a new march composed by flugel horn player John Hayes and played by a volunteer band conducted by Jack Emmott.

Not for the first time, the percussion section was being coached by Denis, but what was new was the fact that it now boasted a glockenspiel! Denis was also the Conductor, the Band was back in its first home in Thornton Grammar School and the concert was in Bradford's showpiece, St. George's Hall.

The August course in 1960 was held in Brighton, with another famous venue for the course-end concert - The Dome. T. J. Powell, who had earlier been an instrumental tutor, was invited back as Guest Conductor and included in the programme his own composition *Snowdon Fantasy* as well as a new arrangement by Leonard Davies of the *French Military March* by Saint-Saëns. As was becoming all-too-common, there were good reports of the Band's playing but disappointment expressed at the lack of support of the South's brass band public. This course was to be David James's last, and the Hannaford Medal this year was awarded to the cornet player who was to be his successor as Leader, John Clay.

1961 was the Band's 10th year, and a certain amount of looking back was done. There were now 120 pieces in the library, and a happy trend established over the previous five courses was that concerts were now being sponsored by outside organisations. Notice was given of auditions to be held at Easter, the stated age-range now having been modified to 12-17. There was also comment that the growing number of youth bands, though to be applauded, was having an adverse effect on applications - a situation which has, in fact, worsened with the passage of time.

The August course was held in Weymouth, again with Eric Ball as Guest Conductor. This was the most southerly course held to date, and it was noted that the longest journey to play with the Band was made by David Nichol - travelling all the way from Aberdeen. There was also a brother-and-sister partnership from Jersey - Marian and Geoffrey Mahy. Denis was once again missing - on tour in New Zealand.

The new auditions policy was obviously working, despite opposition from other youth bands; the waiting lists were looking very healthy, and it was stated that it would have been possible to muster a band of over 200. At last, also, donations were 'coming in nicely', and a suggestion was mooted that it would be a good idea to form an Old Boys' (and Old Girls') Association. The idea seems not to have been tried at the time, but it was put to an unsuccessful test a few years ago, when the FRIENDS OF THE NYBB was formed. The response from former members was so poor that in fact, membership was thrown open to *any* interested person.

This course saw the Band's first visit to Dorset and though the waiting lists were looking good more auditions were carried out. The Band's second TV programme - the first for ITV - was filmed, with interviews and some music from *Carmen* for a programme called *Day by Day*. In keeping with current trends the end-of-course concert, on the Pier Bandstand was sponsored - by Weymouth's Entertainment and Publicity Manager. An excellent audience turned out - possibly in excess of 1,000.

Later in the year the deaths of two of the Band's greatest supporters were announced - those of Mr. W. F. Hannaford JP and Mr. Ernest Huntley - husband of Connie of the famous table-cloth.

Several members from the 1950s who went on to achieve fame have been mentioned. During the 1960s this trend escalated and a pair of those present in August 1961 were Roy Roe and Brian Rankine. Roy was destined to become one of our great soprano cornet players and is now well-known both as conductor and adjudicator and Brian, after earning the title *Champion Soloist of Great Britain* (in 1965) went into the profession, playing trumpet with the BBC Midland Light Orchestra, Syd Lawrence, and the BBC's Big Band and Radio Orchestra.

Having completed its first ten years, in the run-up to the Easter course of 1962 a 4-page centre spread appeared in *The British Bandsman* posing the question,

DO WE NEED A NATIONAL YOUTH BRASS BAND OF GREAT BRITAIN?

It was a hard-hitting, straight-to-the-point feature. The improvements in the Band's financial state had been, apparently, only temporary, and the feature declared that,

'Unless the band world itself gives it the support we ask for, there's a very real possibility of the NYBB having to close down before long.'

The feature gave a résumé of the Band's history, an outline of the way it

George Chisholm and Sir Adrian chat to a group of cornet players. John Clay, Leader, is on the extreme left

was organised, some glowing press quotes, a comprehensive list of conductors, tutors, house staff and office staff, and raised some serious questions about finance and how much was needed, Denis stating:

> "With a loss of from £200 to £300 to be made good each year, if this appeal could raise £5,000 the Band would be free of financial worry for a very long time. This probably seems an immense sum to you. So it is, but it is not unattainable if the brass band world took this appeal seriously and acted generously. *After all, it is the band world that is the ultimate gainer.* How many of you have said *if only we had had something like this when WE were young!*
>
> If you think of the number of bands and bandsmen in Britain and then do a little arithmetic, you would find that our aim could be achieved if every band in the country were to donate two shillings for each of its members, or if every bandsman were to donate the price of a packet of cigarettes, sufficient money would be provided to make the continuance of the NYBB sure.
>
> Don't forget the band's 10th birthday concert, April 28th in the Duke's Hall, Royal Academy of Music, London, with Sir Adrian Boult conducting. If you live near enough to London do try to come along. But please, in the meantime, make YOUR donation, as a 10th birthday gift to the band.
>
> *Thank You."*

Then followed a 'Donation Form' to make it as easy as possible to contribute to the NYBB's future.

It had been hoped that Sir Malcolm Sargent, the band's President, would be Guest Conductor for the 10th anniversary concert but in the event, Sir Adrian Boult made his second appearance. BBC TV filmed a programme featuring the Band conducted by Sir Adrian and introduced by jazz trombonist George Chisolm. This went out on Wednesday, 2nd May, nation-wide, at the peak viewing time of 6.20 p.m.

Even with all the hype, and Boult, there was again a disappointing attendance at the concert, despite all the usual entreaties. It was also revealed that the 'Appeal' had not been fruitful, 'indicating complete indifference to the usefulness of the NYBB.'

With regard to this, two rather interesting and opposite views were publicised. The Yorks & District Brass Band Association recommended member bands to give donations for the next three years, but the Council of Brass Band Associations announced that a proposal to give financial support to the NYBB was 'deferred until a later date.'

Shortly before the course the Band lost another of its stalwarts with the death of Edith Alston - really Mrs. Leonard Davies, who had helped with theory and aural lessons almost since the formation of the Band.

In May 1962 it was announced that the NYBB had a new-found friend in the shape of comedian Jimmy Edwards. In addition to his talents as a comic-cum-euphonium/trombone player, Jimmy also apparently had a desire to conduct. One of his first ventures into this field was in a massed band concert organised specifically to raise funds for the NYBB. Stan Reakes was instrumental in setting up this, the first of a number of events in which Jimmy Edwards participated, with the combined bands of City of Coventry, Coventry Festival, Jaguar Cars and The Langley Band. All gave their services, and the proceeds were donated to the Youth Band. Trumpet player Eddie (*Oh My Papa*) Calvert was also involved and Denis, Mrs. Wright and Leonard Davies were present to represent the NYBB, which benefited to the tune of over £300.

In August 1962 the Band went even further into the South West - to St. Austell. There were two concerts in Truro's City Hall, both well attended, and the NYBB was indebted to Mr. Reg. Trudgian, the Cornwall Brass Band Association and the Cornwall County Youth Music Committee for hosting the Band. Unfortunately, a few boisterous members brought discredit to the NYBB and had to be reprimanded - not a unique incident, but a quite unusual one throughout the Band's history.

Shortly after this course the NYBB suffered another blow at the hands of 'The Great Reaper' - when 28-year-old Derek Sanderson, who had been tutoring lower cornets for three years, died.

During November Jimmy Edwards put on another of his concerts for the Youth Band. This took place in the Palace Theatre, Manchester, and the bands involved were CWS (Manchester), Wingates and Mossley.

But now to 1963. More and more youngsters were coming into the Band and going on to make their marks as players, teachers or conductors. Amongst the names in the 1963 bands were:

Ian Copland	Robert Morgan (now Chairman of Gloucester BBA)
Tony Cresswell	Roger Payne
Martin Eastwood	Leighton Rich (Head of Brass, County of Hampshire)
Ray Farr	Peter Skellern (singer, pianist and entertainer)
Stan James	James Watson
John Maines	Keith Wilkinson
Phillip McCann	

Jimmy Edwards pursued his interests in the NYBB even further this year, first with another massed band concert, this one at the famous Victoria Palace in London, with Hanwell, Luton, and Morris Motors, along with George Chisolm. This was in March and a month later Jimmy chartered a

---

SUNDAY, 31st MARCH, 1963

AT

THE VICTORIA PALACE. LONDON

COMMENCING   -   -   7-30 P.M.

JIMMY EDWARDS

WITH

HANWELL BAND
Musical Director: ERIC BRAVINGTON

LUTON BAND
Musical Director: ALBERT COUPE

MORRIS MOTORS BAND
Musical Director: G. V. BROOKES

Guest Artist: GEORGE CHISHOLM

**Seats: 5/-; 7/6; 10/6; 15/-; £1; Boxes: £3
Bookable at the Theatre, or by Post from the
Box Office, Victoria Palace. Victoria Street,
London, S.W.1.   (Telephone VIC. 1317)**

PROCEEDS IN AID OF
THE NATIONAL YOUTH BRASS BAND

Clarence Raybould (left) with Mrs. Wright and Denis

plane to fly to Birmingham to conduct a couple of items in the NYBB's Easter concert.

The Guest Conductor was Harold Gray, Assistant Conductor of the Birmingham Symphony Orchestra, and a musician who also had a special interest in youth music-making. Denis missed this course because he was adjudicating in Canada. A newcomer to the staff was Derek Garside, then at the height of his playing career with CWS (Manchester) Band.

The final concert, in Birmingham Town Hall, attracted a large crowd - no doubt Jimmy Edwards' presence was an added attraction. Jennifer Gillingham succeeded John Clay as Leader, becoming the first of seven young ladies who to date have held the prestigious position.

In August the Band returned to Wallasey. Leonard Davies conducted and Phillip McCann[4] became Leader, a position he held with distinction for eight courses.

Other news from 1963 was that Jimmy Edwards and Bill Hume (who had been a member of the Council since the Band's inception) were made Vice-Presidents. The shattering news of the resignation of Leonard Davies, due to ill-health, was announced in February 1964. There had been an inkling that all was not well in January when a news item said that "owing to re-organisation in the NYBB" applicants for audition were to write direct to Denis. Leonard's replacement was Stan Reakes, who had contributed so much to the Birmingham course of a year earlier. Stan tells me that Denis was always keen to move around the country as much as possible, and that he himself spent a great deal of time visiting potential venues to assess whether or not they were suitable.

Easter saw another milestone in the Band's history with its 25th course. This took place in Gloucester. Denis conducted and the Band cut its first disc, a 10" LP for Keepoint called *Youth Makes Music*. Another fact worth noting from this course is that three Swedish boys attended, to become the first non-British members of the National Youth Brass Band of Great Britain. They were members of the LKU Band from Malmö.

The August course was held in Wrexham. Maurice Miles[5] was Guest Conductor and a young lad by the name of John Wallace[6] was in the cornet section.

By the end of 1964 the Keepoint LP appeared on the market. It created lots of interest both in Britain and overseas, and made a profit which, naturally enough, was ploughed back into the band-fund. Towards the end of January 1965 Dr. Harold Hind reviewed it in *The British Bandsman,* speaking very highly of both the quality of playing and the choice of programme.

Notice was also given that the Easter course of 1965 was to be in Huddersfield, that the Guest Conductor was to be Clarence Raybould[7] and that the concert, to be in Huddersfield Town Hall, would be sponsored by the Huddersfield Brass band Association.

In February Jimmy Edwards did yet another massed band concert, this one in the Guildhall, Portsmouth, with BMC Morris Motors, Bournemouth T. A. and Southsea bands. The famous pianist Semprini, giving his services, made an appearance in the concert, from which the Lord Mayor's Charity and the NYBB each received a cheque for £200.

Staff changes for the Easter course saw James Shepherd taking over from Jack Emmott as a tutor and Peter Room joining the House-staff. Peter Later became Senior House-master, serving in this capacity for several years, becoming a member of the Council, and later being elected a Vice-President.

Once again a successful course and concert were reported, much help having been given by Huddersfield Association's President, Mrs. Evelyn Bray. Clarence Raybould, in an interview with *The British Bandsman* spoke highly of his week with the Band, adding,

'During my long life-time of music-making in many countries, my recent experience with the NYBB stands out as one of the very happy and friendly encounters in that musical life.'

The course was again tinged with sadness, as one of the Band's flugel horn players, Jim Smith, had been killed in a motor cycle accident. His parents came to Huddersfield to present a music desk in his memory.

In February 1965 Boosey & Hawkes made their historic announcement that they would not be selling any more high-pitched instruments after 31st March. However, Denis decreed that the NYBB would continue to play in high pitch for a few more courses, realising that the bands with which most members played would not be converting for some time.

New members of staff for August included Denis Carr, who looked after lower cornets and horns for several years, and also served on the Council. Alex Mortimer had been engaged to direct this course, but had to withdraw due to illness, and Denis himself took over - at very short notice.

Continuing the Swedish connection - three boys from Malmö having played with the NYBB at Easter 1964, three boys and a girl came to Cardiff, at the request of Kurt Hedburg. In a letter to me Kurt, who had recently formed a band in the village of Vaxtorp commented:

'I can still remember how awful my youngsters felt when they heard all the clever players from Great Britain perform before being placed in their sections. As Denis Wright was a kind man he suggested that they were placed on 2nd and 3rd cornet - without audition. The bass player and the baritone player had no problems with nerves, and of course we were there to learn.'

Waiting lists were looking quite healthy, but instead of the by now customary in-course auditions, a nationwide scheme was planned for the Autumn similar to, but on a less grand scale than the 1958 series, with auditions taking place in eight centres.

Plans for Easter 1966 were released early in the year. Harold Gray was to return as Guest Conductor, but Denis and Mrs. Wright were to miss this course because they would be on tour in the Far East. The Band was to play at a lunch-time Service in Coventry Cathedral - possibly the first time this

Denis's last concert with the NYBB.

THE TOWN HALL, EUSTON ROAD, LONDON, N.W.1.

Saturday, 1st April, 1967, at 7.30 p.m.

The

National   Youth

Brass   Band

of Great Britain

CONDUCTED BY

Denis Wright

PROGRAMME . . . . SIXPENCE

had happened, and a BBC recording was to be made on Friday - the first for a few years.

March brought the sad news of the death of the Band's first Secretary, Leonard Davies, from a heart attack. You'll remember that he'd had to resign from the Band two years earlier.

Auditions were held during the August course, there being vacancies - unusually - in the cornet section as well as in basses and percussion. The Editorial in an August edition of *The British Bandsman* re-stated some of the aims and objectives of the Band as it approached its 30th course. A highlight of this was to be a recording for the BBC Third Programme (a fore-runner of Radio 3) with an all-original programme comprising the *Heroic March* (from Fletcher's *Epic Symphony*), the *Elegy* (from *Downland*), Eric Ball's Overture *Call of the Sea* and Denis's *Glastonbury*. Eric Ball was Guest Conductor and the concert, in Portsmouth's Guildhall, was a great success, mainly due to the help of Wesley Johnstone - then Portsmouth's Music Advisor.

Again there were going to be auditions during the Autumn at various centres, and notice was given that the course for the following Easter was to be held at St. George's School, Harpenden, where Denis had served both as pupil and master. it was also announced that Denis had composed his *Trio Concerto*, to be premièred at the course-end concert. This proved to be Denis's last composition.

Another group of well-known names appears during the mid-1960s, including Neil Jowett, David Essex, Peter Christian, Nigel Boddice (now Principal trumpet with the BBC Scottish Symphony Orchestra) and quite a crop of euphonium players, including Russell Booker[8] who played with GUS and Graham Cobley who was for a number of years the principal euphonium of Sun Life Stanshawe.

However, a shock announcement appeared in *The British Bandsman* of 11th March in 1967:

'At the recent Annual General Meeting of the National Youth Brass Band Dr. Denis Wright announced that as from Easter he would be relinquishing the position of Music Advisor. He had recently found it increasingly difficult to give sufficient time to the work and it was likely that in the near future he would have again to be absent from courses because of overseas commitments.'

It seems that Denis felt that he had made his contribution and that with more necessary work to be done overseas, he ought to stand down at the Youth Band.

Also with this announcement came news of more staff changes; Bill Hume was replaced by Harry Mortimer as a Trustee and A. J. Molinari, for many years Secretary of the National Brass Band Club and also a member of the Council retired, and was succeeded in both rôles by Bill England who, some years later was to replace Stan Reakes as Secretary of the NYBB, a position he holds to this day.

Naturally, Denis had given much thought to his own successor and he chose a man whose name was fast coming to the fore in the band world,

Geoffrey Brand. He was a man of wide experience, had started his playing days in the Salvation Army, had become a professional trumpet player, playing under Beecham in the RPO, and later serving as a member of the orchestra of the Royal Opera at Covent Garden. Like Denis, he had worked for the BBC for many years and so his musical experience covered a much wider area than that of bands alone. However, amongst his duties at the BBC had been a responsibility for all band broadcasts, so he was well in touch with current developments in banding.

Geoffrey had already been asked to be Guest Conductor for the August course in 1967. Now Denis invited him to be his successor as Music Advisor and, 'after considerable thought' Geoffrey had accepted, remaining in office until the end of 1974, when he was succeeded by Arthur Butterworth.

I have had a variety of observations about Denis's state during the course. Phillip McCann, on his final course, didn't notice that there was anything seriously wrong. Alf Jarvis said the tutors were aware that he was ill, 'but he didn't allow it to look too obvious - he camouflaged it well!' He does say, however, that Denis was rather unsteady on the rostrum during the Saturday concert. Nigel Boddice, on the other hand, a youngster of about 14 and on his first course was very worried at the amount of coughing Denis was doing. Stan Reakes goes even further, saying 'He shouldn't really have been on that course.'

However he was, and he expressed the opinion that,

> "In the 15 years of the Band's existence, that was the best all-round ensemble there had been."

And in the context of this, as early as 1955, Denis had stated that working with the NYBB gave him greater pleasure and musical satisfaction than almost anything else in his life's work.

The British Bandsman reported that there were three items of special interest in the concert, a *Folk Song Suite* which Denis had written for an octet and which was performed, as was the custom, without conductor, 'a spirited performance' of the march *County Palatine,* conducted by its composer, Maurice Johnstone - Denis's old friend, and the first performance of Denis's new *Trio Concerto*, with Phillip McCann, Eoin McCallum and Russell Booker featured on cornet, trombone and euphonium. The concert had been arranged in collaboration with the National Brass Band Club.

The NYBB was presented at this time with a shield, by Messrs. Chappell & Co. Ltd., the music publishers for whom Denis had worked during the 1930s, and in whose Educational Department former Band member David Seville was now working. The Band already had the Newman Cup, being presented each Easter to the student considered to have made the most progress. The Chappell Shield, as this new trophy was to be called, would be presented each August, it was decided, to the student considered to have given the most outstanding service to the Band - both in a playing capacity and in general behaviour and example. On this first occasion the shield went to Phillip McCann, just completing his eighth course as Leader. Also during the Final Assembly when, traditionally, these awards are announced and presented, there was a surprise for Denis when the members of the Band presented him with a stop watch and a table lighter, to mark the occasion of his last course as Music Advisor. In thanking the members he said that he was not ceasing his connection with the Band, adding that he hoped, whenever possible, to look in on future courses.

Alas, this was not possible. He was dead within a matter of weeks. That the NYBB is still going strong, and in many details doing things introduced by Denis during the early years of the Band's existence is undoubtedly 'The Lasting Tribute'. There is a Latin phrase from *Odes* (Horace: Book 3, 30:1) which, translated, means *I have raised a monument more durable than brass*. I'd like to close this chapter with a paraphrase on it meaning *he has raised a lasting monument of brass*, for that is surely what the NYBB is.

Exegi monumentum aeratum perenne.

Notes

[1] *Forty Years Young* - the title of the CD issued to commemorate the 40th Anniversary.

[2] *Maurice Murphy* first came to fame in 1947, winning the Juvenile Solo Championships at the Royal Albert Hall when he was aged 12. He had played with Harton and Crookhall and had been influenced by both Norman Ashcroft and Jack Atherton. He subsequently moved into the Leeds area, becoming an apprentice electrician at YEWCO - where (naturally) he played in the band - prior to moving to Fairey's and later becoming principal cornet with Black Dyke. He then went into the orchestral world, playing first with the BBC Northern Orchestra and, since 1976, as principal trumpet with the LSO. Maurice was the first of a chain of distinguished Leaders and one of many members of the NYBB to carve national and international reputations for themselves through their music.

[3] *David James* was leader for four courses and went on to study at the Royal Academy. Whilst still in the NYBB he was chosen to be one of the two Principal Trumpets in the Student Orchestra of Great Britain when it visited Vienna in December 1959. After leaving the Academy he joined the BBC Scottish Symphony Orchestra on Principal trumpet, remaining there for almost 17 years. He left the orchestral scene in 1978 to become a brass band conductor. He worked with several top bands, including Grimethorpe and Carlton Main, and has become one of Britain's most respected cornet/trumpet teachers and clinicians.

[4] *Phillip McCann* went on to become Principal Cornet with Yorkshire Imperial, Fairey Engineering, Men o' Brass and for 15 outstanding years with Black Dyke. Though now a successful conductor and teacher, he is still in demand as a cornet soloist, and has recently completed his 5th album of solos in the series *The World's Most Beautiful Melodies*.

[5] *Maurice Miles* was a founder-conductor of the short-lived Yorkshire Symphony Orchestra and also worked for the BBC. More recently he has directed conducting classes at the Royal Academy and at the Royal Military School of Music, Kneller Hall.

[6] At the time he joined the NYBB *John Wallace* was a member of Tullis Russell Mills Band in Scotland. He is now Principal Trumpet of The Philharmonia and a world-famous trumpet soloist, having shot to fame playing the trumpet obligato in Handel's *Let the Bright Seraphim,* sung by Kiri Te Kanawa, and seen and heard by millions on the occasion of the Royal Wedding of Prince Charles and Princess Dianne.

[7] *Clarence Raybould* spent his early years as a conductor working with Beecham, followed by nine years as Chief Assistant Conductor to Boult with the BBC Symphony Orchestra. At the time he conducted the NYBB he had been conductor of the National Youth Orchestra of Wales since its formation.

[8] *Russell Booker* and his wife Irene (née Hooker) have, to this day, the distiction of being the only married couple in the NYBB. They met in the Youth Band, and were married while still both members.

Chapter 27

The Final Years

In 1960 Denis was 65 - and presumably qualified for the Old Age Pension! This is a time when most people stop or at least slow down in their work-a-day activities. In terms of the hectic years of the 1950s there may have been a bit of easing off, but certainly not very much. It is neither possible nor, I suppose, desirable to trace his activities to the last detail, but I hope that this chapter will illustrate the scale and range of his work - right up to the end.

We must remember also that he was still very actively involved in running the National Youth Brass Band, that he undertook a mind-boggling tour of the Antipodes in 1961, an extensive adjudicating assignment in Canada two years later and a working holiday in the Far East in 1966, as well as regular trips to Denmark and Sweden - and all this in addition to assignments mentioned in this chapter, dealing with the years 1960-1967.

Conducting and Adjudicating

Denis's first important conducting engagement during this period came during 1960, when he took part in the BBC Light Music Festival, conducting a performance of his own transcription of Handel's *Hallelujah Concerto*, with George Thalben-Ball at the organ and Black Dyke. Later in the year he directed the second course of the Cornwall Youth Band.

In 1961 he conducted the inaugural concert of the Yorkshire Schools Brass Band in Carlton Grammar School, Bradford, the scene of the NYBB's first concert in 1952. The Yorkshire Schools Brass Band held monthly rehearsals, but otherwise was modelled on similar lines to, and aimed to prepare youngsters for the National Youth Brass Band.

A particularly interesting conducting engagement popped up in 1965. Pre-recorded, it was broadcast at 9.30a.m. in the BBC's Music Programme (Radio 3) on 20th February, the day of Denis's 70th birthday. By co-incidence it also commemorated 40 years' service to brass bands, and in an interview with Tom Naseby Denis admitted to a 'skeleton in the cupboard' in that he had never played a brass instrument. The programme, played by Black Dyke under Denis's baton, was an all-Wright affair, consisting of the Prelude, *St. Nicholas Eve, Canzonetta and Rondo* from the *Cornet Concerto* (with soloist James Shepherd), the *Scherzo* from *Music for Brass* and *Tintagel*. Later in 1965 he conducted the last of his 11 massed band concerts for Brighouse &

Rastrick Band in Huddersfield Town Hall. Brighouse's guests on this occasion were Cammell Laird and CWS (Manchester).

In accordance with tradition there were a number of times when Denis was called upon to adjudicate at a contest and then conduct the massed band concert which followed. The first of these occurred when he adjudicated Edinburgh Festival's brass band contest in 1960 and then conducted the massed bands. In October of the same year he adjudicated the 2nd Section Finals in London and was an Associate conductor in the Gala concert in the Royal Albert Hall. He returned to Edinburgh in 1965 to adjudicate the Edinburgh Charities Contest, following which he conducted the combined bands of Kinneil Colliery and Scottish CWS.

Between January and April 1961, along with Maurice Johnstone, Denis adjudicated the BBC North Region's knock-out competition *Northern Brass* (devised and produced by William Relton). This involved adjudicating one heat between two bands each week, with the last two bands left in the competition meeting for the Finals, for which Denis and Maurice were joined on the adjudicating panel by Stanford Robinson. The title on this occasion went to Yorkshire Imperial Metals Band, and after a tense final they were joined by the other three semi-finalists - Goodshaw, Hammonds and Harton Colliery - for a massed band concert in which the conducting was shared by Denis, Maurice and Harry Mortimer.

By 1967 the competition had left the North Region and gone national, with

Denis with the Cornwall Youth Band, 1960

On stage at the Royal Albert Hall at the 1961 Nationals. (The other adjudicators are Frank Wright and Harold Moss; Frank Phillips is on the right and members of a jubilant Black Dyke may be seen in the background)

the title *Challenging Brass*. This involved, initially, adjudicating 28 pre-recorded 20-minute programmes prior to the Finals, live, in the Royal Festival Hall. For the Finals Denis sat alongside his namesake Frank and the distinguished composer Malcolm Arnold. This was the last time Denis adjudicated.

Straight adjudicating appointments during these last seven years included the Belle Vue September contests of 1960, 1963, 1965 and 1966. The 1966 contest was his 19th appearance as adjudicator at this mecca of brass bands, including some of the Spring Festivals. During these years he also adjudicated at a number of Area Contests in various sections, including the 2nd section contest in Huddersfield Town Hall in 1962, to which I referred in the Foreword, when he awarded 1st prize to the 'Slawit' Band, conducted by a certain Roy Newsome. There were also Coal Board Contest Finals (CISWO) at Blackpool in 1962 and 1966, the Junior Solo Championships at Coalville in 1963, and numerous other local contests.

Outside his brass band work, Denis again adjudicated in the choral classes at the Llangollen International Eisteddfod in 1960 and 1962, and also in 1962 he accepted the conductorship of Manor House Operatic Society in Hampstead. This was the hospital with the founding of which his father had helped. The Society's aim was to raise funds for the Hospital.

Still outside the brass band field, as Vice-President of Wembley Operatic

Society he also became its musical Director, in 1963 directing *South Pacific* and in 1964 *Kismet*.

Returning to 1965, and no doubt as a follow-up to his work as an adjudicator at Llangollen in earlier years, Denis was invited to be Guest Conductor of the first ever massed brass band concert at this world-famous Eisteddfod. The major classes in this festival sing and play to vast audiences in a huge marquee and on this occasion, under Denis's baton, Black Dyke, Brighouse and Foden's played to an audience of around 11,000.

There was, in a manner of speaking, a posthumous long-playing record, and perhaps it should be pointed out that Denis seems to have had very limited involvement in commercial recordings. James Scott tells me that as early as 1964 when his band, Cammell Laird, were runners-up in the Nationals, Denis approached him about doing a recording with them, with Denis himself conducting. James readily agreed and the recording duly took place. For whatever reason, the disc did not see the light of day until after Denis's death. It was reviewed by Dr. Harold Hind in *The British Bandsman* of 1st July 1967 and began as follows:

> 'It is extremely sad to realise that Dr. Denis Wright was not spared to see the release by Realty Records Ltd. of the first in the series BRASS PROM for which he conducted Cammell Laird Works Band in an attractive and well-played programme, mostly of works of which he was the arranger.'

Musical Writings

Brass band compositions dating from the beginning of the 1960s were *Salzburg Suite* (1960), *St. Nicholas Eve* (1962), *Carol Sinfonietta* and the *Trio Concerto* (1966). These were all discussed in Chapter 20 and call for no further comment.

As a follow-up to *Messiah* (1946), the Cherubini *Requiem* (1951) and miscellaneous choral and vocal items for use with brass band accompaniment, Denis made his last such transcription in 1960. It was in preparation for the New Zealand tour the following year and is referred to on page 187. It was, of course, his transcription of excerpts from another Handel oratorio, *Judas Maccabæus*. Lasting some 40 minutes, it incorporated 17 of the 68 numbers in the complete work and was therefore far less comprehensive a transcription than *Messiah*.

Novello's had published three books of pieces suitable for school bands or ensembles in the early 1950s, arranged by Denis. In 1966 he produced a fourth book, this one published by Chesters and called *Music for Junior Bands and Brass Ensembles*. It contained a selection of 12 mainly well-known and moderately easy pieces, scored for brass band instruments, but with optional parts for flute, clarinet and french horn, thus catering for the rising numbers of young players on these instruments who were unable to get into their school orchestras. This book must have been one of the early stepping-stones towards the rise of the school wind or concert band.

There were also several song-settings, arranged during his editorship for Ascherberg, Hopwood and Crew, plus a couple of original motets for Cary's - the church music branch of Ascherberg's.

Even when adding the collection of miscellaneous band arrangements this does not represent a prolific writing period in Denis's life, and the only piece of any real significance is his very last, the *Trio Concerto*.

Books

In 1963 the last of Denis's books appeared - *The Complete Bandmaster*. This was one of a set of 24 books planned for inclusion in the music division of the Commonwealth and International Library of Science, Technology, Engineering and Liberal Studies. The 24 were part of a 1,000-volume series to be published between 1964 and 1967, so Denis's contribution was but a small item in a very grand scheme. Nevertheless, he expressed his delight at being given the opportunity "to get a lifetime of brass in between one set of covers."

Denis came under a bit of fire from the National Schools Brass Band Association for not including a chapter about them. He offered an immediate apology along with an explanation of the difficulties of getting absolutely everything into one quite small volume. Evidently there were no hard feelings, as Denis was invited, a couple of years later, to be Guest Conductor at the Association's 12th Annual Festival, with a band of some 300 children drawn from all parts of England.

There was a note in *The British Bandsman* during July 1966 to the effect that *Scoring for Brass Band* was being temporarily withdrawn from sale as Denis was revising it and enlarging it, and bringing it up to date with more modern music examples. The new, revised, 4th edition came out in 1967, and in its Preface Denis revealed that the book, first published in 1935, owed its origins to the two articles he had written for *Musical Times*. These were discussed in Chapter 22. Further revisions took place prior to the publishing of the 5th edition by Studio Music in 1986.

The Royal Academy of Music

During the middle part of 1962 Denis deputised for one of the professors at the Royal Academy of Music in London who was in hospital, and he was very thrilled when the Academy's Principal, Sir Thomas Armstrong, offered him a permanent post on the part-time staff, to teach harmony and composition. He took up this appointment in 1963.

In 1965, while still teaching at the Academy, Denis became one of the first recipients of a new award, becoming an Honorary Associate of the Royal Academy of Music (Hon. A.R.A.M.) It was an award bestowed on outstanding musicians who were not ex-students of the Academy. (It will be recalled that Denis studied at the Royal College of Music.) In 1966 Denis was 'promoted', becoming a full Honorary Member of the Royal Academy of Music (Hon. R.A.M.), a distinction awarded to musicians in recognition of outstanding services to music.

By now Denis had given up teaching at the Academy due to all his other commitments, but he was being called on to act as examiner in conducting and composition, both for internal examinations and for the LRAM diploma.

National Association of Brass Band Conductors

Apart from the temporary altercation during the 1950s Denis had maintained closed links with this organisation since its inception during the war, and had been a regular contributor to its official magazine, *The Conductor*. During his late years the link continued, as Denis continued as a Vice-President.

Most of his involvement during the 1960s seems to have been as adjudicator of various competitions for composers or arrangers. A feature of these was that he was generally present to make verbal comments on the work, and also to present each competitor with a written comment.

One session outside of this series was a talk he gave to Scottish delegates in 1965 on the day following the Edinburgh Charities contest, which he had adjudicated. The title of his talk was *How to make the most of rehearsal time*, and the band which was on call to assist was Carlton Main Frickley Colliery Band from Yorkshire - a band for which he was long supposed to have had a soft spot.

Miscellaneous Ventures - but Mainly Educational

Throughout these closing years Denis continued as Honorary Director of Examinations for the Bandsman's College of Music, setting and marking papers, and often presiding at the practical examinations. As already mentioned, he seems to have withdrawn to some extent from the AOMF Scholarship, but in 1965 another Scholarship was set up, this one in memory of the late Harry Heyes, a noted Midlands band personality. The emphasis was on musicianship rather than performance and the winner was to receive two years' free training in Theory and General musicianship. The Scholarship was administered by the Birmingham & District Brass Band Association, and they invited Denis to be the Examiner for the first year.

Denis continued giving talks and being involved in discussions of one sort or another. In October 1960 he gave the address at the Bandsman's Annual Service at St. Sepulchre's. At around the same time he discussed his *Salzburg Suite* in *The British Bandsman* and in *The Conductor* contributed an article headed *Whither Brass Band Music?* In 1962 he chaired a meeting of The British Institute of Recorded Sound, at which the principal speaker was Eric Bravington, conductor of Hanwell and orchestral manager of the London Philharmonic Orchestra. Denis chaired the meeting and also introduced some recordings, including one of a quintet from the NYBB playing the *St. Anthony Chorale*.

The following year saw Denis presenting two 20-minute programmes in the BBC Concert Series for schools. The first explained the difference between brass and military bands, demonstrating the tone colours of a range of instruments and giving an outline of their historical backgrounds. He also reviewed the differences in styles between English and overseas bands. The second programme was a concert which emphasised the possibilities of children participating in the performance of brass band music. Later in the same year he was discussing Bantock and *Prometheus Unbound* in an article in *The British Bandsman*.

The Course That Never Was

What was intended to be one of Denis's biggest ventures, possibly ultimately taking on as much significance as the NYBB itself was hinted at in a preliminary announcement in *The British Bandsman* of 3rd December 1966. It told of a Band Conductor's Summer School which was to take place in Shrewsbury from the 5th to the 12th of August the following year. Later it emerged that this was to be run at Radbrook College - the same venue as the NYBB's August course but one week earlier.

The background to this project is that Denis had come to the conclusion that, at the time, there were no means in band circles for the training of conductors. A plan for a Brass Band Conductors' course was drawn up, "Formulated by Eric Ball, Editor of *The British Bandsman*, Maurice Johnstone, late BBC Head of Music (Sound) and Denis Wright, OBE, D.Mus, Director of Examinations, Bandsman's College of Music."

The plan put forward the argument for the need for such a course and a list of the kind of people who would benefit from it, outlines of how it could be organised and what needed to be taught. It also gave an estimate of advertising and staffing costs and to what extent it would need subsidising, along with suggestions as to the best venues and time of year. The plan was put to the Council of the NYBB with a view to the course being run under its auspices. Mrs. Wright comments:

> 'The Council considered a proposal by the Chairman (Dr. Denis) that the idea should be developed and a course organised for conductors, primarily with the object of catering for the further education of ex-members of the NYBB. The council approved the idea in principle, but since such a project would be outside the terms of the Constitution, which had an age limit of 18, it decreed that the NYBB could not be formally involved, and decided not to agree to the proposal.'[1]

However, Denis was not going to be put off and he decided that, with help from Mrs. Wright, he would go ahead himself and set up the first *Brass Band Conductors' Summer School*. Advertising was started and a plan for the week prepared. Denis would be Course Director and would be assisted by Eric Ball, Harry Mortimer (engagements permitting) and an un-named instrumental tutor. A publicity hand-out stated that,

> 'The course will be run on lines already found effective by Dr. Wright some years ago when he directed two similar courses for the Workers' Educational Association and later for the Universities of Western Australia at Perth and Canterbury University, New Zealand'.

Aspects of instruction would include:

> The physical side of conducting
> The musicianly qualities needed by a conductor
> Rehearsal technique
> Teaching of instrumentalists
> Aural training for young players
> Tuning the band

Scoring for band and smaller ensemble
Score reading

The minimum age was to be 20 and the course would be 'open to ladies as well as men'. The course fee, fully inclusive, would be £12.12s and a deposit of £2.2s was required with the application. The hand-out also gave details of music to be studied and a general outline of how the week would run.

The advertisements brought an immediate response, with several applications and deposits arriving. Sadly, with the unexpected death of Denis, the whole project became a non-starter. He would have been the lynch-pin and the motivator for the course and Mrs. Wright felt, in her grief, that the only way open to her was to cancel the course and refund the deposits she had already received.

And so we can see that, right to the very end, Denis was still pressing forward with his plan to educate the brass band movement.

Conclusion

A 1965 publicity leaflet stated that in addition to numerous large-scale works for brass band, Denis had transcribed over 800 works by other composers and that he had adjudicated over 300 band contests and music festivals in many parts of the world. These claims represent but a small part of his contribution to brass bands and say nothing about his work in other musical spheres.

In the foregoing chapters I have attempted to show the scale and scope of this remarkable man's work, and to indicate his influence on the progress of brass bands - much of which is in danger of being completely forgotten.

One thing I have failed to mention. It might well be assumed that with such an active musical life there would be room for nothing else. In fact, he had a passion for fly-fishing, and spent many happy hours involved in this activity - especially in the English Lakes.

I've written this book out of a sense of admiration for the man and in an attempt to put into perspective the work he did in his quest for recognition for the brass band. I've done it also in the hope that for future generations of bandsmen the name Denis Wright will mean rather more than simply a name on a piece of music.

Note

[1] This is quoted from the Minutes of the NYBB's Annual General Meeting of January 1967.

One that didn't get away

Chapter 28

Obituary

I began Chapter 21 by quoting part of a tribute written about Denis by Tom Atkinson. It seems appropriate to round off the book and at the same time precis much of what I've written by quoting extracts from some of the numerous tributes which appeared in print shortly after his death on 20th April 1967. First some of the comments made by Denis's old friend Maurice Johnstone in *The Conductor*.

'After World War I several British composers of national and international renown were inspired by John Henry Iles to compose challenging test-pieces for brass band. Regrettably, most of them ventured only once into this new (to them) and richly explorable territory. Not so Denis Wright. The winning of a £100 prize (which caused him as much astonishment as delight) in 1924 (he means 1925 RN) for a Crystal Palace test-piece was the beginning of a career virtually devoted to the brass band in all its manifestations.

For over 40 years this accomplished and versatile man of music applied himself to putting the best into and getting the best out of bands and their music. Apart from examining for educational bodies, Denis Wright did little else but compose, conduct, adjudicate, arrange and organise for the band movement.

With a masterly gift for scoring and transcribing that came from experience and imagination, he arranged for brass a wide range of adaptable music chosen from the world's concert repertoire, from *1812* to *Chanson de Nuit*. His unswerving principle was that only the best was good enough for brass, and he believed that bands were no less important in the nation's musical life than choirs and orchestras.

Within a few years, Wright's position in the band world was unique. He became internationally famous as conductor, adjudicator and examiner. His books on brass band technique, written from practical experience, were immediately recognised as standard works. After he retired from the BBC his services as a creator and improver were in demand from Huddersfield to Hong Kong, from Swansea to Sydney. At every band centre that he visited as conductor and trainer he exercised with notable results that very rare power to transmute the unequal abilities of enthusiastic amateurs into a total musical refinement and skill.

Perhaps Denis Wright's most outstanding contribution to the band movement was the formation and direction of the National Youth Brass Band. The opportunities it afforded to young players for instrumental training and playing together were as unique as those of the National Youth Orchestra, upon which brilliantly successful organisation it was modelled.

Denis and his assistant tutors looked after the music; his highly capable wife looked after the administration and, with a matron and house-master, cared for their well-being and extra-musical happiness. At the last course, in April shortly before he died, Denis told me it was without question the finest collection of players he had had in the 16 years of the organisation's existence.

When I joined the BBC's music staff in 1935, my fringe knowledge of our bands and their music involved me in a pleasurable extension of my editorial responsibilities. It soon became evident that the importance of band music in the radio programmes required the supervision of an acknowledged expert, and Denis was appointed as the Corporation's first Brass and Military Band Supervisor. Thus his influence and inspiration within this special field were hugely extended. In those days, the very man for the job.

Denis had few interests beyond this special field. He was a solitary, for whom the occasional companionship of a few intimates and reading and fishing completed his life. His mind seemed to be wholly applied to the betterment of bands. Earlier this year he was planning to combine a course for young conductors with the youth band meeting. To the legacy of his music he has added an imperishable memory of industry for a cause. A master trainer and visionary is much rarer than even a good composer. May other leaders soon emerge to maintain his ideals and inspire their band-mates.'

Denis's other BBC colleague, Kenneth A. Wright wrote at least two quite lengthy tributes. Here is part of the one which appeared in *British Mouthpiece* of 13th May 1967:

'During the war years (World War II) he was my Assistant Overseas Music Director: a magnificent colleague through difficult days of bombing, tense waiting for D-Day, broadcasts to occupied countries and exiled communities and afterwards to a Europe happier but in flames, and an Empire undergoing the agonies which precede, and follow, self-determination. In charge of the BBC's Transcription Service he not only administered a vast output of all types of music, but arranged and conducted much of it himself, only a small proportion of it for brass or military band.

In his world tours - four to Australasia, two to Canada, plus Rhodesia and South Africa - he worked not only with festivals, local Associations, Examination Boards, and Orchestras, but also with several Commonwealth Universities. He was everywhere acclaimed as a conductor as well as an adjudicator, educationalist and adviser. Everywhere, too, people loved him for his gentle manner and extreme modesty. It gave him great satisfaction when in 1963 Sir Thomas Armstrong invited him to become a Harmony Professor at the Royal Academy of Music. That same year, in Llangollen, Sir Thomas was sitting next to me at lunch when he caught sight of Denis's new book, *The Complete Bandmaster*, lying on the table. Pointing to the author's name he said: *You know, the more I know that man, the greater my regard for him, and my trust.*

Dr. Denis Wright, OBE and Hon. R.A.M. for his services to music, will be greatly missed. Bandsmen, students and audiences all over the world have lost a fine musician and a true friend.'

Understandably, a whole series of tributes appeared in *The British Bandsman*. Here are some extracts from just a few of them:

Eric Ball:

'The passing from our midst of so leading - and often dominant - a personality will leave a gap which no one else is likely to fill, mainly because Denis Wright's position in the brass band movement has been unique. In it he served his day and more than one generation well.

His is not the spectacularly-won fame which comes to the star soloist, the virtuoso contest-conductor: rather has his work become woven in depth into the texture of the movement.

Already a practising musician in an altogether different sphere, he came into brass band work many years ago when great winds of change were blowing: when the idea of original music for bands was something new and controversial and when a new school of conductors were seeking a more expressive, orchestral style of performance than had hitherto been the rule.

Denis's music and arrangements will for a long time keep his name well-known when many of his contemporaries are forgotten. As I write I hear in my mind the haunting strains of *Elaine* from his *Tintagel* Suite. That, of all his music, is something I would wish to remember, and with it, its composer.'

Harry Mortimer:

'As one who had the privilege of making so much music with him during our 40 years of friendship, to me personally this is a great loss, because one always felt that he was there to ask and so willing to proffer good and wise advice. I shall ever be grateful for the help and guidance which he gave me when I took over from him at the BBC in 1942.

Although we shall remember him for the music he created, he was known all over the world, where he travelled as conductor and adjudicator, as DR. DENIS, the perfectionist in everything he undertook. Those of us who knew him more intimately, will never forget his integrity both as a man and as a musician.'

Dr. Harold Hind:

'I feel shattered to hear of the passing of Dr. Denis Wright, for we were contemporaries.

We took our degrees of Mus. Doc. at Edinburgh within a year of each other and his book on the brass band (his first of three) almost coincided with mine. As a matter of fact, Denis held up his first book, to let mine get going!

Undoubtedly the greatest figure in the contemporary brass band world, he was a willing helper to all who consulted him on their problems. Future historians of the brass band movement will name him as the *most outstanding* of all times in brass band personnel.'

Peter Wilson:

'To attempt any sort of appraisal of his life and work is quite outside the scope of this letter, and hardly necessary. I would like, however, as a representative of the younger generation of conductors, to place on record this simple tribute to a sincere and kindly musician who was always ready to help and advise on matters musical and otherwise.

In time we will perhaps come to appreciate more fully the value of Denis Wright's very considerable contribution to brass bands, for his writings and compositions will endure. Meantime we remember him for the quietly effective way he had of drawing the best from those with whom he came in contact. Our loss is very great.'

Arthur Irons:

'I first became associated with Dr. Denis Wright as Bandmaster of Crystal Palace when he was the Musical Director. In those days he was treated with a certain hostile resentment (or at best, amused tolerance) by the brass band world.

I have always wondered why Denis remained in our midst - not having the initial experience of playing a brass instrument as a boy. But he made up for any lost time with his hundreds of arrangements, his original works and his tireless efforts as a teacher. His knowledge was profound. Whenever I found myself bewildered by a harmonic progression, he could always explain it. If some modulation appeared unsatisfactory, he could suggest an improvement. A weak arrangement of a piece could always be strengthened by reference to Denis. What seemed so incredible was his assurance and his lightning response to a question.

Denis was a kindly and human man. His quiet reserve may have given the impression that he was cold and aloof; nothing was farther from the truth. His great work for the NYBB revealed his fundamental humanism.'

My final quote is from an obituary which appeared in the Michaelmas (1967) edition on the Royal Academy of Music's Magazine. It was written by Margaret Hubicki, a colleague of Denis's at the Academy. She concluded with the following:

'Dr. Wright endeared himself to people throughout the world for his gentle manner, extreme modesty, delightful sense of humour and for being someone in whom complete trust could be put. He will be greatly missed by those he so generously helped and they will always associate him with the words he often quoted and which most fittingly represented his point of view: ***It is not what you expect to get out of music that matters, but what you put into it***.

In *The British Bandsman* of 29th April 1967 there was a statement which read: 'Incidentally, Dr. Denis Wright has been far from well since Easter and is having to relinquish a number of engagements during the next few weeks. He hopes to be back to normal by the beginning of July.'

Alas, it was not to be. He was already at rest as we were reading.

1967   *Denis Wright*   *Composer*

(Recorded in perpetuity. The name as it appears in the Book of Remembrance which lies in the Musician's Chapel of the Church of the Holy Sepulchre, London.)

Compositions

a) Test pieces (in chronological order)

1925	Joan of Arc[1]	Overture	R.Smith
1927	The White Rider	Symphonic Poem	R.Smith
1930	Tintagel	Symphonic Suite	B & H/R.Smith(1956)
1933	Princess Nada	Symphonic Legend	R.Smith
1933	The Sea (Thalassa) (BB & MB)	Overture	B & H/Molenaar(1970)
1944	Overture for an Epic Occasion	Overture	R.Smith
1948	Music for Brass	Suite	R.Smith
1951	Atlantic	Symphonic Sketch	R.Smith
1953	Glastonbury[2]	Overture	Paxton
1956	Tam o' Shanter's Ride	Symphonic Sketch	R.Smith
1960	Salzburg Suite	Suite	R.Smith
1962	St. Nicholas Eve (BB & MB)	Prelude	Ms

b) Concert pieces (in chronological order)

1926	Hanover	Fantasia	R.Smith
1935	Deep Harmony[3]	Chorale Prelude	Duckworth/Molenaar(1967)
1935	Carnival[4]	Suite	Ms
1937	Overture in the Olden Style	Overture	Jamesons
1937	A Scottish Fantasy (BB & MB)	Concert piece	Chappell
1940	A Handelian Suite[1]	Suite	B & H
1942	Fanfare for Brass[5]	Fanfare	Ms
1951	Two Lyric Pieces	Concert piece	Parr
1956	Echo Minuet	Concert piece	Sound Music/Peter Maurice
1957	Cornish Holiday[6] (BB and MB) (also for Orchestra)	Concert Piece	Mills Music
1958	Casino Carnival[6]	Concert piece	Mills Music
1966	Carol Sinfonietta	Concert piece	Paxton
1966	Passing Hours	Concert piece	Molenaar

c) Miscellaneous light pieces (in alphabetical order of title)

	Clarion Call	Novello
	Dancing with the Daffodils	Universal
1950	In Grindzing (BB & MB)	Peter Maurice/Studio
	Malaga - Serenade	Ms
	Song at Moonrise	Jameson's (St. Brides)

d)   Marches (in alphabetical order of title)

1931	Ever Forward	Lareine & Co
1935	Empire Jubilee[7] (BB & MB)	Novello

1944 Commonwealth Star (BB & MB)		Peter Maurice/Studio
1947 Homeward Bound (MB & Orch)		Bosworth
Pride of Coventry		Ms (B&H)BBC N91
Up Anchor		Paxton

e) Solos, etc. (in alphabetical order of title)

1931 Columbine - Caprice for Cornet & Orchestra (arr. Chignell)		Ms
1933 Merry Mountaineers	Cornet duet	B & H
1933 Two Little Finches	Cornet duet	B & H
1941 Concerto for Cornet (BB,MB & Orch)	Cornet Solo	Chappell/Studio
1941 La Mantilla	Cornet solo	R.Smith
1967 Trio Concerto	Concerto	Ms

f) Ensembles (in alphabetical order of title)

1945 Miniature Suite	Octet	R.Smith
1945 Sonatina	Septet	R.Smith
1960 Age of Chivalry	Trombone Quartet	Weinberger
1960 Romantica	Standard quartet	Weinberger/Studio
Quartet for Trombones	Trombone quartet	Ms
Tuba Tunes	Bass quartet	Ms

Notes

[1] Also scored for orchestra
[2] Also known as *The Little Overture*
[3] Originally for organ
[4] Includes *Valse Interlude* - published separately by Parr in 1955
[5] Used regularly on war-time broadcasts
[6] Composed for orchestra and brass band
[7] Originally for piano. Band version assigned to Novello in 1952

Appendix 2

Transcriptions

(Classified and in alphabetical order of titles)

a) Marches

1951	Aida - Grand March	Verdi	Ms/Parr/Studio
1951	Festival March (for Festival of Britain)	William Alwyn	Chappell
1940	Imperial March	Elgar	Novello
1938	March of the Bowmen (Robin Hood Suite)	Frederick Curzon	B & H
1936	March Polovtsienne (Prince Igor)	Borodin	B & H
1937	March Solonelle (MB)	German	Chappell
1953	Men of Harlech (March Paraphrase) (BB & MB)	Stanford Robinson	Novello
1965	Pomp & Circumstance March No. 2	Elgar	B & H
1942	W.R.N.S. March, The	Richard Addinsell	K.Prowse
1949	Youth of Britain	Eric Coates	Ms

b) Overtures

1936	Academic Festival Overture	Brahms	R.Smith
1949	Chandos Overture	Handel	Jamesons (St Brides)
1947	Children's Overture, A	Quilter	Chappell
1944	1812 Overture	Tchaikovsky	R.Smith
1937	Fledermaus, Die	Strauss	Ms/Jamesons (St.Bri.)
1944	Franz Schubert	Suppe	Paxton
1945	Mastersingers, The	Wagner	Ms
	Miltary Overture	Mendelssohn	Ms
1935	Miniature Overture (Nutcracker Suite)	Tchaikovsky	B & H
1948	Plymouth Hoe Overture	John Ansell	Chappell
	Scotsman of Chatou, The	Delibes	Ms
1946	Son and Stranger	Mendelsohn	Ms
1932	Thievish Magpie	Rossini	B & H
	Toreador, The	Adam	Ms
	Tragic Overture	Brahms	Ms/ Studio
1940	Two Blind Men of Toledo	Mehul	B & H

c) Solos

1946	Baraza (Piano)	Bliss	Ms

1961	Chanson Indoue (Sop/Horn)	R-Korsakov	Paxton
1947	Concertante Symphonique - Scherzo (Piano)	Litolff	Ms
1947	Concerto in A minor (Piano)	Grieg	Ms
1946	Concerto in A minor (Piano)	Schumann	Ms
1952	Concerto No. 9 - 'Hallelujah' (Organ)	Handel	Ms
1946	Introduction & Allegro Spiritoso (Euph)	Senaille	Paxton
1934	Largo al Factotum (Euph)	Rossini	B & H
1944	Lullaby (Cornet)	Brahms	Ms/Chester
1937	Rondo from Horn Concerto No 4 (Euph)	Mozart	B & H
1950	Trumpet Piece for a Ceremonial Occasion (Cornet)	Scull	N.Richardson
1949	Trumpet Voluntary (Cornet)	Clarke	EMI/Studio
1935	Trumpet Voluntary (Cornet)	Purcell	B & H
1935	Una voce poco fa (Cornet)	Rossini	B & H

d)   Miscellaneous

1955	Air from Suite in D	Bach	Ms/R.Smith (1957)
	Andalouse	Massenet	Ms
1946	Arlesienne Suite, L'	Bizet	Paxton
1955	Bartered Bride (Polka)	Smetana	Parr/Paxton
1955	Berenice (Minuet)	Handel	Ms
1965	Bouree	Bach	Paxton
1936	Capricco Italien	Tchaikovsky	B & H
	Carillon (BB & MB)	Elgar	Elkin
1937	Carmen (Suite)	Bizet	B & H
1940	Chanson de Matin	Elgar	Novello/Paxton (1974)
1949	Chanson de Nuit	Elgar	Novello
1966	Cid, Le	Massenet	Ms/R.Smith (1980)
1958	Cortege	Chaminade	Ms (Enoch, Paris)
1936	Dance of the Apprentices (later added to M'sing. suite)	Wagner	Hawkes
	Elegia (Organ Sonata No. 4)	Charles Proctor	Feldmans/Legnick
1945	Elegy (BB & MB)	Thalben-Ball	Paxton
1955	Fantasia on British Sea Songs	Henry J. Wood	Chappell
	Finale for a Peace Festival	Rheinberger	Ms
1946	Gay Gallantry	Percy Fletcher	B & H
	Intro & Fugue from Sonata on 94th Psalm (MB)	Reubke	Ms
1937	Irish Tune from County Derry	Percy Grainger	Schott
	Kinderscenen (Scenes from Childhood)	Schumann	Ms
1955	Largo (from 'New World' Symphony)	Dvorak	Ms/Paxton
1943	Lohengrin - Introduction to Act III	Wagner	Paxton
1936	London Again (Suite) (MB)	Eric Coates	Chappell
1964	Marching Song	Holst	Novello/R.Smith

1960 Mastersingers Suite (see also Dance of App.)	Wagner	Paxton
1954 Minuet & Galop (Orpheus in the Underworld)	Offenbach	R Smith
1937 Mock Morris	Percy Grainger	Schott
Moorside Suite (MB)	Holst	R.Smith (1983)
Mother, The (Moderen)	Nielsen	Ms
1959 Music for the Royal Fireworks	Handel	F.Richardson
1936 Nimrod (Enigma Variations) (BB & MB)	Elgar	Novello
Phoenix, The	Bliss	Novello
1955 Plain Man's Guide to the Brass Band, The	Various	Ms/Paxton
1937 Polonaise (Christmas Night)	Rimsky-Korsakov	B & H
Prelude & Fugue (St. Ann)	Bach	Ms
1942 Preludes, Les (MB)	Liszt	Ms
1949 Purcell Suite	Purcell	Feldman/Studio
1937 Rebel Maid (Four Dances)	Phillips	Chappell
1936 Rosamunde (Ballet suite)	Schubert	B & H
1966 Saul and David (Prelude Act II)	Nielsen	Hansen/Studio
1935 Serenade Lyrique (BB & MB)	Elgar	Chappell
1937 Shepherd's Hey	Percy Grainger	Schott
1938 Slavonic Dance No. 2	Dvorak	Ms (Lengnick)
1940 Slavonic Dance No. 8	Dvorak	Hansen/Studio
1949 Sleigh Ride	Mozart (K 605)	Ms
1935 Slavonic Rhapsody No. 2	Friedmann	B & H
1948 Solemn Melody (MB)	Walford Davies	Novello
1935 Song of Loyalty (MB)	Eric Coates	Chappell
1937 Springtime (Suite) (MB)	Eric Coates	Chappell
1938 Swan Lake Ballet	Tchaikovsky	B & H
1942 Sylvia Ballet	Delibes	Chappell
1941 Symphony No. 5 - Themes	Beethoven	R.Smith
1944 Symphony No. 8 - Selection	Beethoven	B & H
1939 Symphony No. 5 - Minuet	Schubert	Chappell
1944 Symphony No. 8 (Unfinished) - 1st Mvt.	Schubert	Paxton
1964 Symphony No. 5 - Andante cantabile	Tchaikovsky	Ms
1937 Symphony No. 5 - March	Tchaikovsky	Ms
1955 Symphony No. 6 (Pathetique) All. con grazia (5/4)	Tchaikovsky	Ms
1937 Three Sketches from 'Kenilworth' (cantata) (MB)	Sullivan	Novello
1937 Toccata and Fuge in D minor (MB)	Bach	Chappell
1964 Trepak (Nutcracker Suite)	Tchaikovsky	Midland
1941 William Tell - Ballet Music	Rossini	R.Smith
1935 Valse des Fleurs (Nutcracker Suite)	Tchaikovsky	B & H

e)   Vocal Music

	Arm, Arm Ye Brave (Judas Maccabeus)	Handel	Ms
1958	Be Not Afraid (Elijah)	Mendelssohn	Ms
1946	Blue Danube (Choral Waltz)	Strauss	Ms
	Border Ballad (TTBB)	Cowan	Ms
	Down Among the Dead Men		Ms
	Hear Ye, Israe (Elijah)	Mendelssohn	Ms
	Heavens are telling, The (Creation)	Haydn	Ms
1960	It Comes From the Misty Ages (Banner of St George)	Elgar	Ms
1960	Judas Maccabeus - extracts	Handel	Ms
	King Shall Rejoice, The	Handel	Ms
1948	Let the Bright Seraphim (Sop + SATB)	Handel	Ms/Novello
1948	Let Their Celestial Concerts	Handel	Ms
	Lost Chord, The	Sullivan	Ms
	Men of Harlech	Trad/Evans	Ms
	Love's Old Sweet Song	Molloy	Ms
1946	Messiah (complete)	Handel	Ms
	National Anthem	Trad/Elgar	Ms
	O Peaceful England	German	Ms
1938	Prize Song (Mastersingers)	Wagner	Ms
1951	Requiem in D minor (TTB) (for Treorchy MVC)	Cherubini	Ms
1939	Sound An Alarm (Judas Maccabeus)	Handel	Ms
	Yeomen of England (TTBB)	German	Ms

Arrangements

(Classified and in alphabetical order of titles)

a) Marches

Year	Title	Composer	Publisher
1938	Army, the Navy & the Air Force, The (MB)	Herman Darewsky	Keith Prowse
1957	Amethyst	Leighton Lucas	Robbins/Studio
1956	Balmoral	Noble	Dix/Studio
1946	Banner of Victory	Roger Barsotti	Bosworth
1944	Barracuda	Richardson/Lowry	Paxton
1940	Calling All Workers	Eric Coates	Chappell
1950	Comrades of Friendship		Joshua Duckworth
1937	Down the Mall	John Belton	Ascherberg
1960	Down With the Curtain	Charles Shadwell	Ascherberg
1941	Empire is Marching, The	Dudley Glass	Chappell
1952	Empire March (MB)	Montague Phillips	Novello
1946	Fiesta		Peter Maurice
1942	Flying High	Herman Dostal	Ascherberg
1942	Granada (BB & MB)	Leo Torrance	Ascherberg
1942	H.M.Qeen Elizabeth (MB)	Adela Verne	Paxton
1940	Home Guards (BB & MB)	Ernest Longstaffe	Ascherberg
1939	Knight of the Garter (MB)	Reginald King	Peter Maurice
	Lenore	Joseph Raff	Parr
1946	Lilliburlero	Trad/Wood	Paxton
	Maginot Line, The	John Belton	Liber
	March for the Flight of an Air Balloon[1]	Samuel Wesley	M/s
1943	Marching On (BB & MB)	George Walter	Ascherberg
	March of the Houssas	Leslie-Smith	Chappell
	Massed Bands of the Horse Guards (MB)	M. North	Chappell
1944	N.F.S. March (BB & MB)	Margaret Longstaffe	M/s
1947	Normandy	Ernest Batten	M/s
1943	Portugese March (MB)	C. R. Pinto	M/s
1956	Royal Review	Arnold Steck	Chappell
1960	Royal Edinburgh	Macpherson	Chappell
1935	Silver Jubilee (MB)	Ralph Letts	Chappell
1946	Six Bells	Thomas Wood	Paxton
	Soldiers of the Fleet	Margaret Bell	J.B.Cramer
1950	Spirit of Freedom	G. H. Willcocks	N.Richardson
1945	Tenacity	Roger Barsotti	Bosworth
1948	Time Marches On	John Belton	Ascherberg

1938	To Your Guard (MB)	W. J. Hughes	Chappell
	United Nations[2]	Robinson-Cleaver	Ms
	Valour of Youth	Richard Bell	Chappell

b)   Selections

1957	Around the World in 80 Days (MB)	Victor Young	Chappell
1942	Britain on Parade (BB & MB)	King Palmer	Paxton
1955	Can-Can	Cole Porter	Chappell
1950	Carousel	Richard Rodgers	Chappell/Studio
1939	Cavalleria Rusticana	Mascagni	B & H
1950	Cinderella	David/Hoffman/ Livingstone	Chappell
	Cloak of Night	Valerie d' Orme	Jamesons
1939	Country Girl, A	Lionel Monckton	Chappell
1935	Dance Memories (MB)	Herman Finck	Chappell
1946	Dancing Years, The	Ivor Novello	Chappell
1936	Dream of the Waltz (BB & MB)	Various	Chappell
1962	Early 20s, The	Various	Chappell
1941	Edward German Melodies	German/Robinson	Chappell
1939	Famous Musical Plays	Sigmund Romberg	Chappell
1953	Fantasy on National Airs	Various	Paxton
1937	Firefly, The (MB)	Rudolph Friml	Chappell
1936	Follow the Sun (MB)	Arthur Schwartz	Chappell
1938	Gems of Irish Song (BB & MB)	Various	Chappell
1936	Glamorous Night	Ivor Novello	Chappell
1950	Gondoliers, The	Sullivan	Chappell
1939	Gulliver's Travels	Leo Robin	Chappell
1951	Hans Christian Anderson	Frank Loesser	Chappell
1950	H.M.S. Pinafore	Sullivan	Chappell
1949	Irene	Harry Tierney	Francis Day
1937	Jerome Kern Melodies (BB & MB)	Jerome Kern	Chappell
1954	King and I, The	Richard Rodgers	Chappell/Studio
1950	King's Rhapsody	Ivor Novello	Chappell
1936	King Steps Out, The (MB)	Kreisler/Fields	Chappell
1955	Kismet	Forrest (Borodin)	Chappell/Studio
1949	Land of Song - Welsh Fantasy	Various	N.Richardson
1937	Land Without Music (MB)	Oscar Straus	Chappell
1934	Leek, The (Welsh Melodies)	W. H. Myddleton	B & H
1936	Lionel Monckton Melodies (BB & MB)	Monckton/Robinson	Chappell
1965	Mary Poppins	Richard Sherman	Chappell
1935	Milestones of Melody	Various	Chappell
1950	Mikado, The	Sullivan	Chappell/Studio
1933	New Sullivan Selection	Sullivan	Chappell/Studio
1943	Oklahoma	Richard Rodgers	Chappell/Studio
1937	On the Avenue (MB)	Irving Berlin	Chappell
	Pagoda of Jade, The	Harold Arlen	Ascherberg
1960	Paris Calling	Various	Ascherberg

1932	Panorama of Famous Songs (BB & MB)	Various	Chappell
1950	Patience	Sullivan	Chappell
1960	Paul Rubens Melodies	Rubens/Robinson	Chappell
1950	Pirates of Penzance, The	Sullivan	Chappell
1936	Please Teacher (MB)	Waller/Tunbridge	Chappell
1935	Radio Parade of 1935	Various	Chappell
1949	Rio Rita	Harry Tierney	Francis, Day & Hunter
	Rise 'n' Shine	Robert Stolz	Chappell
1935	Roberta (MB)	Jerome Kern	Chappell
1937	Rosalie (MB)	Cole Porter	Chappell
1934	Rose de France (MB)	Sigmund Romberg	Chappell
1935	Schubert Waltzes	Schubert	Ms
1934	Second New Sullivan Selection	Sullivan	Chappell
	Seeing Stars (MB)	Martin Broones	Chappell
1937	Shall we Dance? (MB)	George Gershwin	Chappell
1938	Snow White and the Seven Dwarfs	Frank Churchill	Chappell/Studio
1946	Song of Paradise	Reginald King	Peter Maurice
1946	Songs of Long Ago	King Palmer	Paxton
1961	Songs of the Rising Tide	George Fraser	George Fraser
1959	Sound of Music, The	Richard Rodgers	Chappell/Studio
1939	Sousa on Parade	King Palmer	Paxton/Novello
1951	South Pacific	Richard Rodgers	Chappell
1934	Streamline (MB)	Vivian Ellis	Chappell
	Strike Up the Band	George Gershwin	Chappell
1936	Student Prince, The (MB)	Sigmund Romberg	Chappell
1935	Sweet Adeline (MB)	Jerome Kern	Chappell
1934	Sweethearts of Yesterday	Henry Hall	Chappell
1937	Swing Time (MB)	Jerome Kern	Chappell
1937	Tchaikovsky Waltzes (BB & MB)	Tchaikovsky	Chappell
1936	Top Hat (MB)	Irving Berlin	Chappell
1945	Victory Parade	Various	Peter Maurice
1935	Viennese Memories of Lehar	Franz Lehar	Chappell
1947	Waltzing Through Old Vienna	I. Geiger	Bosworth
1957	West Side Story	Bernstein	Chappell/Studio
1937	White Horse Inn, The	Ralph Benatzky	Chappell/Studio
1950	Yeomen of the Guard, The	Sullivan	Chappell

c)   Solos (etc.)

1938	Busybodies (cornet or xylophone duet)	Frederick Curzon	B & H
1963	Carnival Variations (cornet trio)	Jacoby	Ascherberg
1951	Count Your Blessings (cornet)	Reginald Morgan	Ascherberg
1938	Floral Dance (trombone)	Katie Moss	Chappell
1937	I Love the Moon (cornet)	Paul Rubens	Chappell
1934	Indian Love Call (cornet)	Rudolph Friml	Chappell
1944	Lullaby (cornet)	Brahms	Ms
1936	Lucille (cornet)	Percy Code	B & H
1938	Mairie my Girl (trombone)	G.Aitkens	Chappell

| 1946 | Rose of Tralee, The | Glover/Spencer | Paxton |
| 1937 | Trees (cornet)(MB) | Oscar Rasbach | Chappell |

d)   Miscellaneous

	Ain't cha comin' out?	Ruby/Kalman	Chappell
	Amontillado	Valerie d' Orme	Jamesons
	Arabian Scenes	Hermann Lohr	Chappell
1949	Autumn Evensong	H. A. Rimmer	Ascherberg
	Bei mir bist du Schoen		
	(Means that you're grand)	Shalon Secunda	Chappell
1945	Bells of St. Mary's	A.Emmett Adams	Ascherberg
1960	Brahms on Brass	Brahms	Paxton
1939	British Grenadiers, The[3]	Stanford Robinson	Stainer & Bell
	Busybodies	Frederick Curzon	B & H
	Butterfly Kisses	Langham	Jamesons (St Brides)
	Can I Forget You	Jerome Kern	Chappell
1945	Cavalry of the Steppes	Lev Knipper	Bosworth
	Chanson (In Love) (MB)	Rudolph Friml	Chappell
	Chanson Solonelle	Graham Gill	Gill/Chesters
	Chanson Triste	Tchaikovsky	Novello
1952	Chrysanthemun Waltz		
	(Wild Roses)	Franz Lehar	Glocken Verlag
1943	Concerto Pastiche	Tchaikovsky/Palmer	Paxton
	Coronation Bells	Partridge	Peter Maurice
1963	Cuban National Anthem		
	(La Bayames)	Figueredo	Cramer
	Dance of the May Flies	Dorothy Atkinson	Jamesons
	Dancing Toys (Black and Blue)	Ronnie Hill	Stirling Music
	Dinner on the Train	Wreford/Butler	Ms
	Doing an Irish Jig	Vivian Ellis	Chappell
1950	Dolores	Waldteufel	Ascherberg
1948	Dream of Olwen, The	Charles Williams	Lawrence Wright
	Drink to me Only	Trad.	Graham Gill
1951	El Relicario	Jose S. Padilla	Ascherberg
1937	Escapada (BB & MB)	Sid Phillips	Lawrence Wright
	Fairy Ring	Guy Langham	Jamesons
	F. D. R. Jones	Harold Rome	Chappell
	Fleet's Lit Up, The	Vivian Ellis	Victoria Mus. Pub.
	Floral Dance, the	Katie Moss	Chappell
	Flying Trapeze, The	Mabel Wayne	Chappell
	Forget-me-not	Allan Macbeth	Ascherberg
	Fountain Lake Fanfare	Rob. Russ. Bennett	Chappell
1943	From the Fold Country	Thos.F.Dunhill	Ms
1956	Gay Gordons, The	Theo Bonheur	Paxton
1946	Gipsy Flower	A.Ferraris	Paxton
	Goodnight Angel	Allie Wrubel	Chappell
1938	Heigh-Ho (Snow White)	Frank Churchill	Chappell
1947	Her Majesty Queen Elizabeth	Verne	Paxton
	Indian Summer	Dorothy Atkinson	Jamesons
1941	Indian Summer	Victor Herbert	Chappell
1949	In the Soudan		
	(Dervish Chorus)	Sebek	B & H

	In Your Arms Tonight (MB)	Henry Geehl	Chappell
	It All Depends on Me	Phil Park	Chappell
1963	Jamaican National Anthem	Lightbourne	Ms
1943	Kelligree's Soiree, The	K. A. Wright	Paxton (1970)
	Kiss Me Goodnight (MB)	Bernie	Chappell
1944	Lady of Spain	Tolchard Evans	Peter Maurice
1950	Legend	Robert Docker	Lawrence Wright
	Love Walked In	George Gershwin	Chappell
	Masquerade	Hermann Lohr	Chappell
	Masquerade is Over, The	Allie Wrubel	Chappell
	Melody d' Amour	Hermann Lohr	Chappell
1960	Merry Widow Waltz	Franz Lehar	Glocken-Verlag/Studio
	Mightier Yet	George Grant	Lawrence Wright
	Moonlight and Shadows	Robin/Hollander	Victoria Mus. Pub.
	Moonlight Memories	James Coleman	City Music Pub
	Moon Over Miami	Dorothy J.Burke	Chappell
	Moths Round a Candle	Dorothy Atkinson	Jamesons
	Music Maestro Please	Allie Wrubel	Chappell
	Music of the Night	Eric Coates	Chappell
1935	My Gipsy Flower	A. Ferraris	Paxton
1944	National Anthem		
	(with fanfare Rule Britannia)	Trad.	Paxton
1963	Netherlands National Anthem	Nassouwe	Ms
	Night is Young, The	Dana Suesse	Chappell
	Now it can be Told	Irving Berlin	Chappell
	Oh! Joanna	Henry Hall	Chappell
	One day when we were young	Oscar Straus	Chappell
	Our Song (For You Alone)	Jerome Kern	Chappell
1955	Palace of Dreams	Jack Waller	Chappell
1939	Phantom Brigade, The	Myddleton	B & H
1939	Portrait of a Toy Soldier	Montague Ewing	Liber
1945	Prayer at Eventide, A	Reginald A.King	Ascherberg
1935	Robber Symphony Suite (M.B.)	Feher	Chappell
1937	Rose of My Heart	Hermann Lohr	Chappell
1937	Rose of Spain	A. Ferraris	Paxton
	Rule Britannia (see National Anthem)		
	Says My Heart (Coconut Grove)	Burton Lane	Victoria Mus. Pub.
	Scent of Roses, The	Waldteufel	Ascherberg
	Sentry Go	Dorothy Atkinson	Jamesons
1951	Serenade - Frasquita	Franz Lehar	Weinberger
	Serenite	Graham Gill	Graham Gill
	She is Far from the Land (MB)	Frank Lambert	Chappell
	Signposts - suite	Hermann Lohr	Chappell
1952	(Les) Sirens - Waltz	Waldteufel	Ascherberg
	Sleepy Lagoon	Eric Coates	Chappell
1942	Soldiers in the Park (BB & MB)	Lionel Mockton	Chappell
	Somewhere at Sea	Henry Hall	Chappell
1945	Song of Paradise	Reginald King	Peter Maurice
	Star Spangled Banner (The)	Smith	Ms
1937	Sympathy (Firefly)	Rudolph Friml	Chappell
1939	There'll Always be an England	Parker/Charles	Chappell
1937	This Year's Kisses	Irving Berlin	Chappell

1936	Three Blind Mice	Adolf Lotter	B & H
	Through a Stained Glass		
	Window	Montague Ewing	Jamesons
	Trees (MB)	Oscar Rasbach	Chappell
	Two Sleepy People	Hoagy Carmichael	Victoria Mus. Pub.
	Umbrella Man	Rose/Stock	Chappell
1940	Waltzing Matilda	Marie Cowan	Ascherberg
1939	West Country Suite	Ashworth-Pope	Graham Gill
	Whistle While You Work	Frank Churchill	Chappell
1952	Wild Roses	Franz Lehar	Glocken-Verlag/Studio
	Will You Remember? (Maytime)	Sigmund Romberg	Chappell
1934	Wonder Bar	Harry Warren	Feldman
	Ye Olden Chimes	Ernest Batten	Chappell

e)   Ensembles

	Adagio & Allegro (quintet)	Ewald (Ed. DW)	Ms
1938	Bal Masque	Percy Fletcher	B & H
1935	Canzonas 1, 5, 7, 8		
	(large brass ensemble)	G Gabrieli	Ms
1938	Demande et Reponse		
	(2 tpt/2 tbn)	Coleridge Taylor	B & H
	Drink to me only		
	(octet or quartet)	Traditional	Graham Gill
	Emperor's Hymn (Th. & Var.)		
	(sextet)	Haydn	Ms
1942	Gavotte (octet & piano)	Gossec	Ms
1960	Into. & Allegro Spiritoso		
	(wind ensemble)	Senaille	Paxton
1964	Little Folk Song Suite, A		
	(octet)[4]	Trad	Ms
	Lullaby (octet)	Brahms	Ms
	Minuet from Serenade in D		
	(sextet)	Brahms	Ms
	Ottone overture (octet)	Handel	Ms
1942	St. Ann Fugue (octet)	Bach	Ms
1940	Traumeri (octet)	Schumann	Graham Gill

Notes

[1] Composed by Samuel Wesley for the flight of Mr. Lunardi's Air Balloon, at the desire of Sir Watkin Lewes, to whom it is dedicated by the composer. The brass band Ms is in the library of Fairey's, but does not indicate when or why it was scored for brass band.

[2] Denis Wright's Ms is in Fairey's library, but there is no indication of its date.

[3] Also for use with mixed or male voice choir.

[4] There is a later version of this for septet, with alternative instrumentation (brass band or orchestral brass) and with a changed key scheme.

Appendix 4

Pseudonyms

Arrangements as "Frank Denham"
(All published by Chappell)

a) Marches
1933	Knightsbridge (London Suite) (MB)	Eric Coates
1933	London Bridge	Eric Coates
1937	Palace of Varieties	Ernest Longstaffe
1938	Wandering the King's Highway	Leslie Coward

b) Selection
1938	Operette (Waltz Medley)	Noel Coward

c) Miscellaneous
1937	Did You Mean it? (Fox-trot)	Mort Dixon
1937	Donkey Serenade, The (Firefly)	Friml/Stothart
1937	Little Old Lady	Hoagy Carmichael
1935	Lovely to Look At (Sweet Adeline)	Jerome Kern
1937	Lover Come Back to Me (The New Moon)	Sigmund Romberg
1941	Papa Niccolini	Edwards & George
1936	Top Hat (Top Hat) (MB)	Irving Berlin
1933	Whistler and His Dog, The	Arthur Pryor

(According to PRS there are almost 100 more 'Frank Denham' arrangements which I have been unable to locate. I suspect that most of them would be commercial dance band arrangements).

Compositions/Arrangements as "Walter Stewart"

1940	Baby's Sweetheart (arr.)	Concert piece	W. Corri	B & H
1941	Britain on Parade (arr.)	Selection	Various	Paxton
1942	Dashing Away with the Smoothing Iron	Concert piece	Trad.	Paxton
	Gremlin's Parade	Concert piece	D. Wright	Ms
1942	Trumpet Tune in 17th C. Style[1]	Solo	D. Wright	Paxton
	Helston Furry, The	Concert piece	Trad.	Ms

Compositions as "John Savernacke"
(in Music for Brass Ensemble Book 3)

1959 Canzona in the Italian Style	Ensemble piece	D. Wright	Novello
1959 My Lady Daphne's Delight	Ensemble piece	D. Wright	Novello

Composition as R.C.Lanyon

Hilltop Shrine - Reverie	Concert piece	D. Wright	Ms

Note

[1] Also scored for orchestra.

Appendix 5

Collections

1953 Champion Slow Melody Books - No. 1   **R.Smith**
Three graded solos for Bb instruments, edited and piano accompaniments arranged by Denis Wright

Mendelssohn:	If with all your Hearts (Elijah)
Gluck:	Che Faró
Mozart:	Romance from the Clarinet Concerto

1953 Champion Slow Melody Book 2 (Eb inst./Bass Tbn)   **R.Smith**
Three graded solo for Eb instruments (or bass trombone), edited and piano accompaniments arranged by Denis Wright

Wagner:	O Star of Eve (Tannhauser)
Beethoven:	Romance (originally for violin)
Bach:	Air (from the Suite in D)

1965 Cornet pieces with piano accompaniment   **Paxton**

Mendelssohn:	Christmas Piece
Handel:	Air from Ptolemy
Tchaikovsky:	Canzonetta
Charpentier:	March in Rondo Form

1949 Eight Famous Pieces for Cornet Solo   **Ascherberg**
(with pianoforte accompaniment)

Haydn Wood:	A Bird Sang in the Rain
Reginald Morgan:	Count Your Blessings
Lao Silésu:	Love, Here is my Heart
Pietro Mascagni:	Intermezzo (Cavalleria Rusticana)
Meyer Lutz:	Pas de Quatre (Faust up to date)
A. van Biene:	The Broken Melody
E. Waldteufel:	Pomone Waltz
Allan Macbeth:	Intermezzo - Forget-me-not

1941 Eight Quartets   **R.Smith**

Bach:	Gavotte; Bouree
Handel:	Gigue (Berenice); March
Mozart:	Minuet
Beethoven:	Minuet in G
Morley:	It was a Lover and his Lass
Tallis:	Canon

1953   Famous Cornet Solos   **Chappell**

Lehar:	You are my Heart's Delight
Forster:	Rose in the Bud
Lohr:	Little Grey Home in the West
Clay:	I'll Sing Thee Songs of Araby
Haydn Wood:	A Brown Bird Singing
I. de Laren:	Garden of Sleep
Aitkens:	Mairie my Girl

1958   Music for Brass Ensemble Book 1   **Novello**

Scales; Studies; Marionette March;
The Minstrel's Song; Canon at the octave: Berceuse;

Gluck:	March from 'Alceste'
adapt. Corelli:	Sarabande
Trad:	The Londonderry Air
adapt. Handel:	Gavotte
Handel:	March from 'Scipio'
Arcadelt:	Ave Maria
Handel:	Minuet

Chorale (Spiritual Songs 1539 - harm. Mendelssohn)

Handel:	March - See the Conquering Hero Comes

1958   Music for Brass Ensemble Book 2   **Novello**

Mozart:	March from 'The Magic Flute'
Tchaikovsky:	Legend
Mendelssohn:	Song Without Words No. 9
Handel:	Gavotte; Air; Allegro Spiritoso
Wright:	March on Two Old Welsh Airs
Mendelssohn:	Nocturne from 'A Midsummer Night's Dream'
Mozart:	Minuet from 'Don Giovanni'
Brahms:	Melody - My pretty one, why go barefoot?
Haydn:	St. Anthony Chorale; Minuetto
Purcell:	March
Schumann:	A Little Folk Song (Volksliedchan)
Mendelssohn:	Song Without Words No. 16
Handel:	March from 'Occasional Oratorio'

1959   Music for Brass Ensemble Book 3   **Novello**

Schumann:	Hunting Song; The Little Wanderer
	New Year's Song
Savernake (D.W.):	Canzona in the Italian Style
	My Lady Daphne's Delight
Wright:	March on Two Old English Tunes
Purcell:	Prelude; Gay Air; Hornpipe
Bach:	Prelude from 'Six Little Preludes & Fugues'
Beethoven:	Theme from Piano Sonata No. 12
Holborne:	Pavan (The Cradle)
	Gaillard (The New Year's Gift);
	Almayne (The Night Watch)
Haydn:	Rondo from 'Divertimento for Wind Instruments'
Handel:	Bouree & Hornpipe from 'The Water Music'

1966 Music for Junior Bands & Brass Ensembles   **Chester**
(for full brass band, with optional clarinet, saxophone and French horn)

Brahms:	Lullaby; Waltz No. 15
Tchaikovsky:	March of the Toy Soldiers
Mozart:	Sleigh Ride
Mendelssohn:	Christmas Piece
Bach:	Fugue No. 8
Traditional:	The Lincolnshire Poacher
	O Varmland, so lovely
	Rander's March
Handel:	Two Minuets
Purcell:	Gay Air; Minuet; Hornpipe
Schubert:	Entr'acte (Rosamunde)

1969 Six Solos for Cornet or Trumpet, Euphonium or Baritone Paxton
(with pianoforte accompaniment)

Mendelssohn	Christmas Piece
Handel	Air from Ptolemy
Bach	Bourée
Handel	Two Minuets
Tchaikovsky	Canzonetta
Charpentier	March in Rondo Form

Three Operatic Arias (Wagner)   **R.Smith (1969)**

Sigmund's Love Song	Valkyrie
O Star of Eve	Tannhauser
Walther's Prize Song	Mastersingers

Three Operatic Arias for E flat Horn   **(1980)**
(with pianoforte accompaniment)

Virtuoso Album of Cornet Solos   **Ms**
(Dedicated to Jack Mackintosh)

Columbine (Caprice) (also for cornet and orchestra)
Tarantelle Brillante
Forked Lightning (Humoresque)

Music not written for Band or Brass Solo

a) Orchestral/choral works

i) Compositions (all Ms)

	Ballad of Princess Nada, The	SSA & strings
	Dance Suite, op. 17 (Orch)	B & H/Ms (BBC 2260)
1930	Joan of Arc	full orchestra
1940	Pibroch of Donhuil Dhu (D. Mus exercise)	double chorus & orchestra
1936	Sennecherib (Cantata - B. Mus. Exercise)	
1940	Suite for Orchestra (D. Mus exercise)	full orchestra
	Suite for Strings (Prelude, Minuet, Air, Gigue)	strings
	Suite in 18th Century Style	full orchestra (BBC 13130)
	Two Arthurian Sketches	full orchestra
	Variations & Fugue on a Theme of Handel (Brahms Op. 24)	full orchestra

ii) Transcriptions/Arrangements (small orchestra)

1934	Conversation Piece	Noel Coward	Chappell
1936	Follow the Fleet (Selection)	Irving Berlin	Chappell
1935	Robber Symphony, The	F. Feher	Chappell
1935	Roberta (Selection)	Jerome Kern	Chappell
1935	Snow Waltz (simplified)	F. Feher	Chappell
1935	Sweet Adeline (Selection)	Jerome Kern	Chappell
1936	Things to Come	Arthur Bliss	Chappell

b) Songs

				(Words)
1960	At the Fair (2-part)	Ponchielli	Ascherberg	
1961	Ave Maria (2 voices)	J. Archadelt	L. J. Cary & Co	
1924	Bellman Tom	Denis Wright	Perry & Gill	Margaret Owen
1961	Boot, Saddle, to Horse & Away (2-part)	George Dyson	Ascherberg	
1935	Coloured Fields (2-part)	Eric Coates	Chappell	
1965	Come Join the Fife & Drum (Grenadiers)	Waldteufel	Ascherberg	S.Douglas
1964	Dreaming, Dreaming (SATB)	Waldteufel	Ascherberg	
1961	Drummer Curly (2-part)	A. Moffat	Ascherberg	
1960	England (SATB)	C. H. H. Parry	Ascherberg	
1961	Fishing	Alec Rowley	Ascherberg	
1919	Give Me Your Hand	Denis S. Wright	Escott & Co	Edmund John
1960	Habanera (Carmen) (SSA)	Bizet	Ascherberg	
1917	Heroes (unaccompanied)	Denis S. Wright	Stainer & Bell	

1918	In Absence (tenor or soprano)	Denis S. Wright	Stainer & Bell	Denis S. Wright
1921	Is it Love?	Denis S. Wright	Escott & Co	Lawrence P. Russ
1918	Love Wakes and Weeps (SSAA)	Denis S. Wright	Stainer & Bell	Sir Walter Scott
1961	Maria Mater Gratië (motet for 2 v.)	Denis S. Wright	L. J. Cary & Co	Motets
1963	Mass of San Augustin (2 v. & org)	Denis S. Wright	L. J. Cary & Co	
1960	Mother, You Know the Story	Mascagni	Ascherberg	
1961	Music When Soft Voices Die	Charles Wood	Ascherberg	
1924	Mystic Ring, The	Denis S. Wright	Dix & Co	Violet Tinsley
1965	My Heart Ever Faithful (SSA)	Bach	Ascherberg	
1965	My Mother Bids me Bind my Hair	Haydn	Ascherberg	
1920	Night Wind 'neath the Trees	Denis S. Wright	Weekes & Co	Walter Stewart
1960	On With the Motley (TTBB)	Leoncavallo)	Ascherberg	
1924	Out Beaconsfield Way	Denis S. Wright	Perry & Gill	Margaret Owen
1925	Pibroch of Donhuil Dhu	Denis Wright	Elkin & Co	Walter Scott
1935	Sigh No More, Ladies (2-part)	Eric Coates	Chappell	
1965	Scent of Roses, The (SATB)	Waldteufel	Ascherberg	
1964	Southern Maid So Fair (SATB)	Waldteufel	Ascherberg	S.Douglas
1935	Summer Afternoon (2-part)	Eric Coates	Chappell	
1935	Sweet-and-twenty (2-part)	Eric Coates	Chappell	
1961	Trees in England, The	Charles Wood	Ascherberg	
1930	Two Passiontide Songs	Denis Wright	Novello	Rev. J. Troutbeck
	(1) Beloved Saviour wilt thou answer (2) Jesus, thou knowest death			
1964	Virgin's Slumber-song, The (SA)	Max Reger	Ascherberg	
1960	Your Glasses now Raise (2-part)	Verdi	Ascherberg	

c) Instrumental pieces
i) Piano Selections

1961	Carmen (easy-to-play)	Bizet	Ascherberg
1960	Carmen (easy-to-play)	Bizet	Ascherberg
1935	Flying Trapeze	Benatzky & Wayne	Chappell
1935	Glamorous Night (as F. Denham)	Ivor Novello	Chappell
1935	Gay Deceivers	M. Broones	Chappell
1960	Il Trovatore (easy-to-play)	Verdi	Ascherberg
1952	Lovely to Look At	Jerome Kern	Chappell
1935	Stop Press	Irving Berlin	Chappell
1934	Streamline	Vivian Ellis	Chappell

ii) Miscellaneous

1926	Deep Harmony - Chorale Prelude (organ)	Denis Wright	J. Duckworth
1935	Empire Jubilee March (piano)	Denis Wright	Chappell
1920	Impressions of Serbia (piano)	Denis S. Wright	Escott & Co
1925	Odd-moment studies (piano)	Denis S Wright	Perry & Gill
1919	Phantasy-Dialogue (cello & piano)	Denis S. Wright	Escott & Co

(d) Collections

1955	Arrangements for Strings & Piano		Novello

Easy grade	Tchaikovsky:	Morning Prayer; Elegy; Happy Tune
	Schumann:	Humming Song; Chorale; The Reaper's Song
	Muir:	The Maple Leaf
	Welsh Air:	Loudly Proclaim
	Handel:	March from the 'Occasional Overture'
	Tchaikovsky:	Hymn to the Trinity
	Driver:	Song of the Flower
	Ogilvy:	Humoresque
	Spurling:	In the Church
Intermediate	Tchaikovsky:	Chanson Triste
	Chopin:	Three Preludes
	Handel:	Let the Bright Seraphim
	Schubert:	Who is Sylvia?
	Fletcher:	Toy Soldiers' March
	Tchaikovsky:	Happy Dream
	Austin:	Romance
	Greenhill:	Queen Mab Summons her Court
	Dunhill:	The Lavender Lady
	Ogilvy:	Lyric-Caprice
	Mayer:	Village Dance
	Rathbone:	Evensong
	Tchaikovsky:	Graceful Dance
	Schumann:	Christmas Eve; New Year's Eve; Northern Song
	Greenhill:	The Cuckoo
	Bach:	Preludes 4 and 6; Gracious Lord of All our Being
	Handel:	Pastoral Symphony from 'Messiah'
Advanced	Blower:	Solitude
	Schumann:	The Inn
	Beethoven:	Solemn March
	Cowan:	December - Christmas Morn
	Handel:	Where e're you walk
	Schubert:	Sonatina in D major (1st movement)
	Bach:	Largo from Concerto in D minor for two violins
	Fletcher:	Toy Soldiers' March
	Cowen:	Country Dance; Graceful Dance
	Rameau:	La Bouree de Vincent

1967 **Boy's Book of Gilbert & Sullivan**   **Ascherberg**
There lived a King   No Possible Doubt Whatever
The Flowers that Bloom   I am the Captain of the Pinafore
With Cat-like Tread   Behold the Lord High Executioner

1967 **Girl's Book of Gilbert & Sullivan**   **Ascherberg**
Little Buttercup   Poor Wandering One
A Man who would Woo a Fair Maid   Kind Sir You Cannot Have the Heart
For he's Going to Marry Yum-Yum   A Regular Royal Queen

1959 **Strings Collection by D. S. S. Wright (Edited W. H. Reed):**
(Elementary School Orchestra Series)
Allegro spiritoso   Melody
Country Dance   The Minstrel Boy

Cradle Song	Patrol
Left Right	Sarabande
March in Rondo Form	The Vicar of Bray

Music for String Players (Intermediate)

Caprice	Happy Dream
Chorale	The Merry Peasant
Elegy	Northern Song
Graceful Dance	Pastoral Symphony
Lord of All Our Being	Soldiers' March

1949 W. H.Reed's School Orchestral Series (revised Denis Wright)   Novello

Bobby Shaftoe	Trad.
Cradle Song	Schubert
School March	W.H.Reed
The Vicar of Bray	Trad.

Bibliography

Autobiography, Denis Wright, unpublished, date unknown
The Brass Band Conductor, Denis Wright, Joshua Duckworth, 1948
The Brass Band Movement, Russell and Elliott, Dent, 1936
Brass Bands, Arthur R. Taylor; Granada, 1979
Brass Bands in the 20th Century, Ed. Violet & Geoffrey Brand, Egon, 1979
The British Bandsman Centenary Book, Alf Hailstone, Egon, 1987
Challenging Brass, S.P.Newcomb, Powerbrass Music, New Zealand 1980
The Complete Bandmaster, Denis Wright, Pergamon Press, 1963
Durham County Brass Band League - 50 Golden Years, Ed. Massey, County Durham
Books, 1992
The Evolution of the Wind Band, Denis Wright, unpublished thesis, 1940
Labour and Love, Arthur R. Taylor, Elm Tree Books, 1983
List of Prize Winners, (published annually by Belle Vue, Manchester)
The LSO at 70, Maurice Pearton, Victor Gollancz, 1974
The Macmillan Encyclopedia, Macmillan, 1981
The Manor House Hospital, Samuel J. Woodall, Routledge & Kegan Paul, 1966
Music on Record 1 Brass Bands, Ed. Gammond and Horricks, Patrick Stephens, 1980
The Oxford Dictionary of Music, Michael Kennedy, O.U.P., 1985
Scoring for Brass Band (4th edition), Denis Wright, John Baker, 1967
Scoring for Brass Band (5th edition), Denis Wright, Studio Music, 1986
Special Music Recordings, BBC 1945 (2 volumes)
Welfare in Trust, William Roberton, Carnegie U.K. Trust, 1964

Past copies of *The British Bandsman,* 1925-1967
Past copies of *Brass Band News,* 1925-1967
Various other newspaper articles
Programmes, papers and documents from personal collections
Papers and documents supplied by Mrs. Wright
Scores for the compositions discussed in the text
Music catalugues of publishers and various bands
Library of National Youth Brass Band of Great Britain

Index

Absent Minded Beggar 14, 95

Adelaide Choir & Orch. (Dublin) 202-4

Alcock, Walter 16, 19, 24

Alexander Palace 125

Alexandra Choir 175-6

All-Star Band 205-6

A.O.M.F. 49, 51-2, 145, 159-60, 200, 206, 216, 244

Area contests 131, 133, 139, 203, 241

Armstrong, Sir Thomas 243, 249

Arnold, Malcolm 241

Ascherberg, Hopwood and Crew 143, 242

Ashpole, Alfred 209

Askew, Antony 180

Atkinson, Arthur 210

Atkinson Tom 152, 214, 221, 248

Australia 185, 188-90, 197, 202, 207
ABC 189
Adelaide 206
Australasian Bandsman 188-9
Ballarat (South Street) 189-90
Brisbane 185, 188-9, 197
Brisbane Ch. Soc. 176
Dalley-Scarlet, R. 176-7
Melbourne 185, 189
National Ch'ships. 219
New South Wales B.B.A. 188
Ozoompah! 188
Queensland Ch'ships. 189, 197
Q'land Solo & Quart. Ch'ships. 185, 188
Sydney 188-9, 197
Univ. of Western Aust. 189
Western Aust. Ch'ships. 189
Western Command Band 189
Western Group Concert Band 188

Autobiography 8, 9, 11, 22, 24, 26-7, 53, 78-9, 90-1, 94, 161

Bach, J.S. 60, 145

Bachelor of Music 42, 162

Ball, Eric 12, 47, 151, 156, 194, 203, 218, 224, 228-9, 236, 245, 250
Call of the Sea 236
Exodus 169

Bandsman's Coll. of Mus. 49-50, 57, 188-9, 200, 202, 206, 244
B.B.C.M. 49-50, 159, 185, 188-9

Bandsman's Little Book, The 168

Bandsman's World 166

Bantin, Francis 73-4

Bantock, Sir Granville 31, 40, 83-4, 104, 106
Oriental Rhapsody 40, 125
Prometheus Unbound 125, 244

Barbirolli, Sir John 104

Bardgett, Herbert 177

Bath, Hubert 25
Honour & Glory 40, 108, 125

Bax, Arnold 31

Beecham, Sir Thomas 76

Beethoven: Egmont Ov. 76, 78, 226
Sonata Pathetique 40
Symphony No. 5 51, 54, 94-8, 104, 126

Bell, Alfie 177

Belle Vue 13, 37, 39-40, 46-7, 54, 72-3, 86, 98, 100, 125-6, 129, 158, 169, 202, 204-207, 241

Bennett, Herbert 211

Berryman, John 154, 210, 218-220, 227

Besses o' th' Barn Band 51, 54, 96, 181, 209

Binary form 111-2

Bickershaw Coll. Band 108, 177

Birmingham & Dist. B.B.A. 244

Bizet 60
L'Arlesienne 76

Blackburn Choral Society 177

Black Dyke Mills Band 10, 22, 34-6, 39, 54, 59, 74, 77, 79, 85, 94, 96, 104, 108-9, 141, 176-8, 180, 209, 224, 238-9, 242

Blaencym Choral Society 174

Bliss, Sir Arthur 19, 31, 47, 77, 87, 100, 209
Baraza 106, 159

Kenilworth 77, 109, 125

Blue Coat School Band 55

Boldon Coll. Band 37

Book of Remembrance 204

Boosey, Leslie 166

Boosey's 48, 145

Boosey & Hawkes 11, 158, 234

Booth, Webster 106

Boult, Sir Adrian 16, 51, 54, 63, 94-6, 98, 102-4, 106, 141, 155, 201, 219, 226, 230-1

Bourgeois, Derek 151

Bournemouth Symph. Orch 27

Bournemouth T.A. Band 234

Boys' Band Assoc. of Yorkshire 210

Bradford Festival Ch. Soc. 177

Brahms: Academic Festival Ov. 54, 60, 106, 108, 125, 169
Eb Trio 93
Lullaby 108
Requiem 204

Braithwaite, Warwick 93

Brand, Geoffrey 12, 150, 152-3, 194, 237

Brass Band Conductor, The 52, 159, 161

Brass Band News 11, 23-4, 34-7, 39, 45, 50, 60, 104, 153, 213

Brass Band Scoring 26

Bravington, Eric 244

Bridge, Frank 31

Bridge, Sir Frederick 16, 19

Brighouse & Rastrick Band 10, 42, 79, 85, 104, 106, 201, 209, 239, 242

Brighton Silver Band 208

Britannia B'ding Soc. Band 178, 180

British Bandsman 11, 14, 19, 2 3-4, 31-2, 34, 39, 42, 52, 74, 98, 142, 152, 162-3, 168-9, 177, 182-4, 188, 192, 194, 197, 202, 204, 206, 210-11, 213-4, 218, 226, 234, 236-7, 239, 242-5, 250

British Broadcasting Corp (BBC) 42, 44, 50, 75, 77-9, 89, 94-5, 98, 100, 103, 107, 125, 141, 153, 157-8, 161, 172, 178, 180-3, 197, 200, 204-7, 214, 221-2,

224, 227, 229, 236-7, 239, 244, 248-9, 250, 252
Ass. Overseas Director 89, 107
Band Section 77, 80, 84, 98, 154, 169
Br. & Mil. Band Supervisor 86, 100, 154, 249
Broadcast formation 88-9, 101
Challenging Brass 241
Concert Orchestra 205-6
Home Guard Band 85-6
Light Music Festival 148, 205, 239
Men's Chorus 54, 87, 108
Military Band 77, 80, 83-4, 89, 92-3, 98, 108, 170
Music Department 77, 80, 85, 90, 154, 169
Music While You Work 82
Northern Orchestra 93, 108
Overseas Services 108, 154, 170
Saturday Bandstand 82-3
Scottish Orchestra 93, 108
Sounding Brass and Voices 82, 89, 156, 173, 177, 201
Transcription Service 10, 44, 107-8, 157, 185, 201, 203, 205-6, 209, 221, 225, 249
Westminster Orchestra 44, 157, 200-1
British Imperial Military Band 201
British Mouthpiece 249
British Open Ch'ships. 50, 110
Brown, Ernest 43-4, 48, 54, 76, 152, 219
Bulawayo Symph. Orch. 197
Burton Constable 12
Butterfield Tank Wks. Band 55, 204
Butterworth, Arthur 52, 106, 237

Cable & Wireless Band 203-4
Callender's Cable Wks. Band 39, 46-8, 50, 76-7, 79
Cambridge Railway Band 44
Cammell Laird Wks. Band 240, 242
Canada 187, 197-8, 207, 239, 249
Carlisle St. Stephens Band 39
Carlton Main Frick. Coll.

Band 39, 106, 108, 201, 244
Carnegie Trust 207, 209
Catley, Gwen 106
Catelinet, Philip 89, 203
Central Band of R.A.F. 108, 110
Chappell & Co. 42, 75, 78, 148, 158, 167, 237
Cherubini: Requiem 202, 242
Cheshire, Harry 108
Chesters 242
Chislett, W.A. 34
Chobham Band 219
Chorale Prelude 145
Cimarosa 60
  Impressario, The 183
CISWO 241
City of Coventry Band 231
Clayton, Colin 106, 108
Clayton, Elgar 110, 160, 186
Clydebank Burgh Band 104
Coates, Eric 31
  Calling All Workers 109
Cobbett, Walter 93, 99
Coldstream Guards Band 170
Cole, Gracie 50-2, 57, 83, 109, 145, 160
Coleridge-Taylor 188
Colombo 197
Complete B'master. 52, 159, 161, 243, 250
Concert Overture 24-5, 27
Conductor, The 155, 244, 248
Cook, K: Bandsman's Ev'thing. Within 160, 200
  Oh Listen to the Band 160
Cornwall Youth Band 208, 239
Counterpoint 112
Coventry Festival Band 231
Coward, Noel 75
Creswell Coll. Band 29, 36, 201
Crystal Palace Contest 13-4, 24, 28-9, 31, 34-40, 42, 45, 50, 60, 68, 72, 74, 95, 125, 144, 157, 169-70, 248
Crystal Palace Band 43-4, 53-4, 60, 67-8, 75, 77-8, 87, 89-90, 152, 156, 251
Cundell, Edric 207
CWS (M/c) Band 150, 177, 201, 231, 240

Daily Herald Contest 74, 126, 128, 133, 189

Daily Mail 97-8
Daily Telegraph 31, 39, 77, 97
Davies, Leonard 152, 200, 209, 212-13, 215, 219-20, 224-5, 227-8, 231, 233, 236
Davies, Walford 31
Daw Mill Coll. Band 225
Decca 93
Delibes 60
Delius 31
Denham, Frank 158
Denmark 190-7, 199
  Aarlborg 196, 199
  Concord Brass Band 192, 194, 196
  FDF Bands 190, 192, 194, 196, 199
  Hamlet Festival 194
  Møller, Herbert (see Møller)
  Tivoli (Concert Hall/Gdns.) 194, 196
Dennison, Kenneth 153-4, 157, 160, 220
Dewsbury Mus. Soc. 177
Doctorate 27, 55, 90-1, 94, 143, 160, 170
Duckworth, Joshua 145
Dvôrak 60
  New World Symph. 226

East Grinstead 19, 42
  Amateur Op. Soc. 17, 42, 75
Edge Hill L.M.S. Band 78
Edinburgh Charities 240, 244
Edinburgh Festival 201, 205, 240
Elgar 31, 46-7, 59-60, 76, 94, 108, 225
  Severn Suite 27, 40, 47, 59-60, 76, 125, 225
Elland Silver Band 220
Empire Memorial Trust 204, 225
England, W.J. (Bill) 203, 215, 236
Evans, Richard 157, 210, 216-8, 221-2
Evolution of the Wind Band 90, 160, 170-1

Fairey Aviation Wks. Band 52, 83-4, 94, 98, 104, 106, 108, 110, 153, 159, 182-3, 185-6, 199, 201, 238
Farrington, Harry 187, 199, 220
Firbeck Coll. Band 50-1

Fletcher, Percy 24-5, 46
  Epic Symphony 40, 59,
  109, 125, 236
  Labour and Love 24, 59,
  108, 153
Foden's Motor Wks Band 22,
  35-6, 39, 46, 48, 54, 68-9,
  74, 77, 83, 92, 94, 96,
  104, 106, 108-10, 159, 182,
  201, 242
Form 111
Friary Silver Band 45, 67-8,
  75
Fugue 112, 115

Garside, Derek 150, 233
Gartside, Peter 55, 177, 196
Gay, Bram 106, 109-10, 160
Gay, Noel 75
Geehl, Henry 17, 19, 25-7,
  39, 46, 109, 115
  Oliver Cromwell 17, 25
  On the Cornish Coast 17,
  25
  Robin Hood 125
German, Edward 31, 60
Gilbert and Sullivan 169
Gladney, John 12, 58, 70, 71
Glasgow Corp. Gas Board
  Band 148
Goodshaw Band 240
Grainger, Percy 60
Grand Shield 42, 44,46, 67,
  73
Greenwood, J.A. 12, 29, 37,
  70-1, 74
  Bravura 109
Gregson, Edward 9, 12, 151
Grenadier Guards Band 108
Grieg: Piano Concerto 159,
  187
Grimethorpe Coll Band 50,
  52, 108
Groves, Charles 209
Guildhall School of Music
  49, 159

Halifax Choral Society 176
Halifax Home Guard Band
  85-6
Hallé Choir 177
Hallé Orchestra 110
Halliwell, William 12, 22,
  70-1, 74
Hammonds Sauce Wks.
  Band 240
Hampshire Youth Band 154,
  225
Handel: Hallelujah Concerto
  55, 204, 239
  Judas Maccabæus 187,242

Messiah 158, 173-8, 180,
  185-6, 202, 204, 242
  Sound an Alarm 89
Hanwell Silver Band 232,
  244
Harlesden Philharmonic 27,
  44
Harmonicon, The 167, 171
Hartmann, J: La Belle
  Americaine 108
Harton Coll. Band 22, 37,
  240
Hawkes 46-7, 123
Haydn: Creation, The 204
  Trumpet Concerto
  206, 227
Hely-Hutchinson, Victor 150
Heyes, Harry 220, 244
Hind, Harold 91, 150, 234,
  242, 250
  Brass Band, The 169
Historicus 163
Hoby, Charles 22, 27, 29,
  169
Holbrooke, J: Clive of India
  125
Holland 182-4, 194
Holst 19, 31, 46-7, 59, 109-
  10
  Moorside Suite 40, 42, 47,
  59, 109, 125, 142
Hong Kong 199
Hopkins, Antony 203-4
Horwich R.M.I. Band 34, 36
Howarth, Elgar 12. 50, 160
  Mosaic 205
Howells, Herbert 19, 40, 47
  Pageantry 40, 108, 125
Hubicki, Margaret 251
Huddersfield Choral Society
  177-8, 180
Hume, Bill 84, 213, 233, 236

Iles, John Henry 12-13, 15,
  17, 19, 22-3, 32, 37, 44, 46,
  54, 67, 72-4, 94-6, 98,
  100, 126-7, 211, 221, 248
Iles Silver Medal 205, 207
International Staff Band
  (SA) 169
Ireland, John 19, 31, 46-7,
  59, 221
  Comedy Overture 109, 125
  Downland Suite 40, 59,
  109, 125, 226, 236
Irish Championships 157
Irish Guards Band 94, 108,
  206, 224
Irons, Arthur 152, 251
Irwell Springs Band 22, 74

Jackson, Enderby 12-15

Jacob, Gordon 203
Jaeger, C.H. 206, 224
Jaguar Cars Band 231
Jarnefelt: Praeludium 71
Jenkins, Alan 176
Jenkins, Cyril 24-5, 46
  Coriolanus 24, 86
  Life Divine 24
  Victory 40, 125
Johannesburg 197
John Dickinson Band 153
Johnstone, Maurice 76-7, 93,
  98, 240, 245, 248
  County Palatine 76, 222,
  237
  Pennine Way 76, 109
  Tempest, The 76, 108, 110,
  126
Joyce, Eileen 104, 106, 158-9
Junior Solo Ch'ships. 241

Keighley, Thomas 40, 47, 49,
  163
  Crusaders, The 40, 42. 125
  Lorenzo 40, 78, 125
Ketelby, Albert W. 31
Kentner, Louis 104
Kinneil Coll. Band 240
Kitson, C.H. 55, 90

Lambert, Constant 31
Langford, Gordon 145, 148-9
Langley Band 231
Leicester Contest 45, 51
Levy, Jules 93. 99
Lewis, Sgt-Maj. 93
Life Guards (Trumpeters)
  106
Liszt 121
  Preludes, Les 44
Litolff, H: Con. Symph.
  (Scherzo) 159
Llangollen International
  208, 241
London & Home Counties
  B.B.A. 204
London Brass Players 159
London Symphony
  Orchestra 44-5
Longstaffe, M: N.F.S. March
  110
Loveridge, Iris 159
Lumb, (Peet) Elizabeth 11,
  205, 210, 212, 221, 228
Luton Choral Society 106
Luton (Red Cross) Band 67,
  74, 77, 175-6, 232

Mackintosh, Jack 92, 201,
  203

McCann, Phillip 150, 210, 232-3, 237-8
Manor House Hospital 45
Operatic Society 44, 241
Markham Main Coll Band 201
Marsden Coll Band 22, 34-5, 37, 70
Massed Bands 10, 13, 23, 44, 54, 68, 94-5, 100, 103-4, 148, 156, 158, 183-4, 194, 196, 201, 239, 242
Massey, Ron 178
Melody Maker, The 164
Mendelssohn: Elijah 44, 186, 203
Italian Symph. 71
Merchant, David 207
Minuet (& Trio) 112, 140, 148
Molinari, A.J. 207, 236
Mollenaar's 11, 47, 123
Møller, Herbert 11, 161, 190, 192, 196
Morris, Haydn: Springtime 40
Morris Motors Band 232, 234
Mortimer, Alex 150, 176, 216, 235
Mortimer, Fred 67, 83, 106, 109, 203
Mortimer, Harry 12, 67, 84, 86, 92-4, 99-100, 103-4, 106-10, 147, 154, 156, 160, 170, 175-6, 178, 189, 194, 201, 203, 205, 207, 211, 214, 218, 227, 236, 240, 245, 250
Moss, Harold 51-2, 209
Mossley Band 231
Mottl, Felix 102
Mozart 60, 140, 145
Munn & Felton's Wks. Band 84, 199
Murphy, Maurice 178, 210, 214, 216, 218, 238
Musical Opinion 31
Musical (Progress &) Mail 159, 164-8
Musical Standard 31
Musical Times17, 31, 93, 168-9, 176, 226, 243
Musicus 163

N.A.B.B.C. 154-5, 200-1, 203, 205, 208-9, 211, 225, 244
N.B.B.C. 19, 160, 203-4, 207, 225, 237
National Ch'ships. 14-5, 17, 22-4, 32, 37, 48, 67-8, 71,

73-4, 106, 125-8, 133, 150, 159, 207, 209, 240, 242
N.S.B.B.A. 243
N.Y.B.B. 8-10, 55, 62, 141, 148, 150, 153-4, 160, 186-7, 189, 196, 200, 202, 207, 209, 210-238, 239, 245, 247-9, 251
Alston, Edith 228, 231
Amys, Renee 216
Ashcroft, Norman 220, 238
Auditions 218, 227-9, 235
Austin, R.E. 212
Blackburn, Michael 214
Boddice, Nigel 236-7
Booker, Russell 150, 236-8
Boult, Geoffrey 216
Bray, Evelyn 234 PoGSON
Broadbent, Brian 216
Brown, Judith 216
Burnham, Norman 214, 216, 221
Butterworth, Ken 216
Calvert, Eddie 231
Cardwell, Trevor 227
Carlton Grammar School 214, 216, 239
Carr, Denis 234
Carr, John R. 212
Chappell Shield 224, 237
Chisolm, George 231-2
Christian, Peter 236
Clay, John 210, 228, 233
Cobley, Graham 236
Copland, Ian 232
Creasey, A.V. 212
Clough, John 216
Cresswell, Tony 154, 232
Dinsdale, Grace 216
Eastwood, Martin 232
Emmott, Jack 228
Edmunds, Cliff 214, 221
Edwards, Jimmy 231-4
Essex, David 236
Evans, Brian 218
Farr, Ray 232
Ford, Bryce 218
Forty Years Young 215, 238
Friends of the NYBB 229
Gillingham, Jennifer 210, 233
Gray, Harold 233, 235
Hannaford Medal 222, 225
Hannaford, Mrs. 222
Hannaford, W.F. 212, 222, 229
Harris, Brian 225
Hawley, H.B. 216, 221
Haydock, William 213
Hayes, John 228
Hooker, Irene 238
Huntley, Connie 224-5, 229

Hurst, Rex 187
Iles, Eric 221
James, David 219, 227-8, 238
James, Stan 232
Jarvis, Alf 224, 228, 237
Jerwood, W.G. 213
Johnstone, Wesley 236
Jowett, Neil 236
Kaye, George 214, 221
Lang, Willie 214
Little, Reg 213
Longson, Jennifer 216
McCallum, Eoin 150, 237
Mahy, Marian & Geoffrey 229
Maines, John 232
Mead, Allan 154, 225
Miles, Maurice 234, 238
Monkman, Colin 216
Morcombe, Tommy 213
Morgan, Robert 232
Mulholland, Robert (Jr.) 216
Murphy, Maurice (see Murphy)
Newman, Clarence 225
Newman Cup 225, 237
Nichol, David 229
Parsons, Anthony 218, 220
Payne, Roger 232
Penrose, R.H. 213
Perrin, I. 213
Powell, T.J. 220-1, 228
Rankine, Brian 229
Raybould, Clarence 234, 238
Reakes, Stan 215, 227, 231, 233, 237
Rich, Leighton 232
Robinson, Ann 216
Roe, Roy 229
Room, Peter 234
Rothery, Frank 222
Sanderson, Derek 231
Semprini 234
Seville, David 224, 228, 237
Shepherd, James 234, 239
Skellern, Peter 232
Smith, Jim 234
Taylor, Douglas 220
Teal, Peter 216
Teasdale, Maurice 213
Tetley, Ernest 224
Thatcher, Sir Reginald 221
Thornton Grammar School 214, 228
Trugian, Reg 231
Tuck Shop 228
Tyrell, F.G. 213
Wainwright, Stanley 225
Wallace, John 234, 238

Watson, James 232
Wilkinson, Keith 232
Williams, A.G. 213
✓ Wood, Joe 214
National Youth B.B. of
  Scotland 207-9
National Youth Orchestra of
  G.B. 211, 249
Nellist, Ralph 210
Nelson Old Band 74
(New) Musical Educator 52,
  161, 168, 172
News Chronicle 42
✓ Newsome, Roy 178, 241
New Zealand 184-8, 197,
  201-2, 207, 229
  Auckland Choral Society
    187
  Auckland University 184-
    186
  BBCM 185
  Canterbury University
    184-5, 187-8
  Christchurch 185-7
  Dunedin 186
  Dunedin Choral Society
    186
  Dunedin Ladies' Band 185
  Griffiths, Vernon 185, 187,
    202
  Hamilton 187
  Hawera 184, 187
  Hokitika 185
  Invercargill 185, 197
  Junior Solo Ch'ships 187
  Mulholland, Robert (Sr.)
    185
  Napier Band 185
  National Ch'ships 184,
    188. 197
  National Youth B.B. (N.Z.)
    186-7
  Nelson 188
  NZ B'casting Service 186
  Timaru Band 177, 185
  St. Kilda Band 186
  Smith, Frank 185
  Waitemata Silver Band
    187
  Wellington 184-5, 187
  Woolston Band 185
Northern Brass 141, 240
Northern Echo, The 180
Novello, Ivor 31, 75
Novello & Co. 11, 110, 158,
  242

O.B.E. 207
O'Donnell family 89, 98
  B.Walton 77, 98, 170
  P.S.G. 27, 93, 98
  R.P. 99, 110

Offenbach 60
Ord Hume, J. 58, 67, 70, 74
  B.B. & C.F. 183
  Brilliant 108
Owen, Alexander 12, 50, 58,
  70-1

Parc & Dare Band 108, 174
Parker, Handel 145
Parkhead Forge Band 106
Parr School of Music 212
Paxton's 147, 158
Pearce, Arthur O. 109
Phillips, Frank 103
Pinner Orchestra 44, 201
Pitch - standardisation 204
Prelude 129
Price, R.Maldwyn 109, 212,
  221
Programme Music 131, 142
PYE Records 177

Radio Malaysia 130
Radio Times 170
Railton, Ruth 211
Rascher, Sigmund 93, 99
Raunds Temperance Band
  44
Rawsthorne, Alan 31
Read, David 106
Rebel Maid, The 43
Regal Zonophone 34, 39
Relton, William 240
Rimmer, Drake 207
Rimmer, William 12, 51, 58,
  70-1, 74, 78, 108
Rimsky-Korsakov 60
Ringham, Maisie 52, 83
Robinson, Stanford 104, 240
Rogers, Richard: South
  Pacific 242
Rondo form 111, 147
Rossini 60
Round, Harry 24
Royal Academy of Music 45,
  243, 250
Royal Albert Hall 14, 40, 51,
  54, 94, 96, 98, 100, 102,
  106, 127-8, 150, 157, 159,
  189, 201, 207, 209, 240
Royal Artillery Band 93
Royal College of Music 16,
  19, 27
Royal Festival Hall 241
Royal Horse Guards Band
  108
Royal Marines 27, 29, 98,
  108
Royal Mil. Sch. of Mus.
  (trumpeters) 106
Rubbra, Edmund 31

Rugby S.A. Band 190
Rushden Temperance Band
  183

St. Andrew's Sch.
  (E.Grinstead) 17, 162, 164
St. George's Sch.
  (Harpenden) 16, 42, 76,
  150, 165, 236
St. Hilda's Band (Leeds)177,
  180
St. Hilda's Coll. Band 22, 28,
  34, 36-7, 48, 74
St. Sepulchre's Church 204,
  244
Salvation Army 12, 197,
  200, 237
Sargent, Sir Malcolm 103-4,
  106, 159, 211, 231
Scale - degrees of 113
Scherzo 112, 117, 130
Schubert 60
  Serenade 109
  Unfinished Symphony
    100, 104
Schumann: Piano Concerto
  55, 104, 158
Scoring for Brass Band 52,
  90, 159-61, 243
Scots Guards Band 108
Scott, James 106, 242
Scottish Amateur Mus. Ass.
  207, 209
Scottish C.W.S. Band 104,
  240
Serbia 16, 20-1, 38
Sheffield Phil. Choir 177
Singapore 197
Slaithwaite Band 241
Smith, R. & Co. 11, 14, 17,
  23, 46, 48, 54, 74, 100,
  119, 144, 158
Solomon, John 44-5
Sonata form 111-2, 131, 134,
  145
Sonata-rondo 112, 147
Soulsby, Alan 159
South African B'casting.
  Corp. 197
South London Philharmonic
  44
South Moor Coll. Band 22
Southsea Silver Band 228,
  234
Sowerby Bridge Band 74
Sparke, Philip 151
Spotlight on Service 207,
  209
Stanford, Sir CharlesV. 16,
  19, 24
Stewart (Steuart) 16, 147
  Britain on Parade 109

Dashing away with the s'ing iron 109, 148
Tpt. Tune in 17th Cent. Style 109, 147
Stockport Citadel Band & Songsters 176
Strauss, Johann 60
  Blue Danube, The 106
Subject 112, 124
Sullivan 14, 95
Sweden 192, 194-197
  Hansson, Bertil 192, 194
  Hedburg, Kurt 194, 196, 235
  Limhamn Church Youth Band 194
  LKU Band 196, 234
  Malmö 194, 196, 235
  Vaxtorp 196
Swift, Edwin 12, 58, 70, 71
Symphonic Poem 112

Taylor, Arthur 48
Tchaikovsky 60
Templemore Avenue Band 177
Ternary form 111-2
Tertis, Lionel 93, 99
Thalben-Ball, George 239
Theme & variations form 113
Thompson, George 50, 52
Thomson, Maud 204, 224
Times, The 31, 97-8
Tippett, Sir Michael 31
Tovey, Sir Donald 55
Treorchy Male Voice Choir 202
Trinity College of Music 25, 49, 159
Turner, Eva 95

U.N.E.S.C.O. 185, 189, 197, 199, 203-4
University College Salford 9, 11
U.S. Army Air Force Band 108, 110

Vaughan Williams, R. 19, 31
Verdi 60
Vinter, Gilbert 98, 110, 142

Wagner 60, 101-2, 130
  Lohengrin 100-1
  Mastersingers, The 66, 89, 162
  Ring, The 42
Waldteufel 60

Walsworth, Ivor 89
Walton, Sir William 31
W.E.A. 187, 197, 200-201, 245
Weber: Freischutz, Der 71, 78
Welsh Guards Band 108
Wembley Operatic Society 241-2
Wessex B.B.A. 209
Whiteley, Herbert 19, 22, 24, 26, 28-9, 32, 46, 60, 70, 74
Widdop, Walter 89
Willcocks, G.H. 94
Wilson, Peter 11, 251
Wingates Temp. Band 36, 39, 74, 231
Winner (record company) 34, 39
Wood, Arthur 109
Wood, Charles 16, 19
Wood, Sir Henry 101-4
Wright & Round 11, 100
Wright, Denis: Age of Chivalry 148
  Atlantic 131, 133
  Ballad of Princess Nada 123
  Carnival Suite 47, 145
  Carol Sinfonietta 148-9, 242
  Casino Carnival 148, 207
  Commonwealth Star 148
  Cornet Concerto 92-4, 96, 109, 145, 147, 170, 239
  Cornish Holiday 148, 206
  Deep Harmony (Chorale Prelude) 144
  Early piano pieces 143-4
  Glastonbury 133-4, 203, 221, 236
  Handelian Suite 47, 109, 145, 183
  Hanover 42, 143, 162
  Joan of Arc 17, 19, 24-7, 32, 35, 37-8, 42, 60, 91, 115, 117, 119-21, 144, 162
  La Mantilla 51, 109, 145
  Merry Mountaineers 145
  Miniature Suite 148
  Music for Brass 129-31, 239
  Overture for an Epic Occasion 127-8, 158, 209
  Overture in the Olden Style 47, 145
  Plain Man's Guide to the Brass Band 185
  Princess Nada 38-40, 42, 59, 109, 121, 125, 158, 168
  Romantica 148

St. Nicholas Eve 141, 239, 242
Salzburg Suite 139, 242, 244
Scottish Fantasy 47, 109, 145
Sea, The (Thalassa) 47, 123
Sennecherib 42
Sonatina 148
Suite for Orchestra 27, 90-1
Tam o' Shanter's Ride 42, 135, 139, 142, 147, 205, 220
Tintagel 46-7, 60, 91, 109, 115, 119-21, 165, 206, 239, 250
Trio Concerto 150, 236-7, 242-3
Two Little Finches 145
Two Lyric Pieces 148
White Rider, The 38-40, 44, 59, 75, 109, 117, 119, 121, 125, 162, 227
Wright, Dudley 16, 45
Wright, Ethel 16
Wright, Frank 154, 209, 241
  Brass Today 209
Wright, Kenneth A. 53, 76-7, 86, 108. 126, 249
  Pride of Race 76, 108, 125
Wright, Maud 8, 10-11, 86, 91, 161-2, 178, 182, 185, 198-9, 214, 224, 231, 235, 245, 247

Yeomen of the Guard, The 43
Yorkshire Imperial Metals Band 238, 240
Yorkshire Miners' Gala 106
Yorkshire Schools Brass Band 239

Ziegler, Anne 106